THE MAID

A Novel

NITA PROSE

Ballantine Books
New York

Published in the United States by Ballantine Books, an imprint of Random House, a division of Penguin Random House LLC, New York.

BALLANTINE and the HOUSE colophon are registered trademarks of Penguin Random House LLC.

LIBRARY OF CONGRESS CATALOGING-IN-PUBLICATION DATA

Names: Prose, Nita, author.
Title: The maid: a novel / Nita Prose.
Description: First edition. | New York: Ballantine Books, [2022]
Identifiers: LCCN 2020057416 (print) | LCCN 2020057417 (ebook) |
ISBN 9780593356159 (hardcover; acid-free paper) |
ISBN 9780593356166 (ebook)
Subjects: GSAFD: Suspense fiction.
Classification: LCC PR9199.4.P7768 M35 2022 (print) |
LCC PR9199.4.P7768 (ebook) | DDC 813/.6—dc23
LC record available at https://lccn.loc.gov/2020057416
LC ebook record available at https://lccn.loc.gov/2020057417

Printed in the United States of America on acid-free paper

randomhousebooks.com

1st Printing

First Edition

Book design by Virginia Norey

—

PROLOGUE

I am your maid. I'm the one who cleans your hotel room, who enters like a phantom when you're out gallivanting for the day, no care at all about what you've left behind, the mess, or what I might see when you're gone.

I'm the one who empties your trash, tossing out the receipts you don't want anyone to discover. I'm the one who changes your sheets, who can tell if you slept in them and if you were alone last night or not. I'm the one who straightens your shoes by the door, who puffs up your pillows and finds stray hairs on them. Yours? Not likely. I'm the one who cleans up after you drink too much and soil the toilet seat, or worse.

When I'm done with my work, I leave your room pristine. Your bed is made perfectly, with four plump pillows, as though no one had ever lain there. The dust and grime you left behind has been vacuumed into oblivion. Your polished mirror reflects your face of innocence back at you. It's as though you were never here. It's as though all of your filth, all of your lies and deceits, have been erased.

I am your maid. I know so much about you. But when it comes down to it: what is it that you know about me?

Monday

CHAPTER 1

I am well aware that my name is ridiculous. It was not ridiculous before I took this job four years ago. I'm a maid at the Regency Grand Hotel, and my name is Molly. Molly Maid. A joke. Before I took the job, Molly was just a name, given to me by my estranged mother, who left me so long ago that I have no memory of her, just a few photos and the stories Gran has told me. Gran said my mother thought Molly was a cute name for a girl, that it conjured apple cheeks and pigtails, neither of which I have, as it turns out. I've got simple, dark hair that I maintain in a sharp, neat bob. I part my hair in the middle—the exact middle. I comb it flat and straight. I like things simple and neat.

I have pointed cheekbones and pale skin that people sometimes marvel at, and I don't know why. I'm as white as the sheets that I take off and put on, take off and put on, all day long in the twenty-plus rooms that I make up for the esteemed guests at the Regency Grand, a five-star boutique hotel that prides itself on "sophisticated elegance and proper decorum for the modern age."

Never in my life did I think I'd hold such a lofty position in a grand hotel. I know others think differently, that a maid is a lowly nobody. I know we're all supposed to aspire to become doctors and lawyers and rich real-estate tycoons. But not me. I'm so thankful for my job that I pinch myself every day. I really do. Especially now, without Gran. Without her, home isn't home. It's as though all the color has been drained from the apartment we shared. But the moment I enter the Regency Grand, the world turns Technicolor bright.

As I place a hand on the shining brass railing and walk up the scarlet steps that lead to the hotel's majestic portico, I'm Dorothy entering Oz. I push through the gleaming revolving doors and I see my true self reflected in the glass—my dark hair and pale complexion are omnipresent, but a blush returns to my cheeks, my raison d'être restored once more.

Once I'm through the doors, I often pause to take in the grandeur of the lobby. It never tarnishes. It never grows drab or dusty. It never dulls or fades. It is blessedly the same each and every day. There's the reception and concierge to the left, with its midnight-obsidian counter and smart-looking receptionists in black and white, like penguins. And there's the ample lobby itself, laid out in a horseshoe, with its fine Italian marble floors that radiate pristine white, drawing the eye up, up to the second-floor terrace. There are the ornate Art Deco features of the terrace and the grand marble staircase that brings you there, balustrades glowing and opulent, serpents twisting up to golden knobs held static in brass jaws. Guests will often stand at the rails, hands resting on a glowing post, as they survey the glorious scene below—porters marching crisscross, dragging suitcases behind them, guests lounging in sumptuous armchairs or couples tucked into emerald love seats, their secrets absorbed into the deep, plush velvet.

But perhaps my favorite part of the lobby is the olfactory sensation, that first redolent breath as I take in the scent of the hotel itself at the start of every shift—the mélange of ladies' fine perfumes, the dark musk of the leather armchairs, the tangy zing of lemon polish that's used twice daily on the gleaming marble floors. It is the very scent of animus. It is the fragrance of life itself.

Every day, when I arrive to work at the Regency Grand, I feel alive again, part of the fabric of things, the splendor and the color. I am part of the design, a bright, unique square, integral to the tapestry.

Gran used to say, "If you love your job, you'll never work a day in your life." And she's right. Every day of work is a joy to me. I was born to do this job. I love cleaning, I love my maid's trolley, and I love my uniform.

There's nothing quite like a perfectly stocked maid's trolley early in the morning. It is, in my humble opinion, a cornucopia of bounty and beauty. The crisp little packages of delicately wrapped soaps that smell of orange blossom, the tiny Crabtree & Evelyn shampoo bottles, the squat tissue boxes, the toilet-paper rolls wrapped in hygienic film, the bleached white towels in three sizes—bath, hand, and washcloth—and the stacks of doilies for the tea-and-coffee service tray. And last but not least, the cleaning kit, which includes a feather duster, lemon furniture polish, lightly scented antiseptic garbage bags, as well as an impressive array of spray bottles of solvents and disinfectants, all lined up and ready to combat any stain, be it coffee rings, vomit—or even blood. A well-stocked housekeeping trolley is a portable sanitation miracle; it is a clean machine on wheels. And as I said, it is beautiful.

And my uniform. If I had to choose between my uniform and my trolley, I don't think I could. My uniform is my freedom. It is the ultimate invisibility cloak. At the Regency Grand, it's dry cleaned daily in the hotel laundry, which is located in the dank bowels of the hotel down the hall from our housekeeping change rooms. Every day before I arrive at work, my uniform is hooked on my locker door. It comes wrapped in clingy plastic, with a little Post-it note that has my name scrawled on it in black marker. What a joy it is to see it there in the morning, my second skin—clean, disinfected, newly pressed, smelling like a mixture of fresh paper, an indoor pool, and nothingness. A new beginning. It's as though the day before and the many days before that have all been erased.

When I don my maid uniform—not the frumpy *Downton Abbey* style or even the Playboy-bunny cliché, but the blinding-white starched dress shirt and the slim-fit black pencil skirt (made from stretchy fabric for easy bending)—I am whole. Once I'm dressed for my workday, I feel more confident, like I know just what to say and do—at least, most of the time. And once I take off my uniform at the end of the day, I feel naked, unprotected, undone.

The truth is, I often have trouble with social situations; it's as though everyone is playing an elaborate game with complex rules they all know, but I'm always playing for the first time. I make etiquette mistakes with alarming regularity, offend when I mean to compliment, misread body language, say the wrong thing at the wrong time. It's only because of my gran that I know a smile doesn't necessarily mean someone is happy. Sometimes, people smile when they're laughing at you. Or they'll thank you when they really want to slap you across the face. Gran used to say my reading of behaviors was improving—*every day in every way, my dear*—but now, without her, I struggle. Before, when I rushed home after work, I'd throw open the door to our apartment and ask her questions I'd saved up over the day. "I'm home! Gran, does ketchup really work on brass, or should I stick to salt and vinegar? Is it true that some people drink tea with cream? Gran, why did they call me Rumba at work today?"

But now, when the door to home opens, there's no "Oh, Molly dear, I can explain" or "Let me make you a proper cuppa and I'll answer all of that." Now our cozy two-bedroom feels hollow and lifeless and empty, like a cave. Or a coffin. Or a grave.

I think it's because I have difficulty interpreting expressions that I'm the last person anyone invites to a party, even though I really like parties. Apparently, I make awkward conversation, and if you believe the whispers, I have no friends my age. To be fair, this is one hundred percent accurate. I have no friends my age, few friends of any age, for that matter.

But at work, when I'm wearing my uniform, I blend in. I become part of the hotel's décor, like the black-and-white-striped wallpaper that adorns many a hallway and room. In my uniform, as long as I keep my mouth shut, I can be anyone. You could see me in a police lineup and fail to pick me out even though you walked by me ten times in one day.

Recently, I turned twenty-five, "a quarter of a century" my gran would proclaim to me now if she could say anything to me. Which she can't, because she is dead.

Yes, dead. Why call it anything other than what it is? She did not pass away, like some sweet breeze tickling the heather. She did not go gently. She died. About nine months ago.

The day after her death was a lovely, balmy day, and I went to work, as usual. Mr. Alexander Snow, the hotel manager, was surprised to see me. He reminds me of an owl. He has tortoiseshell glasses that are very large for his squat face. His thinning hair is slicked back, with a widow's peak. No one else at the hotel likes him much. Gran used to say, *Never mind what others think; it's what you think that matters.* And I agree. One must live by her own moral code, not follow like a sheep, blindly.

"Molly, what are you doing here?" Mr. Snow asked when I showed up for work the day after Gran died. "I'm so sorry for your loss. Mr. Preston told me that your grandmother passed away yesterday. I already called in a replacement for your shift. I assumed you'd take today off."

"Mr. Snow, why did you assume?" I asked. "As Gran used to say, when you assume, you make an A-S-S out of U and ME."

Mr. Snow looked like he was going to regurgitate a mouse. "Please accept my condolences. And are you sure you don't want the day off?"

"It was Gran who died, not me," I replied. "The show must go on, you know."

His eyes widened, which perhaps suggests shock? I'll never understand it—why people find the truth more shocking than lies.

Still, Mr. Snow relented. "As you wish, Molly."

A few minutes later, I was downstairs in one of the housekeeping change rooms donning my maid's uniform as I do every day, as I did just this morning, as I'll do tomorrow even though someone else—not my gran—died today. And not at home but at the hotel.

Yes. That's right. Today at work, I found a guest very dead in his bed. Mr. Black. *The* Mr. Black. Other than that, my workday was as normal as ever.

Isn't it interesting how one seismic event can change your memory of what occurred? Workdays usually slide together, the daily tasks blending into one another. The trash bins I empty on the fourth floor meld into those on the third. I would swear I'm cleaning Suite 410, the corner room that overlooks the west side of the street, but actually I'm at the other end of the hotel, in Room 430, the east-side corner room, which is the mirror inverse of Suite 410. But then something out of the ordinary occurs—such as finding Mr. Black very dead in his bed—and suddenly the day crystalizes, turns from gas to solid in an instant. Every moment becomes memorable, unique from all the other days of work that came before.

It was today, around three in the afternoon, nearing the end of my shift, when the seismic event occurred. I'd cleaned all of my assigned rooms already, including the Blacks' penthouse on the fourth floor, but I needed to return to the suite to finish cleaning their bathroom.

Don't think for a moment that I'm sloppy or disorganized in my work just because I cleaned the Black penthouse twice. When I clean a room, I attack it from top to bottom. I leave it spotless and pristine—no surface left unwiped, no grime left behind. *Cleanliness is next to godliness,* my gran used to say, and I believe that's a better tenet to live by than most. I don't cut corners, I shine them. No fingerprint left to erase, no smear left to clear.

So it's not that I simply got lazy and decided *not* to clean the Blacks' bathroom when I scoured the rest of their suite this morning. *Au contraire,* the bathroom was guest-occupied at the time of my first sanitation visit. Giselle, Mr. Black's current wife, hopped in the shower soon after I arrived. And while she granted me permission (more or less) to clean the rest of the penthouse while she bathed, she lingered for rather a long time in the shower, so much so that steam began to snake and billow out of the crack at the bottom of the bathroom door.

Mr. Charles Black and his second wife, Giselle Black, are longtime repeat guests at the Regency Grand. Everyone in the hotel knows them; everyone in the whole country knows of them. Mr. Black stays—or rather, stayed—with us for at least a week every month while he oversaw his real-estate affairs in the city. Mr. Black is—was—a famous impresario, a magnate, a tycoon. He and Giselle often graced the society pages. He'd be described as "a middle-aged silver fox," though, to be clear, he is neither silver nor a fox. Giselle, meanwhile, was oft described as "a young, lithe trophy socialite."

I found this description complimentary, but when Gran read it, she disagreed. When I asked why, she said, *It's what's between the lines, not on them.*

Mr. and Mrs. Black have been married a short time, about two years. We at the Regency Grand have been fortunate that this esteemed couple regularly grace our hotel. It gives us prestige. Which in turn means more guests. Which in turn means I have a job.

Once, over twenty-three months ago, when we were walking in the Financial District, Gran pointed out all the buildings owned by Mr. Black. I hadn't realized he owned about a quarter of the city, but alas, he does. Or did. As it turns out, you can't own property when you're a corpse.

"He does not own the Regency Grand," Mr. Snow once said about Mr. Black when Mr. Black was still very much alive. Mr. Snow punctuated his comment with a funny little sniff. I have no idea what that sniff was supposed to mean. One of the reasons why I've become fond of Mr. Black's second wife, Giselle, is because she tells me things plainly. And she uses her words.

This morning, the first time I entered the Blacks' penthouse, I cleaned it from top to bottom—minus the occupied bathroom because Giselle was in it. She did not seem herself at all. I noted upon my arrival that her eyes were red and puffy. Allergies? I wondered. Or could it be sadness? Giselle did not dally. Rather, soon upon my arrival, she ran off to the bathroom and slammed the door shut behind her.

I did not allow her behavior to interfere with the task at hand. On the contrary, I got to work immediately and cleaned the suite vigorously. When it was in perfect order, I stood outside the closed bathroom door with a box of tissues and called out to Giselle the way Mr. Snow had taught me. "Your rooms have been restored to a state of perfection! I'll return later to clean the bathroom!"

"Okay!" Giselle replied. "No need to yell! Jeez!" When she eventually emerged from the bathroom, I handed her a tissue in case she was indeed allergic or upset. I expected a bit of a conversation, because she is often quite talkative, but she quickly whisked herself away to the bedroom to get dressed.

I left the suite then and worked through the fourth floor, room after room. I fluffed pillows and polished gilt mirrors. I spritzed smudges and stains from wallpaper and walls. I bundled soiled sheets and moist towels. I disinfected porcelain toilets and sinks.

Halfway through my work on that floor, I took a brief respite to deliver my trolley to the basement, where I dropped off two large, heavy bags of sullied sheets and towels at the laundry. Despite the airlessness of the basement quarters, conditions aggravated by the bright fluorescent lights and very low ceilings, it was a relief to leave those bags behind. As I headed back to the corridors, I felt a great deal lighter, if a tad dewy.

I decided to pay a visit to Juan Manuel, a dishwasher in the kitchen. I zoomed through the labyrinthine halls, making the familiar turns— left, right, left, left, right—rather like a clever trained mouse in a maze. When I reached the wide kitchen doors and pushed through, Juan Manuel stopped everything and immediately got me a large drink of cold water with ice, which I appreciated greatly.

After a short and agreeable chat, I left him. I then replenished my clean towels and sheets in the housekeeping quarters. Next, up I went to the fresher air of the second floor to begin cleaning a new set of rooms, which suspiciously yielded only small change in tips, but more on that later.

By the time I checked my watch, it was around three o'clock. It was time to circle back to the fourth floor and clean Mr. and Mrs. Black's bathroom. I paused outside their door to listen for evidence of occupancy. I knocked, as per protocol. "Housekeeping!" I said in a loud but politely authoritative voice. No reply. I took my master keycard and buzzed into their suite, dragging my trolley behind me.

"Mr. and Mrs. Black? May I complete my sanitation visit? I would very much like to return your room to a state of perfection."

Nothing. Clearly, or so I thought, husband and wife were out. All the better for me. I could do my work thoroughly and without disturbance. I let the heavy door close behind me. I surveyed their sitting room. It was not as I'd left it a few hours earlier, neat and clean. The curtains had been drawn against the impressive floor-to-ceiling windows overlooking the street below, and there were several small minibar bottles of scotch knocked over on the glass table, a tumbler beside it half-empty, an unsmoked cigar beside that, a crumpled napkin on the floor, and a divot on the divan where the drinker's bottom had left its mark. Giselle's yellow purse was no longer where I'd seen it in the morning, on the bureau by the entrance, which meant she was traversing the town.

A maid's work is never done, I thought to myself as I pulled the pillow off the divan, plumped it, returned it to its spot, and smoothed any lingering divan imperfections. Before cleaning up the table, I decided to check the state of the other rooms. It was looking very much like I'd have to clean the entire suite from scratch.

I headed to the bedroom at the back of the suite. The door was open, and one of the hotel's plush, white bathrobes was strewn on the floor just outside the threshold. From my vantage point, I could see the bedroom closet, with one door still open, exactly as I'd left it in the morning because the safe inside was also open and was preventing the closet door from closing properly. Some of the safe's contents were still intact—I could see that much immediately—but the objects that had caused me some consternation in the morning were notably missing. In some ways, this was a relief. I turned my attention away from the closet, stepped carefully over the bathrobe on the floor, and entered the bedroom.

And only then did I see him. Mr. Black. He was wearing the same double-breasted suit he had on earlier when he bowled me over in the hallway, only the paper in his breast pocket was gone. He was lying down, flat on his back on the bed. The bed was creased and disheveled, as though he'd tossed and turned a lot before settling on his back. His head was resting on one pillow, not two, and the other two pillows were askew beside him. I would have to locate the mandatory fourth pillow, which I most certainly put on the bed this morning when I made it, because the devil is, as they say, in the details.

Mr. Black's shoes were off, on the other side of the room. I remember that distinctly because one shoe pointed south and the other east, and immediately I knew it was my professional duty to point both shoes in the same direction, and smooth out the nasty tangle of laces before I left the room.

Of course, my first thought upon beholding this scene was not that Mr. Black was dead. It was that he was napping soundly after having enjoyed more than one afternoon tipple in the sitting room. But upon further observation I noted some other oddities in the room. On the bedside table to the left of Mr. Black was an open bottle of medication, a bottle I recognized as Giselle's. Various small blue pills had cascaded out of the bottle, some landing on the bedside table and others on the floor. A couple of pills had been trampled, reduced to a fine powder that was now ground into the carpet. This would require high vacuum suction, followed by a spot of carpet deodorizer to return the carpet pile to a state of perfection.

It isn't often that I enter a suite to find a guest sound asleep in bed. If anything, much to my dismay, it's more common that I stumble across guests in another state entirely—in flagrante, as they say in Latin. Most guests who decide to sleep or to engage in private activities are courteous enough to employ the "Do Not Disturb: Zzzing" door hanger I always leave on the front bureau for such eventualities. And most guests call out immediately if I inadvertently catch them at an inopportune moment. But not so with Mr. Black; he did not call out and order me to "bugger off," which is how he would normally dismiss me if I arrived at the wrong time. Instead, he remained soundly asleep.

It was then that I realized I had not heard him breathe during the ten seconds or more I'd been standing at his bedroom door. I do know something about sound sleepers, because my gran happened to be one, but no sleeper rests so deeply that he gives up breathing entirely.

I thought it prudent to check on Mr. Black and ensure that he was quite all right. This, too, is a maid's professional duty. I took a small step forward to scrutinize his face. That's when I noticed how gray he appeared, how puffy and how . . . distinctly unwell. I gingerly moved even closer, right to his bedside, where I loomed over him. His wrinkles were entrenched, his mouth drawn down in a scowl, though for Mr. Black that can hardly be considered unusual. There were strange little marks around his eyes, like red and purple pinpricks. Only then did my mind suddenly ring alarm bells. It was at that moment that I fully cued to the disturbing fact that there was more wrong with this situation than I'd realized at the outset.

I eased a hand forward and tapped Mr. Black's shoulder. It felt rigid and cold, like a piece of furniture. I put my hand in front of his mouth in the desperate hope that I'd feel some breath come out of him, but to no avail.

"No, no, no," I said as I put two fingers to his neck, checking for a pulse, which I did not find. I took him by the shoulders and shook. "Sir! Sir! Wake up!" It was a silly thing to do, now that I think about it, but at the time it still seemed largely impossible that Mr. Black could actually be dead.

When I let him go, he plunked down, his head banging ever so slightly against the headboard. I backed away from the bed then, my own arms rigid by my sides.

I shuffled to the other bedside table, where there was a phone, and I called down to the front desk.

"Regency Grand, Reception. How can I help you?"

"Good afternoon," I said. "I'm not a guest. I don't usually call for help. This is Molly, the maid. I'm in the penthouse suite, Suite 401, and I'm dealing with a rather unusual situation. An uncommon mess, of sorts."

"Why are you calling Reception? Call Housekeeping."

"I *am* Housekeeping," I said, my voice rising. "Please, if you could alert Mr. Snow that there's a guest who is . . . permanently indisposed."

"Permanently indisposed?"

This is why it's always best to be direct and clear at all times, but in that moment, I can admit that I'd lost my head, temporarily.

"He is very dead," I said. "*Dead* in his *bed*. Call Mr. Snow. And please dial emergency services. Immediately!"

I hung up after that. To be honest, what happened next all feels surreal and dreamlike. I recall my heart clanging in my chest, the room tilting like a Hitchcock film, my hands going clammy and the receiver almost slipping from my grasp as I put it back in its place.

It was then that I looked up. On the wall in front of me was a gilt-framed mirror, reflecting not only my terrified face back at me but everything I'd failed to notice before.

The vertigo got worse then, the floor tilting like a funhouse. I put a hand to my chest, a futile attempt to still my trembling heart.

It's easier than you'd ever think—existing in plain sight while remaining largely invisible. That's what I've learned from being a maid. You can be so important, so crucial to the fabric of things and yet be entirely overlooked. It's a truth that applies to maids, and to others as well, so it seems. It's a truth that cuts close to the bone.

I fainted not long after that. The room went dark and I simply crumpled, as I sometimes do when consciousness becomes overwhelming.

Now, as I sit here in Mr. Snow's luxurious office, my hands are shaking. My nerves are frayed. What's right is right. What's done is done. But still, I tremble.

I employ Gran's mental trick to steady myself. Whenever the tension got unbearable in a film, she'd grab the remote control and fast-forward. "There," she'd say. "No point jangling our nerves when the ending's inevitable. What will be will be." That is true of the movies, but less true in real life. In real life, the actions you take can change the results, from sad to happy, from disappointing to satisfactory, from wrong to right.

Gran's trick serves me well. I fast-forward and pick up my mental replay at just the right spot. My trembling immediately subsides. I was still in the suite but not in the bedroom. I was by the front door. I rushed back into the bedroom, grabbed the phone receiver for the second time, and called down to Reception. This time, I demanded to speak with Mr. Snow. When I heard his voice on the line saying, "Hello? What is it?" I made sure to be very clear.

"This is Molly. Mr. Black is dead. I am *in his room*. Please call emergency services immediately."

Approximately thirteen minutes later, Mr. Snow entered the room with a small army of medical personnel and police officers filing in behind him. He led me away, guiding me by the elbow like a small child.

And now, here I sit in his office just off the main lobby in a firm and squeaky maroon leather high-backed chair. Mr. Snow left some time ago—perhaps an hour, maybe more? He told me to stay put until he returned. I have a lovely cup of tea in one hand and a shortbread biscuit in the other. I can't remember who brought them to me. I take the cup to my lips—it's warm but not scalding, an ideal temperature. My hands are still trembling slightly. Who made me such a perfect cup of tea? Was it Mr. Snow? Or someone else in the kitchen? Perhaps Juan Manuel? Maybe it was Rodney at the bar, a lovely thought—Rodney brewing me a perfect cup of tea.

As I gaze down at the teacup—a proper porcelain one, decorated with pink roses and green thorns—I suddenly miss my gran. Terribly.

I put the shortbread biscuit to my lips. It crunches nicely between my teeth. The texture is crisp, the flavor delicate and buttery. Overall, it is a delightful biscuit. It tastes sweet, oh so very sweet.

CHAPTER 2

I remain alone in Mr. Snow's office. I must say, I am concerned to be running so behind on my room-cleaning quota, not to mention on my tip collection. Usually, by this time in my workday, I'd have cleaned at least a full floor of rooms, but not today. I worry what the other maids will think and if they'll have to pick up the slack. So much time has passed, and Mr. Snow still hasn't come to fetch me. I try to settle the fear that's bubbling in my stomach.

It occurs to me that a good way to sort myself is to track back through my day, recollecting to the best of my ability everything that occurred up to the moment I found Mr. Black dead in his bed in Suite 401.

Today started out as an ordinary day. I came through the stately revolving doors of the hotel. Technically, employees are supposed to use the service door at the back, but few employees do. This is a rule I enjoy breaking.

I love the cold feeling of the polished brass banisters leading up the scarlet steps of the hotel's main entrance. I love the squish of the plush carpet under my shoes. And I love greeting Mr. Preston, the Regency Grand's doorman. Portly, dressed in a cap and a long trench coat adorned with gold hotel crests, Mr. Preston has worked at the hotel for over two decades.

"Good morning, Mr. Preston."

"Oh, Molly. Happy Monday to you, my dear girl." He tips his hat.

"Have you seen your daughter recently?"

"Why, yes. We had dinner on Sunday. She's arguing a case in court tomorrow. I still can't believe it. My little girl, standing up there in front of a judge. If only Mary could see her now."

"You must be proud of her."

"That I am."

Mr. Preston was widowed more than a decade ago, but he never re-married. When people ask why not, his answer is always the same: "My heart belongs to Mary."

He's an honorable man, a good man. Not a cheater. Have I mentioned how much I detest cheaters? Cheaters deserve to be thrown in quicksand and to suffocate in filth. Mr. Preston is not that kind of man. He's the kind you'd want as a father, though I'm hardly an expert on that subject, given that I've never had a father in my life. Mine disappeared at the same time my mother did, when I was "just a wee biscuit" as my gran used to say, which I have come to understand as sometime be-tween the age of six months to a year, at which point Gran took over my care and we became a unit, Gran and me, me and Gran. Until death did us part.

Mr. Preston reminds me of Gran. He knew her too. It's never been clear to me how they met, but Gran was friendly with him and quite close with his wife, Mary, may-she-rest-in-peace.

I like Mr. Preston because he inspires people to behave properly. If you're the doorman at a fine, upstanding hotel, you see a lot of things. Like businessmen bringing in sultry young playthings when their middle-aged wives are a thousand miles away. Like rock stars so drunk they mistake the doorman's podium for a urinal. Like the young and beautiful Mrs. Black—the second Mrs. Black—exiting the hotel in a rush, mascara running down her tear-stained cheeks.

Mr. Preston applies his personal code of conduct to lay down the law. I once heard a rumor that he got so mad at that same rock star that he tipped off the paparazzi, who swarmed the star so much he never stayed at the Regency Grand again.

"Mr. Preston, is it true?" I once asked. "Were you the one who called the paparazzi that time?"

"Never ask what a gentleman did or didn't do. If he's a true gentleman, he did it with good cause. And if he's a true gentleman, he'll never tell."

That's Mr. Preston.

After passing him this morning, I swung through the massive front lobby and dashed down the stairs into the maze of hallways leading to the kitchen, the laundry rooms, and, my favorite rooms of all, the housekeeping quarters. They may not be grand—no brass, no marble, no velvet—but the housekeeping rooms are where I belong.

Like I always do, I put on my fresh maid uniform and collected my housekeeping trolley, making sure it was replenished and ready for my rounds. It was not replenished, which is no surprise, since my supervisor, Cheryl Green, was the one on shift last night. Chernobyl is what most employees at the Regency Grand call her behind her back. To be clear, she's not from Chernobyl. In fact, she's not from Ukraine at all. She's lived her entire life in this city, as have I. Let it be known that while I do not think highly of Cheryl, I refuse to call her—or anyone—names. *Treat others as you wish to be treated,* Gran used to say, and that's a tenet I live by. I've been called many a thing in my quarter century, and what I've learned is that the common expression about sticks and stones is backward: sticks and stones often hurt far less than words.

Cheryl may be my boss, but she's definitely not my superior. There is a difference, you know. You can't judge a person by the job they do or by their station in life; you must judge a person by their actions. Cheryl is slovenly and lazy. She cheats and cuts corners. She drags her feet when she walks. I've actually seen her clean a guest's sink with the same cloth she used to clean their toilet. Can you believe such a thing?

"What are you doing?" I asked the day I caught her in flagrante. "That's not sanitary."

Shoulder shrug. "These guests barely tip. This'll teach them."

Which is illogical. How are guests to know that the head maid just spread microscopic fecal matter around their sink? And how are they to know this means they need to tip better?

"As low to the ground as a squirrel's behind," is what Gran said when I told her about Cheryl and the toilet cloth.

This morning, upon my arrival, my trolley was still full of damp, soiled towels and used soaps from the day before. If I were the boss of things, let me tell you this: I would relish the chance to restock the trolleys.

It took me some time to replenish my wares, and by the time I was finished, Cheryl was finally arriving for her shift, late as usual, dragging her floppy feet behind her. I wondered if she'd rush to the top floor today as she usually did "to do her first rounds," meaning to sneak to the penthouse suites that are mine to clean and steal my biggest tips off the pillows, leaving only the loose change behind for me. I know she does this, though I can't prove it. That's just the kind of person she is—a cheater—and not the Robin Hood kind. The Robin Hood kind takes for the greater good, restoring justice to those who've been wronged. This kind of theft is justified, whereas other kinds are not. But make no mistake: Cheryl is no Robin Hood. She steals from others for one reason only—to better herself at the expense of others. And that makes her a parasite, not a hero.

I said my halfhearted hello to Cheryl, and then greeted Sunshine and Sunitha, the two other maids on shift with me. Sunshine is from the Philippines.

"Why are you named Sunshine?" I asked her when we first met.

"For my bright smile," she said as she put a hand on one hip and made a flourish with her feather duster.

I could see it then, the similarity—how the sun and Sunshine were similar. Sunshine is bright and shiny. She talks a lot, and guests love her. Sunitha is from Sri Lanka, and unlike Sunshine, she barely says a word.

"Good morning," I'll say to her when she's on shift with me. "Are you well?"

She'll nod once and say a word or two and little else, which suits me just fine. She's agreeable to work with and she does not slack or dilly-dally. I take no exception to other maids, provided they do their jobs well. One thing I will say: both Sunitha and Sunshine know how to make up a room spotlessly, which, maid to maid, I respect.

Once my trolley was set, I rolled down the hall to the kitchen to visit Juan Manuel. He is a fine colleague, always quite pleasant and collegial. I left my trolley outside the kitchen doors, then I peeked through the glass. There he was, at the giant dishwasher, pushing racks of dishes through its maw. Other kitchen workers milled about, carrying food trays with silver covers, fresh triple-layer cakes, or other decadent delights. Juan Manuel's supervisor was nowhere to be seen, so now was a good time to enter. I crept along the perimeter until I reached Juan Manuel's workstation.

"Hello!" I said, probably too loudly, but I wanted to be heard above the whirring machine.

Juan Manuel jumped and turned. "*Híjole,* you scared me."

"Is now a good time?" I asked.

"Yes," he replied, wiping his hands on his apron. He ran over to the large metal sink, grabbed a clean glass, and filled it with ice-cold water, which he handed to me.

"Oh, thank you," I said. If the basement was warm, the kitchen was an inferno. I don't know how Juan Manuel does his job, standing for hours in the unbearable heat and humidity, scraping half-eaten food from plates. All that waste, all those germs. I visit him every day, and every day I try not to think about it.

"I've got your keycard. Room 308, early checkout today. I will clean the room now so it's ready for you whenever you want it. Okay?" I'd been slipping Juan Manuel keycards for at least two months, ever since Rodney explained Juan Manuel's unfortunate situation.

"*Amiga mía,* thank you so much," Juan Manuel said.

"You'll be safe until nine tomorrow morning, when Cheryl arrives. She's not supposed to clean that floor at all—but with her, you just never know."

It was then that I noticed the angry marks on his wrist, round and red.

"What are those?" I asked. "Did you burn yourself?"

"Oh! Yes. I burned myself. On the washer. Yes."

"That sounds like a safety infraction," I said. "Mr. Snow is very serious about safety. You should tell him and he'll have the machine looked at."

"No, no," Juan Manuel replied. "It was my mistake. I put my arm where it shouldn't go."

"Well," I said. "Do be careful."

"I will," he answered.

He did not make eye contact with me during this part of the conversation, which was most unlike him. I concluded he was embarrassed by his mishap, so I changed the subject.

"Have you heard from your family lately?" I asked.

"My mother sent me this yesterday." He pulled a phone from his apron pocket and called up a photo. His family lives in northern Mexico. His father died over two years ago, which left the family short of income. Juan Manuel sends money home to compensate. He has four sisters, two brothers, six aunts, seven uncles, and one nephew. He's the oldest of his siblings, about my age. The photo showed the entire family seated around a plastic table, all of them smiling for the camera. His mother stood at the head of the table proudly holding a platter of barbecued meat.

"This is why I'm here, in this kitchen, in this country. So my family can eat meat on Sundays. If my mother met you, Molly, she'd like you right away. My mother and me? We are alike. We know good people when we see them." He pointed to his mother's face in the photo. "Look! She never stops smiling, no matter what. Oh, Molly."

Tears came to his eyes then. I didn't know what to do. I didn't want to look at any more pictures of his family. Every time I did, I felt an odd sensation in the pit of my stomach, the same feeling I got when I once accidentally knocked a guest's earring into the black hole of a drain.

"I must be off," I said. "Twenty-one rooms to clean today."

"Okay, okay. It makes me happy when you visit. See you soon, Miss Molly."

I rushed out of the kitchen to the quiet, bright hallway and the perfect order of my trolley. Instantly, I felt much better.

It was time to go to the Social, the restaurant bar and grill inside the hotel, where Rodney would be starting his shift. Rodney Stiles, head bartender. Rodney, with his thick, wavy hair, his white dress shirt with the top buttons tastefully undone, revealing just a little of his perfectly smooth chest—well, almost perfectly smooth, minus one small round scar on his sternum. Anyhow, the point is, he isn't hairy. How any woman could like a hairy man is beyond me. Not that I'm prejudiced. I'm just saying that if a man I fancied was hairy, I'd get the wax out, and I'd rip the strips off him until he was clean and bare.

I have not yet had the opportunity to do this in real life. I've had only one boyfriend, Wilbur. And while he didn't have chest hair, he turned out to be a heartbreaker. And a liar and a cheat. So perhaps chest hair isn't the worst thing in the world.

I breathe deeply to cleanse my mind of Wilbur. I'm blessed with this ability—to clean my mind as I would a room. I picture offensive people or recall uncomfortable moments, and I wipe them away. Gone. Erased, just like that. My mind is returned to a state of perfection.

But as I sit here, in Mr. Snow's office, waiting for him to return, I'm having trouble keeping my mind clean. It returns to thoughts of Mr. Black. To the feeling of his lifeless skin on my fingers. And so on.

I take a sip of my tea, which is now cold. I will focus once more on the morning, on remembering every detail. . . . Where was I?

Ah, yes. Juan Manuel. After I left him, I headed to the elevator with my trolley, taking it up to the lobby. The doors opened and Mr. and Mrs.

Chen were standing there. The Chens are regular guests, just like the Blacks, though the Chens are from Taiwan. Mr. Chen sells textiles, so I'm told. Mrs. Chen always travels with him. That day, she was wearing a wine-colored dress with a lovely black fringe. The Chens are always flawlessly polite, a characteristic I find exceptional.

They acknowledged me right away, which, let me just say, is rare for hotel guests. They even stepped aside so I could exit the elevator before they entered.

"I thank you for being repeat guests, Mr. and Mrs. Chen."

Mr. Snow taught me to greet guests by name, to treat them as I would family members.

"It is we who thank you for keeping our room so orderly," said Mr. Chen. "Mrs. Chen gets to rest while she's here."

"I'm getting lazy. You do everything for me," Mrs. Chen said.

I am not one for attention-seeking behavior. I prefer to acknowledge a compliment with a nod, or silence. At that moment, I nodded, curtsied, and said, "Please enjoy your stay."

The Chens shuffled onto the elevator and the doors closed.

The lobby was moderately busy, with new guests arriving and some checking out. At a glance, it appeared clean and orderly. No touch-ups required. Sometimes, however, guests will leave a newspaper in a state of disarray on a side table, or discard a coffee cup on the clean marble floor, where it spills its last drops and leaves an ominous blot. Whenever I notice such infelicities, I address them immediately. Strictly speaking, cleaning the lobby is not my job, but as Mr. Snow has said, good employees think outside of the box.

I pushed my trolley to the entrance of the Social Bar & Grill and parked it. Rodney was behind the bar, reading a newspaper spread on the bar top.

I walked in briskly to show that I am a woman with confidence and a sense of purpose.

"I've arrived," I said.

He looked up. "Oh, hey Molly. Here for the morning papers?"

"Your assumption is one hundred percent correct." Every day, I picked up a stack of newspapers to deliver to guest rooms as I made my rounds.

"Have you seen this?" he asked, pointing to the newspaper in front of him. He wears a very shiny Rolex watch. Even though I'm not much of a brand person, I'm well aware that Rolex is an expensive brand, which must mean Mr. Snow recognizes Rodney's superior abilities as a bartender and pays him more than a usual bartender's salary.

I looked at the headline Rodney pointed at: "FAMILY FEUD ROCKS BLACK EMPIRE."

"May I see that?"

"Sure." He turned the article my way. It featured several photos, a large one of Mr. Black in his classic double-breasted suit, fending off reporters who were sticking cameras in his face. Giselle was on his arm, perfectly styled from head to toe, wearing dark sunglasses. Judging from her outfit, the photo was taken recently. Perhaps yesterday?

"Looks like trouble's brewing in the Black family," Rodney said. "Seems his daughter, Victoria, is forty-nine percent shareholder of the Black business empire, and he wants those shares back."

I scanned the article. The Blacks had three children, all of them grown-up. One of the boys lived in Atlantic City, the other flitted from Thailand to the Virgin Islands or wherever else the party happened to be. In the article, Mrs. Black—the first Mrs. Black—described her two sons as "flakes" and was quoted saying, "The only way Black Properties & Investments will survive is if my daughter, Victoria, who essentially already runs the organization, becomes a half shareholder, at least." The article went on to describe the nasty legal jabs between Mr. Black and his ex-missus. A host of other power magnates were referenced in the article, rallying on one side or the other. The article suggested that Mr. Black's second marriage to Giselle two years ago—a woman less than half his age—marked the beginning of destabilization within the Black empire.

"Poor Giselle," I said aloud.

"Right?" Rodney replied. "She doesn't need this."

A thought occurred to me. "How well do you know her, Giselle?"

Rodney whisked the paper away and slid it under the bar, bringing out a fresh stack for me to take upstairs. "Who?"

"Giselle," I said.

"Mr. Black doesn't let her come down here to the bar. You probably have more contact with her than I do."

He was right. I did. I do. An unlikely and pleasing bond—dare I say friendship?—has recently formed between us, between the young and beautiful Giselle Black, second wife of the infamous property mogul, and me, Molly, insignificant room maid. I don't talk about our bond much because Mr. Preston's adage applies equally to gentlewomen as to gentlemen: best to keep my lips pressed shut.

I waited for Rodney to extend the conversation, leaving the kind of ample room that a single-but-not-desperate female might leave were she romantically interested in the eligible bachelor before her whose cologne hinted of bergamot and exotic masculine mystique.

I was not disappointed—not entirely, at least.

"Molly, your newspapers." He leaned on the bar, the muscles in his forearms contracting attractively. (Since this was a bar and not a dinner table, the no-elbows-on-the-table rule did not apply.) "And Molly, by the way, thanks. For what you're doing to help my friend, Juan Manuel. You're really a . . . special girl."

I felt a surge of warmth rush to my cheeks as if Gran had just pinched them. "I'd do the same for you, probably more. I mean, that's what you do for friends, right? You help them out of binds?"

He put one of his hands on my wrist and subtly squeezed. The sensation was extremely pleasing and I realized suddenly how long it had been since I'd been touched at all, by anyone. He pulled away long before I was ready. I waited for him to say something more, to ask me on another date, perhaps? I wanted nothing more than a second rendezvous with Rodney Stiles. Our first occurred well over one year ago and remains a highlight of my adult life.

But I waited in vain. He turned to the coffee station and began making a fresh pot.

"You'd better get upstairs," he said. "Or Chernobyl's going to drop a bomb on you."

I laughed—more of a guffaw/cough, actually. I was laughing with Rodney, not at Cheryl, which surely made it okay.

"Speaking with you has been delightful," I said to Rodney. "Perhaps we can do it another time?" I prompted.

"You bet," he said. "I'm here all week, haha."

"Of course you are," I said, matter-of-factly.

"It was a joke," he replied with a wink.

Though I did not get the joke, I most definitely understood the wink. I floated out of the bar and collected my trolley. I could hear my heart in my ears, the excitement pumping.

Through the lobby I wheeled, nodding at guests as I walked. "Discreet courtesy, invisible but present customer service," Mr. Snow often says. This is a manner I've cultivated, though I must admit it comes rather easily to me. I believe my gran taught me a lot about this way of being, though the hotel has offered me ample opportunity to practice and perfect.

This morning, I carried a happy tune in my head as I took the elevator up to the fourth floor. I headed to Mr. and Mrs. Black's suite, Suite 401. Just as I was about to knock on their door, it opened, and Mr. Black stormed out. He was dressed in his trademark double-breasted suit, with a paper sticking out of his left breast pocket, on it, the word "DEED" in little curlicue letters. He nearly knocked me over with the brute force of his exit.

"Out of my way."

He often did this—bowled me over or treated me like I was invisible. "My apologies, Mr. Black," I said. "Have an enjoyable day."

I stuck my foot in the door to keep it open, then decided I should still knock. "Housekeeping!" I called.

Giselle was seated on the divan in the sitting room, wearing a bathrobe, her head in her hands. Was she crying? I was not entirely sure. Her hair—sleek, long, and dark—was disheveled. It made me quite nervous, her hair in that state.

"Is this a good time for me to return your suite to a state of perfection?" I asked.

Giselle looked up. Her face was red, her eyes swollen. She grabbed her phone off the glass tabletop, got up, and ran to the bathroom, slamming the door behind her. She switched on the fan, which, I noted, sounded loud and clunky. I would have to report that to the Maintenance Department. Next, she turned on the shower.

"Well then!" I called loudly through the bathroom door. "If you don't mind, I'll just tidy up in here while you prepare yourself to seize the day!"

No answer.

"I said, I'll just clean in here! Since you haven't actually answered me...."

Nothing. It was unlike Giselle to behave in this manner. She was usually quite talkative whenever I cleaned her suite. She'd engage me in conversation, and in her presence, I felt something I rarely did with others. I felt comfortable—like I was sitting at home on the sofa with Gran.

I called out to her one more time. "My gran always said that the best way to feel better is by tidying up! If you feel sad, just grab a duster, Buster!"

But she couldn't hear me above the running water and the clunky whirring of the fan.

I busied myself with cleaning, starting in the sitting room. The glass tabletop was a mess of smudges and fingerprints. People's propensity to generate filth never ceases to amaze me. I grabbed my ammonia bottle and set to work, returning the table to a high and mighty shine.

I surveyed the room. The curtains were open. Fortunately, the windows had not been smeared by fingerprints, which was at least one blessing. On the bureau by the door were some envelopes, opened. A ripped corner lay curled on the floor. I retrieved it and threw it in the trash. Beside the correspondence was Giselle's yellow purse with the gold chain-link strap. It looked valuable, but you'd never know it from the way she flung it about. The zipper at the top was open, and sticking out was a flight itinerary. I'm not one to snoop, but I couldn't help notice it was for two one-way flights to the Cayman Islands. Were this my purse, I would always close the zipper and make sure my precious valuables weren't about to fall out. I took it upon myself to place the purse exactly parallel to the mail and arrange the chain strap neatly.

I surveyed the room. The carpet had been well trampled—the pile disturbed on both sides, as if someone, Mr. Black or Giselle or both, had been pacing back and forth. I took my vacuum from my trolley and plugged it in.

"Pardon the ruckus!" I called out.

I vacuumed the room in straight lines until the carpet plumped right up and looked like a newly swept Zen garden. I've never actually visited a Zen garden in real life, but Gran and I used to holiday together on the sofa, side by side in our living room.

"Where shall we travel tonight?" she would ask. "To the Amazon with David Attenborough or to Japan with *National Geographic?*"

That night I chose Japan, and Gran and I learned all about Zen gardens. This was before she was sick, of course. I no longer engage in armchair travel because I can't afford cable or even Netflix. Even if I did have the money, it wouldn't be the same to armchair travel without Gran.

Right now, as I sit in Mr. Snow's office replaying my day, it strikes me again just how odd it was that Giselle stayed in the bathroom for so long this morning. It was almost as though she didn't want to speak with me.

After vacuuming, I moved on to the bedroom. The bed was rumpled, no tip on the pillows, which was a disappointment. I will admit that I've come to count on the generous tips from the Blacks. They've gotten me through the last few months now that I'm a one-salary household and can't count on Gran's earnings to help pay the rent.

I set about removing the bedsheets and crisply made up the bed, complete with perfect hospital corners and four plump, hotel-standard pillows—two hard, two soft, two pillows each, for husband and wife. The closet door was ajar, but when I went to shut it, I couldn't because the safe inside was open. I could see one passport inside the safe, not two, some documents that looked very legal, and several stacks of money—crisp, new $100 notes, at least five stacks in total.

It's hard to admit this, even to myself, but I am in the midst of a financial crisis. And while I'm not proud of the fact, it is nevertheless the truth that the piles of money sitting in that safe tempted me, so much so that I tidied the rest of the room as fast as I could—shoes pointing straight, negligee folded on the dressing chair, and so on, just so I could leave the bedroom and finish cleaning the rest of the suite quickly.

I returned to the sitting room, where I tended to the bar and the mini fridge. Five small bottles of Bombay gin were missing (hers, I presumed) and three mini bottles of scotch (definitely his). I replenished the stock and then emptied all the trash cans.

I heard the shower turn off, at long last, and the fan as well. And then I heard the unmistakable sound of Giselle sobbing.

She sounded very sad, so I announced that the suite was clean, took a tissue box from my trolley, and waited outside the bathroom door.

Eventually, she emerged. She was wrapped in one of the hotel's fluffy white bathrobes. I've always wondered what it must be like to wear one of those robes; it must feel like being hugged by a cloud. She had a bath towel around her hair, too, in a perfect swirl, like my favorite treat—ice cream.

I held the tissue box out to her. "Need a tissue for your issue?" I asked.

She sighed. "You're sweet," she said. "But a tissue isn't going to cut it."

She walked around me and into the bedroom. I could hear her rooting around in her armoire.

"Are you quite all right?" I asked. "Can I help you in any way?"

"Not today, Molly. I don't have the energy. Okay?"

Her voice was different, like a flat tire if it could talk, which of course it can't except in cartoons. It was evident to me that she was most upset.

"Very well," I said in a chipper voice. "May I clean your bathroom now?"

"No, Molly. I'm sorry. Please, not right now."

I did not take this personally. "I'll come back later to clean it then?"

"Good idea," she said.

I curtsied in response to her compliment, then retrieved my trolley and buzzed myself out the door.

I set about cleaning the other rooms and suites on that floor, feeling increasingly unsettled as I did so. What was wrong with Giselle? Normally, she talked about where she was going that day, what she was doing. She solicited my opinion about whether she should wear this or that. She said pleasing things. "Molly Maid, there's no one like you. You're the best, and never forget it." The warmth would rise to my face. I'd feel my chest expand a bit with every kind word.

It was also unlike Giselle to forget to tip me.

We're all entitled to a bad day now and again, I heard Gran say in my head. *But when they are all bad days, with no pleasant ones, then it's time to reconsider things.*

I moved on to Mr. and Mrs. Chen's room a few doors down. Cheryl was just about to enter.

"I was going to take the dirty sheets downstairs for you, as a favor," she said.

"That's quite all right, I've got it," I replied, pushing past her with my trolley. "But thank you for your kindness." I buzzed through, allowing the door to shut abruptly on her scowling face.

On the pillow in the Chens' bedroom was a crisp twenty-dollar bill. For me. An acknowledgment of my work, of my existence, of my need.

"That's kindness, Cheryl," I said out loud as I folded the twenty and tucked it into my pocket. As I cleaned, I fantasized about all the things I would do—spray bleach in her face, strangle her with a bathrobe tie, push her off the balcony—if ever I caught Cheryl red-handed, stealing tips from one of my rooms.

CHAPTER 3

I hear footsteps coming down the hallway toward Mr. Snow's office, where I remain obediently seated in one of Mr. Snow's squeaky maroon high-backed leather chairs. I don't know how long I've been here—it feels like more than one hundred and twenty minutes—and while I've tried my best to distract myself with thoughts and recollections, my nerves are increasingly frayed. Mr. Snow steps in. "Molly, thank you for waiting. You've been very patient."

It's only then that I realize there is someone behind him, a figure in dark blue. The figure steps forward. It's a police officer, a female. She's large, imposing, with broad athletic shoulders. There's something about her eyes that I do not like. I'm used to people looking past me, around me, but this officer, she looks right at me—dare I say *through* me?—in a deeply unsettling manner. The teacup in my hand is stone cold. My hands are cold too.

"Molly, this is Detective Stark. Detective, this is Molly Gray. She's the one who found Mr. Black."

I'm not sure what the protocol is for greeting a detective. I've received training from Mr. Snow on how to greet businessmen, heads of state, and Instagram stars, but never did he mention what to do in the case of detectives. I must resort to my own ingenuity and my memories of *Columbo*.

I stand, then realize the teacup is still in my hand. I shuffle over to Mr. Snow's mahogany desk, where I'm about to place it down, but there is no coaster. I spot the coasters on the other side of the room on a shelf filled with sumptuous, leather-bound volumes that would be laborious to clean but also quite satisfying. I take one coaster, return to Mr. Snow's desk, place it down, square it to the desk's corner, and then set my rose-ornamented cup upon it, careful not to spill so much as a drop of the cold tea.

"There," I say. Then I approach the detective and meet her discerning eye. "Detective," I say, just as they do on television. I perform a somewhat curtsy by placing one foot behind the other and nodding my head curtly.

The detective glances at Mr. Snow then back at me.

"What an awful day for you," the detective says. Her voice is not without warmth, I don't think.

"Oh, it wasn't all awful," I say. "I've just been running through it in my mind. It was actually mostly pleasant, until approximately three o'clock."

The detective looks at Mr. Snow again.

"Shock," he says. "She's in shock."

Perhaps Mr. Snow is correct. The next thought I have suddenly seems most urgent to articulate out loud. "Mr. Snow, thank you so much for the cup of tea and the lovely shortbread biscuit. Did you bring them? Or did someone else? I truly enjoyed both. May I ask, what brand is the shortbread?"

Mr. Snow clears his throat. Then he says, "Those are made in our own kitchens, Molly. I would be happy to bring you more another time. But right now, it's important to discuss something else. Right now, Detective Stark has a few questions for you, seeing as how you were first on the scene of Mr. Black's . . . of his . . ."

"Death bed," I say, helpfully.

Mr. Snow looks down at his well-polished shoes.

The detective crosses her arms. I do believe her eyes are drilling into mine in a meaningful way, yet I'm not sure what that meaning is exactly. If Gran were here, I would ask her. But she is not here. She will never be here again.

"Molly," Mr. Snow says. "You're not in trouble in any way. But the detective would like to talk to you as a witness. Perhaps there are details you noticed about the scene or about the day that would be helpful to the investigation."

"The investigation," I say. "Do you presume to know how Mr. Black died?" I ask.

Detective Stark clears her throat. "I presume nothing at this point."

"How very sensible," I say. "So you don't think that Mr. Black was murdered?"

Detective Stark's eyes open wide. "Well, it's more likely he died of a heart attack," she says. "There's petechial hemorrhaging around his eyes consistent with cardiac arrest."

"Petechial hemorrhaging?" Mr. Snow asks.

"Tiny bruises around the eyes. Happens during a heart attack, but it can also mean . . . other things. At this point, we don't know anything for sure. We'll be doing a thorough investigation to rule out foul play."

This puts me in mind of a very funny joke that Gran used to tell: What do you call a poor rendition of *Hamlet* performed by chickens? Fowl play.

I smile at the recollection.

"Molly," says Mr. Snow. "Do you realize the gravity of this situation?" His eyebrows knit together, and then I realize what I've done, how my smile has been misinterpreted.

"My apologies, sir," I explain. "I was thinking of a joke."

The detective uncrosses her arms and places both hands squarely on her hips. Again, she stares at me in that way of hers. "I'd like to bring you to the station, Molly," she says. "To take your witness statement."

"I'm afraid that won't be possible," I say. "I haven't completed my shift and Mr. Snow counts on me to do my fair share as a maid."

"Oh, that's quite all right, Molly," Mr. Snow says. "This is an exceptional circumstance, and I do insist that you help Detective Stark. We will remunerate you for your full shift, so don't worry about that."

It's a relief to hear this. Given the current state of my finances, I simply can't afford to lose wages.

"That's very good of you, Mr. Snow," I say. Then another thought occurs to me. "So I'm not in any trouble, is that correct?"

"No," says Mr. Snow. "Isn't that right, Detective?"

"No, not at all. We just need to know what you saw today, what you noticed, especially at the scene."

"You mean in Mr. Black's suite?"

"Yes."

"When I found him dead."

"Uh, yes."

"I see. Where shall I take my soiled teacup, Mr. Snow? I'm happy to return it to the kitchen. 'Never leave a mess to be discovered by a guest.'"

I'm quoting from Mr. Snow's most recent professional-development seminar, but alas, he doesn't acknowledge my witty rejoinder.

"Don't worry about the cup. I'll take care of it," he says.

And with that, the detective leads the way, ushering me out of Mr. Snow's office, through the illustrious front lobby of the Regency Grand Hotel and out the service door.

CHAPTER 4

I am in the police station. It feels odd not to be either at the Regency Grand or at home in Gran's apartment. I have trouble calling it "my apartment," but I suppose it's mine now. Mine and mine alone for as long as I can manage to pay the rent.

Now here I am in a place I've never been before, a place I certainly never expected to be in today—a small, white, cinder-block room with only two chairs, a table, and a camera in the upper-left corner, blinking a red light at me. The fluorescent illumination in here is too sharp and blinding. While I have a great appreciation of bright white in décor and clothing, this style choice is definitely not working. White only works when a room is clean. And make no mistake: this room is far from clean.

Perhaps it's an occupational hazard: I see dirt where others don't. The stains on the wall where a black briefcase likely grazed it, the coffee rings on the white table in front of me, two round, brown o's. The gray thumbprints smeared around the doorknob, the geometric treads left on the floor from an officer's wet boots.

Detective Stark left me here just a few moments ago. Our car ride over was pleasant enough. She let me sit in the front of the car, which I appreciated. I'm no criminal, thank you very much, so there's no need to treat me like one. She tried to make small talk during the drive. I'm not good at small talk.

"So how long have you worked at the Regency Grand?" she asked.

"It's now approximately four years, thirteen weeks, and five days. I may be off by a day, but no more. I could tell you exactly if you have a calendar."

"Not necessary." She shook her head slowly for a few seconds, which I took to mean I'd offered too much information. Mr. Snow taught me "KISS," which isn't what you think. It stands for Keep It Simple, Stupid. To be clear, he wasn't calling me stupid. He was suggesting that sometimes I overexplain, which I've learned can be annoying to others.

When we reached the station, Detective Stark greeted the receptionist, which was rather good of her. I do appreciate when so-called superiors properly greet their employees—*No one is too high or too low for common courtesy*, Gran would say.

Once we were in the station, the detective led me to this small room at the back.

"Can I get you anything before we begin our chat? How about a cup of coffee?"

"Tea?" I asked.

"I'll see what I can do."

Now she's back with a Styrofoam cup in her hand. "Sorry, there's no tea to be had in this cop shop. I brought you some water instead."

A Styrofoam cup. I detest Styrofoam. The way it squeaks. The way dirt clings to it. The way even the slightest nick with a fingernail leaves a permanent scar, but I know to be polite. I won't make a fuss.

"Thank you," I say.

She clears her throat and sits in the chair across from mine. She has a yellow note pad and a Bic pen, the top chewed. I will my mind not to think about the universe of bacteria dwelling on the top of that pen. She puts her pad down on the table, the pen beside it. She leans back and looks at me in that penetrating way of hers.

"You're not in any trouble, Molly," she says. "I just want you to know that."

"I'm well aware," I say.

The yellow pad is askew, approximately forty-seven degrees off from being square with the corner of the table. Before I can stop them, my hands move to rectify this untidiness, shifting the pad so it's parallel with the table. The pen is also askew, but there is no power on Earth great enough to make me touch it.

Detective Stark watches me, her head cocked to one side. This may be uncharitable, but she looks like a large dog listening for sounds in the forest. Eventually, she speaks.

"It seems to me that Mr. Snow might be right about you, that you're in shock. It's common for people in shock to have trouble expressing their emotions. I've seen it before."

Detective Stark does not know me at all. I suppose Mr. Snow didn't tell her much about me either. She thinks my behavior is peculiar, that I'm out of sorts because I found Mr. Black dead in his bed. And while it was shocking and I am out of sorts, I'm feeling much better now than I was a few hours ago, and I'm most certain that I'm behaving quite normally indeed.

What I really want is to go home, to make myself a proper cup of tea, and perhaps text Rodney about the day's events in the hopes that he might console me in some way or offer himself for a date. If that doesn't transpire, not all is lost. I might take a nice bath and read an Agatha Christie novel—Gran has so many of them, all of which I've read more than once.

I decide not to share any of these thoughts. Instead, I agree with Detective Stark insofar as I can without complete deception. "Detective," I say, "you may be right that I am in shock, and I'm sorry if you think I'm not quite myself."

"It's perfectly understandable," she says, and her lips lift into a smile—at least, I think it's a smile? I can rarely be certain.

"I'd like to ask you what you saw when you entered the Blacks' suite this afternoon. Did you see anything out of place or unusual?"

During each and every shift, I encounter a panoply of things that are "out of place" or "unusual"—and not just in the Black suite. Today, I found a curtain rod ripped from its hinges in a room on the third floor, a contraband hot plate left in plain sight on a bathroom counter on the fourth floor, and six very giggly ladies trying to hide air mattresses under a bed in a room meant for two guests only. I did my due diligence and reported all of these infractions—and more—to Mr. Snow.

"Your devotion to the high standards of the Regency Grand knows no bounds," Mr. Snow said, but he did not smile. His lips remained a perfect horizontal line.

"Thank you," I replied, feeling quite good about my report.

I consider what it is the detective really wants to know and what I'm prepared to divulge.

"Detective," I say, "the Black suite was in its usual state of disarray when I entered this afternoon. There wasn't much out of the ordinary, except the pills on the bedside table."

I offer this up on purpose, because it's a detail that even the most nitwitted investigator would have noticed at the scene. What I don't want to discuss are the other things—the robe on the floor, the safe being open, the missing money, the flight itinerary, Giselle's purse being gone the second time I went into the room. And what I saw in that mirror in Mr. Black's bedroom.

I've watched enough murder mysteries to know who the prime suspects tend to be. Wives often top the list, and the last thing I want is to cast any doubt on Giselle. She's blameless in all of this, and she's my friend. I'm worried for her.

"We're looking into those pills," the detective says.

"They're Giselle's," I say, despite myself. I cannot believe her name popped right out of my mouth. Perhaps I really am in shock, because my thoughts and my mouth aren't working in tandem the way they usually do.

"How do you know the pills are Giselle's?" the detective asks, never looking up from the pad she writes on. "The container wasn't labeled."

"I know because I handle all of Giselle's toiletries. I line them up when I clean the bathroom. I like to organize them from tallest to smallest, though I'll sometimes ascertain first if a guest prefers a different method of organization."

"A different method."

"Yes, such as makeup products, medicines, feminine-hygiene products..."

Detective Stark's mouth opens slightly.

"Or shaving implements, moisturizers, hair tonics. Do you see?"

She is silent for too long. She's looking at me like I'm the idiot when clearly she's the one unable to grasp my very simple logic. The truth is that I know the pills are Giselle's because I've seen her pop them into her mouth several times while I've been in her room. I even asked about them once.

"These?" she said. "They calm me down when I freak out. Want one?"

I politely declined. Drugs are for pain management only, and I'm acutely aware of what can happen when they're abused.

The detective carries on with her questions. "When you arrived in the Blacks' room, did you go straight to the bedroom?"

"No," I say. "That would be against protocols. First, I announced my arrival, thinking that perhaps someone was in the suite. As it turns out, I was one hundred percent correct on that assumption."

The detective looks at me and says nothing.

I wait. "You didn't write that down," I say.

"Write what down?"

"What I just said."

She gives me an unreadable look, then picks up her *plume de peste* and jots down my words, smacking the pen against the pad when she's done. "So then what?" she asks.

"Well," I say, "when no one answered, I ventured into the sitting room, which was quite untidy. I wanted to clean it up, but first I thought it right to look around the rest of the suite. I walked into the bedroom and found Mr. Black in bed, as though he were resting."

Her chewed pen cap wags at me menacingly as she scratches down my words. "Go on," she prompts.

I explain how I approached Mr. Black's bedside, checked for breath, for a pulse, but found none, how I called down to Reception for help. I tell her all of it, up to a point.

She writes furiously now, occasionally pausing to look at me, putting that germ factory of a pen in her mouth as she does so.

"Tell me something, do you know Mr. Black very well? Have you ever had conversations with him, beyond just about cleaning their suite?"

"No," I reply. "Mr. Black was always aloof. He drank a lot and did not seem partial to me at all, so I stayed clear of him as much as possible."

"And Giselle Black?" the detective asked.

I thought of Giselle, of all the times we'd conversed, of the intimacies shared, hers and mine. That's how a friendship is built, one small truth at a time.

I thought back to the very first time, many months ago, when I met Giselle. I'd cleaned the Blacks' suite many times before, but I'd never actually met Giselle. It was in the morning, probably around nine-thirty, when I knocked on the door and Giselle let me in. She was wearing a soft pink dressing gown made of satin or silk. Her dark hair cascaded onto her shoulders in perfect waves. She reminded me of the starlets in the old black-and-white movies that Gran and I used to watch together in the evenings. And yet there was something very contemporary about Giselle as well, like she bridged two worlds.

She invited me in and I thanked her, rolling my trolley in behind me.

"I'm Giselle Black," she said, offering me her hand.

I didn't know what to do. Most guests avoid touching maids, especially our hands. They associate us with other people's grime—never their own. But not Giselle. She was different; she was always different. Perhaps that's why I'm so fond of her.

I quickly wiped my hands on a fresh towel from my trolley and then reached out to shake her hand. "I'm pleased to make your acquaintance," I said.

"And your name?" she asked.

Again, I was flummoxed. Guests rarely asked my name. "Molly," I mumbled, then curtsied.

"Molly the Maid!" she roared. "That's hilarious!"

"Indeed, madame," I replied, looking down at my shoes.

"Oh, I'm no 'madame,'" she said. "Haven't been for a long time. Call me Giselle. Sorry you have to clean this shithole every day. We're a bit of a mess, me and Charles. But it's nice to open the door and find everything all fresh after you've been here. It's like being reborn every single day."

My work had been noticed, acknowledged, appreciated. For a moment, I wasn't invisible.

"I'm at your service . . . Giselle," I said.

She smiled then, a fulsome smile that reached all the way to her feline green eyes.

I felt the blood rush to my cheeks. I had no idea what to do next, what to say. It's not every day that I engage in a real conversation with a guest of such stature. It's also not every day that a guest acknowledges my existence.

I picked up my feather duster and was about to begin my work, but Giselle kept the conversation going.

"Tell me, Molly," she said. "What's it like being a maid, cleaning up after people like me every day?"

No guest had ever asked me this. How to respond was not a subject covered in any of Mr. Snow's comprehensive professional development sessions on service decorum.

"It's hard work," I said. "But I find it pleasing to leave a room pristine and to slip out and disappear without a trace."

Giselle took a seat on the divan. She twirled a lock of her chestnut mane between her fingers. "That sounds incredible," she said. "To be invisible, to disappear like that. I have no privacy, no life. Everywhere I go, I have cameras in my face. And my husband's a tyrant. I always thought being the wife of a rich husband would solve all of my problems, but that's not how it turned out. That's not how it is at all."

I was speechless. What was the appropriate response? I had no time to figure that out, because Giselle started talking again. "Basically, Molly, what I'm saying is, my life sucks."

She got up from the divan, went to the minibar, and grabbed a small bottle of Bombay gin, which she poured into a tumbler. She returned to the divan with her drink and plopped back down.

"We all have problems," I said.

"Oh really? What are yours?"

Another question for which I was not prepared. I remembered Gran's advice—*Honesty is the best policy.*

"Well," I began. "I may not have a husband, but I did have a boyfriend for a while, and because of him, I now have money problems. My beau . . . he turned out to be . . . well, a bad egg."

"A beau. A bad egg. You talk kind of funny, you know that?" She took a big gulp from her glass. "Like an old lady. Or the queen."

"That's because of my gran," I said. "She raised me. She wasn't very educated in the official sense—she never went beyond high school, and she cleaned houses all of her life, until she got sick. But she schooled herself. She was clever. She believed in the three E's—Etiquette, Elocution, and Erudition. She taught me a lot. Everything, in fact."

"Huh," said Giselle.

"She believed in politeness and treating people with respect. It's not your station in life that matters. It's how you conduct yourself that counts."

"Yeah. I get that. I think I would have liked your gran. And she taught you to talk like that? Like Eliza from *My Fair Lady*?"

"I suppose she did, yes."

She got up from the divan and stood right in front of me, her chin held high, taking me in.

"You have incredible skin. It's like porcelain. I like you, Molly the Maid. You're a bit weird, but I like you." She then skipped off to the bedroom and returned with a brown men's wallet in her hand. She rummaged through it and pulled out a new $100 bill. She put it in my hand.

"Here. For you," she said.

"No, I couldn't possibly—"

"He won't even notice it's gone. And even if he does, what's he going to do about it, kill me?"

I looked down at the bill in my hand, crisp and feather-light. "Thank you," I managed, my voice a hoarse whisper. It was the biggest tip I'd ever received.

"It's nothing. Don't mention it," she replied.

That's how it started, the friendship between Giselle and me. It continued and grew with each one of her extended stays. Over the course of a year, we became quite close. She would sometimes send me on errands so that she didn't have to face the paparazzi that often waited right outside the hotel's front door.

"Molly, I've had quite a day. Charles's daughter called me a gold digger, and his ex-wife told me I have terrible taste in men. Will you slip out and buy me barbecue chips and a Coke? Charles hates it when I eat junk, but he's out this afternoon. Here." She'd pass me a $50 bill, and when I'd return with her treats, she'd always say the same thing. "You're the best, Molly. Keep the change."

She seemed to understand that I don't always know the right way to behave or what to say. Once, I came at my usual time to clean the room, and Mr. Black was seated at the bureau by the door, perusing paperwork and smoking a filthy cigar.

"Sir. Is now a good time for me to return your suite to a state of perfection?" I inquired.

Mr. Black peered at me over his glasses. "What do *you* think?" he asked, then, like a dragon, exhaled smoke right in my face.

"I think it's a good time," I replied and turned on my vacuum.

Giselle rushed out of the bedroom. She put her arm around me and gestured for me to turn the machine off.

"Molly," she said, "he's trying to tell you it's a really bad time. He's trying to tell you to basically fuck off."

I felt horrible, like a complete fool. "My apologies," I said.

She grabbed my hand. "It's okay," she said quietly so Mr. Black wouldn't hear. "You didn't mean anything by it." She saw me to the door and mouthed, *I'm sorry* before holding it open so I could push my trolley and myself out of the suite.

Giselle is good like that. Instead of making me feel stupid, she helps me understand things. "Molly, you stand too close to people, you know that? You have to back off a bit, not get right in people's faces when you talk to them. Imagine your trolley is between you and the other person, even if it's not really there."

"Like this?" I asked, standing at what I thought was the correct distance.

"Yes! That's perfect," she said, and she grabbed both of my arms and squeezed. "Always stand that far away, unless it's, like, me or another close friend."

Another close friend. Little did she know, she was my one and only.

Some days while I was cleaning the suite, I got the sense that despite being married to Mr. Black, she felt lonely and craved my company as much as I craved hers.

"Molly!" she yelled one day, greeting me at the door in silk pajamas even though it was close to noon. "I'm so glad you're here. Clean the rooms fast and then we're doing a makeover." She clapped her hands with joy.

"Excuse me?" I said.

"I'm going to teach you how to apply makeup. You're really pretty, Molly, you know that? You have perfect skin. But your dark hair makes you look pale. And the problem is you don't try very hard. You have to enhance what nature gave you."

I cleaned the suite quickly, which is hard to do without cutting corners, but I managed. It was lunchtime, so I figured it was acceptable to take a break. Giselle seated me at the vanity in the hallway outside of the bathroom. She brought out her makeup case—I knew it well since I reorganized each of her cosmetics every day, putting the caps back on things she'd left open and placing each tube or container back in its proper slot.

She rolled up her pajama sleeves, put her warm hands on my shoulders, and looked at me in the mirror. It was a lovely feeling, her hands resting on my shoulders. It reminded me of Gran.

She picked up her hairbrush and started brushing my hair. "Your hair, it's like silk," she said. "Do you straighten it?"

"No," I said. "But I wash it. Regularly and thoroughly. It's quite clean."

She giggled. "Of course it is," she said.

"Are you laughing with me or at me?" I asked. "There's a big difference, you know."

"Oh, I know," she said. "I'm the butt of many a joke. I'm laughing with you, Molly," she said. "I'd never laugh at you."

"Thank you," I said. "I appreciate that. The receptionists downstairs were laughing at me today. Something about the new nickname they gave me. To be honest, I don't fully understand it."

"What did they call you?"

"Rumba," I said. "Gran and I used to watch *Dancing with the Stars,* and the rumba is a very lively partner dance."

Giselle winced. "I don't think they meant the dance, Molly. I think they meant Roomba, as in the robotic vacuum cleaner."

Finally, I understood. I looked down at my hands in my lap so Giselle wouldn't notice the tears springing to my eyes. But it didn't work.

She stopped brushing my hair and put her hands back on my shoulders. "Molly, don't listen to them. They're idiots."

"Thank you," I said.

I sat stiffly in the chair, staring at myself and Giselle in the mirror as she worked on my face. I was concerned that anyone could come in and find me sitting down with Giselle Black, having my makeup done. How to handle guests placing you in this exact situation had never been covered in Mr. Snow's professional-development seminars.

"Close your eyes," Giselle said. She wiped them, then dabbed cool foundation all over my face with a fresh makeup sponge.

"Tell me something, Molly," she said. "You live alone, right? You're all by yourself?"

"I am now," I said. "My gran died a few months ago. Before that, it was just the two of us."

She took a powder container and brush and was about to use it on my face, but I stopped her. "Is it clean?" I asked. "The brush?"

Giselle sighed. "Yes, Molly. It's clean. You're not the only person in the world who sanitizes things, you know."

This pleased me immensely because it confirmed what I knew in my heart. Giselle and I are so different, and yet, fundamentally, we are very much alike.

She began using the brush on my face. It felt like my feather duster, but in miniature, like a little sparrow was dusting my cheeks.

"Is it hard, living alone like that? God, I'd never last. I don't know how to make it on my own."

It had been very hard. I still greeted Gran every time I came home, even though I knew she wasn't there. I heard her voice in my head, heard her traipsing about the apartment every day. Most of the time, I wondered if that was normal or if I was going a bit soft in the head.

"It's hard. But you adapt," I said.

Giselle stopped working and met my eyes in the mirror. "I envy you," she said. "To be able to move on like that, to have the guts to be fully independent and not care what anyone thinks. And to be able to just walk down a street without being accosted."

She had no idea how I struggled, not the slightest clue. "It's not all a bed of roses," I said.

"Maybe not, but at least you don't depend on anyone. Charles and I? It looks so glamorous from the outside, but sometimes . . . sometimes it's not. And his kids hate me. They're close to my age, which I admit is kind of weird. His ex-wife? She's weirdly nice to me, which is worse than anything. She was here the other day. Do you know what she said to me the second Charles was out of earshot? She said, 'Leave him while you still can.' The worst part is I know she's right. Sometimes I wonder if I made the right choice, you know?"

"As a matter of fact, I do," I said. I'd made my own wrong choice—Wilbur—something I still regretted every single day.

Molly picked up some eye shadow. "Close your eyes again." I did so. Giselle continued to talk as she worked. "A few years ago, I had one goal and one goal only. I wanted to be swept off my feet by a rich man who would take care of me. And I met this girl—let's call her my mentor. She showed me the ropes. I went to all the right places, bought a couple of the right outfits. 'Believe and you will receive,' she used to say. She'd been married to three different men, divorced three times, taking each man for half his net worth. Isn't that incredible? She was set. A house in Saint-Tropez and another in Venice Beach. She lived alone, with a maid, a chef, and a driver. No one telling her what to do. No one bossing her around. I'd kill for that life. Who wouldn't?"

"Can I open my eyes now?" I asked.

"Not yet. Almost, though." She switched to a thin brush that felt cool and tender on my eyelids.

"At least you don't have a man telling you what to do, a man who's a hypocrite. Charles cheats on me," she said. "Did you know that? Gets jealous if I so much as glance at another man, but he has at least two mistresses in different cities. And those are just the ones I know about. He has one here too. I wanted to strangle him when I found out. He pays off the paparazzi so they don't leak the truth about him. Meanwhile, I have to give him a full report on where I'm going every time I leave this room."

I opened my eyes and sat up straight in my chair. I was most distressed to learn this about Mr. Black. "I detest cheaters," I said. "I despise them. He shouldn't do that to you. It's not right, Giselle."

Her hands were still close to my face. She'd rolled her pajama sleeves up well past her elbows. From that vantage point, I could make out bruises on her arms, and as she leaned forward and her top shifted, I saw a blue-and-yellow mark on her collarbone too.

"How did you get those?" I asked. There had to be a perfectly reasonable explanation.

She shrugged. "Like I said, things aren't always great between Charles and me."

I felt a familiar churn in my stomach, bitterness and anger frothing just below the surface, a volcano that I would not let erupt. Not yet.

"You deserve better treatment, Giselle," I said. "You're a good egg."

"Meh," she said. "I'm not that good. I try, but sometimes . . . sometimes it's hard to be good. It's hard to do the right thing." She picked a blood-red shade of lipstick from her kit and began applying it to my lips.

"You're right about one thing, though. I deserve better. I deserve a Prince Charming. And I'll make that happen, eventually. I'm working on it. Believe and you will receive, right?" She put the lipstick down and picked up a large hourglass timer from the vanity. I'd seen it there often enough. I had polished its glass curves with ammonia and the brass with metal cleaner to bring it to a high shine. It was a beautiful object, classic and graceful, a pleasure to touch and to behold.

"You see this timer?" she said, holding it in front of me. "The woman I met, my mentor? It was a gift from her. It was empty when she gave it to me, and she told me to fill it with sand from my favorite beach. I said, 'Are you crazy? I've never even seen the ocean. What makes you think I'm going to a beach anytime soon?'

"Turns out she was right. I've seen a lot of beaches these past few years. I was escorted to many of them even before I met Charles—the French Riviera, Polynesia, the Maldives, the Caymans. The Caymans are my favorite. I could live there forever. Charles owns a villa there, and the last time he took me, I filled this timer with sand from the beach. I turn it over sometimes and just watch the sand run through. Time, right? You gotta make things happen. Make what you want out of your life before it's too late. . . . And done!" she said, stepping away so I could see my reflection in the mirror.

She stood behind me, hands on my shoulders again.

"See?" she said. "Just a bit of makeup, and suddenly you're a hottie."

I turned my head from side to side. I could barely see my old self anymore. I knew that I somehow looked "better," or at least more like everyone else, but there was something very off-putting about the change.

"Do you like it? It's like duckling to swan, like Cinderella at the ball."

I knew the etiquette for this, which was a relief. When someone compliments you, you're supposed to thank them. And when they do something kind for you—even if you didn't want them to—you're supposed to thank them.

"I appreciate your efforts," I said.

"You're welcome," she replied. "And take this," she said, picking up the beautiful timer. "It's a gift. From me to you, Molly."

She put the glowing object into my hands. It was the first gift I'd received since Gran died. I couldn't recall the last time I'd been given a gift by someone other than Gran. "I love it," I said. I meant it. This was something I valued much more than any makeover. I couldn't believe it was now mine, to cherish and polish from this day forth. It was filled with sand from a far-off, exotic place that I would never see. And it was a generous gift from a friend.

"I will keep it here in my hotel locker in case you ever want it back," I said. The truth is that as much as I loved the timer, I couldn't bring it home. I wanted only Gran's things at home.

"Really, I love it, Giselle. I will admire it every day."

"Who are you kidding? You already do admire it every day."

I smiled. "Yes, I suppose you're right," I said. "May I make a suggestion?"

She stood there with a hand on her hip while I tidied her makeup kit and cleaned up the vanity.

"You might consider leaving Mr. Black. He hurts you. You're better off without him."

"If only it were that easy," she said. "But time, Miss Molly. Time heals all wounds, as they say."

She was right. As time passes, the wound doesn't hurt as much as it did at first, and that's always a surprise—to feel a little bit better and yet to miss the past.

No sooner had that thought crossed my mind than I realized how late it was. I checked my phone—1:03 P.M. My lunch hour was over minutes ago!

"I have to go, Giselle. My supervisor, Cheryl, will be very upset with my tardiness."

"Oh, her. She was sniffing around here yesterday. She came in asking if we were pleased with the cleaning services. I said, 'I've got the best maid ever. Why wouldn't I be pleased?' And she stood there with that dumb look on her face and said, 'I'll do a much better job for you than Molly. I'm her supervisor.' And I'm like, 'Nope.' I pulled out a tenner from my purse and handed it to her. 'Molly's the only maid I need, thanks,' I said. Then she left. She's a real piece of work, that one. Gives new meaning to the term 'resting bitch face,' if you know what I'm saying."

Gran taught me not to use foul language, and I rarely do. But I could not deny Giselle's appropriate use of language in this particular instance. I started to smile despite myself.

"Molly? Molly." It was Detective Stark.

"I'm sorry," I said. "Can you repeat the question?"

"I asked if you know Giselle Black. Did you ever have any dealings with her? Conversations? Did she ever say anything about Mr. Black that struck you as odd? Did she ever mention anything that might help our investigation?"

"Investigation?"

"As I mentioned, it's likely that Mr. Black died of natural causes, but it's my job to rule out other possibilities. That's why I'm talking to you today." The detective wipes a hand across her brow. "So, again I'll ask: did Giselle Black ever talk to you?"

"Detective," I say, "I'm a hotel maid. Who would want to talk to me?"

She considers this, then nods. She is entirely satisfied with my response.

"Thank you, Molly," she says. "It's been a tough day for you, I can see that. Let me take you home."

And so she did.

—

Chapter 5

With a turn of the key, I open the door to my apartment. I walk across the threshold and close the door behind me, sliding the dead bolt across. Home sweet home.

I look down at the pillow on Gran's antique chair by the door. She sewed the Serenity Prayer on it in needlepoint: *God grant me the serenity to accept the things I cannot change, the courage to change the things I can, and the wisdom to know the difference.*

I take my phone from my pants pocket and place it on the chair. I unlace my shoes and wipe the bottoms with a cloth before putting them away in the closet.

"Gran, I'm home!" I call out. She's been gone for nine months, but it still feels wrong not to call out to her. Especially today.

My evening routine is no longer the same without her. When she was alive, we spent all our free time together. In the evening, the first thing we'd do was complete that day's cleaning task. Then we'd make dinner together—spaghetti on Wednesdays, fish every Friday, provided we could find a good deal on filets at the grocery store. Then we'd eat our meals side by side on the sofa as we watched reruns of *Columbo*.

Gran loved *Columbo,* and so do I. She often commented on how Peter Falk could use a woman like her to sort him out. "Look at that overcoat.

It's in extreme need of a wash and an iron." She'd shake her head and address him on the screen as if he were real and right there in front of her. "I do wish you wouldn't smoke cigars, dear. It's a filthy habit."

But despite the bad habit, we both admired the way Columbo could see through the conniving plots of the ne'er-do-wells and make sure they got their just deserts.

I don't watch *Columbo* anymore. Just another thing that doesn't seem right now that Gran is dead. But I do try to keep up with our nightly cleaning routines.

> Monday, floors and chores.
> Tuesday, deep cleaning to give meaning.
> Wednesday, bath and kitchen.
> Thursday, dust we must.
> Friday, wash-and-dry day.
> Saturday, wild card.
> Sunday, shop and chop.

Gran always drilled into me the importance of a clean and orderly home.

"A clean home, a clean body, and clean company. Do you know where that leads?"

I could not have been more than five years old when she taught me this. I looked way up at her as she spoke. "Where does it lead, Gran?"

"To a clean conscience. To a good, clean life."

It would take years for me to truly understand this, but it strikes me now how right she was.

I take out the broom and dustpan, the mop and bucket from the cleaning cupboard in the kitchen. I begin with a good sweep, starting at the far corner of my bedroom. There isn't much floor space, since my queen bed takes up most of the room, but dirt has a way of hiding under things, of lodging in the cracks. I lift the bed skirts and do a sweep under the bed, pushing any clinging dust forward and out of the room. Gran's landscape paintings of the English countryside hang on every wall, and every one of them reminds me of her.

What a day it has been, what a day indeed. It is one I'd rather forget than remember, and yet it doesn't work that way. We bury the bad memories deep, but they don't go away. They're with us all the time.

I carry on sweeping through the hallway. I make my way to the bathroom, with its old, cracked black-and-white tiles that nevertheless shine brightly when polished, something I do twice weekly. I sweep up a few of my own stray hairs from the floor, then back out of the bathroom.

Now, I'm right in front of Gran's bedroom door. It's closed. I pause. I won't go in there. I haven't crossed that threshold in months. And it won't be today.

I sweep the parquet from the farthest end of the living room, around Gran's curio cabinet, under the sofa, right through the galley kitchen and back to the front door. I've left minute piles of detritus behind me—one outside my bedroom door, another outside the bathroom, one here by the front entrance, and one in the kitchen. I sweep each pile into the dustpan and then have a look at the contents. Quite a clean week, overall—a few crumpet crumbs, some dust and clothing fibers, some strands of my own dark hair. Nothing left of Gran that I can see. Nothing at all.

I whisk the dirt into the trash bin in the kitchen. Then I fill the bucket with warm water and add some of that nice Mr. Clean, Moonlight Breeze scent (Gran's favorite), into the bucket. I carry the bucket and mop into my bedroom and start at the far corner. I'm careful not to splash any water onto my bed skirts and definitely not on the lone-star quilt that Gran made for me years ago, faded now from use and wear, but nonetheless a treasure.

I complete my circuit, ending again at the entrance, where I encounter a very stubborn black scuff mark at the door. I must have done that with my black-soled work shoes. I scrub, scrub, scrub. "Out, damn spot," I say aloud, and eventually it fades before my eyes, revealing the gleam of parquet beneath.

It's funny the way memories bubble up whenever I clean. I do wonder if that's the same for everyone—for everyone who cleans, that is. And though I've had a rather eventful day, it's not today that I'm thinking about, not Mr. Black and all of that wretched business, but a day long ago when I was about eleven years old. I was asking Gran about my mother, as I did from time to time—What kind of person was she? Where had she gone and why? I knew she'd run off with my father, a man Gran described as a "bad egg" and "a fly-by-night."

"What was he during the day?" I asked.

She laughed.

"Are you laughing with me or at me?"

"With, my dear girl! Always with."

She went on to say it was no surprise that my mother got caught up with a fly-by-night, because Gran had made mistakes, too, when she was young. That's how she got my mother in the first place.

It was all so confusing at the time. I had no idea what to think about any of it. It makes more sense now. The older I get, the more I understand. And the more I understand, the more questions I have for her—questions she can no longer answer.

"Will she ever come back to us? My mother?" I asked back then.

A long sigh. "It won't be easy. She has to escape him. And she has to want to get away."

She didn't, though. My mother never returned. But that's okay with me. There's no point mourning someone you never knew. It's hard enough mourning someone you did know, someone you'll never see again, someone you miss dreadfully.

My gran worked hard and cared for me well. She taught me things. She hugged me and fussed over me and made life worth living. My gran was also a maid, but a domestic one. She worked for a well-to-do family, the Coldwells. She could walk to their mansion from our apartment in half an hour. They complimented her work, but whatever she did for them, it was never enough.

"Can you clean up after our soirée on Saturday night?"

"Can you get this stain out of our carpet?"

"Do you garden as well?"

Gran, ever willing and good-natured, said yes to every request, no matter what toll it took on her. In so doing, she saved up a very nice nest egg over the years. She called it "the Fabergé."

"Dear girl, would you pop down to the bank and deposit this in the Fabergé?"

"Sure, Gran," I'd say, grabbing her bank card and walking down five flights of stairs, out of the building, and down two blocks to the ATM.

As I got older, there were times I worried for Gran, worried she was working too hard. But she dismissed my concerns.

"The devil makes work for idle hands. And besides, one day it will just be you, and the Fabergé will see you through when that day comes."

I didn't want to think about that day. It was hard to imagine life beyond Gran, especially since school was a special form of torture. Both elementary and high school were lonely and trying. I was proud of my good grades, but my peers were never my peers. They never understood me then and rarely do now. When I was younger, this vexed me more than it does today.

"No one likes me," I'd tell Gran when I got picked on at school.

"That's because you're different," she explained.

"They call me a freak."

"You're not a freak. You're just an old soul. And that's something to be proud of."

When I was nearing the end of high school, Gran and I talked a lot about professions, about what I wanted to do in my adult life. There was only one option of any interest to me. "I want to be a maid," I told her.

"Dear girl, with the Fabergé, you can aim a little higher than that."

But I persisted, and I think deep down Gran knew better than anyone what I am. She knew my capabilities and my strengths; she was also keenly aware of my weaknesses, though she said I was getting better— *The longer you live, the more you learn.*

"If being a maid is what you're set on, so be it," Gran said. "You'll need some work experience, though, before you enter a community college."

Gran asked around and through an old contact who was a doorman at the Regency Grand, she learned of an opening for a maid at the hotel. I was nervous at my interview, felt sweat pooling indiscreetly at my armpits as we stood outside the hotel's imposing, red-carpeted front steps with the stately black-and-gold awning looming over it.

"I can't go in there, Gran. It's far too posh for me."

"Balderdash. You deserve to enter those doors as much as anyone. And you will. Go on, then."

She pushed me forward. I was greeted by Mr. Preston, her doorman friend.

"It's a pleasure to meet you," he said, bowing slightly and tipping his hat. He looked at Gran in a funny way that I couldn't quite comprehend. "It's been a while, Flora," he said. "It is good to see you again."

"It's good to see you too," Gran replied.

"Better get you inside then, Molly," Mr. Preston said.

He guided me through the shiny revolving doors and I took in the glorious lobby of the Regency Grand for the very first time. It was so beautiful, so opulent, I almost felt faint at the sight of it—the marble floors and staircases, the gleaming golden railings, the smart, uniformed Reception staff, like neat little penguins, tending to well-dressed guests who milled about the stately lobby.

I followed breathlessly as Mr. Preston led me through the ornate ground-floor corridors, decorated with dark wainscoting, clamshell wall sconces, and the kind of dense carpet that absorbs all sound, leaving radiant silence to delight the ears.

We turned right then left, then right, passing office after office until at last we came to an austere black door with a brass nameplate that read: MR. SNOW, HOTEL MANAGER, THE REGENCY GRAND. Mr. Preston knocked twice, then opened the door wide. To my utter astonishment, I found myself in a dark, leathery den, with mustard brocade wallpaper and looming bookshelves, an office I could easily have believed was 221B Baker Street and belonged to none other than Sherlock Holmes himself.

Behind a giant mahogany desk sat the diminutive Mr. Snow. He stood to greet me the moment we walked in. When Mr. Preston discreetly padded out of the room, leaving us to our interview, I can readily admit that while my palms were sweating and my heart palpitated wildly, so enamored was I with the Regency Grand that I was bound and determined to land myself the coveted position of maid.

Truth be told, I don't remember much about our interview itself, except that Mr. Snow expounded on comportment and rules, decorum and decency, which was not just music to my ears but rather a heavenly and sacred hymn. After our chat, he led me through the hallowed corridors—left, right, left—until we were back in the lobby, clipping down a steep flight of marble stairs to the hotel basement, which, he informed me, housed the housekeeping and laundry quarters alongside the hotel kitchen. In a cramped, airless closet-cum-office that smelled of algae, must, and starch, I was introduced to the head maid, Ms. Cheryl Green. She looked me up and down, then said, "She'll have to do."

I began my training the very next day and was soon working full-time. Working was so much better than going to school. At work, if I was teased, it was at least subtle enough to ignore. Wipe, wipe, and the slight was gone. It was also terrifically exciting to receive a paycheck.

"Gran!" I'd say as I returned home after making my very own deposit to the Fabergé. I'd pass her the deposit receipt and she'd smile ear to ear.

"I never thought I'd see the day. You're such a blessing to me. Do you know that?"

Gran brought me close and hugged me tight. There's nothing in the world quite like a Gran hug. It may be the thing I miss the most about her. That, and her voice.

"Do you have something in your eyes, Gran?" I asked when she pulled away.

"No, no, I'm quite fine."

The more I worked at the Regency Grand, the more I put into the Fabergé. Gran and I began talking about post-secondary options for education. I attended an information session about the hotel management and hospitality program at a nearby community college. It was tremendously exciting. Gran encouraged me to apply, and to my surprise, I was accepted. At college, I'd learn not only how to clean and maintain an entire hotel but also how to manage employees, just like Mr. Snow did.

However, just before classes were about to begin, I attended an orientation session, and that's where I met Wilbur. Wilbur Brown. He was standing in front of one of the display tables, reading the literature. There were pads and pens being offered for free. He grabbed several and shoved them into his backpack. He wouldn't move out of the way, and I very much wanted to browse the brochures.

"Excuse me," I said. "Might I access the table?"

He turned to me. He was stocky, wore very thick glasses, and had coarse, black hair.

"Sorry," he said. "I didn't realize I was in your way." He looked at me, unblinking. "I'm Wilbur. Wilbur Brown. I'm going into accounting in the fall. Are you going into accounting in the fall?" He offered me his hand. He shook it and shook it until I had to yank my arm away to make the shaking stop.

"I'm going into hotel management," I said.

"I like girls who are smart. What kind of guys do you like? Math guys?"

I'd never considered what kinds of "guys" I liked. I knew I liked Rodney at work. He had a quality I'd heard referred to on television as "swagger." Like Mick Jagger. Wilbur did not have swagger, and yet, he had something else: he was approachable, direct, familiar. I wasn't afraid of him the way I was of most other boys and men. I probably should have been.

Wilbur and I began dating, much to Gran's delight.

"I'm so happy you've found someone. It's simply delightful," she said.

I'd come home and tell her all about him, how we went grocery shopping together and used coupons, or how we walked in a park and counted out 1,203 steps from the statue to the fountain. Gran never inquired about the more personal aspects of our romance, for which I'm grateful, because I'm not sure I would have known how to explain how

I felt about the physical parts, except that while it was all new and different, it was also quite pleasant.

One day, Gran asked me to invite Wilbur round to the apartment, and so I did. If Gran was disappointed by him, she certainly hid it well.

"He's welcome round here anytime, your beau is," she said.

Wilbur started visiting regularly, eating with us and staying after dinner to watch *Columbo*. Neither Gran nor I enjoyed his incessant TV commentary and questions, but we bore it stoically.

"What kind of a mystery reveals the killer from the beginning?" he'd ask. Or, "Can't you see the butler did it?" He'd ruin an episode by talking through it, often pointing out the wrong culprit, though to be fair, Gran and I had seen every episode several times, so it didn't really matter.

One day, Wilbur and I went to an office-supply store together so he could buy a new calculator. He seemed very off that day, but I didn't question it, even when he told me to "Hurry up, already" as I tried to keep up with his compulsive stride. Once inside the shop, he picked up various calculators and tried them out, explaining the function of each button to me. Then, once he had chosen the calculator he liked best, he slipped it into his backpack.

"What are you doing?" I asked.

"Will you shut your damn mouth?" he replied.

I don't know what shocked me more—his language or the fact that he walked out of the store without paying for the calculator. He'd stolen it, just like that.

And that's not all. One day, I came back home from work with my paycheck. He visited that evening. Gran wasn't doing so well by this point. She'd been losing weight and was much more quiet than normal. "Gran, I'm going to pop down and deposit this in the Fabergé."

"I'll go with you," Wilbur offered.

"What a gentleman you have there, Molly," Gran replied. "Off you two go, then."

At the ATM, Wilbur began asking me all kinds of questions about the hotel and what it was like to clean a room. I was more than happy to explain the peculiar joy of making hospital corners with freshly pressed sheets and how a polished brass doorknob in the sunshine turns the whole world to gold. I was so engrossed in sharing that I didn't notice him watching me type in Gran's PIN.

That night, he left abruptly, right before *Columbo*. For days, I texted him, but he didn't reply. I'd call and leave him messages, but he wouldn't answer. It's funny, but it never occurred to me that I didn't know where he lived, had never been to his home, didn't even know his address. He always made excuses for why it was best to go to my place, including that it was always nice to see Gran.

About a week later, I went to take out the rent money. I couldn't find my bank card, which was odd, so I asked Gran for hers. I went to the ATM. And that's when I discovered that our Fabergé was empty. Completely drained. And it was then I knew that Wilbur was not just a thief but a cheat as well. He was the very definition of a bad egg, which is the worst kind of man.

I was ashamed that I'd been duped, that I'd fallen for a liar. I was ashamed to my core. I considered calling the police and seeing if they could track him down, but in the end, I knew that would mean telling Gran what he'd done, and I just couldn't do it. I couldn't break her heart like that. One broken heart was plenty, thank you very much.

"Where has he been, your beau?" Gran asked after a few days of not seeing him.

"Well, Gran," I said, "it seems he's decided to go his own way." I do not like to lie outright, and this was not an outright lie but rather a truth that remains the truth provided no further details are requested. And Gran didn't inquire further.

"That's a shame," she said. "But not to worry, dear. There are plenty of fish in the sea."

"It's better this way," I said, and I think she was surprised that I wasn't more upset. But the truth is I *was* upset. I was furious, but I was learning how to hide my feelings. I was able to keep my rage under the surface where Gran couldn't see it. She had enough to contend with, and I wanted her to concentrate all of her energy on getting well.

Secretly, I imagined tracking Wilbur down myself. I had vivid fantasies about running into him at the college campus and garroting him with the straps of his backpack. I imagined pouring bleach into his mouth to make him confess what he'd done, to Gran, to me.

The day after Wilbur robbed us, Gran had a doctor's appointment. She'd been to several in the weeks prior, but every time she came home, the news was the same.

"Any results, Gran? Do they know why you're unwell?"

"Not yet. Maybe it's all in your ol' Gran's head."

I was pleased to hear this, because a fake illness is far less frightening than a real one. But still, part of me had misgivings. Her skin was like crepe paper, and she barely had an appetite anymore.

"Molly, I know it's Tuesday, deep cleaning, but do you think we could tackle that task another day perhaps?" It was the first time ever that she asked for a reprieve from our cleaning routine.

"Not to worry, Gran. You rest. I'll do our evening chore."

"Dear girl, what would I do without you?"

I didn't say it out loud, but I was starting to wonder what I myself would do if ever I were without Gran.

A few days later, Gran had another appointment. When she came home, something was different. I could see it in her face. She looked puffy and strained.

"It seems I am a little bit sick after all," she said.

"What kind of sickness?" I asked.

"Pancreatic," she said quietly, her eyes never straying from mine.

"Did they give you medicine?"

"Yes," she said. "They did. It's a sickness that unfortunately causes pain, so they're treating that."

She hadn't mentioned pain before that, but I suppose I knew. I could see it in the way she walked, how she struggled to sit down on the sofa each night, how she winced when she got up.

"But what is the illness exactly?" I asked.

She never answered me. Instead, she said, "I need a lie-down, if that's all right. It's been a long day."

"I'll make you a tea, Gran," I said.

"Lovely. Thank you."

Weeks went by and Gran was quieter than normal. When she made breakfast, she didn't hum. She came home from work early. She was losing weight rapidly and taking more and more medication each day.

I didn't understand. If she was taking medicine, why wasn't she getting better?

I launched an investigation. "Gran," I said, "what illness do you have? You never told me."

We were in the kitchen at the time, cleaning up after dinner. "My dear girl," she said. "Let's have a seat." We took our spots at our country-style dining set for two, which we'd salvaged years earlier from a bin outside of our building.

I waited for her to speak.

"I've been giving you time. Time to get used to the idea," she eventually said.

"Used to what idea?" I asked.

"Molly, dear. I have a serious illness."

"You do?"

"Yes. I have pancreatic cancer."

And just like that, the pieces clicked, the full picture emerged from the murky shadows. This explained the loss of weight and the lack of energy. Gran was only half herself, which is why she needed full and proper medical care so she could make a complete recovery.

"When will the medicine take effect?" I asked. "Maybe you need to see a different doctor?" But as she doled out the details, the truth began to sink in. Palliative. Such an operatic word, so lovely to say. And so hard to contemplate.

"It can't be, Gran," I insisted. "You will get better. We simply have to clean up this mess."

"Oh, Molly. Some messes can't be cleaned. I've had such a good life, I really have. I have no complaints, except that I won't have more time with you."

"No," I said. "This is unacceptable."

She looked at me then in such an unreadable way. She took my hand in hers. Her skin was so soft, so paper-thin, but her touch was warm, right to the end.

"Let's just be clear-eyed about this," she said. "I'm going to die."

I felt the room close in around me, felt it tilt on one end. For a moment, I couldn't breathe at all, could not so much as move. I was sure I was going to pass out right at the kitchen table.

"I've told the Coldwells I can't work anymore, but don't you worry, there's still the Fabergé. I hope that when my time comes, the good Lord takes me quickly, without too much pain. But if there is pain, I've got my prescription to help with that. And I have you. . . ."

"Gran," I said. "There has to be a—"

"There's one thing you must promise me," she said. "I will not go to the hospital under any circumstances. I won't spend my end days in an institution surrounded by strangers. There's no substitute for family, for the ones you love. Or for the comforts of home. If there's anyone I want by my bedside, it's you. Do you understand?"

Sadly, I did. I'd tried as hard as I could to ignore the truth, but it was now impossible. Gran needed me. What else was I to do?

That evening, Gran tired out long before *Columbo,* so I tucked her into bed, kissed her on the cheek, and said good night. Then I cleaned the kitchen cupboards and every dish we owned, one by one. I could not stop my tears from falling as I polished every bit of silver, not that we had much, but we had a little. When I was done, the entire kitchen smelled of lemons, but I couldn't shake the feeling that dirt lurked in the cracks and crevices, and unless I cleaned it, the contagion would spread into every facet of our lives.

I still hadn't said a thing to Gran about the Fabergé and Wilbur, how he'd left us penniless. How I could no longer pay tuition for college, how I was struggling to even keep up with the rent. Instead, I simply worked more shifts at the Regency Grand, took on more hours so that I could have enough to pay for everything—including Gran's pain-management medications and our groceries. We were late on the rent, which was another thing I didn't mention. Whenever I met our land-lord, Mr. Rosso, in the hall, I pleaded for more time to pay, explaining that Gran was sick and we were down to just my income.

Meanwhile, as Gran's health worsened, I read college brochures aloud to her at her bedside, explaining all the courses and workshops I was excited about, even though I knew I'd never make it to the first class. Gran closed her eyes, but I could tell she was listening because of the peaceful smile on her face.

"When I'm gone, you just use the Fabergé whenever you need to. If you keep working part-time, there will still be enough for rent for at least two years, and that's not including your tuition. It's all yours, so use it to make your life easier."

"Yes, Gran. Thank you."

I've been daydreaming and I didn't realize it. I'm standing by the front door of our apartment. My mop leans against the wall and I'm clutching Gran's serenity pillow to my chest. I don't remember when I put down my mop or when I picked up this pillow. The parquet floor is clean, but it's battered and scarred from decades of foot traffic, from the daily wear and tear of our domestic life. The overhead light bears down on me, too bright, too warm.

I'm all alone. How long have I been standing here? The floors are dry. My phone is ringing. I lean over and grab it from Gran's chair.

"Hello, this is Molly Gray speaking."

There's a pause on the other end of the line. "Molly. This is Alexander Snow from the hotel. I'm glad you're home."

"Thank you. Yes. I've been home for some time. The detective drove me here herself after she questioned me. Rather good of her, I thought."

"Yes. And thank you for agreeing to talk to her. I'm sure your insights will help the investigation."

He pauses again. I can hear his shallow breathing on the other end of the line. It is not the first time he has called me at home, but a call from Mr. Snow is a rare occurrence.

"Molly," he says again. "I realize this has been a very trying day for you. It's been hard on many of us, especially Mrs. Black. News has been spreading about Mr. Black's . . . demise. As you can imagine the entire staff is very upset and disturbed."

"Yes. I can imagine," I say.

"I realize that tomorrow is your one day off in weeks and that you went through a lot today, but it seems that Cheryl has taken the news of Mr. Black's death quite badly. She says the experience has caused her 'extreme trauma,' so she won't be coming in tomorrow."

"But she wasn't the one to find him dead," I say.

"Everyone reacts to stress in different ways, I suppose," he replies.

"Yes, of course," I reply.

"Molly, do you think you could come in her place and work the day shift tomorrow? Again, I'm sorry that—"

"Of course," I say. "An extra day of work isn't going to kill me."

Another long pause.

"Is that all, Mr. Snow?"

"Yes, that's all. And thank you. We'll see you tomorrow morning."

"You will indeed," I say. "Good night, Mr. Snow. Don't let the bed bugs bite."

"Good night, Molly."

TUESDAY

CHAPTER 6

I will admit to having bad dreams last night. I dreamed that Mr. Black walked through the front door of my apartment, gray and ashen, like the living dead. I was sitting on the sofa, watching *Columbo*. I turned to him and said, "No one comes here, not since Gran died." He started laughing—laughing at me. But I focused my laser gaze on him, and his limbs turned to dust, a fine charcoal particulate that spread around the room and into my lungs. I started gagging and coughing.

"No!" I yelled. "I didn't do this to you! It wasn't me! Get out!"

But it was too late. His grime was everywhere. I woke up gasping for air.

It's now six A.M. It's time to rise and shine. Or just rise.

I get out of bed and make it properly, careful to position Gran's quilt so that the star in the middle points due north. I go to the kitchen, where I put on Gran's paisley apron and prepare tea and crumpets for one. It's too quiet in the mornings. The scratchy grate of my knife against the toasted crumpet is an offense to my ears. I eat quickly, then shower and leave for work.

I'm locking the apartment door behind me when I hear someone clearing their throat in the hallway. Mr. Rosso.

I turn to face him. "Hello, Mr. Rosso. Up early this morning?"

I'm expecting the basic civility of a good morning, but all I get is, "Your rent is overdue. When will you pay up?"

I put my keys in my pocket. "The rent will be paid in a few days' time, and at that point, I will make good on every penny I owe you. You knew my gran, and you know me. We are law-abiding citizens who believe in paying our fair share. And I will do so. Soon."

"You'd better," he says, then shuffles back to his apartment, closing the door behind him.

I do wish people would pick up their feet when they walk. It's most slovenly to shuffle like that. It leaves a very poor impression.

Now, now, let's not judge others too harshly. I hear it in my head in Gran's voice, a reminder to be gracious and forgiving. It's a fault of mine, to be quick to judge or to want the world to function according to my laws.

We must be like bamboo. We must learn to bend and flex with the wind.

Bend and flex. Not my strong suits.

I head down the stairs and out of my building. I decide to walk all the way to work—a twenty-minute jaunt that's pleasant enough in good weather, though today the clouds are broody and threaten rain. I breathe a sigh of relief the second I set eyes on the bustling hotel. I'm a professional half hour early for my shift, as is my way.

I greet Mr. Preston at the front doors.

"Oh Molly. Tell me you're not working today."

"I am. Cheryl called in sick last night."

He shakes his head. "Naturally. Molly, are you all right? You had quite a scare yesterday, so I hear. I'm terribly sorry . . . about what you saw."

My dream flashes in my head for a moment, mixed with the real vision of Mr. Black, dead in his bed. "No need to be sorry, Mr. Preston. It's not your fault. But I'll admit, this whole situation has been a bit . . . trying. I'll keep calm and carry on." A thought occurs to me. "Mr. Preston, did Mr. Black receive any visitors yesterday, friendly or . . . otherwise?"

Mr. Preston adjusts his cap. "Not that I noticed," he says. "Why do you ask?"

"Oh, no reason," I say. "The police will investigate, I'm sure. Especially if something is amok."

"Amok?" Mr. Preston fixes me with a serious stare. "Molly, if ever you need anything—any help at all—you just remember your ol' friend Mr. Preston, you hear?"

I am not the kind to impose on other people. Surely Mr. Preston knows that much about me by now. His face is stern, his eyebrows knit with concern that even I can read clearly.

"Thank you, Mr. Preston," I say. "I appreciate your kind offer. Now, if you don't mind, I'm sure there's extra cleaning to tackle today since there were many officers and paramedics traipsing through this hotel yesterday. I fear not all of their boots are as clean as yours."

He tips his hat and turns his attention to some guests who are trying, unsuccessfully, to hail a cab.

"Taxi!" he calls out, then turns back to me for a moment, "Take good care, Molly. Please."

I nod and make my way up the plush red stairs. I push through the shiny revolving doors, jostling against guests heading in and out. In the front lobby, I see Mr. Snow by the reception desk. His glasses are akimbo, and a lock of hair has escaped his gelled-back coiffure. It wags back and forth on his head like a disapproving finger.

"Molly, I'm so glad you're here. Thank you," he says. He holds the day's newspaper in his hand. It's hard not to notice the headline: WEALTHY TYCOON CHARLES BLACK TURNS UP DEAD IN THE REGENCY GRAND HOTEL.

"Have you read this?" he asks.

He passes me the paper and I scan the article. It explains how a maid found Mr. Black dead in his bed. My name, thank goodness, is not mentioned. Then it talks about the Black family and the strife between his children and his ex-wife. "Rumors have been swirling for years around the legitimacy of Black Properties & Investments, with allegations of fraudulent dealings and embezzlement being shut down by Black's powerful team of attorneys."

Halfway through the article, I catch the name Giselle and read more carefully. "Giselle Black, Mr. Black's second wife, is thirty-five years his junior. She is the presumed heir to the Black fortunes, which have been the subject of family feuds in recent years. After Giselle Black's husband was found dead, she was seen leaving the hotel wearing dark glasses, accompanied by an unknown male. According to various staff members at the hotel, the Blacks are regular guests at the Regency Grand. When asked if Mr. Black conducted business at the hotel, Mr. Alexander Snow, the hotel manager, had no comment. According to lead detective Stark, foul play has not yet been ruled out as Mr. Black's cause of death."

I finish reading the article and pass the paper back to Mr. Snow. I suddenly feel unsteady on my feet as the implications of that final line sink in.

"Do you see, Molly? They're suggesting that this hotel is . . . is . . ."

"Foul," I offer. "Unclean."

"Yes, exactly."

Mr. Snow attempts to straighten his glasses, with limited success. "Molly, I must ask you, did you or have you, at any time, noticed any . . . questionable activities in this hotel? With the Blacks or any other guests?"

"Questionable?" I say.

"Nefarious," he explains.

"No!" I reply. "Absolutely not. If I had, you'd have been the first to know."

Mr. Snow releases a pent-up sigh. I feel sorry for him, for the burden he carries—the mighty reputation of the Regency Grand Hotel itself rests on his slight shoulders.

"Sir, may I ask you a question?"

"Of course."

"The article mentions Giselle Black. Do you know: is she still staying here? In the hotel, I mean?"

Mr. Snow's eyes dart left and right. He steps away from the reception desk and the smartly uniformed penguins manning it. He signals for me to do the same. Gaggles of guests are roaming the lobby; it's unusually busy this morning. Many of them hold newspapers in hand, and I suspect that Mr. Black may be the topic on the tip of many tongues.

Mr. Snow gestures to an emerald settee in a shadowy corner by the grand staircase. We make our way there. It's the first time I've ever sat on one of these settees. I sink into the soft velvet, no springs to circumvent, unlike our sofa at home. Mr. Snow perches beside me and speaks in a whisper. "To answer your question, Giselle is still staying here at the hotel, but you're not to pass that along. She has nowhere else to go, do you understand? And she's distraught, as you can imagine. I've moved her to the second floor. Sunitha will clean her room from now on."

I feel a nervous flutter in my stomach. "Very well," I say. "I best be off. This hotel won't clean itself."

"One more thing, Molly," Mr. Snow says. "The Black suite? It's out of bounds today, obviously. The police are still conducting their investigation in the room. You'll notice security tape, and a police guard posted outside the door."

"So when should I clean that suite?"

Mr. Snow stares at me for a long time. "You're not to clean it, Molly. That's what I'm trying to tell you."

"Very well. I won't then. Goodbye."

And with that, I stand, turn on my heel, and head down the marble stairs to my basement locker in the housekeeping quarters.

I'm greeted by my trusty uniform, crisp and clean, encased in plastic wrap, hung on my locker door. It's as though yesterday's upheavals never happened, as though every day conveniently erases the one that came before. I quickly change, leaving my own clothes in my locker. Then I grab my maid's trolley—which is, miracle of miracles, fully stocked and replenished (no doubt owing to Sunshine or Sunitha, and certainly not to Cheryl).

I head through the labyrinth of too-bright hallways until I make it to the kitchen, where Juan Manuel is scraping the remnants of breakfasts into a large garbage can and putting plates into the industrial dishwasher. I've never been in a sauna, but I imagine it must feel like this—minus the offensive odor of a medley of breakfast foods.

As soon as Juan Manuel sees me, he puts down the spray nozzle and eyes me with concern.

"*Dios te bendiga*," he says, crossing himself. "I am glad to see you. Are you okay? I've been worried about you, Miss Molly."

It's becoming upsetting that everyone is making such a fuss about me today. I'm not the one who died.

"I'm quite fine, thank you, Juan Manuel," I say.

"But you found him," he whispers, eyes wide. "Dead."

"I did."

"I can't believe he's really gone. I wonder what it means," he says.

"It means he's dead," I say.

"What I'm saying is, what will it mean for the hotel?" He takes a few steps closer to me, so close he's only half a trolley's width away.

"Molly," he whispers. "That man. Mr. Black? He was powerful. Too powerful. Who will be the boss now?"

"The boss is Mr. Snow," I say.

He looks at me strangely. "Is he? Is he really?"

"Yes," I reply with utmost confidence. "Mr. Snow is most definitely the boss of this hotel. Now, can we stop discussing this? I really need to get to work. Today, I'll make some new arrangements for tonight. I've just heard that the fourth floor is under surveillance. The police are still up there. I need you to stay in Room 202 tonight, okay? Second floor, not the fourth. To avoid the police."

"Okay. Don't worry. I'll stay clear."

"And Juan Manuel, I shouldn't be telling you this, but Giselle Black is staying somewhere on the same floor. On the second. So be careful. There may be investigators, even on her floor. You have to keep a low profile until this investigation is over. Understood?"

I hand him a keycard for Room 202. "Yes, Molly. Understood. You need to keep a low profile, too, okay? I worry about you."

"There's nothing to worry about," I say. "I best be off." Then I exit the kitchen and wheel my trolley to the service elevator. I step in, the air instantly fresher and cooler, and I ride up to the lobby, where I'll retrieve my daily stack of papers from the Social.

Even from afar, I can spot Rodney behind the bar. When he sees me, he rushes out to greet me.

"Molly! You're here." He puts his hands on my shoulders. I feel them like electricity, warming me to my core. "Are you all right?"

"Everyone keeps asking me that. I'm all right," I say. "Perhaps a hug would not be too much to ask of you?"

"Of course!" he says. "You're actually just the person I wanted to see today." He folds me into his chest. I rest my head on his shoulder and take in the scent of him.

It's been so long since I've been hugged that I don't know what I'm supposed to do with my arms. I opt to wrap them around his back and rest them on his shoulder blades, which are even stronger than I would have imagined.

He pulls away before I'm ready. It's only then that I notice his right eye. It's swollen and purple, as though he's been punched. "What happened to you?" I ask.

"Oh, it was stupid. I was helping Juan Manuel with a bag in his room, and I . . . I ran into the door. Ask him. He'll tell you."

"You should ice that. It looks sore."

"Enough about me, I want to hear how *you're* doing." He looks around the bar as he says this. Groups of middle-aged women eat breakfast together, teaspoons tinkling against ceramic, laughter echoing as they while away the morning hours before their theater matinees. A few families are filling up on stacks of pancakes before a day full of museums and sightseeing. And two lone-wolf business travelers peck at continental breakfasts, their eyes glued to their phones or the newspapers splayed in front of them. Who is Rodney looking for? Surely it's none of these guests. But if not them, who?

"Listen," Rodney says in a hush. "I heard you found Mr. Black yesterday and that they took you to the cop shop to ask you questions. I can't talk now, but why don't you come by after your shift? We can grab a quiet booth and you can tell me everything. Every last detail, okay?" He reaches for my hand and squeezes it in his. His eyes are deep pools of blue. He is concerned. Concerned for me. For a moment, I wonder if he's going to kiss me, but then I realize how daft that is—kissing a fellow employee in the middle of the bar and grill. Of course he wouldn't do that. But it's a pity nonetheless.

"It would be lovely to meet you later," I say, aiming for coy nonchalance. "So five P.M.? Sharp? Is this a date?"

"Uh, yeah. Okay."

"I'll see you then," I say, and start to walk away.

"Don't forget your newspapers," he says. He grabs a stack from the floor and plops them on the bar.

"Oh, silly me." I struggle with the full stack as I carry them to my trolley. He's now distracted behind the bar, pouring a coffee for a customer. I try to make eye contact with him one last time, but to no avail.

That's fine. We'll have plenty of time for eye contact tonight.

—

CHAPTER 7

L ife is a funny thing. One day can be quite shocking, and so can the next. But the two shocks might be as different from each other as night from day, as black from white, as good from evil. Yesterday, I found Mr. Black dead; today, Rodney asked me on a date. Technically, I suppose we won't be "going" on a date but "staying" on a date because it will happen at our place of work. But that's a matter of semantics. The date part is what's most relevant.

It has been well over a year since Rodney and I went on our last date. *Good things come to those who wait*, Gran always said, and yes, Gran, you were right about that. Just when I thought Rodney wasn't interested in me, then he reveals that he is. And his timing is impeccable. Yesterday was a jolt to my system. Today is also a jolt but in a much more pleasant and exciting way. It goes to show you that you just never know what surprises life has in store for you.

I push my trolley through the lobby and head toward the elevator. Another group of ladies, probably on a "girls' getaway," rushes past me. They close the elevator in my face, something I'm used to. The maid can wait. The maid goes last. Finally, I get an elevator all to myself and push number 4. The button glows red. I feel queasy as I go back to the fourth floor for the first time since finding Mr. Black dead in his bed. *Pull yourself together,* I think. *You don't have to enter that suite today.*

The doors chime and open. I push my trolley out but immediately bash into something. I look up to discover I've just run into a police officer, his eyes so glued to his phone that he's entirely unaware that he's blocking the elevator. Regardless of who's at fault, I know exactly what I'm supposed to do. I learned this in an early training session with Mr. Snow: the guest is always right, even when they are paying no mind whatsoever to whom they may be inconveniencing.

"My sincerest apologies, sir. Are you all right?" I ask.

"Yeah, I'm fine. But watch where you're going with that thing."

"I appreciate the advice. Thank you, Officer," I say as I maneuver my trolley around him. What I really want is to run right over his toes since he refuses to step out of the way, but this would be inappropriate. Once I'm past him, I pause. "May I be of assistance to you in any way? A hot towel, perhaps? Some shampoo?"

"I'm fine," he says. "Excuse me."

He steps around me and I watch as he heads toward the Black suite. There is bright-yellow caution tape across the door. He stands to the side of it, leaning against the wall, one foot crossed over the other. I can see already that if he lolls around like that all day, he'll leave a stain that will be a challenge to erase. I'd love to take my broom handle and flick him off the wall, but never mind. It's not my place.

I head to the far end of the floor to begin my work in Room 407. I'm pleased to find it empty, the guests checked out. There's a five-dollar bill on the pillow, which I pick up and put in my pocket with quiet thanks. *Every penny counts,* as Gran always said. I busy myself with stripping the bed and laying fresh sheets. My hands are a bit shaky today, I must admit. Every once in a while, a flash of Mr. Black enters my mind—sallow face, cold to the touch—and all the things I witnessed after. A bolt of electricity flashes through me. There's nothing to be antsy about, though. Today is not yesterday. Today is a brand-new day. To ease my nerves, I concentrate on happy thoughts. And nothing is happier to me right now than thoughts of Rodney.

As I clean, I replay our burgeoning relationship in my mind. I remember when I first began working at the hotel and didn't know him well. Every day, as I collected my newspapers at the start of my shift, I tried to linger a bit longer. Slowly, over time, we became quite cordial—dare I say congenial? But it was one day over a year and a half ago when our affection was cemented.

I was on the third floor, cleaning my rooms. Sunshine was cleaning one half of the floor and I was tackling the other. I entered Room 305, which was not on my roster for that shift, but the front desk had told me it was vacant and needed to be cleaned. I didn't even bother knocking since I'd been told it was empty, but when I pushed through the door with my trolley, I came face-to-face with two very imposing men.

Gran taught me to judge people by their actions rather than by their appearances, so when I looked upon these two behemoths with shaved heads and perplexing facial tattoos, I immediately assumed the best of them rather than the worst. Maybe these guests were a famous rock duo I'd never heard of? Or perhaps they were trendy tattoo artists? Or world-renowned wrestlers? Since I prefer antiques to pop culture, how would I know?

"My sincerest apologies, sirs," I said. "I was told that all the guests in this room had vacated. I'm terribly sorry to disturb you."

I smiled then, as per protocol, and waited for the gentlemen to respond. But neither said a word. There was a navy-blue duffel bag on the bed. One of the giants had been packing away a piece of equipment when I intruded, some kind of machine or scale that he was about to put in the bag. Now, he stood stock-still with the odd apparatus in one hand.

Just when I was feeling slightly uncomfortable with the amount of silence that lingered, two people stepped out of the bathroom behind the two men. One was Rodney, in his crisp, white shirt, with sleeves rolled, revealing his lovely forearms. The other was Juan Manuel, who was holding a brown paper package, his bagged lunch or dinner, perhaps? Rodney's hands were balled into fists. He and Juan Manuel were clearly surprised to see me, and to be perfectly honest, I, too, was surprised to see them.

"Molly, no. Why are you here?" Juan Manuel asked. "Please, you need to leave right away."

Rodney turned to Juan Manuel. "What, are you the boss now? You're suddenly in charge?"

Juan Manuel took two steps backward and became entranced by the position of his feet on the floor.

I decided this was the moment to step in and smooth the rift between them. "Technically speaking," I said, "Rodney is the bar manager. Which means that in the strictly hierarchical sense, he is the highest-ranking employee among us at the present moment. But let's remember that we're all VIPs, every last one of us," I said.

The two behemoths looked from Rodney and Juan Manuel to me several times in quick succession.

"Molly," Rodney said. "What are you doing here?"

"Isn't it obvious?" I answered. "I'm here to clean the room."

"Yeah, I get that part. But this room wasn't supposed to be on your roster today. I told them downstairs . . ."

"Told whom?" I asked.

"Look, it doesn't matter. That's not the point."

Juan Manuel suddenly rushed past Rodney and grabbed my arm. "Molly, don't worry about me. Run downstairs now and you go tell—"

"Whoa," said Rodney. "Let go of her, right now." It wasn't a suggestion. It was an order.

"Oh, it's quite all right," I said. "Juan Manuel and I are acquaintances and I'm not in the least uncomfortable." It was only then that it dawned on me exactly what was going on. Rodney was jealous of Juan Manuel. This was a masculine display of romantic rivalry. I took this as a very good sign, since it revealed the true extent of Rodney's feelings for me.

Rodney eyed Juan Manuel in a way that conveyed his clear displeasure, but then he said something entirely surprising. "How's your mother, Juan Manuel?" he asked. "Your family's in Mazatlán, right? I've got friends in Mexico, you know. Good ones. I'm sure they'd be happy to check in on your family."

Juan Manuel let go of my arm then. "No need," he said. "They are fine."

"Good. Let's keep it that way," he replied.

How lovely that Rodney was concerned about the well-being of Juan Manuel's family, I thought. The more I got to know him, the more his true nature revealed itself to me.

At this moment, the two behemoths spoke up. I was looking forward to being properly introduced so that I could commit their names to memory for future reference, perhaps even make sure they received chocolate turn-down service in the evenings.

"What the hell is going on here?" one of them asked Rodney.

"Who the fuck is she?" the other added.

Rodney stepped forward. "It's okay. Don't worry. I'll fix this."

"You better. And fuckin' fast."

Now, I must say that this repeated use of foul language took me aback, but I have been trained to act as a consummate professional at all times, with all manner of people, be they polite or impolite, clean or slovenly, potty-mouthed or well-spoken.

Rodney got right in front of me. In a low voice, he said, "You weren't supposed to see any of this."

"See what?" I asked. "The colossal mess all of you have made in this room?"

One of the behemoths spoke up then. "Lady, we've just cleaned everything up good."

"Well," I said. "You've done a substandard job. As you can see, the carpet needs a vacuum. Your footprints are all over it. See that? How the pile is disturbed by the front door, and then over there, by the bathroom? It looks like a herd of elephants tromped through here. Not to mention this side table. Who ate powdered doughnuts without a plate?

And these big, fat fingerprints. No offense, but how could you not notice those? They're all over the glass top. I'll have to polish every doorknob too."

I took a spray bottle and paper towel from my trolley and began spritzing the table. I cleaned up the whole mess in a flash. "See? Isn't that better?"

The behemoths' faces mirrored each other—their long mouths agape. Clearly, they were quite impressed with my efficient cleaning techniques. Juan Manuel, meanwhile, was obviously embarrassed. He was still staring at his shoes.

No one spoke for a good, long while. Something was amiss, but I was hard-pressed to say what. It was Rodney who broke the silence. He turned his back on me and addressed his friends. "Molly is . . . she's a very special girl. You can see that, right? How she's . . . unique."

What a lovely thing for him to say. I felt truly flattered and avoided eye contact for fear that I was blushing. "I'm happy to clean up after your friends anytime," I said. "In fact, it would be my pleasure. You just have to tell me what room you're staying in and I'll ask for it to be added to my roster."

Rodney addressed his friends again. "Can you see how helpful she could be? And she's discreet. Right, Molly? You're discreet?"

"Discretion is my motto. Invisible customer service is my goal."

Both men suddenly moved in on me, pushing Rodney and Juan Manuel out of the way.

"So you're not a squawker, right? You won't talk?"

"I'm a maid, not a gossip, thank you very much. I'm paid to keep my mouth shut and return rooms to a state of perfection. I pride myself on getting the job done and then disappearing without a trace."

The two men glanced at each other and shrugged.

"You good?" Rodney asked them. They nodded, then turned to the duffel bag on the bed. "And you?" Rodney asked Juan Manuel. "All good?"

Juan Manuel nodded, but his lips were a sharp line.

"Okay, Molly," Rodney said as he looked at me with those piercing blue eyes of his. "Everything will be fine. You just do your job like you usually do, okay? You leave this place spotless so no one will ever know Juan Manuel and his buddies were here. And you keep quiet about it."

"Of course. And if you'll excuse me, I really should get to work."

Rodney came in close to me. "Thank you," he whispered. "We'll talk more about this later. Let's meet up tonight, okay? I'll explain everything."

It was the first time he proposed such a rendezvous. I could barely believe my ears. "I would love that!" I said. "So it's a date?"

"Sure. Yeah. Meet me in the lobby at six. We'll go somewhere and talk privately."

And with that, the behemoths grabbed the duffel bag, pushed past me, and opened the hotel room door. They looked down the hallway, left then right. Then they gestured for Rodney and Juan Manuel to follow. All four of them promptly vacated the room.

The rest of that morning went by in a blur of activity. As I cleaned furiously, yearning for six o'clock to come, I suddenly realized that I'd worn old but serviceable slacks and one of Gran's high-collared blouses to work that morning. This would not do at all, not for a first date with Rodney.

I finished the room I was cleaning and pulled my trolley into the hall. I searched for Sunitha on the other side of the floor.

"Knock-knock," I said, though the suite she was cleaning was wide open. She stopped what she was doing and looked at me. "I need to run an errand. If Cheryl comes up here, would you tell her . . . that I'll be back shortly?"

"Yes, Molly. It's well past lunchtime and you never stop. You're allowed to take a break, you know." She began to hum as she continued cleaning.

"Thank you," I said, dashing out of the room and down the hall to the elevator. I rushed out the revolving front doors.

"Molly? Everything all right?" Mr. Preston asked as I sailed by him.

"Splendid!" I called back. I took to the sidewalk, jogging. I raced around the corner to a little boutique I passed every day on my way to

work. I'd always admired the lovely lemon-yellow sign and the manne-
quin in the window, smartly dressed in a chic new outfit every day. This
was not a place I'd normally shop. It was meant for the guests of the
hotel, not for their maid.

I grabbed the door handle and stepped inside. A shopkeeper approached me instantly.

"You look like you need some help," she said.

"Yes," I replied, a bit breathlessly. "I need an outfit posthaste. I have a
date tonight with a subject of potential romantic intrigue."

"Whoa," she said. "You're in luck. Romantic intrigue is my specialty."

About twenty-two minutes later, I was leaving the store with a large
lemon-yellow bag containing a polka-dot top, something called "skinny
jeans," and a pair of "kitten heels" that did not have kittens on them so
far as I could tell. I nearly fainted when the shopkeeper announced the
total, but it seemed a breach of decorum to back out of payment when
the items were already bagged. I paid using my debit card, then rushed
back to the hotel. I tried not to think about the rent money I'd just spent
and how I'd replace it.

I was back at work at 12:54, just in time to start work again. Mr. Preston did a double-take when he saw my shopping bag, but he refrained
from comment. I hurried down the marble stairs to the housekeeping
quarters, where I stowed my new purchases in my locker. Back to work
I went, Cheryl never the wiser.

That night, at exactly six P.M., I showed up in the hotel lobby dressed
in my new outfit. I'd even managed to style my hair a bit with a curling
iron from the lost and found, making it sleek and smooth the way I'd
seen Giselle do with her flat iron. I watched as Rodney entered the lobby
and looked for me, his eyes brushing right past me and then back, because he failed to recognize me at first glance.

He approached. "Molly?" he said. "You look . . . different."

"Different good or bad?" I asked. "I put my trust in a local shopkeeper, and I hope she didn't lead me astray. Fashion is not my forte."

"You look . . . great." Rodney's eyes darted about the room. "Let's get
out of here, okay? We can go to the Olive Garden down the street."

I could not believe it! It was fate. A sign. The Olive Garden is my very favorite restaurant. It was Gran's favorite too. Every year, on her birthday and on mine, we'd ready ourselves for a big night out together, complete with endless garlic bread and free salad. The last time we went to the Olive Garden together, Gran turned seventy-five. We ordered two glasses of Chardonnay to celebrate.

"To you, Gran, on three-quarters of a century, one quarter left to go, at a minimum!"

"Hear, hear!" said Gran.

The fact that Rodney had chosen my favorite dining establishment? We were star-crossed, meant to be.

Mr. Preston eyed us as we exited the hotel. "Molly, are you all right?" he asked as he offered his arm, steadying me as I wobbled uncertainly down the staircase in my new feline heels. Rodney had raced down the stairs ahead of me and was waiting on the sidewalk, checking his phone.

"Not to worry, Mr. Preston," I said. "I'm very well indeed."

Once we were at the bottom step, Mr. Preston assumed a low tone. "You're not going out with him, are you?" he asked.

"As a matter of fact," I whispered, "I am. So if you'll excuse me . . ." I gave his arm a little squeeze and then teetered up to Rodney on the sidewalk.

"I'm ready. Let's go," I said. Rodney began walking without glancing up from the important, last-minute business he was taking care of on his phone. Once we were away from the hotel, he put his phone away and slowed his pace.

"Sorry about that," he said. "A bartender's work is never done."

"That's quite all right," I replied. "Yours is a very important job. You're an integral bee in the hive."

I hoped he was impressed by my reference to Mr. Snow's employee-training seminar, but if he was, he did not show it.

All the way to the restaurant, I babbled on about any and all topics of interest I could think of—the advantages of real feather dusters versus synthetic ones, the waitresses he worked with who rarely remembered my name and, of course, my love for the Olive Garden.

After what seemed like a long time but was probably only sixteen and a half minutes, we arrived at the entrance of the Olive Garden. "After you," Rodney said, politely opening the door for me.

A helpful young waitress seated us in a perfectly romantic booth tucked to one side of the restaurant.

"Want a drink?" Rodney asked.

"That sounds lovely. I'll have a glass of Chardonnay. Will you join me?"

"I'm more of a beer kind of guy."

The waitress returned and we ordered our drinks. "Can we order food right away?" Rodney asked. He looked at me. "Ready?"

Indeed I was, ready for anything. I ordered what I always ordered. "The Tour of Italy, please," I said. "Because how can you go wrong with a trio of lasagna, fettucine, and chicken parmigiana?" I smiled at Rodney in a way I hoped was somewhat coquettish.

He looked down at his menu. "Spaghetti and meatballs."

"Yes, sir. Would you like free salad and garlic bread?"

"No, that's fine," Rodney answered, which, I'll admit, was a minor disappointment.

The waitress then left and we were alone under the warm ambient glow of the pendant light. Taking Rodney in from such a close vantage point made me forget all about salad and garlic bread.

He rested his elbows on the table, an etiquette faux pas that was forgivable this one time since it offered me a fine view of his forearms.

"Molly, you're probably wondering what was going on today. With those men. In that hotel room. I didn't want you to go away thinking anything bad or to start talking about what you saw. I wanted a chance to explain."

The waitress returned with our drinks.

"Here's to us," I said, holding my wine stem delicately between two fingers as Gran had taught me (*A lady never touches the bowl—it leaves unsightly fingerprints*). Rodney picked up his beer stein and clinked it against my glass. Being quite thirsty, he gulped half of his beverage before setting it back down on the tabletop with a clang.

"Like I was saying," he said. "I wanted to explain what you saw today." He paused and stared at me.

"You really do have the most arresting blue eyes," I said. "I hope you don't find it inappropriate of me to point that out."

"Funny. Someone else told me the same thing recently. Anyhow, here's what I need you to know. Those two men in that room? They're Juan Manuel's friends, not mine. Do you understand?"

"I think that's lovely," I said. "I'm glad he's made some friends here. His entire family is in Mexico, as you know. And I think he may feel lonely from time to time. That's something I can understand, having felt lonely myself from time to time. Not now, of course. I don't feel lonely at all in this particular moment."

I took a deep, delicious sip from my glass.

"So here's the thing you probably don't know about my buddy Juan Manuel," Rodney said. "He's actually not a documented immigrant at the moment. His work permit ran out a while back and he's now working under the table at the hotel. Mr. Snow doesn't know that. If Juan Manuel were caught, he'd be kicked out of the country and would never be able to send money home ever again. You know how important his family is to him, right?"

"I do," I said. "Family is very important. Wouldn't you agree?"

"Not so much," he said. "Mine disowned me years ago." He took another gulp of his beer, then wiped his mouth with the back of his hand.

"I'm very sorry to hear that," I said. I couldn't imagine why anyone would turn down a chance to be familial with a fine man like Rodney.

"Right," he said. "So those two men you saw in that room? That bag they had? That was Juan Manuel's bag. It wasn't theirs. It definitely wasn't mine. It was Juan Manuel's. Got it?"

"I understand, yes. We all have baggage." I paused, allowing ample time for Rodney to pick up on my clever double entendre. "That's a joke," I explained. "Those men were literally carrying baggage, but the expression usually refers to psychological baggage. You see?"

"Yeah. Okay. So the thing is that Juan Manuel's landlord figured out his papers expired. He kicked him out of his apartment a while back.

Now he has nowhere to live. I've been helping Juan Manuel sort things out. You know, like with the law, because I know people. I do what I can to help him make ends meet. All of this is a secret, Molly. Are you good at keeping secrets?"

He locked eyes with me, and I felt the great privilege of being his confidante.

"Of course I can keep a secret," I said. "Especially yours. I have a locked box near my heart for all of your confidences," I said as I mimed locking a box on my chest.

"Cool," he replied. "So there's more. It's like this. Every night, I've secretly been putting Juan Manuel up in a different room at the hotel so that he doesn't have to sleep on the streets. But no one can know, you understand? If anyone found out what I was doing . . ."

"You'd be in a lot of trouble. And Juan Manuel would be homeless," I said.

"Yeah. Exactly," he replied.

Yet again, Rodney was proving what a good man he was. Out of the goodness of his heart, he was helping a friend. I was so moved I was at a loss for words.

Fortunately, the waitress returned and filled the silence with my Tour of Italy platter and Rodney's spaghetti and meatballs.

"Bon appétit," I said.

I had a few extremely satisfying mouthfuls, then put my fork down. "Rodney, I'm very impressed by you. You're a fine man."

Rodney's mouth bulged with a meatball. "I try," he said, chewing and swallowing. "But I could use your help, Molly."

"Help how?" I asked.

"It's getting harder for me to know which hotel rooms are vacant. Let's just say there are key staffers who used to slip me info, but they might not be so into me anymore. But you . . . you're beyond suspicion, and you know which rooms are free every night. Plus, you're so good at cleaning things up, just like you proved today. It would be amazing if you could tell me which room is empty on any given night and if you could make sure you're the one to clean it before and after we—I mean, Juan Manuel and his friends—stay there. You know, just make sure there's no sign of anyone having ever been there at all."

I carefully placed my cutlery on the edge of my plate. I took another sip of wine. I could feel the effects of the beverage reaching my extremities and my cheeks, making me feel liberated and uninhibited, two things I hadn't felt in . . . well, as long as I could recall.

"I would be delighted to help you in any way I can," I said.

He put his fork down with a clatter and reached for my hand. The sensation was pleasingly electric. "I knew I could count on you, Molly," he said.

It was a lovely compliment. I was struck speechless again, lost in those deep blue pools.

"And one more thing. You won't tell anyone about any of this, right? About what you saw today? You won't say a word, especially not to Snow. Or Preston. Or even Chernobyl."

"That goes without saying, Rodney. What you're doing is vigilante justice. It's making something right in a world that's so often wrong. I understand that. Robin Hood had to make exceptions in order to help the poor."

"Yeah, that's me. I'm Robin Hood." He picked up his fork again and popped a fresh meatball into his mouth. "Molly, I could kiss you. I really could."

"That would be wonderful. Shall we wait until after you swallow?"

He laughed then and quickly gobbled the rest of his pasta. I didn't even have to ask: I knew he was laughing with me, not at me.

I was hoping we could linger longer and order dessert, but as soon as his plate was finished, he promptly asked the waitress for the bill.

When we were leaving the restaurant, he held the door open for me, a perfect gentleman. Once we were outside, he said, "So we have a deal, right? One friend helping another?"

"Yes. At the beginning of my shift, I'll tell Juan Manuel what room he can stay in that night. I'll give him a keycard and the room number. And

I'll pop in early every morning to clean the room he and his friends were in the night before. Cheryl's tardiness is legendary, so she won't even notice."

"That's perfect, Molly. You really are a special girl."

I knew from *Casablanca* and *Gone with the Wind* that this was the moment. I leaned forward so he could kiss me. I think he was aiming for my cheek, but I moved in such a way as to suggest I was not opposed to a kiss on the mouth. Unfortunately, the connection was a little misaligned, though my nose was not entirely disappointed by the unexpected affection.

In that moment, when Rodney kissed me, it didn't matter where his lips landed. In fact, nothing except the kiss mattered to me at all, not the splotch of red sauce on his collar, not the way he reached for his phone right after, not even the piece of limp basil stuck between his teeth.

CHAPTER 8

I t's almost the end of my shift. Playing over our first date in my mind has made the day go by quickly and has amplified my anticipation for our date tonight. It has also helped me avoid memories of yesterday. For the most part, I've been successful at keeping the flashbacks at bay. There was just the one instance when I remembered Mr. Black, dead in his bed, and for some reason, in my mind, suddenly, it was Rodney's face on Mr. Black's body, as though they were twinned, inextricably linked.

What utter rubbish. How could I imagine them connected like that, when they exist on polar opposites of so many spectrums—old versus young, dead versus alive, evil versus good? I shook my head back and forth to erase the nasty image. And just like with an Etch-a-Sketch, a good shake was all it took to wipe my mind clean.

The other intrusive thoughts I've had today are of Giselle. I know she's still staying in the hotel, but I don't know where, which room on the second floor. I do wonder how she's doing, what with her husband dead. Is she happy about this turn of events? Or is she sad? Is she relieved to be free from him or concerned about her future? What does she stand to inherit, if anything at all? If the newspapers are right, she's the heir apparent to the family fortune, but Mr. Black's first wife and kids will no doubt have something to say about that. And if I've learned anything about the way money works, it's that it magnetizes toward those born with it, leaving those who need it most without.

It weighs on me—what will become of Giselle.

This is the problem with friendships. Sometimes you know things you shouldn't know; sometimes you carry other people's secrets for them. And sometimes, that burden takes its toll.

It's four-thirty P.M., only half an hour before I'm due to meet Rodney at the Social for our date. Our second date—progress!

I scoot down the hall with my trolley to let Sunshine know I'm done cleaning all my rooms, including the one Juan Manuel stayed in last night.

"You're a quick one, you are, Miss Molly!" Sunshine says. "I've got more rooms to finish, myself."

I say goodbye for the day, then pass by the police officer on my way to the elevator, but he barely registers my presence. I take the elevator to the basement. I peel off my maid uniform and change into my regular clothes, some jeans and a floral blouse—not quite what I would have chosen for a date with Rodney, but I've no more money to spend on excesses such as kitten heels and polka dots. Besides, if Rodney's truly a good egg, he'll judge by the yolk, not by the shell.

At five to five, I'm downstairs at the front of the Social, waiting by the Please Be Seated sign, looking around for Rodney. He sees me, comes from the back of the restaurant right to my side.

"Just in time, I see."

"I pride myself on punctuality," I reply.

"Let's go to a booth at the back."

"Privacy. Yes, that seems appropriate."

We walk through the restaurant to the most secluded—and romantic—booth at the back.

"It's very quiet here now," I say, taking in the empty chairs, the two waitresses by their service station talking to each other because there's hardly a customer in sight.

"Yeah. Wasn't like this earlier. Lots of cops. And reporters." He looks around the room, then at me. His bruised eye looks a bit better than it did this morning, but it's still swollen.

"Listen, I'm really sorry about what happened to you yesterday, finding Mr. Black and all that. Plus, being taken to the cop shop. That must have been intense."

"It was a disruptive day. Today is going much better. Especially now," I add.

"So tell me, when you were with the cops, I hope nothing about Juan Manuel came up."

This is a perplexing line of inquiry. "No," I say. "That has nothing to do with Mr. Black."

"Right. Of course it doesn't. But you know. Cops can be nosy. I just want to make sure he's safe." He runs the fingers of one hand through his thick, wavy hair. "Can you tell me what happened, what you saw in that suite yesterday?" he asks. "I mean, I'm sure you're feeling really scared, and maybe it would help to say it all out loud to, you know, a friend."

He reaches his hand out to touch mine. It's amazing, the human hand, how much warmth it conveys. I've missed physical contact, what without Gran in my life. She used to do exactly this, put her hand over mine to draw me out and get me to talk. Her hand let me know that no matter what, everything would be okay.

"Thank you," I say to Rodney. It surprises me; it comes out of nowhere—the urge to cry. I fight it as I tell him about yesterday. "It all seemed like a normal day until I went to finish cleaning the Blacks' room. I stepped inside and saw that the sitting room was untidy. I was only supposed to clean the bathroom, but then I went into the bedroom to see if that was a mess as well, and there he was, laid out on the bed. I thought he was napping, but . . . it turns out he was dead. Very dead."

At this, Rodney takes his other hand so that he's cradling mine in both of his. "Oh, Molly," he says. "That's just awful. And . . . did you see anything in the room? Anything out of place or suspicious?"

I tell him about the safe being open, how the money was gone, along with the deed I'd seen in Mr. Black's breast pocket earlier in the day.

"And that's it? Nothing else out of the ordinary?"

"Actually, yes," I say. I tell him about Giselle's pills spilled on the floor.

"What pills?" he asks.

"Giselle has an unmarked bottle. It was that bottle, spilled by Mr. Black's bedside."

"Shit. You're kidding me."

"I'm not."

"And where was Giselle?"

"I don't know. She wasn't in the suite. In the morning, she seemed quite upset. I know she was planning a trip, because I saw her flight itinerary sticking out of her purse." I shift in my chair, bringing my chin to rest on my hand coquettishly, like a starlet in a classic film.

"Did you tell the cops that? About the itinerary? Or the pills?"

I'm growing increasingly impatient with this line of interrogation, yet I know that patience is a virtue, a virtue that, among others, I hope he attributes to me.

"I told them about the pills," I say. "But I didn't want to say much else. To be honest, and I hope you'll keep this confidential, Giselle has been more than just a guest. She's . . . well, she's become a friend to me. And I'm quite worried about her. The nature of the police questions, they were . . ."

"What? They were what?"

"It was almost as though they were suspicious. Of her."

"But did Black die of natural causes or not?"

"The police were fairly certain that was the case. But not completely."

"Did they ask anything else? About Giselle? About me?"

I feel something slither in my stomach, as though a sleeping dragon were just roused from its torpor. "Rodney," I say, with an edge in my voice that I have trouble hiding. "Why would they ask about you?"

"That was stupid," he says. "No idea why I said that. Forget it."

He pulls his hands away and I immediately wish he would put them back.

"I guess I'm just worried. For Giselle. For the hotel. For all of us, really."

It occurs to me then that I'm missing something. Every year at Christmas, Gran and I would set up a card table in the living room and work on a puzzle together as we listened to Christmas carols on the radio. The harder the puzzle, the happier we were. And I'm feeling the same sensation I felt when Gran and I were challenged by a really hard puzzle. It's as if I'm not quite putting the pieces together properly.

Then it occurs to me. "You said you don't know Giselle well. Is that correct?"

He sighs. I know what this means. I've exasperated him, even though I didn't mean to.

"Can't a guy be concerned for someone who seems like a nice person?" he asks. There's a sharp clip to his consonants that reminds me of Cheryl when she's up to something unsanitary.

I must course-correct before I put Rodney off me entirely. "I'm sorry," I say, smiling widely and leaning forward in my chair. "You have every right to be concerned. It's just the way you are. You care about others."

"Exactly." He reaches into his back pocket and takes out his phone. "Molly, take my number," he says.

A frisson of excitement flitters through me, removing any and all slithering doubt. "You want me to have your phone number?" I've done it. I've mended fences. Our date is back on track.

"If anything happens—like the police bother you again or ask too many questions—you just let me know. I'll be there for you."

I take out my phone and we exchange numbers. When I write my name in his phone, I feel inclined to add an identifier. "Molly, Maid and Friend," I type. I even add a heart emoji at the end as a declaration of amorous intent.

My hands feel jittery as I pass back his phone. I'm hoping he'll look at my entry and see the heart, but he doesn't.

Mr. Snow enters the restaurant then. I see him by the bar, grabbing some paperwork before leaving. Rodney is slouching in the seat opposite me. He should not be shy about remaining in the workplace after the end of his shift—Mr. Snow says that's a sign of an A++ employee.

"Listen, I've gotta go," Rodney says. "You'll call if anything comes up?"

"I will," I say. "I most definitely will make phone contact."

He gets up from the booth and I follow him out the lobby and through the front doors. Mr. Preston is just outside the entrance.

I wave and he tips his hat.

"Hey, any cabs around here?" Rodney asks.

"Of course," Mr. Preston says. He walks to the street, blows his whistle, and waves down a taxi. When it pulls over, Mr. Preston opens the back door. "In you go, Molly," he says.

"No, no," Rodney replies. "The cab's for me. You're going . . . somewhere else, right, Molly?"

"I'm going east," I say.

"Right. I'm west. Have a good night!"

Rodney gets in and Mr. Preston closes the door. As the taxi pulls away, Rodney waves at me through the window.

"I'll call you!" I yell after him.

Mr. Preston stands beside me. "Molly," he says. "Be careful with that one."

"With Rodney? Why?" I ask.

"Because that, dear girl, is a frog. And not all frogs turn out to be princes."

CHAPTER 9

I walk home briskly, full of energy and butterflies from my time with Rodney. I think back to Mr. Preston's uncharitable comment about frogs and princes. It occurs to me how easy it is to misjudge people. Even an upstanding man like Mr. Preston can sometimes get it wrong. Minus the smooth chest, Rodney entirely lacks amphibious qualities. My chiefest hope is that while he is not a frog, Rodney will turn out to be the prince of my very own fairy tale.

I wonder to myself what the etiquette is around wait times before I dial Rodney's phone number. Should I call him immediately to thank him for our date or should I wait until tomorrow? Perhaps I should text him instead? My only experience with such matters was with Wilbur, who despised talking on the phone and used text messages for time- or task-related correspondence only: "Expected arrival time: 7:03," "Bananas on sale: 0.49 cents. Buy while quantities last." If Gran were still around, I'd ask for advice, but that is no longer an option.

As I approach my building, I notice a familiar figure standing outside the front doors. For a moment I'm sure I'm hallucinating, but as I get closer, I see it really is her. She's wearing her large dark sunglasses and carrying her pretty yellow purse.

"Giselle?" I say as I approach.

"Oh, thank God. Molly, I'm so glad to see you." Before I can say anything else, she opens her arms and hugs me tight. I'm at a loss for words, mostly because I can barely breathe. She releases me, tips her sunglasses back so I can see her red-rimmed eyes. "Can I come in?"

"Of course," I say. "I can't believe you're here. I'm . . . I'm so pleased to see you."

"Not as pleased as I am to see you," she says.

I rummage through my pockets and manage to find my keys. My hands shake a little as I open the door and invite her into my building.

She steps in gingerly and looks around the lobby. Crumpled flyers litter the ground, surrounded by muddy footprints and cigarette butts—such a filthy habit. Her face registers disdain at the mess, so much so that I can read it clearly.

"It's unfortunate, isn't it? I do wish every tenant would participate in keeping the entrance clean. I think you'll find Gran's . . . *my* apartment much more sanitary," I say.

I guide her through the entrance and toward the stairwell.

She looks up the looming staircase. "What floor are you on?" she asks.

"Fifth," I say.

"Can we take the elevator?"

"I do apologize. There isn't one."

"Wow," she says, but she joins me in marching up the stairs even though she's wearing impossibly high heels. We make it to the fifth landing and I rush ahead of her to open the broken fire door. It creaks as I pull it. She steps through and we emerge onto my floor. I'm suddenly aware of the dim lighting and burnt bulbs, the peeling wallpaper and the general tattiness of these corridors. Of course, Mr. Rosso, my landlord, hears us approach and chooses precisely that moment to emerge from his apartment.

"Molly," he says. "On your good Gran's grave, when are you going to pay me what's owed?"

I feel a blast of heat rise to my face. "This week. Rest assured. You'll get what's coming to you." I imagine a big red bucket full of soapy water and pushing his bulbous head into it.

Giselle and I keep walking by him. Once we're past, she rolls her eyes comically, which to me is a great relief, since I was concerned she'd think poorly of me for not keeping up with my rent. Clearly, that's not what she's thinking at all.

I put my key in the lock and shakily open my front door. "After you," I say.

Giselle walks in and looks around. I step in behind her, not knowing where to stand. I close the door and slide the rusty dead bolt across. She takes in Gran's paintings in the entry, ladies lounging by lazy riversides, eating picnic delicacies from a wicker basket. She spots the old wooden chair by the door with Gran's needlepoint pillow on it. She picks it up in both hands. Her lips move as she reads the Serenity Prayer.

"Huh," she says. "Interesting." Suddenly, right there in the doorway, her face contorts into a grimace and tears fill her eyes. She hugs the pillow to her chest and begins to sob quietly.

My shaking gets worse. I'm at a total loss. Why is Giselle at my house? Why is she crying? And what am I supposed to do?

I put my keys down on the empty chair.

There's nothing you can ever do but your best, I hear Gran say in my head.

"Giselle, are you upset because Mr. Black is dead?" I ask. But then I remember that most people don't appreciate this kind of direct talk. "Sorry," I say, correcting myself. "What I mean is I'm sorry for your loss."

"You're sorry? Why?" she asks between sobs. "I'm not sorry. I'm not sorry at all." She puts the pillow back in its place, pats it once, then takes a deep breath.

I remove my shoes, wipe the bottoms with the cloth from the closet, and put them away.

She watches me. "Oh," she says. "I guess I should take these off." She removes her glossy black heels with the red bottoms, heels so tall I have no idea how she made it up those five flights of stairs.

She gestures for me to hand her the cloth.

"No, no," I say. You're my guest." I take her shoes, which are fine and sleek, a delight to hold, and I tuck them away in the closet. She takes in our cramped quarters, her eyes traveling up to the flaking living-room ceiling, where circular stains bleed through from the apartment above.

"Don't mind appearances," I say. "There's not much I can do when it comes to how those above conduct themselves."

She nods, then wipes the tears from her cheeks.

I rush to the kitchen, grab a tissue, and bring it to her. "A tissue for your issue," I say.

"Oh my God, Molly," she replies. "You've got to stop saying that when people are upset. They'll take it the wrong way."

"I only meant—"

"I know what you meant. But other people won't."

I'm quiet for a moment as I take this in, storing her lesson in the vault of my mind.

We're still in the entranceway. I'm frozen in my spot, unsure of what to do next, what to say. If only Gran were here. . . .

"This is the part where you invite me into the living room," Giselle says. "You tell me to make myself at home or something like that."

I feel the butterflies in my stomach. "I'm sorry," I say. "We don't . . . I don't have company very often. Or ever. Gran used to invite select friends round from time to time, but since she died, it's been rather quiet here." I don't tell her that she's the first guest to pass through the door in nine months, but that's the God's honest truth. She's also the first guest I've ever entertained on my own. Something occurs to me.

"My gran always said, 'A good cup of tea will cure all ills, and if it doesn't, have another.' Would you like one?"

"Sure," she says. "Can't remember the last time I had tea."

I hurry to the kitchen to put the kettle on. I peek at Giselle from the doorway as she strolls around the living room. I'm glad that it's Tuesday, as I just washed the floors last night. At least I know they are clean to perfection. Giselle walks over to the windows at the far end of the living room. She touches the frilled trim on Gran's flowery curtains, curtains she sewed herself many years ago.

As I place tea in the pot, Giselle moves to Gran's curio cabinet. She crouches to admire the Swarovski menagerie, then takes in the framed photos angled on top. It makes me slightly uncomfortable but also a tad giddy that she's here in my home. While I'm confident that the apartment is clean, it's not appointed in the manner to which a woman of Giselle Black's station would be accustomed. I don't know what she's thinking. Perhaps she's horrified by the way I live. It is not like the hotel at all. It is not grand. This has always been fine by me, but perhaps it's not fine by her. It's a discomfiting thought.

I pop my head out of the kitchen. "Please rest assured that I maintain the highest level of sanitation at all times in this apartment. Unfortunately, on a maid's salary, I'm not able to purchase extravagant items or keep up with modern décor trends. I'm sure to you this home appears dated and old-fashioned. Perhaps a little . . . worn?"

"Molly, you have no idea how things appear to me. You don't really know much about me. You think I've always lived like I do now? Do you know where I'm from?"

"Martha's Vineyard," I say.

"No, that's just what Charles tells everyone. I'm actually from Detroit. And not the nice side of town. This place actually reminds me of home. I mean, home from long ago. Home before I found myself all alone. Before I ran away and never looked back."

I watch from the kitchen doorway as she leans in to inspect a photo of Gran and me taken over fifteen years ago. I was ten years old. Gran enrolled us both in a baking class. In this shot, we're wearing comically large chef hats. Gran is laughing, though I look very serious. I recall being displeased by the flour dusted on our pantry table. It was all over my hands and apron. Giselle picks up the photo next to it.

"Whoa," she says. "Is this your sister?"

"No," I say. "It's my mother. It was taken a long time ago."

"You look exactly like her." I'm well aware of our resemblance, especially in that photo. Her hair is shoulder-length and dark, framing her moon face. Gran always loved that photo. She called it her "twofer," because it reminded her of the daughter she lost and the granddaughter she gained.

"Where does your mom live now?"

"She doesn't," I say. "She's dead. Along with my grandmother."

The water is boiling. I turn off the element and pour the water into a teapot.

"Mine are gone too," she says. "Which is why I left Detroit."

I place the pot on Gran's best and only silver serving tray alongside two proper porcelain cups and two polished teaspoons; a double-eared, cut-crystal sugar bowl; and a small antique pitcher of milk. All of these items store memories—Gran and I foraging in secondhand shops or picking through boxes of discarded items left outside the row of austere mansions on the Coldwells' street.

"I'm sorry about your mother," Giselle says. "And your grandmother."

"You have no reason to be. You didn't have anything to do with it."

"I know I didn't, but that's just what you say. Like you did with me at the door. You said you were sorry about Charles. You offered your condolences."

"But Mr. Black died yesterday, and my mother died many years ago."

"It doesn't matter," Giselle says. "That's just what you say."

"Thank you. For explaining."

"Sure. Anytime."

I truly am grateful for her guidance. With Gran gone, much of the time I feel like a blind person in a minefield. I'm constantly stumbling upon social improprieties hidden under the surface of things. But with Giselle around, I feel like I'm wearing a breastplate and am flanked by an armed guard. One of the reasons why I love working at the Regency Grand is that there's a rule book for conduct. I can rely on Mr. Snow's training to tell me how to act, what to say when, how, and to whom. I find it relieving to have guidance.

I take the tea tray into the sitting room. It rattles in my hands. Giselle sits down on the worst part of the sofa, where the springs poke through a tad, though Gran has covered them with a crocheted blanket. I sit beside her.

I pour two cups of tea. I pick up mine, the one rimmed with gold and decorated in daisy chains, then realize my error. "Sorry. Would you prefer this cup or that one? I'm used to taking the daisies. Gran would take the English cottage scene. I'm a bit of a creature of habit."

"You don't say," Giselle says, and picks up Gran's cup. She helps herself to two heaping teaspoons of sugar and some milk. She stirs the contents. She's never done much housework, that's for sure. Her hands are smooth and flawless, her manicured nails long and polished blood red.

Giselle takes a sip, swallows. "Listen, I know you're probably wondering why I'm here."

"I was worried for you, and I'm glad you're here," I say.

"Molly, yesterday was the worst day of my life. The cops were all over me. They took me to the station. They questioned me like I'm some kind of common criminal."

"I was worried that would happen. You don't deserve that."

"I know. But they don't. They asked me if I got too eager as a potential heir to Charles's estate. I told them to talk to my lawyers, not that I have any. Charles handled all of that. God, it was awful, to be accused of such a thing. Then as soon as I got back to the hotel, Charles's daughter, Victoria, called me."

I feel a tremor jolt me as I pick up my teacup and take a sip. "Ah yes, the forty-nine-percent shareholder."

"That's what she owned before. Now she'll own over half of everything, which is what her mother always wanted. 'Women and business don't mix,' Charles says . . . said. According to him, women can't handle dirty work."

"That's preposterous," I say. Then I catch myself. "Apologies. It's rude to talk ill of the dead."

"It's okay. He deserves it. Anyhow, his daughter said way worse things to me on the phone. Do you know what she called me? Her father's Prada parasite, his midlife mistake, not to mention his killer. She was raging so much, her mother took the phone away from her. Calm as anything, Mrs. Black—the first Mrs. Black—says, 'I apologize for my daughter. We all react to grief in different ways.' Can you believe it? While her lunatic daughter is yelling in the background, telling me to watch my back."

"You don't have to worry about Victoria," I say.

"Oh, Molly, you're so trusting. You have no idea how vicious it is out there in the real world. Everyone wants to see me go down. It doesn't matter that I'm innocent. They hate me. And for what? The police, they suggested that *I* was violent against Charles. Unbelievable!"

I watch Giselle carefully. I remember the day she told me about Mr. Black's mistresses, how she was so angry she really did want to kill him. But thought and action are different things. They're different things entirely. If anyone knows this, I do.

"The police think I killed my own husband," she says.

"For what it's worth, I know you didn't."

"Thank you, Molly," she says.

Her hands are shaking like mine are. She sets her cup down on the table. "I'll never get how a decent woman like Charles's ex-wife could raise such a bitch of a daughter."

"Perhaps Victoria takes after her father," I say. I remember Giselle's bruises and how they came to be. My fingers tighten on the delicate handle of my teacup. If I grip it any harder, it will shatter into a million pieces. *Breathe, Molly. Breathe.*

"Mr. Black, he wasn't good to you," I say. "He was, in my estimation, a very bad egg."

Giselle looks down at her lap. She smooths out the edges of her satin skirt. She is picture-perfect. It's as if a cinema star from the golden age just crawled out of Gran's TV and magically took a seat beside me on the sofa. That thought seems more probable than Giselle being real, a socialite who is actually friends with a lowly maid.

"Charles didn't always treat me well, but he loved me, in his way. And I loved him in my way. I did." Her big green eyes fill with tears.

I think of Wilbur, how he stole the Fabergé. Any fondness I felt for him turned to bitterness in an instant. I would have cooked him in a vat of lye if I could have done so without repercussion. And yet, Giselle, who has just cause to hate Charles, holds on to her love for him. How curious, the way different people react to similar stimuli.

I take a sip of tea. "Your husband was a cheater. And he beat you," I say.

"Wow. Are you sure you don't want to tell it like it is?"

"I just did," I say.

She nods. "When I met Charles, I thought my life was made. I thought I'd finally found someone who would look after me, who had it all and who adored me. He made me feel special, like I was the only woman in the world. Things were okay for a while. Until they weren't. And yesterday, we had a huge fight right before you came in to clean the suite. I told him I was sick of our life, sick of going from city to city, hotel to hotel, all for his 'business.' I said, 'Why can't we just settle down somewhere, like at the villa in the Caymans, and just live and enjoy life like normal people?'

"People don't know this, but when we got married, he made me sign a prenup so none of his properties or assets belong to me. It hurt, that he didn't trust me, but like an idiot, I signed it. From that moment on, things were different between us. The second we were married, I wasn't special anymore. And he was free to give me what he wanted and take it away at any time. That's exactly what he's done throughout our two years of marriage. If he liked the way I acted, gifts would be showered upon me—diamonds and designer shoes, exotic trips—but he was a jealous man. If I so much as laughed at a guy's joke at a party, I'd be punished. And not just by him turning off the money tap." One of her hands flits up to her collarbone. "I should have known. It's not like I wasn't warned."

Giselle pauses, gets up, and retrieves her purse by the door. She rummages around and her hand emerges with two pills. She sets her purse down on the chair by the door, returns to the sofa, and pops the two pills in her mouth, washing them down with some tea.

"Yesterday, I asked Charles if he would consider canceling our prenup or at least putting the Cayman villa in my name. We've been married for two years; he should trust me by now, right? All I wanted was a place to escape to when the pressure gets too much for me. I told him, 'You can keep growing your business, if that's what you want—your Black empire. But at least give me the deed to the villa. With my name on it. A place to call my own. A home.'"

I think back to the itinerary I saw in her purse. If the trip was for her and Mr. Black, why were the flights one-way?

"He lost it on me when I said the word 'home.' He said everyone always lies to him, tries to steal his money, takes advantage of him. He was drunk, storming around the room, saying I was just like his ex-wife. He called me a lot of things—a money-grabber, a gold digger . . . a dime-store whore. He got so mad that he pulled off his wedding ring and threw it across the room. He said, 'Fine, have it your way!' Then he opened the safe, rooted around in there, stuffed some paper in his suit pocket, then pushed past me and stormed out of the room."

I knew what that paper was. I'd seen it in his pocket—the deed to the villa in the Caymans.

"Molly, that's when you came in the suite, remember?"

I did remember—the way Mr. Black pushed past me, just another aggravating human obstacle in his path.

"Sorry I was acting so weird. But now you know why."

"That's quite all right," I say. "Mr. Black was far ruder than you were. And to be honest, I thought you were sad, not mad."

She smiles. "You know what, Molly? You understand more than anyone gives you credit for."

"Yes," I say.

"I don't care what anyone else thinks. You're the best."

I can feel my face flush at the compliment. Before I have a chance to ask what other people think about me, a strange transformation washes over Giselle. Whatever is in the pills she just took, the change happens quickly. It's like she's turning from solid to liquid before my eyes. Her shoulders relax and her face softens. I remember Gran when she was sick, how the medications relieved the pain just like this, for a while at least, how her face would turn from a tight, stony grimace to a look of peaceful bliss so clear that even I could read it instantly. Those pills worked magic on Gran. Until they didn't. Until they weren't enough. Until nothing was enough.

Giselle turns to face me and sits cross-legged on the couch. She wraps Gran's blanket around her legs. "You found him, right? Charles? It was you who first found him?"

"It was me. Yes."

"And they took you to the station? That's what I heard."

"Correct."

"So what did you tell them?" She brings one hand to her lips and nibbles at the skin by her index finger. I want to tell her that nail-biting is a filthy habit and not to ruin her lovely manicure, but I refrain.

"I told the detective what I saw. How I entered the suite to return it to a state of perfection, how I felt perhaps it was occupied, how I entered the bedroom to find Mr. Black lying on the bed. And when I investigated further, I realized he was dead."

"And was there anything weird about the suite?"

"He'd been drinking," I say. "Which I'm afraid I don't consider unusual for Mr. Black."

"You got that right," she says.

"But . . . your pills. They're usually in the bathroom, and they were on the bedside table, open, with some spilled onto the carpet."

Her whole body stiffens. "What?"

"Yes, and some pills had been stepped on and were ground into the carpet, which is problematic for those of us who have to clean the suite after." I wish she wouldn't nibble her nails like a cob of corn.

"Anything else?" Giselle asks.

"The safe was open."

Giselle nods. "Of course. Normally he kept it locked, never gave me the code. But that day, he took whatever it was he wanted and left it open when he stormed out."

She picks up her teacup and takes a polite sip. "Molly, did you tell the police anything about Charles and me? About . . . our relationship?"

"No," I say.

"Did you . . . did you tell them anything about me?"

"I did not hide the truth," I say. "But I also didn't volunteer it."

Giselle stares at me for a second, then leaps forward and hugs me, which catches me off guard. I can smell her expensive perfume. Isn't it interesting how luxury has an unmistakable scent, as unmistakable as fear or death?

"Molly, you're a very special person, you know that?"

"Yes, I know," I say. "I've been told that before."

"You're a good person and a good friend. I don't think I could ever be as good as you, so long as I live. But I want you to know something: whatever happens, don't you think for a second that I don't appreciate you."

She pulls back from me and springs to her feet. A few minutes ago, she was willowy and relaxed; now she's overcharged.

"What are you going to do? Now that Mr. Black is dead?"

"Not much," she says. "The police won't let me go anywhere until the toxicology and autopsy reports are complete. Because if some rich guy turns up dead, then obviously his wife offed him, right? Couldn't be that he died of natural causes, of the stress he caused himself and everyone else around him. Stress that his wife was trying to relieve him from so he wouldn't drop dead."

"Is that what you think happened? He dropped dead, just like that?"

She sighs. Tears spring to her eyes. "There are so many reasons a heart can stop beating."

I feel a lump in my throat. I think of Gran, of her good heart and how it came to a stop.

"Will you continue to stay at the hotel while you wait for the reports?" I ask.

"I don't have much choice. I've got nowhere else to go. And I can barely step outside of the hotel without being mobbed by reporters. I don't own any property. I've got nothing that's mine and only mine, Molly. Not even a crappy apartment like this." She winces. "Sorry. See? You're not the only one who steps in it from time to time."

"That's quite all right. I take no offense."

She reaches out and puts a hand on my knee. "Molly," she says, "I won't know what Charles's will says for a while. Which means I won't know what becomes of me for a while. Until then, I'll stay at the hotel. At least there, the bill is already paid."

She pauses, looks at me. "Will you look after me? At the hotel, I mean. Will you be my maid? Sunitha is nice and all, but it's not the same. You're like a sister to me, you know that? A sister who sometimes says crazy shit and likes dusting way too much, but a sister nonetheless."

I'm flattered that Giselle thinks of me in such a positive light, that she sees past what others don't, that she sees me as . . . family.

"I'd be honored to look after you," I say. "If Mr. Snow is fine with it."

"Great. I'll tell him when I go back." She stands, walks to the door, and grabs her yellow purse. She brings it to the sofa and takes out a stack of bills—a stack that looks all too familiar. She flicks off two crisp hundred-dollar bills and places them on Gran's silver tea tray.

"For you," she says. "You earned it."

"What? This is a lot of money, Giselle."

"I never tipped you yesterday. Consider this your tip."

"But I never finished cleaning the suite yesterday."

"That's not your fault. You just keep that. And let's pretend this conversation never happened."

I, for one, will never be able to forget this conversation, but I don't say that out loud.

She stands and turns to the door, but then stops and faces me. "One more thing, Molly. I've got a favor to ask of you."

I immediately wonder if this will involve ironing or laundry, so I'm surprised by what comes next.

"Do you think you might be able to get into our suite still? It's cordoned off right now. But I left something in there, something I desperately need back. I tucked it up in the bathroom fan."

That explains it, the clunky sound I heard yesterday when she was in the bathroom, showering.

"What is it you want me to retrieve?"

"My gun," she says, her voice neutral and calm. "I'm at risk, Molly. I'm vulnerable now that Mr. Black is gone. Everyone wants a piece of me. I need protection."

"I see," I reply. But in truth, this request produces raging anxiety. I feel my throat closing. I feel the world tilt around me. I think of Mr. Snow's advice—"When a guest asks for something above and beyond, consider it a challenge. Don't dismiss it. Rise to meet it!"

"I'll do my best," I say, but the words catch. "To retrieve your . . . item." I stand in front of her, at attention.

"Bless your heart, Molly Maid," she says, throwing her arms around me again. "Don't believe what anyone says. You're not a freak. Or a robot. And I'll never forget this as long as I live. You'll see. I swear, I won't forget."

She rushes over to the front door, retrieves her glossy high heels from the closet, and slips them on. She's left her teacup behind on the table rather than carrying it to the kitchen as Gran would have. She has not, however, forgotten her yellow purse, which she slings over her shoulder. She opens my front door, blows me a kiss, and waves good-bye.

A thought occurs to me.

"Wait," I say. She's down the hall, nearly at the stairs. "Giselle, how did you know where to find me? How did you get my home address?"

She turns around. "Oh," she says. "Someone at the hotel gave it to me."

"Who?" I ask.

She squints. "Hmm. . . . Can't quite remember. But don't worry. I won't bug you all the time or anything. And thanks, Molly. For the tea. For the talk. For being you."

And with that she flicks her sunglasses down, pulls open the broken fire door, and leaves.

WEDNESDAY

My alarm clock rings the next morning. It's the sound of a rooster crowing. Even all these months later, I hear Gran's feet padding down the hallway, the gentle rap of her knuckles on my door.

Rise and shine, my girl! It's a new day. Shuffle, shuffle, shuffle as she busies herself in the kitchen making us English Breakfast tea and crumpets with marmalade.

But no, it isn't real. It's only a memory. I push the button on my alarm to stop the crowing and immediately check my phone just in case Rodney texted me overnight. Messages: nil.

I put my two feet flat on the parquet floor. No matter. I will go to work today. I will see Rodney there. I will take the temperature of our relationship. I will move things forward. I will help Giselle because she's a friend who needs me. I will know just what to do.

I stretch and get out of bed. Before doing anything else, I pull off all the sheets and the quilt to make the bed properly.

If you're going to do something, do it right.

Very true, Gran. I start with the top sheet, snapping it crisply and replacing it on the bed. Tuck, tuck. Hospital corners. Next, I sort Gran's quilt, smoothing it neatly, pointing the star north as always. I fluff up the pillows, placing them against the headboard at a regimented forty-five-degree angle, two plump hillocks with crochet fringe.

I go to the kitchen and prepare my own crumpets and tea. I notice the grating sound of my teeth against the crust every time I take a bite. Why is it that when Gran was alive I never heard the horrible sounds I make?

Oh, Gran. How she loved the mornings. She would hum a tune and bustle about in the kitchen. We'd sit together at our country-kitchen table for two, and like a sparrow in the sunshine she would chirp and chirp as she pecked at her breakfast.

Today, I will tackle the library at the Coldwells, Molly. Oh, Molly, I wish you could see it. One day, I'll have to ask Mr. Coldwell if I can bring you for a visit. It's a sumptuous room, full of dark leather and polished walnut. And so many books. And you wouldn't believe it, but they barely go in there. I love those books like my own. And today, it's dusting. It's tricky, let me tell you, dusting books. You can't just blow the dust off them like I've seen some maids do. That's not cleaning, Molly. That's merely dirt displacement. . . .

On and on she'd chatter, preparing us both for the day.

I hear myself slurp my tea. Disgusting. I take another bite of crumpet and find I can't eat any more. I throw out the rest, even though it's a horrid waste. I clean my dishes and head to the bathroom for a shower. Since Gran died, I do everything a bit quicker in the morning because I want to leave the apartment as soon as possible. Mornings are too hard without her.

I'm ready. Off I go, out the front door and down the hall to Mr. Rosso's apartment. I knock firmly. I hear him on the other side of the door. Click. It opens.

He stands with his arms crossed. "Molly," he says. "It's seven-thirty A.M. This better be good."

I'm holding the money in my hand. "Mr. Rosso, here's two hundred dollars toward the rent."

He sighs and shakes his head. "The rent is eighteen hundred, and you know it."

"Yes, you are correct, both about the amount that I owe and the fact that I know it. And I'll produce the rest of the rent by the end of today. You have my word."

More head shaking and bluster. "Molly, if it weren't for how much I respected your grandmother . . ."

"End of day. You'll see," I say.

"End of day, or I take the next step, Molly. I evict you."

"That won't be necessary. May I have a receipt registering proof of payment for two hundred dollars?"

"Now? You have the nerve to ask for that right now? How 'bout I get it to you tomorrow, once you're all paid up."

"That's a reasonable compromise. Thank you. Have a good day, Mr. Rosso."

With that I turn and walk away.

I arrive at work well before nine. As usual, I walk the whole way to avoid unnecessary spending on transit. Mr. Preston is standing on the top step of the hotel entrance behind his podium. He's on the phone. He sets the receiver down and smiles when he sees me.

It's a busy morning at the entrance, busier than usual. There are several suitcases outside the revolving door, waiting to be carried to the storage room. Guests hurry in and out, many of them taking photos and chattering about Mr. Black this and Mr. Black that. I hear the word "murder" more than once, said in a way that makes it sound like a day at the fair or an exciting new flavor of ice cream.

"Good morning, Miss Molly," Mr. Preston says. "Are you all right?"

"I'm quite fine," I say.

"You got home safely last night, I hope?"

"I did. Thank you."

Mr. Preston clears his throat. "You know, Molly. If you ever have any problems, any problems at all, remember that you can count on good ol' Mr. Preston for help." His forehead furrows in a curious way.

"Mr. Preston, are you worried?"

"I wouldn't go that far. But I just want you to . . . keep good company.

And to know that if ever you need, I'd be there for you. You just give Mr. Preston a wee nod and I'll know. Your gran was a good woman. I was fond of her and she was so good to my dear Mary. I'm sure things aren't easy without your gran."

He shifts his weight from foot to foot. For a moment, he doesn't look like Mr. Preston, the imposing doorman, but like an overgrown child.

"I appreciate your offer, Mr. Preston. But I'm quite all right."

"Very well," he says with a tip of his hat. Just then, a family with three children in tow and six suitcases demands his attention. He turns to them before I can say a proper goodbye.

I weave my way through the throng of guests, push past the revolving door and into the lobby. I head straight downstairs to the housekeeping quarters. My uniform hangs from my locker door, clean and shrouded in protective film. I dial the code to my lock and my locker springs open. On the upper shelf is Giselle's timer, all that sand from an exotic, faraway place, all that golden brass shining hope in the dark. I sense a presence beside me. I turn to find Cheryl peeking around my locker door, her face severe and downturned—in other words her normal expression.

I try cheery optimism. "Good morning. I do hope you're feeling better today and that you were able to benefit from a day of respite yesterday," I say.

She sighs. "I doubt you really understand, Molly, what it's like to have a condition like mine. I have bowel issues. And stress aggravates things. Stress, such as a dead man discovered in my workplace. Stress that causes gastrointestinal dysfunction."

"I'm sorry you were unwell," I say.

I expect her to go away then, but she doesn't. She just stands in my way. The plastic wrap of my uniform rattles ominously as she brushes against it.

"Too bad about the Blacks," she says.

"You mean about Mr. Black," I say. "Yes, it's most dreadful."

"No. I mean too bad you won't get their tips anymore, now that Black's dead." Her face reminds me of an egg—featureless and bland.

"Actually," I say, "I believe Mrs. Black is still a guest in the hotel."

She sniffs. "Sunitha's looking after Giselle in her new room. I'll oversee her work, of course."

"Of course," I say. It's yet another ploy to steal tips, but it won't last for long. Giselle will talk to Mr. Snow. She will request that I look after her again. So for now, I'll hold my tongue.

"The police are finished in the former Black suite," Cheryl says. "They've turned it upside down. Quite a mess. You'll have to work hard to set it right. Not big tippers either, cops. I'll look after the Chens from now on. Wouldn't want you overworked."

"How considerate," I say. "Thank you, Cheryl."

She stands there for a moment longer, looking into my locker. I see her eyeing Giselle's timer. I want to gouge out her eyes because she's tainting it, just by looking at it with such envy. It is mine. It's *my* gift. From *my* friend. *Mine.*

"Excuse me," I say, and slam the locker door shut.

Cheryl flinches.

"I best be off. I must get to work."

She mutters something unintelligible as I grab my uniform and head for the change room.

Once I'm uniformed and I've replenished my trolley, I make my way to the main lobby. I see Mr. Snow at Reception. He looks frosted over, like a sugar-glazed doughnut melting on a hot day. He beckons me to him.

I'm careful to allow the hordes of guests to pass before me and my trolley, bowing my head to each as they pay me no mind. "After you, ma'am/sir," over and over again. It takes me an extraordinarily long time to navigate the short distance from the elevator to the reception desk.

"Mr. Snow, my apologies. It's very busy today," I say when I arrive at the desk.

"Molly, it's good to see you. Thank you again for coming to work yesterday. And today. Many employees would simply use recent events as an excuse to feign illness. To shirk their duties."

"I would never do that, Mr. Snow. 'Every worker bee has her place in the hive.' You taught me that."

"Did I?"

"You did. It was part of your speech during last year's professional-development day. The hotel is a hive, and every worker in it is a bee. Without each and every one of us, there would be no honey."

Mr. Snow is looking past me into the busy lobby. It could use some attention. A child has left a sweater on one of the high-back chairs. A discarded plastic bag gusts up and then back to the marble floor as a busy porter sweeps past, wheeling a squeaky suitcase in his wake.

"It's a strange world, Molly. Yesterday, I was worried that after recent unfortunate events, guests would cancel their reservations and our hotel would be empty. But today, the opposite has transpired. More guests are booking. Ladies groups are coming in droves for high tea just to snoop around. Our conference rooms are now booked fully for the next month. It seems everyone's an amateur sleuth. They all believe they can waltz right into the hotel and solve the mystery of Mr. Black's untimely demise. Look at Reception. They can barely keep up."

He is right. The penguins behind the counter punch furiously at their screens, call out orders for valets and porters and the doorman.

"The Regency Grand has become a bit of a hot spot," Mr. Snow says. "Thanks to Mr. Black."

"How interesting," I remark. "I was just thinking about how one day can be so utterly grim and the next such a blessing. In this life, you just never know what's around the bend, be it a dead man or your next date."

Mr. Snow coughs into his hand. I hope he's not getting a cold. He comes closer and speaks in a whisper. "Listen, Molly. I'll have you know the police are now finished with their investigation in the Black suite. I hope they haven't uncovered anything unsavory."

"If they have, I'll just clean it up. Cheryl told me I'm to start there today. I'll get right to it, sir."

"What? I expressly told Cheryl to handle it herself. We are in no rush to rent out that suite again. We need to let everything die down a bit. So to speak. I don't want to cause you any more stress than you've already endured."

"That's quite all right, Mr. Snow," I say. "I find it more stressful knowing the suite is in disarray. I'll feel much better when it's back in order, all cleaned up as if nobody ever died in that bed."

"Hush," Mr. Snow says. "Let's not frighten the guests." It's only then that I realize I've abandoned my inside voice.

"My apologies, Mr. Snow," I whisper. And then loudly, for the benefit of anyone who may have been listening, "I'm going to begin cleaning now, a suite, not any suite in particular, just whichever is on my roster."

"Yes, yes," says Mr. Snow. "Best be off then, Molly."

And so I depart, circumventing the many guests and heading for the Social to pick up the morning papers and, hopefully, to see Rodney.

He's behind the bar when I get there, polishing the brass taps. I feel a warm glow the instant I set eyes upon him.

He turns. "Oh, hey," he says, smiling a smile that I know is just for me, mine and only mine. He holds a tea towel in his hands—pure white, not a spot on it.

"I didn't call you," I say. "Or text you. I figured we could wait to speak in person like we are now. But I want you to know that if I didn't follow the protocol you expected, I'd be happy to simply text you or call you at any time, day or night. Just let me know your expectations, and I'll adjust. It won't be a problem."

"Whoa," he says. "Alrighty then." He takes the crisp, white towel and tosses it over his shoulder. "So," he says, "did you get up to anything interesting last night?"

I come in close to the bar. This time, I'll be sure to use my whisper voice. "You are not going to believe this," I say.

"Try me," he replies.

"Giselle came to see me! To my house! She was waiting outside my building when I got home. Can you believe it?"

"Huh. What a surprise," he says, but his tone is odd, as if he isn't very surprised at all. He picks up a bar glass and begins to polish it. Though all the glassware has been properly sterilized in the kitchen downstairs, he's wiping out every errant spot. I appreciate his commitment to perfection. He is a wonder.

"So what did Giselle want?" he asks.

"Well," I say, "that is a secret between friends." I pause, look around the busy restaurant to make sure that no one is paying attention. Nobody so much as glances my way.

"Feeling gun-shy?" he says. There's a playful smile on his face, and I do believe he may be flirting with me. The very thought catapults my heart into double syncopation.

"Funny that you say that," I reply. Before I can think of what else to tell him, Rodney says, "We need to talk about Juan Manuel."

Guilt suddenly overcomes me. "Oh, of course." I've been concentrating so much on Rodney and the excitement of our burgeoning relationship that I've all but forgotten about Juan Manuel. It's clear that Rodney is a better person than I am, always thinking of others and putting himself last instead of first. It's a reminder of how much he has to teach me, of how much I still have to learn.

"How can I help?" I ask.

"I hear the police are gone and that the Black suite is empty. Is that right?"

"I can confirm that," I say. "In fact, it won't be rented out for a while. I'll be cleaning it first thing today."

"That's perfect," Rodney says. He puts down a polished glass and picks up another. "I figure the safest place for Juan Manuel now is the Black suite," he says. "The cops are gone; the room won't be rented out again anytime soon, not for lack of guest interest, though. Have you seen this place today? Every middle-aged, mystery-watching cat lady in town is roaming the lobby hoping to catch a glimpse of Giselle, or whatever. Honestly, it's pathetic."

"I promise you this: no curious busybody is getting into that suite," I say. "I've got a job to do, and I intend to do it. Once the suite is clean, I'll let you know and Juan Manuel can come in."

"Great," Rodney says. "Can I ask you for one more thing? Juan Manuel gave me his overnight bag. Would you mind putting it in the suite? Under the bed or something? I'll let him know it's there."

"Of course," I say. "Anything for you. And Juan Manuel."

Rodney retrieves the familiar navy-blue duffel bag from beside a beer keg and passes it to me.

"Thanks, Molly," he says. "Man, I wish all women were awesome like you. Most are much more complicated."

My heart, beating at double speed already, alights and soars into the air. "Rodney," I ask, "I was wondering. Perhaps one day we can go for ice cream together? Unless you like jigsaws. Do you like jigsaws?"

"Jigsaws?"

"Yes, jigsaw puzzles."

"Uh . . . if those are the choices, I'm more of an ice cream kind of guy. I'm a bit busy these days, but yeah, we'll go out sometime. Sure."

I pick up Juan Manuel's bag, sling it over my shoulder, and start to walk away.

"Molly," I hear. I turn around. "You forgot your newspapers."

He plops a large stack on the bar, and I heave them into my arms.

"Thank you, Rodney. You're too kind."

"Oh, I know," he says, winking. Then he turns his back on me to deal with a waitress and her order.

After that deliriously delicious encounter, I head upstairs. I'm practically floating on air, but as soon as I'm outside the door of the former Black suite, the gravity of memory pins me to the ground. It's been two days since I've been in this suite. The door seems bigger than it used to be, more imposing. I breathe in and out, gathering the strength to enter. Then I use my keycard to buzz through, pulling my trolley in behind me. The door clicks shut.

The first thing I notice is the smell, or the lack of smell—no comingling of Giselle's perfume with Mr. Black's shaving lotion. As I survey the scene before me, I see that all of the drawers in every piece of furniture are open. The pillows from the couch are on the floor, zippers splayed. The living-room table has been dusted for fingerprints and left like that, prints in flagrante. The surface looks a lot like the finger paintings I was forced to do in kindergarten, even though I hated getting my fingers soiled with paint. A coil of caustic yellow caution tape lies abandoned on the floor outside the bedroom door.

I draw another deep breath and walk farther into the suite. I stand at the threshold to the bedroom. The bed has been stripped bare, no sheets, no mattress cover. I wonder if the police took the sheets away with them. This means I will be low on my bedding count and will have to justify the loss to Cheryl. The pillows have been flung akimbo, stripped of their cases, stains glaring like grotesque bull's-eyes. There are three pillows only, not four.

I suddenly feel a bit dizzy. I hold on to the doorframe to steady myself. The safe is open, but there's nothing in it now. All of Giselle's and Mr. Black's clothes have been emptied from the armoires. And Mr. Black's shoes that were on his side of the bed are gone. The bedside tables have been dusted, too, unsightly prints thumbing up through the powder left behind. Perhaps some of them are mine.

The pills are gone, even the crushed ones on the floor have vaporized. In fact, the carpets and floors seem to be the one thing in the suite that have been properly cleaned. Perhaps the police vacuumed, sucked up the traces—the microfibers and particles of the Blacks' private lives, all caught in the confines of a single filter.

I feel a cold shiver run through me, as though Mr. Black himself, in a ghostly vapor, were pushing me aside. *Get out of my way.* I remember the bruises on Giselle's arms, *Oh, it's nothing I can't handle. I do love him, you know.* That ghastly man bowled me over every time I crossed him in the suite or in the hallways, as though I were an insect or a pest that deserved to be quashed. I see him in my mind's eye, a vile, beady-eyed creature, smoking a vile, malodorous cigar.

I feel a pulse of anger beat at my temples. Where is Giselle supposed to go now? What is she supposed to do? I wonder as much about Giselle as about myself. Mr. Rosso issued more threats this morning. *Pay the rent, or get evicted.* My home, this job. They are all I have left. I feel the prick of tears that I do not need right now.

Good things come to those who work hard. Clean conscience, clean life.
Gran always comes to my rescue.

I take her advice. I hustle back to my trolley and put on my rubber gloves. I spritz disinfectant on the glass tabletops, the windows, the furniture. I wipe off all the prints, all the remains of the interlopers who have been in this room. I scour the walls next, addressing the scuffs and dings that I'm certain weren't here before the ungainly detectives arrived. I cover the mattress in immaculate white. I make the bed, letting the crisp sheets billow down. Polished doorknobs, coffee service replenished, clean drinking glasses with paper lids to vouch for their cleanliness. I work by rote, my body moving of its own accord, so many times have I done this, so many days, rooms, guests blending together in a haze. My hands tremble as I polish the gilt mirror that faces the bed. I must focus on the present, not on the past. I wipe and wipe until a perfect image of myself shines back at me.

There is only one corner of the Blacks' bedroom left to clean, the dark corner beside Giselle's armoire. I take my vacuum and run over and over the carpet there. I inspect the walls closely, give both walls a thorough wipe down with disinfectant. There. Erased.

I survey my handiwork, and I see the suite restored. There's a pleasing citrus tang in the air.

It's time.

I have avoided the bathroom, but I can no longer. It, too, has been left in a state of disarray. The towels are missing, the tissues, even the toilet-paper rolls—all gone. There's fingerprint dust on the mirror and around the bathroom sink. I spritz and spray, I polish and replenish. In this smaller room, which due to its function must be disinfected more aggressively, the acrid scent of bleach is so strong that my nasal passages sting. I flip the switch for the fan and hear that familiar clunking sound. I quickly turn it off.

It's time.

I remove my rubber gloves and throw them into my rubbish bin. I grab the small step stool from my trolley and set it up under the fan. I climb onto it. The fan cover pulls down easily. I push in two clips to release it completely. I gingerly place the cover beside the sink. I get back on the step stool and reach one arm up into the dark recess of the fan, farther into the unknown, until my fingertips connect with cold metal. I pull the object down and hold it in both hands. It is smaller than I thought it would be, sleek and black but surprisingly heavy. Substantial. The grip is gritty, like sandpaper or a cat's tongue. The barrel is smooth, with a satisfying shine. Pristine. Polished. Clean.

Giselle's gun.

Never in my life have I held anything like this. It feels alive, though I know it's not.

Who could blame her for having it? If I were her, had been treated the way she has by Mr. Black and others, well . . . it's no wonder. I can feel it, the power in my hands that makes me immediately feel safer, invincible. And yet she didn't use it, this weapon. She didn't use it on her husband.

Where will she go now? What will she do? And what will I? I feel the gravity in the room change, the weight of everything pushes down on my shoulders. I place the gun on the sink, climb back up the stool, and replace the fan's cover. Back down the steps I go, then I take the gun again and carry it into the living room. It rests so nicely in the bowl of my hands. What will I do with it? How will I get it to Giselle?

Then it comes to me. They say television is an idle pursuit, but I maintain that I've learned many a lesson from *Columbo*.

Hidden in plain sight.

I carefully put the gun down on the glass table, then go back to my trolley. I remove Juan Manuel's duffel bag. I head back to the bedroom, where I slide his bag under the bed. Then I return to the sitting room.

I turn my attention to my vacuum cleaner, standing steadfast and at the ready right beside me. I unzip the vacuum bag and take out the dirty filter. I grab a brand-new filter from my trolley and slip the gun inside it. I push the fresh filter into the guts of my vacuum. I zip it up. *Out of sight, out of mind.* I give the vacuum a shove forward and back. Not a sound does it make, my secret, silent friend.

I pick up the dirty filter and am about to toss it into my rubbish bin when a dusty clump falls out and lands with a dull thud on the carpet. I look down at my feet where the carpet is now sullied with dust and grime. In the middle of the nest of dirt, something gleams. I crouch and take the object into my hand. I wipe away the grime. Gold, thick, encrusted in diamonds and other jewels. A ring. A man's ring. Mr. Black's wedding ring. Right there in the palm of my hand.

The good lord gives and the good lord takes away.

I curl my fingers around it. It's as though my prayers have been answered. "Thank you, Gran," I say to myself.

Because it's only then that I know just what to do.

CHAPTER 11

The gun is stowed in my vacuum cleaner. The ring is carefully wrapped in a tissue and tucked in the left cup of my brassiere, right by my heart.

I clean as many other rooms as I can, as fast as I can, using my manual sweeper rather than my power vacuum. At one point, I meet Sunitha in the hallway. She startles when she sees me, which is out of the ordinary. "Oh, so sorry," she says.

"Sunitha, is something wrong?" I ask. "Are you short on cleaning supplies?"

She grabs my arm. "You found him. Dead. You are a very nice girl. Be careful. Sometimes a place seems as clean as fresh snow, but it's not. It's just a trick. You understand?"

I immediately think of Cheryl cleaning sinks with her toilet rags.

"I understand completely, Sunitha. We must always keep clean."

"No," she hisses. "You must be more careful. The grass is green, but there are snakes in it."

And with that, she slithers a white towel in the air, and then drops it into her dirty laundry pile. She looks at me with an expression that does not fit the repertory of any I understand. What has gotten into her? Before I can ask, she pushes her trolley away and into the next room.

I try to put the odd encounter behind me. I concentrate on finishing as soon as I can so that I can skip out to lunch a few minutes early. I'll need every minute.

It's time.

I push my trolley to the elevator and wait for it to arrive. Three times the doors open and guests stare out at me, not making the slightest move to allow me to enter even though there's plenty of room. The maid goes last.

Finally, the doors open and the elevator is empty. I have it to myself all the way down to the basement. I hurry out with my trolley and almost collide with Cheryl as I turn the corner toward my locker.

"Where are you off to in such a rush? And how can you be finished with all those rooms so fast?" she asks.

"I'm efficient," I reply. "Sorry I can't dally. I have an errand to run over the lunch hour."

"An errand? But you usually work straight through your lunch hour," Cheryl says. "How will you maintain your A+ Exceptional Productivity Score if you're running all over the place at lunchtime?"

I'm very proud of my A+ Exceptional Productivity Score. Every year, it earns me a Certificate of Excellence from Mr. Snow himself. Cheryl never completes her daily room-cleaning quota, and my excellence bridges the gap.

But as I look at Cheryl, I catch something in her expression that's always been there, but today I can read it plainly—the curve of her upper lip, the disdain and . . . something else. I hear Gran's voice in my head giving me advice about school bullies.

Don't let them push your buttons.

At the time, I didn't understand that the buttons weren't literal. I understand it now. The pieces slide together in my head.

"Cheryl," I say, "I am aware of my legal right to take a break and will do so today. And any other day that I choose. Is that acceptable, or should I run it by Mr. Snow?"

"No, no," she replies. "It's fine. I'd never suggest anything . . . illegal. Just be back by one P.M."

"I will," I say.

With that, I'm off, zooming by her. I park my trolley outside my locker, grab my wallet, then race back up to the elevator and out the bustling front doors of the hotel.

"Molly?" Mr. Preston calls after me. "Where are you going?"

"I'll be back in an hour!"

I cross the road and walk past the coffee shop directly in front of the hotel. Then I turn onto a side street. The traffic is slower here, with fewer people on the sidewalks. My destination is about seventeen minutes away. I can feel the heat rising into my chest, my legs burning as I force them onward. But no matter. *Where there's a will, there's a way*, as Gran liked to say.

I pass a first-floor office where workers have assembled and are seated in rows, listening to a man in a suit who is gesticulating wildly in front of a podium. Charts and graphs appear on a screen behind him. I smile to myself. I know just what it's like to be a proud employee fortunate enough to be receiving professional development. I look forward to Mr. Snow's next professional-development day about a month from now.

I have never understood why some staff members complain about these events, as if they're some kind of imposition, as if self-improvement and the chance to receive a free education on guest services and hotel hygiene isn't a bonus of employment at the Regency Grand. I relish such opportunities, especially given that I was unable to pursue my dream of a post-secondary education in hotel management and hospitality. This is a bad thought, an unwelcome thought. I see Wilbur's face flash in my mind and I have a sudden desire to punch it. But you can't punch a thought. Or if you can, it does little to change reality.

My stomach rumbles as I walk. I have no lunch, didn't pack one in the morning as I have so little in the cupboards and could barely eat breakfast anyway. I had hoped to find some perfectly untouched crackers and perhaps a small pot of unopened jam left on a breakfast tray outside one of the rooms, maybe even a piece of fruit that I could wash and discreetly tuck away. But alas, today's guests have left me very little.

In total, my tips are $20.45, which is certainly something, but not enough to placate an angry landlord or fill a fridge with anything but a few scant basics. Never mind.

The honey comes from the hive. The bees tend to the honey.

It's Mr. Snow's voice in my head this time. On the last professional-development day, he covered a most important topic: How the Hive Mentality Creates Greater Productivity. I took notes in a fresh, new journal, and I have studied the details at length. In his hour-long lecture, Mr. Snow talked about teamwork, using a most compelling analogy to do so.

"Think of this hotel as a hive," he said as he looked out at his staff over his owl glasses. I was listening intently to his words. "And think of yourselves as bees."

I wrote in my notebook: *Think of yourself as a bee.*

Mr. Snow continued. "We are a team, a unit, a family, a colony. When we adopt a hive mentality, it means we are all working toward the greater good, the greater good of the hotel. Like bees, we recognize the importance of the hotel, our hive. We must cultivate it, clean it, care for it, because we know that without it, there will be no honey. In my notebook: *hotel = hive; hive = honey.*

At this point, Mr. Snow's lecture took a most surprising turn. "Now," he said, gripping both hands on the podium in front of him, "Let us consider the hierarchy of roles within the hive and the importance of all bees, regardless of rank, working to the best of their bee-bilities. There are supervisory bees (here, he straightened his tie) and there are worker bees. There are bees that serve others directly and there are bees that serve indirectly. But no bee is more important than any other bee, do you understand?"

Mr. Snow's hands balled into fists to highlight the importance of this last point. I was scribbling furiously, recording every word as best I could, when suddenly Mr. Snow pointed at me in the crowd.

"Take, for instance, the example of a maid. She could be any maid, anywhere. Within our hotel, she is our perfect worker bee. She toils and travails to ready each honeycomb for the arrival of honey. This is a physically demanding job. It's exhausting and mind-numbingly repetitive, and yet, she takes pride in her work; she does it well each and every day. Her work is largely invisible. But does this make her lesser than the drones or the queen? Does this make her less significant to the hive? No! The truth is that without the worker bee, we have no hive. We cannot function without her!"

Mr. Snow pounded the podium to underline his point. I looked around and saw many eyes upon me. Sunshine and Sunitha, who were in the row in front of me, had turned and were smiling and waving at me. Cheryl, who was a few seats away, was leaning back, her eyes slits, her arms crossed. Rodney and some of the waitresses from the Social were behind me, and as I turned to look over my shoulder, they whispered to one another, laughing at some joke I'd missed.

All around, employees I knew (but most of whom had never spoken to me) were looking my way.

Mr. Snow continued. "We have much to improve upon in this organization. And I'm increasingly becoming aware that our hive does not always operate as a cohesive unit. We create honey for our guests to enjoy, but sometimes, the sweetness is skimmed off the top and isn't shared equitably. Some of our hive is used nefariously, for personal gain rather than for the common good. . . ."

At this, I stopped taking notes because Cheryl began dry coughing in a very distracting manner. I turned around once more and saw Rodney sinking into his chair.

Mr. Snow carried on. "I'm here to remind you that you're all better than that, that we can strive for something more together. That our hive can be the greatest, fittest, cleanest, most luxurious hive of any bees anywhere. But it will take cohesion and cooperation. It will take a commitment to the hive mentality. I'm asking you to help the colony, for the colony. I want you to think about pristine professionalism. Polished poise. I want you to *clean this place up!*"

At this point, I bounded out of my chair and onto my feet. I had fully expected that the entire staff would recognize Mr. Snow's glorious conclusion and would spontaneously burst into applause. But I was the only one on my feet. I was standing alone in a room that was pin-drop silent. I felt myself turn to stone. I knew I should probably sit, but I couldn't. I was frozen. Stuck.

I stayed that way for a very long time. Mr. Snow remained at the podium for a minute or two. Then he straightened his glasses, grabbed his speech, and marched back to his office. Once he was gone, my coworkers shifted in their seats and started talking among themselves. I could hear the whispers all around me. Did they actually think I couldn't?

Molly the Mutant.

Roomba the Robot.

The Formality Freak.

Eventually, the reception-desk penguins and porters, the waitresses and valets got up in their little cliques and began to drift away. I remained where I was until I was the last bee in the room.

"Molly?" I heard behind me. I felt a familiar hand on my arm. "Molly, are you quite all right?"

I turned and saw Mr. Preston standing in front of me. I searched his face for clues. Was he friend or foe? Sometimes this happens. I'll freeze for a moment because everything I've ever learned is gone. Erased.

"It wasn't about you," he said.

"I'm sorry?" I replied.

"What Mr. Snow was saying about how this hotel might not be so squeaky clean, how some employees skim off the top. That wasn't about you, Molly. There are things happening in this hotel, things even I don't fully understand. But you don't have to worry about that. Everyone knows you do your best every day."

"But they don't respect me. I don't think my coworkers like me at all."

He was holding his cap in his hand. He sighed and looked down at it. "I respect you. And I like you very much."

As he looked at me, the warmth in his eyes radiated out. Somehow, that look unlocked me. My legs became mobile again.

"Thank you, Mr. Preston," I said. "I think I should get back to it. The hive never rests and all that."

I broke away from him and went straight back to work.

That was months ago. Now, I'm standing outside a storefront a few blocks away from the hotel. My legs are stuck again, just like they were that day.

I already went in the store. I showed the man behind the counter the goods; he offered me a price. I accepted. In place of what was there before, in the cup of my brassiere, resting against my heart, there is now a thick wad of bills wrapped in a tissue.

I check the time on my phone. This whole transaction, including the walk here, has taken me twenty-five minutes, which is five minutes less than my original estimation, which means I'll arrive back at work approximately five minutes before one, when, as Cheryl so kindly reminded me, the second half of my shift begins.

My stomach twists, like the dragon that resides there just flipped its tail and sent acid sloshing everywhere. Maybe I shouldn't have done this; maybe it was wrong.

I catch my reflection in the glass. I remember Mr. Black's sallow, downturned face, the dark bruises he inflicted, the pain he has caused.

The monster in my belly curls into a tight ball and lies down.

What's done is done.

A lightness descends. I fill myself with breath. I marvel at my reflection in the glass—a maid, in a crisp, white dress shirt with a starched collar. I adjust my posture. I stand tall in a way that would make Gran proud.

Beyond my reflection are the goods on offer in the shop window— a shiny saxophone in a red velvet case, some solid power tools, their cords neatly wrapped into figure eights held tight with elastic bands, a few tired, old cell phones, and some jewelry in a display case. In the middle of the case is a new addition, a ring, a man's ring, a wedding ring, encrusted in diamonds and other jewels, gleaming, an object of obvious and rare luxury—a fine treasure.

I could tell the shopkeeper felt sorry for me when he handed over the agreed-upon sum. The tight lips. The smile that wasn't a smile. I'm beginning to understand the nuances of smiles, their cornucopia of meanings. I save each smile in a dictionary that I keep alphabetized on a shelf in my mind.

"I'm sorry things didn't turn out the way you'd hoped," the shop-keeper said. "With your man, I'm mean."

"With my man?" I replied. "On the contrary," I say. "For the first time in a long time, things are going well with him. Very well indeed."

Chapter 12

I walk briskly the entire way back to the hotel, checking the time frequently. I'm making good progress. It's now five to one, and I'm nearly at the hotel, my time estimation almost exactly right. I'm a bit flushed from the walk, and the wad of bills over my heart is slightly damp, but no matter.

It would appear the hotel has cleared out a bit since the morning; there are fewer guests about. Mr. Preston is alone at his doorman's podium. When he sees me approaching, he steps out from behind it, his arms oddly stiff by his sides. I wave and rush up the stairs, but Mr. Preston calls down before I reach the top.

"Molly," he says, his voice a tense whisper. "Go home."

I stop on the third stair. His expression is odd, as though he very much needs a washroom break.

"Mr. Preston, I can't go home now. I'm only halfway through my shift."

"Molly," he calls down again. "Use the back door. *Please.*"

"Are you quite all right, Mr. Preston? Do you need assistance?"

It's only then that it comes into focus—the absence of guests in the grand entrance, Mr. Preston standing too formally at the podium, his strange, whispered orders. Through the glass of the revolving doors, I can make out Mr. Snow and beside him, a looming, shadowy figure. Detective Stark.

"My dear girl," Mr. Preston says. "Don't go inside."

"It's quite all right," I say as I march up the remaining steps. "A few more questions won't kill me."

I push through the doors. Before I can take more than one step into the lobby, Mr. Snow and Detective Stark block my path. There's something about Detective Stark's posture that I don't like—the way her arms are bowed and her hands outstretched, as if I'm a varmint she's determined to catch before I take flight. I see Cheryl out of the corner of my eye, standing a few trolley-lengths away, but there's something different about her too. It's the first time I've seen a genuine smile on her face—a look of anticipation and excitement.

"Excuse me," I say to Mr. Snow and Detective Stark. "I must not dilly-dally. The rest of my shift begins in approximately three minutes."

"I'm afraid it doesn't," says Detective Stark.

I look to Mr. Snow, but he can barely meet my eye. His glasses are cantilevered to one side. Beads of sweat have formed at his temples. "Molly, the detective is taking you back to the station for more questioning."

"Can't I answer questions here and then get back to work? I have a heavy workload today."

"That won't be possible," says Detective Stark. "There's an easy way and a hard way to do everything. And the easy way is best."

It's an interesting comment, but it's dead wrong. In my line of work, the easy way is the lazy way, not the best way at all. But since we're in the hotel and that technically makes the detective a guest, I will be polite and bite my tongue.

I look around the lobby again and notice that more people have begun to gather. They're not milling about, heading to and fro the way they usually do. They've formed little clusters—by the reception desk, in the lounge chairs, on the marble landing by the grand staircase. They're oddly static. And quiet. They're all looking in one direction. Their cold eyes are looking at me.

"Well, Detective Stark," I say. "I'll accept the easy way." I look at Mr. Snow and add, "But just this once."

Detective Stark gestures for me to lead the way out the revolving doors, which I do, as she follows too closely behind me. As I pass, I take one glance back and see all eyes tracking my departure.

Mr. Preston is outside the door at the top of the stairs. "Here," he says, taking my elbow. "Allow me to help you, Molly."

I'm about to tell him I'm quite all right, but as I look down at the stairs, the red carpet undulates in a vertigo-inducing wave. I hold tightly to Mr. Preston's arm. It feels warm. Comforting.

We are at the bottom of the staircase.

Detective Stark says, "Let's go. It's time."

"Molly, take good care," Mr. Preston says.

"I always do," I reply, not entirely believing my own words.

—

CHAPTER 13

The car ride is silent. This time, I'm seated in the back of the police cruiser instead of up front. I don't like it back here. The vinyl upholstery squeaks under me every time I make the slightest move. A bullet-proof glass barrier separates Detective Stark from me. It is smeared with grubby fingerprints and dark-brown blood stains.

Imagine you're in a limousine, sitting in the back seat, being driven to the opera.

Gran reminds me that entrapment is only a state of mind, that there's always a way out. I join my hands in my lap and breathe deeply. I will admire the view out the window. Yes. I will concentrate on that.

We are at the station in what feels like seconds. Once inside, Detective Stark leads me to the same white room in which I was questioned before. On our way there, I feel more eyes upon me—uniformed officers who gawk as I pass, some of them offering a nod, not to me, but to Detective Stark. I hold my head high.

"Have a seat," the detective says. I sit down in the same seat where I sat before, and Detective Stark sits across from me. She closes the door. She doesn't offer me coffee or even water this time, which is a shame. I could use some water, though I know if I ask for some it will arrive in a dastardly Styrofoam cup.

Shoulders back, chin up, breathe.

Detective Stark has not said a word. She's sitting there in front of me, watching me. The camera in the corner blinks its red eye at me.

I'm the first to break the silence. "How may I be of service to you, Detective Stark?" I ask.

"How can you be of service to me? Well, Molly the Maid. You can start by telling the truth."

"My gran used to say that the truth is subjective. But I've never quite believed that. I believe the truth is absolute," I say.

"Then there's something we agree on," Detective Stark replies. She leans forward and puts her elbows on the scuffed white table between us. I wish she wouldn't. I disapprove of elbows on the table. But I don't say anything.

She is close enough that I can see tiny gold flecks in the irises of her blue eyes. "Since we're talking about truth," she says, "I'd like to share with you the results of Mr. Black's toxicology report. No autopsy report yet, but we'll have that soon enough. Mr. Black had drugs in his system, the same drug that was on his bedside table and strewn on the floor of his bedroom."

"Giselle's medicine," I say.

"Medicine? Benzodiazepine, laced with some other street drugs."

It takes me a moment to change the picture in my head from Giselle at the drugstore counter to her acquiring something illicit in a sordid back alley. Something isn't right. It doesn't make sense.

"Anyhow," Detective Stark says, "It wasn't the pills that killed him. He had a lot in his system, but not enough to kill him."

"What do you believe killed him then?" I ask.

"We don't know yet. But I assure you, we'll get to the bottom of it," she says. "The full autopsy report will determine if the petechial hemorrhaging was due to a cardiac arrest or if something more sinister happened."

It comes back to me in a flash. The room starts to spin. I see Mr. Black, his skin gray and taut, the little pinprick bruises around his eyes, his body stiff and lifeless. After I made the call to the front desk, I looked up. I caught my reflection in the mirror on the wall in front of the bed.

Suddenly, I feel clammy and cold, like I'm about to faint.

Detective Stark purses her lips, bides her time. Eventually, she says, "If you know something, now's your chance to be on the side of good. You do understand that Mr. Black was a very important man? A VIP?"

"No," I say.

"Excuse me?" Detective Stark replies.

"I don't believe that some people are more important than other people. We're all very important in our own way, Detective. For instance, I'm sitting here with you—a lowly hotel maid—and yet clearly there is something very important about me. Otherwise, you wouldn't have brought me here today."

Detective Stark is listening carefully. She zeroes in on my every word.

"Let me ask you something," she says. "Does it ever make you angry? Being a maid, I mean? Cleaning up after rich people? Taking care of their messes?"

I'm impressed by this line of questioning. This is not what I was expecting at all when I was escorted here.

"Yes," I answer truthfully. "I do sometimes feel angry. Especially when guests are careless. When they forget that their actions have an impact on others, when I'm treated like I don't matter."

Detective Stark says nothing. Her elbows remain on the table, which continues to grate on my nerves even though it's only officially a breach of etiquette when there's a meal being served.

"Now let me ask *you* a question," I say. "Does it ever bother *you*?"

"Does what ever bother me?"

"Cleaning up after rich people. Taking care of their messes," I say.

The detective pulls back as though I've sprouted the head of Hydra and one hundred serpents are hissing in her face. What pleases me, though, is that her elbows are no longer on the table.

"Is that how you see this? That my job as a detective is to clean up after a man has died?"

"What I'm saying is that we're not so different, when it comes down to it."

"Is that so?"

"You want this mess cleaned up, and so do I. We both seek a tidy closure to this unfortunate situation. A return to normalcy."

"What I'm seeking is the truth, Molly. About how Mr. Black died. And right now, I also want to know the truth about you. We've uncovered some interesting information in the last forty-eight hours. When we spoke the other day, you said you didn't know Giselle Black particularly well. But as it turns out, that's not true."

I won't give her the satisfaction of flinching. Giselle is my friend. I've never had a friend like her before, and I'm acutely aware of how easy it would be to lose her. I consider how to protect her and tell the truth at the same time.

"Giselle has confided in me in the past. That doesn't mean I know her as well as I'd like. Mr. Black definitely had a temper. It was hard not to notice Giselle's bruises. She confessed he was the cause of them."

"You do realize we've been talking to other employees at the hotel, right?"

"I would have expected as much, yes. I'm sure you'll find them very helpful to your investigation," I say.

"They've told us a lot. Not only about Giselle and Mr. Black. But about you."

I feel my stomach twist. Surely whoever spoke to Detective Stark would have been fair in their commentary, even if I'm not their cup of tea? And if the detective consulted Mr. Snow, Mr. Preston, or Rodney, she would have received a glowing report on my employee conduct and general reliability.

A thought occurs to me. Cheryl. She was "sick" yesterday—though probably not so sick that she couldn't make her way down to this very station.

As if reading my mind, the detective says, "Molly, we've been talking to Cheryl, your supervisor."

"I do hope she was helpful," I reply, though I highly doubt she was.

"We asked Cheryl if she ever cleaned the Blacks' suite when they stayed at the hotel. She said that for a while she did clean their suite alongside you. It was her way of maintaining quality control and keeping her maids sharp."

The acid builds in my stomach. "It was her way of siphoning off tips that were meant for those who do the work rather than for those who stand around watching," I say.

The detective ignores my words entirely. "Cheryl said that she observed a friendly relationship between you and Giselle, a kind of special kinship that was unusual between a guest and a maid, especially for you, since you don't really have friends, so I'm told."

I knew Cheryl was watching me, but I never realized just how much. I take a moment to collect my thoughts before I respond. "Giselle was grateful for my services," I say. "That was the basis for our relationship."

"Tell me, did you ever receive tips from Giselle? Or large sums of money?" she asks.

"She and Mr. Black tipped me well," I answer. I won't go into further details about the countless times Giselle placed brand-new $100 bills into the palm of my hand to thank me for keeping the suite clean. And I won't mention her visit to my home nor the charitable monetary gift she left me last night. It's no one's business except mine.

"Did Giselle ever give you anything besides money?"

Kindness. Friendship. Help. Trust. "Nothing out of the ordinary," I say.

"Nothing at all?"

Detective Stark digs in her pocket and takes out a small key. She opens a drawer in the table between us. She takes out the timer, Giselle's timer, her golden gift to me. The detective places it on the table.

I feel a surge of heat rise to my face. "Cheryl let you into my locker. That's *my* locker, it's my personal space. That's not right, invading someone's privacy, touching their things without permission."

"Those lockers are hotel property, Molly. Please remember you're just an employee, not the owner of the hotel. Now, tell me: are you ready to confess the truth about you and Giselle?"

The truth about Giselle and me is something I barely understand. It's as strange as a baby rhino being adopted by a tortoise. How am I supposed to explain such a thing? "I don't know what to tell you," I say.

"Then let me tell *you* something," Detective Stark replies as her elbows reclaim the table. "You're rapidly becoming a person of interest to us. Do you understand what that means?"

I'm detecting an air of condescension. I've encountered this before—people who assume that I'm a complete idiot just because I don't grasp things that come easily to them.

"You're becoming a VIP, Molly," Detective Stark adds. "And not the good kind. You've proven that you're capable of leaving out important details, of bending the truth to suit you. I'm going to ask you one more time: are you in contact with Giselle Black?"

I deliberate once more and find I'm able to answer this with 100 percent honesty. "I am not currently in contact with Giselle, though as I understand it, she remains a guest at the hotel."

"Let's hope for your sake that's the truth. And let's hope the autopsy report shows a natural cause of death. Until then, you're not to leave the country or attempt to hide from us in any way. You're not under arrest."

"I most certainly hope not. I've done nothing wrong!"

"Do you have a valid passport?"

"No."

She cocks her head to one side. "If you're lying, I'll find out. I can look you up, you know."

"And when you do," I say, "you'll find that I do not have a passport because I've never left the country in my life. You'll also find I'm a model citizen and that I have a completely clean record."

"Don't go anywhere, you understand?"

It's precisely this kind of language that always trips me up. "May I go to my home? May I go to the store? To the restroom? And what about work?"

She sighs. "Yes, of course you can go home and to all the places you'd usually go. And yes, you can go to work. What I'm saying is we'll be watching you."

Here we go again. "Watching me do what?" I ask.

Her eyes drill into mine. "Whatever it is you're hiding, whoever you're trying to protect, we'll find out. One thing I've learned in my business is that you can hide dirt for a while, but at some point, it all comes to the surface. Do you understand?"

"You're asking me if I understand dirt?"

Smudges on doorknobs. Shoe prints on floors. Dust rings on tabletops. Mr. Black dead in his bed.

"Yes, Detective. I understand dirt better than most."

CHAPTER 14

It is three-thirty when Detective Stark dismisses me from the white room. I walk myself out the station door. No courtesy ride home this time. I haven't eaten since the morning, and I haven't had so much as a cup of tea to tide me over.

My stomach roils. The dragon awakes. I have to pause a moment on the sidewalk in front of my building just to keep from fainting.

It's my deception, not hunger, that's having a deleterious effect on my nerves. It's the fact that I haven't disclosed fully about Giselle nor about what I currently have hidden over my heart. That's what has me in such a state.

Honesty is the only policy.

I can see Gran's face, twisted with disappointment, the day I came home from school at the age of twelve and she asked me how my day was. I told her it was ordinary, nothing to report. That, too, was a lie. The truth was, I ran away at lunchtime, which was far from ordinary. The school called Gran. I confessed to Gran why I'd run away. My classmates had formed a ring around me in the schoolyard and ordered me to roll around in the mud and eat it, kicking me while I obeyed their order. They were keenly inventive when it came to tormenting me, and this iteration was no exception.

When the ordeal was over, I went to the community library and spent hours in the bathroom washing the grime off my face and mouth, scraping the earth out from under my fingernails. I watched with satisfaction as the evidence circled down the drain. I was so certain I'd get away with it, that Gran would never find out.

But she did find out. And she had only one question for me after I confessed to being bullied. "Dear girl, why didn't you just tell the truth right away? To your teacher? To me? To anyone?" Then she cried and embraced me with such force that I was never able to answer her question. But I had an answer. I did. I didn't tell the truth because the truth hurt. What happened at school was bad enough, but Gran knowing about my suffering meant she experienced my pain too.

That's the trouble with pain. It's as contagious as a disease. It spreads from the person who first endured it to those who love them most. Truth isn't always the highest ideal; sometimes it must be sacrificed to stop the spread of pain to those you love. Even children know this intuitively.

My stomach settles. Steadiness returns. I cross the street and enter my building. I bound up the stairs to my floor, heading straight for Mr. Rosso's door. I extricate the wad of bills I've placed by my heart for safekeeping. I was aware of them the whole time I was at the police station, but far from being a nuisance, they felt protective, like a shield.

I knock loudly. I hear Mr. Rosso padding down his hallway, then the scratchy squeal of the lock twisting. My landlord's face appears, ruddy and bulbous. I hold out the bills in my hand.

"Here is the rest of this month's rent," I say. "As you can see, I take after my gran. I'm a woman of my word."

He takes the money and counts it. "It's all there, but I appreciate your diligence," I say.

When he's done counting, he nods slowly. "Molly, let's not do this every month, okay? I know your grandmother is gone, but you need to pay your rent on time. You need to get your life in order."

"I'm well aware of that," I say. "As for order, it is my express wish to live as ordered a life as possible. But the world is filled with random chaos that often bedevils my attempts at arrangement. May I have my receipt for full payment, please?"

He sighs. I know what this means. He's exasperated, which does not seem fair. If someone were to place a wad of bills into my hands, rest assured I would not sigh like this. I'd be grateful beyond measure.

"I'll fill out a receipt tonight," he says, "and give it to you tomorrow."

I would much prefer to have that receipt in my hand *tout suite*, but I defer. "That would be acceptable. Thank you," I say. "And have a lovely evening."

He closes his door without so much as a mannered "You too."

I go to my own entrance and turn the key. I step across the threshold and lock the door behind me. Our home. My home. Exactly as I left it this morning. Neat. Orderly. Unnervingly quiet, despite Gran's voice in my head.

There are times in life when we must do things we don't want to. But do them we must.

Normally, I feel a wave of relief flow through me the instant I close the door behind me. Here, I'm safe. No expressions to interpret. No conversations to decode. No requests. No demands.

I take off my shoes, wipe them down, and place them neatly in the closet. I pat Gran's serenity pillow on the chair by the door. I take a seat on the sofa in the living room to collect my thoughts. I am all a muddle, even here, in the peace of my own home. I know I must consider my next steps—should I call Giselle? Or maybe Rodney, for support and advice? Mr. Snow, to apologize for my absence this afternoon, for leaving my rooms without completing my daily quota?—but I find myself overwhelmed by the very thought of it all.

I feel out of sorts in a way I haven't felt in a while, not since Wilbur and the Fabergé, not since the day Gran died.

In that too-bright station room today, Detective Stark laid blame on me, treating me like some sort of common criminal when I'm nothing of the sort. All I want is to turn my head and find Gran sitting on the sofa beside me, saying, *Dear girl. Do not fret yourself into a tizzy. Life has a way of sorting itself out.*

I head to the kitchen and put the kettle on. My hands are shaky. I open the fridge and find it mostly bare—just a couple of crumpets left, which I should save for tomorrow's breakfast. I find a few biscuits in the cupboard and arrange them neatly on a plate. When the water has boiled, I make my tea, adding two sugars to compensate for the lack of milk. I mean to savor each bite of the biscuits, but instead I find myself devouring them greedily and washing them down with big gulps of tea right at the kitchen counter. My cup is empty before I even know it. Instantly, I feel the tea working. Warm energy flows through me again.

When all else fails, tidy up.

It's a good idea. Nothing raises my spirits more than a good tidy. I wash out my teacup, dry it, and put it away. Gran's curio cabinet in the living room could use a bit of attention. I carefully open the glass doors and remove all of her precious treasures—a menagerie of Swarovski crystal animals, each one paid for with backbreaking overtime hours at the Coldwells' mansion. There are spoons, too, silver mostly, collected from thrift shops over the years. And the photos—Gran and me baking, Gran and me in front of a water fountain in a park, Gran and me at the Olive Garden, glasses of Chardonnay raised. And the one photo that is not of us but of my mother when she was young.

I pick it up. My hands still aren't entirely steady. I have to concentrate as I dust and polish the glass frame. If my fingers slip, the frame will fall to the floor, the glass will shatter into hundreds of deadly shards. I get down on my knees to be closer to the ground. It's safer this way. I'm holding the frame in both hands, studying my mother's image. I'm surrounded by all of Gran's lovely things.

Another memory surfaces, not a recent one, one I haven't thought about in a long time. I was about thirteen years old when I walked through the door after school one day to find Gran kneeling on the floor much like I'm doing now. It was Thursday—*dust we must*—and she'd started the chore, her collection strewn about her, a polishing cloth and this photo of my mother in her hands. As soon as I crossed the threshold, I knew something wasn't quite right. Gran was disheveled. Her hair, which was usually perfectly curled and coiffed, was in disarray. There were stains on her cheeks and her eyes were puffy.

"Gran?" I asked, before even wiping down the bottoms of my shoes. "Are you all right?"

She didn't answer. She just stared at me with a glassy, faraway look in her eyes. Then she said, "Dear girl, I'm simply going to tell it to you as it is. Your mother. She's dead."

I found myself glued to the spot where I stood. I knew that my mother was out there in the world somewhere, but to me, she was as abstract a figure as the queen. To me, it was as if she'd died long ago. But to Gran, she meant so much, and this is what had me worried.

Every year as Mother's Day drew near, Gran would begin her thrice-daily peregrinations to our mailbox. She was hoping there'd be a card from my mother. In the early years, cards appeared, signed in shaky scrawl. Gran would be so happy.

"She's still in there somewhere, my little girl," she'd say.

But for years on end, Mother's Day after Mother's Day, no cards arrived and Gran would be glum for the rest of the month. I compensated by splurging on the biggest, cheeriest card I could find, adding a "Gran" before "Mother," filling the inside with evenly spaced x's and o's, and red and pink hearts that I'd color in, careful not to stray outside the lines.

When Gran told me my mother was dead, it wasn't my own pain that I felt. It was hers.

She cried and cried and cried, which was so unlike her that it unsettled me to my core.

I hurried to her side and placed a hand on her back.

"What you need is a good cup of tea," I said. "There's almost nothing that a good cup of tea can't cure."

I rushed to the kitchen and put the kettle on, my hands shaking. I could hear Gran sobbing on the sitting-room floor. Once the water had boiled, I made two perfect cups and brought them to the living room on Gran's silver tray.

"There we are," I said. "Why don't we have a wee sit on the sofa."

But Gran wouldn't move. The polishing cloth was balled up in one of her hands.

I stepped through the obstacle course of treasures and cleared myself a spot beside her on the floor. I put the tray down to one side, picked up both teacups, and positioned them in front of us. I put one hand on Gran's shoulder again.

"Gran?" I said. "Will you sit up? Will you join me for tea?" My voice was trembling. I was terrified. I'd never seen Gran so weak and diminished, as fragile as a baby bird.

Gran eventually sat up. She dabbed at her eyes with the polishing cloth.

"Oh," she said. "Tea."

We sat like that, Gran and me, on the floor, drinking tea, surrounded by Swarovski crystal animals and silver spoons. My mother's photo was beside us, the absent third person at our tea party.

When Gran spoke next, her voice had returned, composed and steady. "Dear girl," she said. "I'm sorry I was so upset. But not to worry, I'm feeling much better now." She took a small sip from her cup and smiled at me. It was not her usual smile. It traveled only halfway across her face.

A question occurred to me. "Did she ever ask about me? My mother?"

"Of course she did, dear. When she'd call out of the blue, it was often to ask about you. I'd update her, of course. For as long as she'd listen. Sometimes that wasn't very long."

"Because she was unwell?" I asked. This was the word Gran always used to explain why my mother had left in the first place.

"Yes, because she was terribly unwell. When she called me, it was usually from the streets. But when I stopped providing funds, she stopped calling."

"And my father?" I asked. "What happened to him?"

"Like I've said before, he was not a good egg. I tried to help your mother see this. I even called old friends to help me coax her away from him, but that proved ineffective."

Gran paused and took another sip of tea. "You must promise me, dear girl, to never get mixed up with drugs." Her eyes filled with tears.

"I promise, Gran," I said.

I didn't know what else to say, so I reached out and hugged her. I could feel her holding on to me in a whole new way. It was the only time I ever felt that I was giving her a hug, rather than the other way around.

When we separated, I didn't know what the correct etiquette was. I said, "What do you say, Gran? When all else fails, tidy up?"

She nodded. "My dear girl, you're a treasure to me. That you are. Shall we tackle this mess together?"

And with that, Gran was back. Perhaps she was dissimulating, but as we arranged all of her trinkets, freshly cleaned and polished, and put them back in the curio cabinet, she chirped and chattered on as though it were an ordinary day.

We never spoke of my mother again after that.

Here I am now, in the same spot as I was that day, surrounded by a menagerie of mementoes. But this time, I'm dreadfully alone.

"Gran," I say to the empty room, "I think I'm in trouble."

I arrange the photos on top of the curio cabinet. I polish each of Gran's treasures and stow them safely behind the glass. I stand in front of the cabinet looking at everything inside. I don't know what to do.

You're never alone as long as you have a friend.

I've been managing on my own through most of this, but perhaps it really is time to call for help.

I go to the front door where I left my phone. I pick it up and dial Rodney.

He answers after the second ring. "Hello?"

"Hello, Rodney," I say. "I hope I haven't caught you at an inopportune moment."

"All good," he says. "What's up? I saw you leave the hotel with the cops. Everyone's talking, saying you're in trouble."

"I'm sorry to report that in this particular case, the gossip may be correct."

"What did the police want?"

"The truth," I say. "About me. About Giselle. Mr. Black didn't die of an overdose. Not exactly."

"Oh, thank God for that. What did he die of?"

"They don't know yet. But it's clear they suspect me. And maybe Giselle too."

"But . . . you didn't tell them anything about her, did you?"

"Not much," I say.

"And you didn't mention Juan Manuel or any of that, right?"

"What does he have to do with anything?"

"Nothing. Nothing at all. So . . . why are you calling me?"

"Rodney, I need help." My voice cracks and I find it difficult to maintain my composure.

He goes quiet for a moment, then asks, "Did you . . . did *you* kill Mr. Black?"

"No! Of course not. How could you even—"

"Sorry, sorry. Forget I even said that. So how are you in trouble exactly?"

"Giselle, she had me go back into the suite because she'd left something behind. A gun. She wanted it back. And she's my friend, so I . . ."

"Jesus." There's a pause on the other end of the line. "Right."

"Rodney?"

"Yes, I'm here," he says. "So where's that gun now?"

"In my vacuum cleaner. By my locker."

"We have to get that gun," Rodney says. I can hear the agitation in his voice. "We have to make it disappear."

"Yes! Exactly," I say. "Oh Rodney, I'm so sorry to involve you in all of this. And please, if the police ever talk to you, you have to tell them I'm not a bad person, that I would never hurt anyone."

"Don't worry, Molly. I'll take care of everything."

I feel raw gratitude climbing up my chest, threatening to spill out of me in blubbering tears, but I won't let that happen in case Rodney finds it unbecoming. I want this experience to draw us closer, not break us apart. I take a deep breath and push my sentiments back down.

"Thank you, Rodney," I say. "You're a good friend. More than that, even. I don't know what I'd do without you."

"I've got your back," he says.

But there's more. I fear that when he hears the rest, he may turn away from me forever.

"There's another spot of . . . information," I say. "Mr. Black's wedding ring. I found it in the suite. And, well. . . . This is very hard for me to admit, but I've recently found myself in some acute financial distress. I took the ring to a pawn shop today so that I could pay my rent."

"You . . . you *what?*"

"It's on display in a shop window downtown."

"I can't believe it. I really can't believe it," he replies. I can hear him almost laughing, as if this is the most wonderful news. Surely he doesn't find this funny. It strikes me that laughs are just like smiles. People use them to express an array of confounding emotions.

"I've made a terrible mistake," I say. "I never thought they'd interrogate me again. I thought my part in all of this was over. If the police find out I pawned Mr. Black's ring, it will appear as though I killed him for financial gain. Can you see that?"

"Absolutely I can," says Rodney. "Wow. It's . . . incredible. Listen, everything's going to turn out just fine. Leave everything to me."

"Will you make the gun go away? And the ring? I should never have taken it. It was wrong. Will you buy it back and make sure that no one ever sees it again? I'll pay you back someday. You have my word."

"Like I said, Molly. Leave everything in my hands. You're at home now?"

"Yes," I say.

"Don't go out tonight. Okay? Don't go anywhere."

"I never do. Rodney," I say. "I can't thank you enough."

"That's what friends are for, right? To help each other out of binds?"

"Right," I say. "That's what friends are for."

"Rodney?" I say into the receiver. I'm about to add that I most desperately would like to be more than just a friend to him, but it's too late. He's hung up without saying goodbye. I've left him with quite a mess to tidy, and he's not wasting a moment.

When all of this is over, I'm going to take him on an all-expenses-paid Tour of Italy. We will sit in our private booth at the Olive Garden under the warm glow of the pendant light, and we will eat mountains of salad and bread, followed by a universe of pasta and topped by a smorgasbord of sweet desserts. Somehow, when we're done, I will pick up the bill.

I will pay for all of this. I know I will.

Thursday

CHAPTER 15

The next morning I'm at the hotel, and I'm late, oh so very late. No matter how hard I work, no matter how many rooms I clean, I can't keep up. I finish one room and an obsidian door, like a great, gaping maw, opens to the next guest room just down the hall. There's dirt everywhere—grit ground into the pile of every carpet, cracks in all the mirrors, greasy smudges on tabletops, and bloody fingerprints smeared across twisted sheets. Suddenly, I'm climbing the grand terrace staircase in the lobby, desperate to get away. My hands clutch the golden serpent balustrades, each one slippery to the touch. The beady reptilian eyes look familiar, then they blink and come to life under my fingers. With each step I take, a new serpent awakens—Cheryl, Mr. Snow, Wilbur, the tattooed behemoths, Mr. Rosso, Detective Stark, Rodney, Giselle, and finally, Mr. Black.

"No!" I scream, but then I hear knocking. I sit bolt-upright in bed, my heart pounding in my chest.

"Gran?" I call out. It comes back to me as it does every morning. I'm alone in the world.

Knock. Knock. Knock.

I check my phone. It's not quite seven in the morning, so my alarm has not yet gone off. Who in their right mind would be rapping on my door at this most inconvenient hour? Then I remember Mr. Rosso, who owes me my receipt for rent paid.

I haul myself out of bed and put my slippers on. "Coming!" I say. "Just one moment!"

I shake away the nightmare and walk down the hallway to the front door. I slide the rusty dead bolt across, then turn the lock and open the door wide.

"Mr. Rosso, while I appreciate you bringing—" But midsentence I stop cold because it's not Mr. Rosso at the door.

An imposing young police officer is standing with his feet apart, blocking all the light. Behind him are two more officers, a middle-aged man who would fit in fine in *Columbo*, and Detective Stark.

"Please excuse me. I'm not properly dressed," I say. I clutch at the collar of my pajamas, which used to be Gran's—pink flannel with a delightful array of multicolored teapots all over them. This is no way to greet guests, even ones impolite enough to arrive unannounced at an inconvenient hour of the morning.

"Molly," Detective Stark says, stepping in front of the young officer. "You're under arrest for unlawful possession of a firearm, possession of drugs, and first-degree murder. You have the right to remain silent and to refuse to answer questions. Anything you say may be used against you in a court of law. You have the right to consult an attorney before speaking to the police and to have an attorney present during questioning now or in the future."

My head is spinning, the floor is tilting under my feet. Tiny teapots spin before my eyes. "Would anyone like a cup of . . ." But I can't finish the question, because my vision dims.

The last thing I remember is my knees turning to marmalade and all the world fading to black.

When I come to, I'm in a holding cell, lying down on a tiny gray cot. I remember my front door, opening it, and the shock of my rights being read to me just like on TV. Was that real? I sit up slowly. I take in the small room with bars. Yes, it's all real. I'm in a jail cell, probably in the basement of the same station I've visited twice before for questioning.

I take a few breaths, willing myself to remain calm. It smells dry and dusty. I'm still wearing my pajamas, which strikes me as entirely unsuitable apparel for this particular situation. The cot I'm sitting on is stained with what Gran would call "unresolvable dirt"—smeared blood and some yellow circular stains that could be many things that I don't want to think about. This cot is an example of a perfectly serviceable item that should immediately be disposed of because there is simply no way to restore it to a state of perfection.

How sanitary is the rest of this cell? I wonder. It occurs to me that a far worse job than being a hotel maid would be working as a janitor in such a place. Imagine the plethora of bacteria and filth that has accumulated here over the years. No, I cannot focus on that.

I put my slippered feet on the floor.

Count your blessings.

My blessings. I'm about to start at number one, but when I look down at my hands, I see they are besmirched. Stained. I have dark black ink marks on every finger. It comes back to me then. Lying on this cot in this cramped, germ-infested cell, two police officers guiding each of my fingers toward a jet-black ink blotter. They didn't even have the decency to allow me to wash my hands after, though I did ask. After that I don't remember much. Perhaps I fainted again. It's hard to say how long ago that was—it could have been five minutes or five hours.

Before I can think about anything else, the young police officer who was at my door at home appears on the other side of the cell bars.

"You're awake," he says. "You're at the police station, do you understand? You passed out at your front door and in here too. We read you your rights. You're under arrest. Multiple charges. Do you remember?"

"Yes," I say. I can't recall what exactly I've been arrested for, but I know it most certainly has to do with the death of Mr. Black.

Detective Stark appears beside the young officer. She's in plainclothes now, but this does nothing to alter the dread I feel the moment her eyes meet mine. "I'll take it from here," she says. "Molly, come with me."

The young officer turns a key in the cell door and holds it open for me.

"Thank you," I say as I pass.

Detective Stark leads the way. Behind me, the young officer follows, making sure I'm hemmed in. I'm escorted down a hallway with three other cells. I try not to look inside them, but it's futile. I catch a glimpse of a sallow-faced man with sores on his face, holding on to the bars of his cell. Opposite him a young woman in torn clothing lies crying in her cot.

Count your blessings.

We go up some stairs. I avoid touching the railings, which are coated with filth and grime. Eventually, we arrive at a familiar room that I've visited twice before. Detective Stark flicks on the lights.

"Sit," she orders. "You've been here so often it must feel like home."

"It's nothing like home," I say, my voice like a blade, cutting and sharp. I sit in the wobbly chair behind the dirty, white table, careful not to touch my back against the rest. My feet are cold despite my fuzzy slippers.

The young officer walks in with a coffee in a dastardly Styrofoam cup, two creamers, and a muffin on a paper plate. And a metal spoon. He puts all of this down on the table, then leaves. Detective Stark closes the door behind him.

"Eat," she says. "We don't want you passing out again."

"That's very thoughtful," I reply, because you're supposed to say something complimentary when offered food. I don't believe she's being authentically caring, but it hardly matters. I'm ravenous. My body craves sustenance. I need it to carry on, to get me through what's next.

I pick up the spoon, turn it over in my hand. There's a dried clump of gray matter on the underside. I put it down immediately.

"Do you take cream in your coffee?" Detective Stark asks. She's taken a seat across from me at the table.

"Just one," I say. "Thank you."

She reaches out for the creamer, opens it, and pours it into the cup. She's about to grab the revolting spoon and stir.

"No!" I say. "I prefer my coffee unstirred."

She stares at me with that look of hers that is becoming easier and easier to interpret—derision and disgust. She hands me the Styrofoam cup. It makes that horrific squeaky sound as I take it in my hand. I can't help but cringe.

Detective Stark pushes the plate with the muffin closer to me. "Eat," she says again, an order not an invitation.

"Thank you very much," I say as I delicately pry the muffin from the paper lining, then sever it into four neat pieces. I pop one quarter into my mouth. Raisin bran. My favorite kind of muffin—dense and nutrient-rich, with random bursts of sweetness. It's as if Detective Stark knew my preference, though of course she didn't. Only Columbo could have figured that out.

I swallow and take a couple of sips of the bitter coffee. "Delightful," I say.

Detective Stark guffaws. I do believe it is a proper guffaw. No other word would suffice. She crosses her arms. This could mean she's cold, but I doubt it. She distrusts me, and the feeling is entirely mutual.

"You realize we've laid charges against you," she says. "For unlawful possession of a firearm, for possession of drugs. And for first-degree murder."

I nearly choke on my next sip of coffee. "That's impossible," I say. "I have never hurt a soul in my life, never mind murdered one."

"Look," she says, "we believe you killed Mr. Black. Or you had something to do with it. Or you know who did. The autopsy report has come in. It's definitive, Molly. It wasn't a heart attack. He was asphyxiated. That's how he died."

I jam another chunk of muffin into my mouth and concentrate on chewing. It's always good to chew every bite ten to twenty times. Gran used to say it aids digestion. I begin counting in my head.

"How many pillows do you leave on every bed that you make up at the hotel?" Detective Stark asks.

I know the answer, obviously, but my mouth is full. It would be impolite to reply right now.

"Four," the detective says before I'm ready to answer. "Four pillows are on every bed. I verified it with Mr. Snow and some of the other maids. But there were only three pillows on Mr. Black's bed when I arrived at the scene of the crime. Where did the fourth pillow go, Molly?"

Six, seven, eight chews. I swallow and am about to speak, but before I do, the detective slams both hands down on the table that divides us, which causes me to nearly jump out of my chair.

"Molly!" she barks. "I just insinuated that you murdered a man in cold blood with a pillow, and you're sitting there, mindfully eating a muffin."

I pause to regulate my pulse, which is racing. I'm not used to being yelled at or accused of heinous crimes. I find it most disconcerting. I sip my coffee to settle my jangling nerves. Then I speak. "I will say it in a new way, Detective. I did not kill Mr. Black. And I most certainly didn't asphyxiate him with a pillow. And for the record, there is no possible way that I could ever possess drugs. I've never seen nor tried one in my life. Also, they killed my mother. And very nearly killed my gran of a broken heart."

"You lied to us, Molly. About your connection to Giselle. She told us you often hung around the Blacks' suite long after you were done cleaning it and that you engaged in personal conversations with her. She also said you took money from Mr. Black's wallet."

"What? That's not what she meant! She meant took as in accepted. She *gave* the money to me." I look from the detective to the camera blinking in the corner of the room. "Giselle always tipped me generously and freely. It was she who took bills from Mr. Black's wallet, not me."

Detective Stark's mouth is a hard line. I straighten my pajamas and sit taller in my chair.

"After everything I've said, that's the one point you want to clarify?"

The straight angles of the room begin to warp and bend. I take a deep breath to steady myself, waiting until the table has corners instead of curves.

It's too much information. I can't process it all. Why can't people just say what they mean? I gather the detective has spoken to Giselle again, but it's impossible to believe that Giselle misrepresented me. She wouldn't do such a thing, not to a friend.

A tremor starts in my hands and travels up my body. I reach for the Styrofoam cup and almost spill it in my haste to bring it to my lips.

I make a quick decision. "I do have one clarification to make," I say. "It is true that Giselle confided in me and that I consider—considered—her a friend. I am sorry for not making this entirely clear to you before."

Detective Stark nods. "Not making this entirely clear? Huh. Is there anything else you decided to 'not make entirely clear'?"

"Yes. In fact there is. My gran always said that if you don't have anything nice to say about someone, it's best to say nothing at all. Which is why I said little about Mr. Black himself. I'll have you know that Mr. Black was far from the fine VIP that everyone seems to think he was. Perhaps you should investigate his enemies. I told you before that Giselle was physically harmed by him. He was a very dangerous man."

"Dangerous enough for you to tell Giselle that she'd be better off without him?"

"I never . . ." But I stop right there, because I did say this. I remember now. I believed it then, and I believe it still.

I fill my mouth with a chunk of muffin. It's a relief to have a legitimate reason not to speak. I return to Gran's chewing imperative. One, two, three . . .

"Molly, we've spoken with many of your coworkers. Do you know how they describe you?"

I pause my regimen to shake my head.

"They say you're awkward. Standoffish. Meticulous. A neat freak. A weirdo. And worse."

I reach ten chews and swallow, but it does nothing to alleviate the lump that has formed in my throat.

"Do you know what else some of your colleagues said about you? They said they could totally picture you murdering someone."

Cheryl, of course. Only she would say such a heinous thing.

"I don't like speaking ill of people," I reply. "But since you're pressing me, Cheryl Green, head maid, cleans sinks with her toilet rag. That's not a euphemism. I mean it literally. She calls in sick when she's well. She spies into people's lockers. And she steals tips. If she's capable of theft and hygiene crimes, how low would she go?"

"How low would *you* go, Molly? You stole Mr. Black's wedding ring and pawned it."

"What?" I say. "I didn't steal it. I found it. Who told you that?"

"Cheryl followed you all the way to the pawn shop. She knew you were up to something. We found the ring in the front window, Molly. The shopkeeper described you perfectly—someone who blends into the background, until she speaks. The kind of person you'd easily forget about under most circumstances."

My pulse is pounding. I can't keep my mind focused. This doesn't reflect well on my character and I must make amends.

"I should not have pawned that ring," I say. "I applied the wrong rule in my head, 'the finders-keepers rule,' when I should have applied the 'do unto others' rule. I regret that choice, but it doesn't make me a thief."

"You've stolen other things," she says.

"I have not," I say, punctuating my disdain with crossed arms, a postural signal of indignance.

"Mr. Snow has seen you stealing food from discarded trays. And small pots of jam."

I feel the floor of my stomach drop out from under me the way it does when the elevator at the hotel is about to go on the fritz. I'm not sure what's more humiliating—that Mr. Snow saw me do this or that he never said a word to me about it.

"He is telling the truth," I admit. "I have liberated discarded food, food that would have ended up in the trash bin anyway. This is 'waste not, want not.' It is not theft."

"It's all a matter of degrees, Molly. One of your colleagues, a fellow maid, said she worries that you can't spot danger."

"Sunitha," I say. "For the record, she's an excellent maid."

"It's not *her* record that's on the line here."

"Did you speak with Mr. Preston?" I ask. "He will vouch for me."

"We did speak to the doorman, actually. He said you were 'blameless'—interesting choice of words—and that we should dig for dirt elsewhere. He mentioned Black's family members, as well as some strange characters coming and going at night. But it was like he was going out of his way to protect you, Molly. He knows something isn't right in the state of Denmark."

"What does Denmark have to do with any of this?" I ask.

Detective Stark sighs loudly. "Bloody hell. It's going to be a long day."

"And Juan Manuel, the dishwasher?" I ask. "Did you talk to him?"

"Why would we talk to a dishwasher, Molly? Who is he, anyhow?"

A son to a mother, a provider to a family, another invisible worker bee in the hive. But I decide not to press further. The last thing I want is for him to be in trouble. Instead, I name the one person who I'm certain would vouch for my reliability. "Have you spoken with Rodney, the bartender at the Social?"

"As a matter of fact, I have. He said he thought you were—quote unquote—'more than capable of murder.'"

All of the energy that has kept my spine upright dissipates in an instant. I slump over and look down at my hands in my lap. A maid's hands. Working hands. Chaffed and dry, despite all the lotion I put on them, the nails cut cleanly short, calluses on the palms. The hands of a much older woman than I actually am. Who would want these hands and the body attached to them? How could I ever think that Rodney would?

If I look up at Detective Stark now, I know the tears will spill from my eyes, so I concentrate on the cheery little teapots on my pajamas—vibrant pink, baby blue, and daffodil yellow.

When the detective speaks, her voice is softer than before. "Your fingerprints were all over the Blacks' suite."

"Of course they were," I say. "I cleaned that suite every day."

"And did you also clean Mr. Black's neck? Because traces of your cleaning solution were found there too."

"Because I checked his pulse before calling for help!"

"You had various plans for killing him, Molly, so why in the end did you choose asphyxiation rather than the gun? Did you really think you wouldn't get caught?"

I will not look up. I will not.

"We found the weapon in your vacuum cleaner."

I feel my insides twisting, the dragon slashing and gnashing. "What were you doing meddling with my vacuum cleaner?"

"What were *you* doing hiding a gun in it, Molly?"

My pulse is pounding. The only other person who knew about both the ring and the gun was Rodney. I can't do it. I can't assemble the pieces in my mind.

"We tested your housekeeping cart," Detective Stark says. "And it tested positive for traces of cocaine. We know you're not the kingpin here, Molly. You're simply not smart enough for that. We believe that Giselle introduced you to Mr. Black, and that she groomed you to work for her husband. We believe you and Mr. Black were well acquainted, and that you were helping him hide the lucrative drug operation he was running through the hotel. Something must have gone wrong between the two of you. Maybe you got angry with him and you retaliated by taking his life. Or maybe you were helping Giselle get out of a bad situation. Either way, you were involved.

"So as I said, this can go one of two ways. You can plead guilty immediately to all charges, including first-degree murder. The judge will take your swift guilty plea and confession into consideration. An early demonstration of regret, plus any information you can provide about the drug-running happening in this hotel, could go a long way in lightening your sentence."

The teapots dance around in my lap. The detective is droning on, but her voice sounds tinny, farther and farther away.

"Or we can do this the long and slow way. We can gather more evi-

dence, and we can end up in court. Either way, Molly the Maid, the jig is
up. So what do you choose?"

I know I'm not thinking straight. And I don't know the proper rules
of etiquette when one is accused of murder. Out of nowhere, I remember *Columbo*.

"You read me my rights earlier," I say. "At the door of my home. You
said I have the right to consult an attorney. If I hire one, do I have to pay
immediately?"

Detective Stark rolls her eyes—exasperation writ so large that I can't
miss it. "Lawyers generally don't expect cash on the spot," she says.

I hold my head up and look straight at her.

"In that case, I'd like one phone call, please. I demand to speak to a
lawyer."

Detective Stark pushes back her chair. It makes an aggravating noise.
I'm certain she's just added to the plethora of unsightly scuff marks already on the floor. She opens the door of the interrogation room and
says something to the young police officer standing guard outside. He
fishes a cell phone from his back pocket and hands it to her. It's my cell
phone. What is he doing with my cell phone?

"Here," the detective says. She drops my phone on the table with a
clunk.

"You took my phone," I say. "Who gave you the right?"

Detective Stark's eyes go wide. "You did," she says. "After you fainted
in the cell, you insisted that we take your phone in case you needed it
later to call a friend."

The truth is that I don't remember, but something vague niggles at
the back of my consciousness.

"Thank you very much," I say. I pick up my phone and press Contacts. I search all eight entries—Giselle, Gran, Cheryl Green, Olive Garden, Mr. Preston, Rodney, Mr. Rosso, Mr. Snow. I consider who is truly
on my side—and who might not be. The names swirl before my eyes. I
wait until I can see clearly. Then I choose and dial. I hear it ringing.
Someone picks up.

"Mr. Preston?" I say.

"Molly? Are you all right?"

"Please pardon me for troubling you at such an inconvenient hour. You're probably getting ready for work."

"Not now. I'm working the late shift today. Dear girl, what's going on?"

I look around the plain white room with the fluorescent lights beating down on me. Detective Stark eyes me with her ice-glazed stare. "The truth is, Mr. Preston, I'm not quite all right. I've been arrested for murder. And more. I'm being held at the station nearest the hotel. And I . . . I hate to say this, but I could really use your help."

Chapter 16

Once I finish my call to Mr. Preston, Detective Stark holds out her hand. In truth, I do not know what for, so I grab my empty Styrofoam cup and pass it to her, thinking we are finished and that she's cleaning the table.

"Are you kidding me?" she says. "Now you think I'm your maid?"

I most certainly do not. If she were anywhere near a half-decent maid, this room would not look as it does—scuffed and scratched, stained and smeared. If I had so much as a napkin and a bottle of water, I could bide my time cleaning up this pigpen.

Detective Stark takes my phone from my hand.

"Will I get that back? I have essential contacts that I'd hate to lose."

"You'll get it back," she says. "Someday." She looks at her watch. "So, is there anything else you'd like to say, while we're waiting for your lawyer?"

"My apologies, Detective. Please don't take my silence personally. First off, I've never been very gifted with small talk and when I'm forced to make it, I often say the wrong thing. Second, I'm aware of my right to remain silent and so I'll begin employing it immediately."

"Fine," she says. "Have it your way."

After what seems like an unholy eternity, there's a loud knock on the door.

"This should be interesting," Detective Stark says, rising from her chair and opening the door.

It's Mr. Preston, in civilian dress. I've rarely seen him out of his doorman's cap and coat. He's wearing a perfectly pressed blue shirt and dark jeans. There's a woman with him dressed much more formally in a tailored navy suit, carrying a black leather briefcase. Her short, curly hair is perfectly coiffed. Her dark-brown eyes immediately give away who she is because they're so much like her father's.

I stand to greet them. "Mr. Preston," I say, barely able to contain my relief at seeing them. I move a bit too quickly and hit my hip bone on the table. It smarts, but it doesn't stop the surge of words that flows from my mouth. "I'm so glad you're here. Thank you so much for coming. It's just that I've been accused of some terrible things. I've never harmed anyone, never touched a drug in my life, and the only time I've ever held a weapon was—"

"Molly, I'm Charlotte," Mr. Preston's daughter says, interrupting me. "It's my professional advice that you remain silent at this time. Oh. And it's very nice to meet you. My dad has told me a lot about you."

"One of you better be an attorney, or I'm going to lose it," Detective Stark says.

Charlotte steps forward, her sharp heels clacking loudly on the cold, industrial floor. "That would be me, Charlotte Preston, of Billings, Preston & García," she says, flicking a business card to the detective.

"Dear girl," Mr. Preston says to me. "We're here now, so don't you worry about a thing. This is all just a big—"

"Dad," Charlotte says.

"Sorry, sorry," he replies, and zips his mouth shut.

"Molly, do you agree to be represented by me?"

I don't say a word.

"Molly?" she prods.

"You instructed me not to speak. Should I speak now?"

"My apologies. I wasn't clear. You can speak, just not anything relating to the charges lain. Let me ask you again: do you agree to be represented by me?"

"Oh yes, that would be most helpful," I say. "Can we discuss a payment plan at a more convenient time?"

Mr. Preston coughs into his hand.

"I'd offer you a tissue, Mr. Preston, but I'm afraid I don't have one on me." I eye Detective Stark, who is shaking her head.

"Please don't worry about payment right now. Let's just concentrate on getting you out of here," Charlotte says.

"You realize that to release her you've got to post bail of $800,000. Now, let me see . . ." Detective Stark says as she puts her index finger to her lips, "I think that's just a spot above a maid's earnings and assets, am I right?"

"You're right, Detective," Charlotte says. "Maids and doormen are often underpaid and undervalued. But litigators? We do all right. Better than detectives, so I'm told. I've personally posted bail with the clerk out front." She smiles at Detective Stark. I can say with one hundred percent certainty that it's not a friendly smile.

Charlotte turns to me. "Molly," she says. "I've arranged for you to have a bail hearing later this morning. I'm not allowed to represent you there, but I've filed some letters already on your behalf."

"Letters?" I ask.

"Yes, from my father, who has provided a character statement, and from me, saying I'll post your bail. If all goes well, you'll be released this afternoon."

"Really?" I ask. "Is it that simple? I'll be released and this will be over?" I look from her to Mr. Preston.

"Hardly," Detective Stark says. "Even if they get you off now, you'll still have to stand trial. It's not like we're dropping the charges."

"Is that your phone?" Charlotte asks me.

"Yes," I say.

"You'll make sure it's kept locked and safe somewhere, right, Detective? You won't be logging that as evidence."

Detective Stark pauses. Her hand is on her hip. "It's not my first rodeo, cowgirl. I've got her house keys, too, by the way, which she insisted I keep after she passed out." The detective fishes my keys from her pocket and drops them on the table. If I had an antiseptic wipe, I'd snatch them up and immediately disinfect them.

"Great," Charlotte says, picking up my keys and phone. "We'll talk to your clerk out front and make sure they log these as personal possessions, not evidence."

"Fine," says Detective Stark.

Mr. Preston is looking down at me, his eyebrows crinkling together. It may be that he's concentrating hard, but I think it's more likely that he's concerned.

"Don't worry," he says. "We'll be waiting for you after the hearing."

"See you on the other side," Charlotte adds. And with that, they turn and leave.

Once they're gone, Detective Stark just stands there, arms crossed, glaring at me.

"What happens now?" I ask. I'm finding it hard to breathe.

"You and your teapots go back to your charming holding cell and wait patiently for your hearing," Detective Stark replies.

I stand and straighten my pajamas. The young officer outside is ready to escort me back to the repugnant cell.

"Thank you very much," I say to the detective before I exit.

"Thank you for what?" she asks.

"For the muffin and the coffee. I do hope you have a more pleasant morning than mine."

CHAPTER 17

It feels awfully strange to be wearing pajamas in the afternoon, and it feels particularly unnerving to be in a courthouse wearing such wholly inappropriate attire. One of Detective Stark's police officers kindly drove me to this courthouse about an hour ago, and now I'm seated in a cramped office on the premises with a very young man who will serve as my attorney in the bail hearing. He asked me my name, reviewed the charges against me, told me we'd be called into the courtroom when the judge was ready, and then claimed he had some emails to read. He took out his phone and has been giving it his fullest attention for at least five minutes. I have no idea what I'm supposed to do in the meantime. No matter. This allows me time to collect myself.

I know from TV that as the accused, I should be wearing a clean blouse, buttoned to the neck, and formal dress slacks. I most certainly should not be wearing pajamas.

"Excuse me," I say to the young attorney. "Would it be possible to go home and change before the hearing?"

His face scrunches up. "You can't be serious," he replies. "Do you know how lucky you are to be seen today?"

"I am serious," I say. "Quite."

He puts his phone in his breast pocket. "Wow. Do I have some news for you."

"Excellent. Please share it, posthaste," I reply.

But he doesn't utter a word. He just stares at me with his mouth open, which surely means I've made some blunder, but what it is I do not know.

Moments later, he proceeds to fire questions my way. "Have you ever done jail time?"

"Not until this morning," I say.

"That wasn't jail," he says. "Jail's way worse than that. Do you have a criminal record?"

"My record is squeaky clean, thank you very much."

"Do you harbor plans of leaving the country?"

"Oh, yes. I'd love to visit the Cayman Islands someday. I've heard it's lovely. Have you been?"

"Just tell the judge you have no plans of leaving the country," he says.

"As you wish."

"The hearing won't take long. They're pretty standard, even in criminal cases like yours. I'll try to get you free on bail. I'm assuming that like everyone else who's ever been accused, you're not guilty and you want out on bail because you're the sole caregiver for your poor, sick grandmother, right?"

"I was. But not anymore," I say. "She's dead. And I'm not guilty on any of the charges, of course."

"Right. Of course," he replies.

I'm grateful for his instant vote of confidence.

I'm about to get into the details of my complete innocence, but his phone buzzes in his pocket. "We're up," he says. "Let's go."

He leads me out of the small office, down a hallway, and into a much larger room with benches on both sides and a wide aisle in the middle. I'm walking down the aisle with him to the front of the courtroom. For a moment, I imagine a similar room with a similar aisle, with the big difference that in my imagination, I'm walking down the aisle as a brideto-be and the man beside me is not this stranger at all but a man very known to me.

My flight of fancy is rudely interrupted when my young attorney says, "Take a seat," and points to a chair in front of a table to the right of the judge.

As I sit, Detective Stark walks into court and seats herself at an identical chair in front of an identical table across the chasm of the aisle.

I feel my jitters return. I clasp my hands tightly in my lap to quell my trembling.

Someone says, "All rise," and I feel the young attorney's hand on my elbow guiding me to my feet.

The presiding judge emerges from a door at the back of the court and plods to his high bench, sitting down in front of it with an audible groan. I do not mean it unkindly when I say that he reminds me of a Brazilian horned frog. Gran and I watched a tremendous documentary about the Amazon rain forest and the Brazilian horned frog. Such a unique creature. It has a long, downturned mouth and protuberant eyebrows, much like the judge before me.

The proceedings begin immediately, with the judge asking Detective Stark to speak. She presents the charges against me. She says many things about the Black case and about my involvement in it. She makes it seem like I'm not a reliable person. But it's the end of her diatribe that stings the most.

"Your Honor," she says, "the charges against Molly Gray are very serious. And while I'm aware that the accused before you presents as a picture of innocence and not a flight risk at all, she has proven herself unreliable. Much like the Regency Grand Hotel where she works, which by all appearances is a fine, upstanding hotel, the more we probe into the life of Molly and her workplace, the more dirt we uncover."

If I could and it were my place to do so, I'd bang a gavel and yell, "Objection!" just like they do on TV.

The judge doesn't move at all, but he does interrupt. "Detective Stark, may I remind you that the hotel is not the subject of this hearing, nor can a hotel stand trial. Can you please get to the point?"

Detective Stark clears her throat. "The point is that we're beginning to question the nature of the connection between Molly Gray and Mr. Black. We've gathered significant evidence of illegal activity between Mr. Black and the seemingly innocent young hotel maid you see before you. I'm deeply concerned about her moral integrity and her ability to abide by the rule of law. In other words, Your Honor, this is a prime example of appearances being deceiving."

I find this incredibly insulting. I may have my faults, but it's balderdash and poppycock to suggest that I don't follow rules. I've devoted my entire life to just that, even when the rules are entirely unsuited to my constitution.

The young attorney is directed to speak on my behalf. He talks quickly and flails his arms dramatically. He explains to the judge that I have a squeaky-clean criminal record, that I lead a woefully uneventful life, am gainfully employed in a menial position offering zero flight risk, that I have never in all my years left the country and have occupied the same address for twenty-five years—ergo, my entire life.

In closing, he poses a question. "Does this young woman really fit the profile for a dangerous criminal and a runner? I mean, really. Take a good look at who you have in front of you. Something doesn't add up."

The judge's froglike jowls are resting on his hands. His eyes are droopy and half-closed. "Who's posting bail?" he asks.

"An acquaintance of the accused," the young attorney answers.

The judge checks a paper in front of him. "Charlotte Preston?" The judge's eyes open slightly and fall on me. "Friends in high places, I see," he says.

"Not usually, Your Honor," I answer. "But lately, yes. Also, I wish to apologize for my wholly inappropriate attire. I was arrested at my front door at an inopportune hour of the early morning and was not afforded a chance to dress in a respectful manner that befits your court."

I don't know if I was supposed to speak, but it's too late now. My young attorney's mouth is wide open, but he's giving me no clues as to what I should do or say.

After a sizable pause, the judge speaks. "We won't judge you on the basis of your teapots, Ms. Gray, but on your propensity to obey the rules and to stay put." His impressive eyebrows undulate to accentuate his words.

"That's welcome news, Your Honor. I'm actually quite gifted when it comes to obeying rules."

"Good to know," he replies.

The young attorney remains completely quiet. Since he's not venturing a word in my defense, I carry on. "Your Honor, I consider myself most fortunate to have made a couple of friends several rungs above my station, but I'm just a maid, you see. A hotel maid. A wrongly accused one."

"You're not standing trial today, Ms. Gray. You understand that if we grant you bail, your movements will be restricted. Home, work, and the city only."

"That accurately summarizes my circumnavigations up to this point in my life, Your Honor, minus travel and nature documentaries on TV, which I'm assuming don't count since they occur from the relative comfort of an armchair. I have no intention nor financial ability to expand my geographic reach, nor would I know how to go about travel all on my own. I'd be worried I wouldn't know the rules in a foreign place and that I'd make an . . . well, a fool of myself." I pause, then realize my faux pas. "Your Honor," I add hastily, with a quick curtsy.

One side of the judge's long, amphibious mouth curls up into something resembling a smile. "I'd hate for anyone here today to be making a fool of themselves," the judge says, then he looks at Detective Stark, who for the first time in the proceedings does not meet his eye.

"Ms. Gray," the judge pronounces, "I hereby grant you your conditional bail. You're free to go."

Chapter 18

At long last, after many forms and formalities, I find myself sinking into the plush leather backseat of Charlotte Preston's luxury car. Once I left the courthouse, I was passed off to a clerk who said she knew Charlotte well and would bring me safely to her. She escorted me to a back door, where Mr. Preston and his daughter, as they had promised, were waiting for me. They whisked me away in this car. I am free, for now at least.

The dashboard of Charlotte's car tells me it's one P.M. I believe this vehicle is a Mercedes, but given that I've never owned a car myself and only ride in them on rare occasions, I'm not up on the finer brands. Mr. Preston sits in the passenger seat while Charlotte drives.

I'm tremendously grateful to be in this car rather than in court or in the filthy basement holding cell in the police station. I suppose I should focus on the bright side rather than on the unpleasantness. This day has afforded me many new experiences, and Gran used to say that new experiences open doors that lead to personal growth. I'm not sure that I've enjoyed the doors that have opened today, nor the experiences I've had, but I do hope they lead to personal growth in the long run.

"Dad, you have Molly's phone and keys, right?"

"Oh, yes," Mr. Preston says. "Thank you for reminding me." He removes them from his pocket and passes them back to me.

"Thank you, Mr. Preston," I say.

Only then does it occur to me. "May I ask where we're going?"

"To your home, Molly," Charlotte said. "We're going to take you home."

Mr. Preston turns around in the passenger seat to meet my eye. "Now, don't you worry, Molly," he says. "Charlotte's going to help you out, pro bono, and we won't stop until everything's back to normal, tickety-boo."

"But what about the bail?" I ask. "I don't have anywhere near that kind of money."

"That's okay, Molly," Charlotte says, never taking her eyes off the road. "I don't actually have to pay that, only if you run away."

"Well, I'm not about to do that," I say, leaning into the space between the two front seats.

"Sounds like old Judge Wight figured that out fairly quickly, or so I'm told," Charlotte says.

"How did you hear that so fast?" Mr. Preston asks.

"The clerks, the assistants, the court reporters. People talk. Treat them well and they give you the inside scoop. Most attorneys walk all over them, though."

"The way of the world," Mr. Preston says.

"I'm afraid so. They also said Judge Wight was in no rush to release Molly's name to the press. Sounds to me like he knows Stark's chasing the wrong fox."

"I don't know how any of this could have happened," I say. "I'm just a maid, trying to do my job to the best of my abilities. I'm . . . I'm not guilty of any of these charges."

"We know that, Molly," Mr. Preston says.

"Sometimes life isn't fair," Charlotte adds. "And if there's one thing I've learned over years of practice, it's that there's no shortage of criminals out there who will prey on a person's difference for their personal gain."

Mr. Preston turns around in his seat again to look at me. Deep wrinkles have emerged on his forehead.

"Life must be hard without your gran," he says. "I know you relied on her a lot. You know, she asked me to look out for you, before she passed."

"Did she?" I say. How I wish she were here. I look out the window through the tears that have formed in my eyes. "Thank you. For looking out for me," I say.

"That's quite all right," Mr. Preston replies.

My building comes into view, and I'm fairly certain that I've never been happier to see it.

"Do you think it's appropriate for me to go to work today as usual, Mr. Preston?"

Charlotte turns to her dad, then looks back to the road ahead.

"I'm afraid not, Molly. It will be expected that you take some time off," Mr. Preston says.

"Would it not be correct to call Mr. Snow?"

"No, not in this case. It's best right now not to contact anyone at the hotel."

"There's visitors' parking at the back of my building," I say. "I've never used it, as the visitors Gran and I used to receive were mostly Gran's friends and none of them had vehicles."

"Do you keep in touch with them?" Charlotte asks as she turns into a free spot.

"No," I reply. "Not since Gran died."

Once we're parked, we get out of the car and I lead the way into the building. "This way," I say, pointing to the stairwell.

"No elevator?" Charlotte asks.

"I'm afraid not," I reply.

We climb silently to my floor and are walking down the hall toward my apartment when Mr. Rosso emerges from his.

"You!" he says, pointing a plump index finger at me. "You brought the police into this building! They arrested you! Molly, you're no good, and you can't live here anymore. I'm evicting you, you hear me?"

Before I can answer, I feel a hand on my arm. Charlotte steps past me and stands a few inches from Mr. Rosso's face.

"You're the slumlord—I mean landlord—I suppose?"

Mr. Rosso pouts the way he always does when I tell him I'm going to be a bit late with the rent.

"I am the landlord," he says. "Who the hell are you?"

"I'm Molly's lawyer," Charlotte replies. "You do realize that this building is in violation of more than a few codes and bylaws, right? Cracked fire door, parking too tightly spaced. And any residential building over five stories has to have a working elevator."

"Too expensive," Mr. Rosso says.

"I'm sure city inspectors have heard that excuse before. Let me offer you some free legal advice. What's your name again?"

"It's Mr. Rosso," I offer helpfully.

"Thank you, Molly," Charlotte replies. "I'll remember that." She turns back to him. "So the free advice is: don't think about my client, don't talk about my client, don't harass or threaten my client with eviction or anything else. Until you hear differently from me, she's got a right to be here, the same as anyone else. You got it? Clear?"

Mr. Rosso's face has turned bright red. I expect him to speak, but surprisingly, he does not. He merely nods, then backs away into his apartment, quietly closing the door behind him.

Mr. Preston smiles at Charlotte. "That's my girl," he says.

I fumble for my keys and unlock my apartment door.

One of the great virtues of Gran's daily cleaning regimen is that the apartment is in a perpetually suitable state to receive unexpected visitors, not that I usually receive any. Besides the unwanted visit from police earlier today and the shocking visit from Giselle on Tuesday, this is one of the few times I'm able to reap the benefits of this advantage.

"Please come in," I say, directing Charlotte and Mr. Preston through my front door. I don't take the polishing cloth out of my closet because I'm still in slippers and they have spongy bottoms that can't effectively be wiped. Instead, I grab a plastic bag from the closet and wrap my slippers in it, TBSL—To Be Sanitized Later. Mr. Preston and Charlotte elect to keep their shoes on, which is fine by me given how grateful I am to them at this particular juncture in time.

"May I take your bag?" I ask Charlotte. "The closets are small, but I'm a bit of a wizard when it comes to spatial organization."

"Actually, I'm going to need it," she says. "To take notes."

"Of course," I say, though I feel the floors tilt under me as I realize what she's here for and what's about to happen next. Up to now I've been concentrating on the new delight of having people—friendly people, helpful people—in my environs. I've tried to ignore the fact that very soon, I'll have to think more deeply about all that has happened to me today and leading up to today. I'll have to share details and recount things I don't actually want to think about. I'll have to explain all that has gone wrong. I'll have to choose what to say.

No sooner have I had these thoughts than I visibly begin to shake.

"Molly," Mr. Preston says, putting a hand on my shoulder. "Would it be all right if I went into the kitchen and prepared us all a pot of tea? Charlotte will tell you, I'm very good at it, for a big old lug, anyhow."

Charlotte strolls into the living room. "He makes a mean cuppa, my daddy does," she says. "Leave that to him, and you can go freshen up, Molly. I'm sure you're eager to change."

"I most certainly am," I say, looking down at my pajamas. "I won't take long."

"There's no rush. We'll be here when you're ready."

I can hear Mr. Preston clanging around in the kitchen and humming to himself while I'm out here in the hall. This is most certainly a breach of proper etiquette. The guests should be seated comfortably in the sitting room and I should be tending to them, not the other way around. And yet, the truth of the matter is, I can't follow protocols in this very moment. I can barely think straight. My nerves are too frayed. While I stand, immobilized in my own hallway, Charlotte joins Mr. Preston in my kitchen. They chatter back and forth to each other, like two birds on a wire. It's the most pleasing sound, like sunshine and hope, and for a moment I wonder what it is I have done to deserve the good fortune of having them both here. My legs gradually regain mobility and I walk over to the kitchen and stand in the threshold. "Thank you," I say. "I can't thank you enough for—"

Mr. Preston interrupts me. "Sugar bowl? I know it must be here somewhere."

"In the cupboard beside the stove. First shelf," I say.

"Off you go then. Leave the rest to us."

I turn and head to the bathroom, where I shower quickly, grateful that there's proper hot water today and relieved to scrub the sour filth of the station and court off my skin. I enter the living room a few minutes later in a white, buttoned-down blouse and dark slacks. I'm feeling quite a lot better.

Mr. Preston is seated on the sofa and Charlotte is sitting across from him on a chair she's brought from the kitchen. He's found Gran's beautiful silver serving tray in the cupboard, the one we bought for a most economical sum at a thrift store so long ago. It's so strange to see it in his large, masculine hands. The full tea service is expertly arranged on the table in front of the sofa.

"Where did you learn to serve a proper tea, Mr. Preston?"

"I wasn't always a doorman, you know. I had to work my way up to that," he says. "And to think, I now have a daughter who's a lawyer." His eyes crinkle up as he looks upon his daughter. It's a look that reminds me so much of gran, I want to cry.

"Shall I pour you a cup?" Mr. Preston asks me. He doesn't wait for an answer. "One lump or two?"

"It's a two sort of day," I say.

"Every day is a two sort of day for me," he says. "I need all the sweetness I can get."

Truthfully, so do I. I need the sugar because I'm feeling a tad faint again. I've had nothing to eat since the raisin-bran muffin in the station this morning. I don't have enough food in my cupboards to serve three people and eating on my own would be the very pinnacle of impropriety.

"Dad, you've got to cut back on sugar," Charlotte says, shaking her head. "You know it's not good for you."

"Ah well," he replies. "Hard to teach an old dog new tricks and all, right, Molly?" He pats his belly and chuckles.

Charlotte puts her teacup on the table. She picks up the yellow pad of paper and a sleek gold pen she's placed on the floor beside her chair. "So, Molly. Have a seat. Are you ready to talk? I'll need you to tell me everything you know about the Blacks and why you think you stand accused of . . . well, many things."

"Wrongly accused," I say as I take a seat beside Mr. Preston.

"That's a given, Molly," Charlotte replies. "I'm sorry I didn't make that immediately clear. My father and I wouldn't be here if we didn't believe that. Dad's convinced you had nothing to do with this. He's long suspected there's nefarious activity taking place at that hotel." She pauses and looks around the room. Her eyes land on Gran's flowered curtains, her curio cabinet, and the English landscape prints on the wall. "I can see why Dad's so sure about you, Molly. But to absolve you, we need to figure out who might actually be guilty of these crimes. We both think you've been played. Do you understand? You've been used as a pawn in Mr. Black's murder."

I recall the gun in my vacuum. The only people who knew about me and that gun were Giselle and Rodney. That thought alone sends a wave of sadness rushing through me. I slump over as it washes away all the gumption from my spine.

"I'm innocent," I say. "I didn't kill Mr. Black." Tears prick my eyes and I drive them back. I don't want to make a fool of myself, I really don't.

"It's all right," Mr. Preston says, giving my arm a little pat. "We believe you. All you have to do is tell the truth, *your* truth, and Charlotte will see to the rest."

"My truth. Yes," I say. "I can do that. I suppose it's time."

I start with a full description of what I saw the day I entered the Black suite and found him dead in his bed. Charlotte furiously jots down my every word. I describe the drinks on the messy sitting-room table, Giselle's spilled pill bottle in the bedroom, the discarded robe on the floor, the three pillows on the bed rather than four. I start to shake as the memory returns.

"I'm not sure that pillows and messiness are the details Charlotte's after here, Molly," Mr. Preston says. "I think she's looking for details that might suggest foul play."

"That's right," Charlotte adds. "Such as the pills. You said the pills were Giselle's. Did you touch them? Were they labeled?"

"No, I didn't touch them. Not that day at least. And the container wasn't labeled. I knew they were Giselle's because she'd often take them in my presence when I was cleaning the suite. Plus, I often saw the bottle in the bathroom. She called them her 'benz friends' or her 'chill pills.' I believe 'benz' is a medicine of some sort? She did not seem ill to me— well, not in the physical sense. But some illnesses are a lot like maids— omnipresent but almost imperceptible."

Charlotte looks up from her pad. "So true," she says. "Benz is short for benzodiazepine. It's an anti-anxiety and depression med. Small white pills?"

"A lovely shade of robin's-egg blue, actually."

"Huh," says Charlotte. "So it was a street drug, not a prescription. Dad, did you ever talk to Giselle? Ever see any odd behavior from her?"

"Odd behavior?" he says, taking a sip of tea. "Odd behavior is par for the course when you're a hotel doorman at the Regency Grand. It was clear that she and Mr. Black were often on the outs. On the day that Mr. Black died, she left in a hurry and was crying. A week before, same thing, but that was after a visit from Victoria, Mr. Black's daughter, and his ex-wife, the first Mrs. Black."

"I remember that day," I say. "Mrs. Black—the first—held the elevator door open for me, but her daughter told me to take the service elevator instead. Giselle told me Victoria disliked her. Perhaps that's why Giselle was crying that day, Mr. Preston."

"Tears and high drama were a rather regular occurrence for Giselle," Mr. Preston says. "I suppose that's not surprising when you consider the man she married. Far be it from me to wish a man ill, but I was not sad to see that man's life come to an early end."

"Why's that?" Charlotte asks.

"You work a door like the Regency Grand for as long as I have, and you can read people in a single glance. He was no gentleman, not to the new Mrs. Black or to the former Mrs. Black. Mark my words, that man was a bad one."

"A bad egg?" I ask.

"A stinking, rotten egg," Mr. Preston confirms.

"Did he have any obvious enemies, Dad? Anyone who might have wanted him conveniently dispatched?"

"Oh, I'm sure he did. I was one of them. But there were others. First off, there were the women—the *other* women. When the Mrs. Blacks, new or old, were not around, there were . . . how should I call them . . . young female callers?"

"Dad, just say sex workers."

"I would call them that if I knew for sure that's what they were, but I never actually saw money exchange hands. Or the other part." Mr. Preston coughs and looks at me. "Sorry, Molly. This is all quite dreadful."

"It is," I say. "But I can corroborate that. Giselle told me that Mr. Black was engaging in extramarital relations. With more than one woman too. It hurt Giselle. Understandably."

"She told you that?" Charlotte asks. "Did you tell anyone else?"

"I most certainly did not," I say. I adjust the top button of my blouse. "Discretion is our motto. Invisible customer service is our goal."

Charlotte looks at her father.

"Mr. Snow's edict for hotel employees," he explains. "He's the hotel manager and self-proclaimed Grand Vizier of hotel hospitality and hygiene. But I'm starting to wonder if his Mr. Clean act is all just a clever front."

"Molly," Charlotte says. "Can you tell me anything that might help me understand the drug and weapons charges against you?"

"I can shed some light, I hope. Giselle and I were more than just maid and guest. She trusted me. She shared her secrets with me. She was my friend." I look to Mr. Preston, fearing I'm disappointing him since I crossed a guest-employee boundary. But he doesn't look upset, just concerned.

"Giselle came to my house the day after Mr. Black died. I didn't tell the police about that. I figured it was a private visit in my own home and therefore none of their concern. She was very upset. And she needed a favor from me. I obliged."

"Oh dear," says Mr. Preston.

"Dad," Charlotte says. Then to me, "What did she ask you to do?"

"To remove the handgun she'd hidden in the suite. In the bathroom fan."

Charlotte and Mr. Preston exchange another look, one I'm all too familiar with—they understand something that I don't.

"But there weren't any gunshots heard, or even reports of wounds on Mr. Black's body," Mr. Preston says.

"No, not according to any news feeds I've seen," Charlotte replies.

"Asphyxiated," I say. "That's what Detective Stark said."

Charlotte's mouth falls open. "Good to know," she says and scribbles something on her yellow pad. "So the gun wasn't the murder weapon. Did you return it to Giselle?"

"I didn't get the chance. I hid it in my vacuum cleaner, expecting to give it to her later. Then at lunch, I left the hotel."

"That's right," says Mr. Preston. "I saw you rushing out the doors and was wondering where you were off to in such a hurry."

I look down at the cup in my lap. Something niggles at my conscience; the dragon in my belly stirs. "I found Mr. Black's wedding ring," I say. "And I pawned it. I know that was wrong. It's just been very hard on my own to make ends meet financially. My gran. She'd be so ashamed of me." I can't bear to look up at either of them. Instead, I just stare into the black hole of my teacup.

"Dear girl," Mr. Preston says. "Your gran understood money troubles better than most. Believe me, I know that much about her and a whole lot more. It's my understanding that she left you some savings, after she passed?"

"Gone," I say. "Frittered away." I can't explain about Wilbur and the Fabergé. There's only so much shame I can confess to at once.

"So you pawned the ring and then went back to work?" Charlotte asks.

"Yes."

"And the police were waiting for you when you came back?"

Mr. Preston steps in. "That's correct, Charlotte. I was there. Couldn't do a damn thing to stop it either, though I tried."

Charlotte shifts her weight in the chair, crosses her legs. "What about the drug charges? Do you understand how those came about?"

"There were traces of cocaine on my maid's trolley. I have no idea how that's even possible. I promised Gran long ago that I'd never in my life touch a drug. Now I fear I've broken my promise."

"Dear girl," Mr. Preston says. "I'm sure she didn't mean it literally."

"Let's go back to the gun," Charlotte says. "How did the police find it in your vacuum cleaner?"

And here's where I must confess the pieces that I've put together myself since my arrest. "Rodney," I say, choking on the two syllables, barely able to spit them up and eject them from my mouth.

"I was wondering when his name would pop up," Mr. Preston says.

"When the police talked to me yesterday, I was afraid. Very afraid. I went straight home and called Rodney."

"He's the bartender at the Social," Mr. Preston adds for Charlotte's benefit. "Smarmy cretin. Write that down."

It hurts to hear Mr. Preston say it. "I called Rodney," I say. "I didn't know what else to do. He's been a loyal friend to me, maybe even a little bit more than a friend. I told him about the police questioning me, about Giselle and the gun in my vacuum cleaner, and about the ring I'd found and pawned."

"Let me guess. Rodney said he'd be all too happy to help a nice girl like you," says Mr. Preston.

"Something to that effect," I say. "But Detective Stark said it was Cheryl, my supervisor, who followed me to the pawn shop. Maybe she's the culprit in all of this? She's definitely untrustworthy. The stories I could tell you."

"My dear Molly," Mr. Preston says with a sigh. "Rodney used Cheryl to tip off the police. Can you see that? He likely used the gun and the ring in your possession to divert suspicion away from himself and toward you. He may very well be connected to the cocaine found on your cart. And to the murder of Mr. Black."

I know Gran would be displeased, but my shoulders slump even more. I can barely keep myself upright. "Do you think that perhaps Rodney and Giselle are in cahoots?" I ask.

Mr. Preston nods slowly.

"I see," I say.

"I'm sorry, Molly. I tried to warn you about Rodney," he says.

"You did, Mr. Preston. You can add the 'I told you so.' I deserve it."

"You do not deserve it," he replies. "We all have our blind spots."

He stands and walks over to Gran's curio cabinet. He looks at the photo of my mother, then puts it down. He picks up the photo of Gran and me at the Olive Garden. He smiles, then returns to his seat on the sofa.

"Dad, what exactly did you see at the hotel that made you suspicious of illegal activity? Do you think there's actual drug-running happening at the Regency Grand?"

"No," I say definitively before he can answer. "The Regency Grand is a clean establishment. Mr. Snow wouldn't have it any other way. The only other issue is Juan Manuel."

"Juan Manuel Morales, the dishwasher?" Mr. Preston asks.

"Yes," I reply. "I certainly wouldn't tell tales under ordinary circumstances, but these are far from ordinary circumstances."

"Go on," Charlotte says.

Mr. Preston leans forward, adjusting himself around the sofa's pointier springs.

I explain everything. How Juan Manuel's work permit expired some time ago, how he has nowhere to live, and how Rodney secretly lets him stay overnight in empty hotel rooms. I explain the overnight bags I drop off, and how I clean up after Juan Manuel and his friends every morning.

"I'll admit," I say, "I really don't know how so much dust can be tracked into a room in just one night."

Charlotte puts her pen down on her pad and addresses her father. "Wow, Dad. What a fine establishment you work at."

"*Par excellence,* as they say in France," I add.

Mr. Preston has his head in his hands and is shaking it back and forth. "I should have known," he says. "The burn marks on Juan Manuel's arms, the way he avoided me whenever I asked how he was doing."

It's only then that the jigsaw pieces connect in my mind. Rodney's behemoth friends, the dust, the parcels and overnight bags. The traces of cocaine on my trolley.

"Oh my lord," I say. "Juan Manuel. He's being abused and coerced."

"He's being forced to cut drugs every night in the hotel," Mr. Preston says. "And he's not the only one being used. They've been using you, too, Molly."

I try to swallow the enormous lump that has formed in my throat.

I see it all clearly, all of it. "I haven't only been working as a maid, have I?" I ask.

"I'm afraid not," Charlotte replies. "I'm sorry to say it, Molly, but you've also been working as a mule."

CHAPTER 19

Charlotte is on the phone having a quiet conversation with someone from her office. Mr. Preston is using the washroom. I'm pacing the living room. I stop at the window and open it a crack in a futile attempt to get some fresh air. Attached to our exterior wall, an empty bird feeder swings in the breeze. Gran and I used to watch birds from this window. We'd admire them for hours as they gobbled bread crumbs we'd leave out. We gave each little bird a name—Sir Chirpsalot, Lady Wingdamere, and the Earl of Beak. But when Mr. Rosso complained about the noise, we stopped our feeding. The birds flew away and never returned. Oh, to be a bird.

As I stare out the window, I catch little snippets of Charlotte's conversation—"background check on Rodney Stiles," "firearms registry for the name Giselle Black," "inspection records for the Regency Grand Hotel."

Mr. Preston emerges from the washroom. "No Juan Manuel?" he asks.

"Not yet," I reply.

About an hour ago, Charlotte and Mr. Preston decided to contact Juan Manuel. I was very unsure about dragging him into my mess.

"It's the right thing to do," Charlotte said. "For many reasons."

"He holds the missing pieces," Mr. Preston added. "He's the only one who might be able to shed light on this fiasco—if we can convince him to talk."

"Won't he be afraid?" I asked. "I have reason to believe that his family has been threatened. And so has he." I can't bear to even mention the other part—the burn marks.

"Yes," said Charlotte. "Who wouldn't be scared? But he'll have a new choice today that he didn't have before."

"What choice?" I asked.

"Between us and them," Mr. Preston replied.

Mr. Preston wasted little time after that. He called someone in the hotel kitchen who called someone else who discreetly checked the staff directory and handed over Juan Manuel's direct cell number, which all of us hastily stored in our phones.

I waited nervously as Mr. Preston dialed his number. What if he turned out to be yet another disappointment, another person who wasn't who I thought they were?

"Juan Manuel?" Mr. Preston said. "Yes, that's right . . ."

I couldn't hear Juan Manuel's responses, but I pictured his puzzled face as he tried to figure out why Mr. Preston was calling.

"I believe you're in some serious danger," Mr. Preston explained. He went on to say that his daughter was a lawyer and that he knew Juan Manuel had been coerced at the hotel.

There was a short pause as Juan Manuel spoke.

"I understand," Mr. Preston said. "We don't want you hurt, and we don't want your family hurt either. You should also know that Molly's in trouble as well. . . . Yes, that's right. . . . She's been framed for Mr. Black's murder," Mr. Preston said.

Another short pause, a bit more back and forth, and then, "Thank you . . . Yes . . . Certainly, we can explain everything in detail. And please know, we'd never do anything to . . . Yes, of course. All decisions will be up to you. . . . I'll text you the address. See you soon."

It's now been over an hour, and Juan Manuel is still not here. All of this waiting and anticipating is having a most deleterious effect on my nerves. To calm myself, I think about what a difference it makes having Mr. Preston and Charlotte on my side. Yesterday, I was alone. This apartment felt bleak and hollow. All of its color and vibrancy drained away the day Gran died. But now it's alive again, revitalized. I look at the feeder outside the window. Perhaps later I will scrounge for crumbs and fill it, no matter what Mr. Rosso says.

I feel overcharged and I can't stay still, which is why I'm now pacing. If I were here by myself, I'd probably scour the floors or scrub the bathroom tiles, but I'm not by myself, not anymore. It's altogether new and odd to have company. It's also a great comfort.

Mr. Preston takes his seat on the sofa.

Charlotte ends her call.

Something is eating away at me, and I decide to voice it. "Don't you think I should call R-Rodney?" I ask. His name trips me up again, but I spit it out. "Perhaps he can offer an explanation? Maybe he has nothing at all to do with the cocaine found on my trolley. It could have been Cheryl, couldn't it? Or someone else? What if Rodney's the one who can actually explain all of this?"

"Absolutely not," says Charlotte. "I've just done a background check on Rodney. Rich family but kicked out at fifteen. Then in a group home. Then petty theft, assault, and various drug charges that never stuck, and a string of different addresses a mile long before landing himself in this city."

"See, Molly? Calling that cretin is a bad idea," Mr. Preston says as he smooths out Gran's crocheted blanket on the sofa. "He'll only lie."

"And then he'll disappear," Charlotte adds.

"What about Giselle? She must know something that can help me. Or Mr. Snow?"

Before either of them can answer, there's a knock at my door.

My breath catches in my throat. "What if it's the police?" The room starts to undulate and I fear I won't make it to the front door.

Charlotte rises from her seat. "You have a legal representative now. The police would have called me if they wanted to contact you."

She comes to my side. "It's okay," she says, putting a reassuring hand on my wrist. It works. I immediately feel a little bit calmer and the ripples in the floor solidify.

Mr. Preston appears on my other side. "You can do this, Molly," he says. "Let's open the door together."

I take a deep breath and walk to the entryway. I open the door.

Juan Manuel is standing before me. He's wearing a pressed polo shirt, tucked into his neat jeans. He's carrying a white plastic takeout bag in one hand. His eyes are wide and his breath is ragged as though he climbed the stairs two by two.

"Hello, Molly," he says. "I can't believe it. I never, ever wanted trouble for you. If I could have—"

He stops midsentence. "Who are you?" he asks, looking past me to Charlotte.

She steps forward. "I'm Charlotte, Molly's lawyer and Mr. Preston's daughter. Please don't be afraid. We have no intention of turning you in. And we know you're in grave danger."

"I'm in too deep," he says. "So deep. I never chose this situation. They made me. They made Molly, too. It's the same but different."

"We're both in trouble, Juan Manuel," I say. "It is most serious."

"Yes, I know," he says.

Mr. Preston speaks up from behind me. "What's in the bag?"

"Leftovers from the hotel," Juan Manuel replies. "I had to make it look like I was leaving for an early dinner break. There are afternoon tea sandwiches in there. I know you like them, Mr. Preston."

"Oh, I do. Thank you," says Mr. Preston. "I'll lay them out. We all need to stay fortified."

Mr. Preston takes the bag and brings it to the kitchen.

Juan Manuel stands at the threshold without moving. Now that he's not holding the bag, it's easy to see that his hands are shaking. So are mine.

"Won't you come in?" I say.

He takes two unsteady steps forward.

"I'm grateful that you've come, especially given your current circumstances. I'm really hoping you'll talk to me," I say. "And to them. I need . . . help."

"I know, Molly. We're both in deep."

"Yes. There are things that happened that I didn't—"

"That you didn't understand—until now."

"Yes," I say. I glance at his scarred forearms, then turn away.

He steps inside and looks around the apartment. "Wow," he says. "This place. It reminds me of home."

He takes his shoes off. "Where can I put my work shoes? Not very clean."

"Oh, that's very thoughtful," I say. I step around him and open the closet. I take out a cloth. I'm about to wipe the bottoms of his shoes when he takes the cloth from me.

"No, no. My shoes. My job."

I stand there not knowing what to do with myself as he carefully wipes his shoes, puts them in the closet, then folds the cloth neatly and tucks it away before closing the closet door.

"I must warn you that I'm not altogether myself. Everything has been very . . . shocking. And I don't normally have visitors, so I'm not used to that either. I'm not very practiced at entertaining."

"For the love of God, Molly," Mr. Preston says from the kitchen. "Just relax and accept some help. Juan Manuel, perhaps you can assist me in the kitchen?"

Juan Manuel joins him, and I excuse myself to use the washroom. The truth is, I need a moment to collect myself. I stare into the mirror and breathe deeply. Juan Manuel is here and we're both in danger. I look like I'm falling apart. There are black circles under my eyes, which are swollen and red. I'm tense and drawn. Like the bathroom tiles that surround me, my cracks are beginning to show. I splash some water on my face, dry it off, and then exit the bathroom, joining my guests in the living room.

Mr. Preston carries in Gran's serving tray full of dainty cucumber sandwiches—crusts removed—mini-quiches and other delectable leftovers. I smell the food and my stomach immediately begins to rumble. Mr. Preston puts the tray on the coffee table. Then he brings an additional chair from the kitchen for Juan Manuel. We all take our seats.

I can't believe it. Here we are in Gran's sitting room, all four of us. Mr. Preston and I are on the sofa, and in front of me are Charlotte and Juan Manuel. Pleasantries are exchanged, as if this were a friendly tea party, though we all know it is not. Charlotte's asking about Juan Manuel's family and how long he's worked at the Regency Grand. Mr. Preston comments on what a reliable and hard worker he is. Juan Manuel looks down at his lap.

"I work hard, yes," he says. "Too hard. But still, I have big problems."

We have tiny plates on our laps filled with little sandwiches, which we are eating, me faster than anyone.

"Eat," says Charlotte. "Both of you. This isn't easy. You'll need to stay strong."

Juan Manuel leans forward.

"Here," he says. "Try these." He places two lovely finger sandwiches on my plate. "I made them."

I pick up a sandwich and take a bite. It's an exquisite taste, fluffy cream cheese and smoked salmon, with a burst of dill and lemon zest at the end. I've never tasted a sandwich more delicious in my life, so much so that it's nearly impossible to follow Gran's chewing imperative. It's gone before I know it.

"Delightful," I say. "Thank you."

We are all silent for a moment, but if others feel uncomfortable I'm not aware. For a brief moment, despite the circumstances, I find myself feeling something I haven't felt in so long, not since before Gran died. I feel . . . companionship. I feel . . . not entirely alone. Then I remember what brought everyone here in the first place, and the anxiety begins to churn again. I put my plate aside.

Charlotte does the same. She picks up the pad and pen by her chair. "Well, we're all here for the same reason, so we better get started. Juan Manuel, I believe my father filled you in about Molly's predicament? And I believe you yourself are in a very challenging situation."

Juan Manuel shifts in his chair. "Yes," he says. "I am." His big brown eyes look into mine. "Molly," he says, "I never wanted to see you involved in this, but when they brought you in, I didn't know what to do. I hope you believe me."

I swallow and consider his words. It takes me a moment to spot the difference—between a bold-faced lie and the truth. But then it sharpens and I can see it clearly in his face. What he's saying is the truth. "Thank you, Juan Manuel. I believe you."

"Tell her what you told me in the kitchen," Mr. Preston suggests.

"You know how every night I stayed in a different room at the hotel? How you gave me a different keycard each night?"

"Yes," I say.

"Mr. Rodney, he wasn't telling you the whole story. It's true, I don't have an apartment anymore. And no work permit now either. When I did, everything was great. I sent money back home. It was needed, because after my dad died, there wasn't enough. My family was so proud of me—'You're a good son,' my mother said. 'You work hard for us.' I was so happy. I was doing things the right way."

Juan Manuel pauses, swallows, then continues to speak. "But then, when I needed my work permit extended, Mr. Rodney said, 'No problem.' He introduced me to his lawyer friend. And that lawyer friend took a lot of my money, but in the end, no permit. I complained to Rodney and he said, 'My lawyer guy can fix anything. You'll have a new permit in a few days.' He told me he'd make sure Mr. Snow didn't find out. But then he said, 'You have to help me, too, you know. You scratch my back, I scratch yours.' I didn't want to scratch his back. I wanted to go back home, to find another way. But I couldn't go back home. I had no savings left."

Juan Manuel goes silent.

"What exactly did Rodney make you do?" Charlotte asks.

"At night, after my shift in the kitchen, I'd sneak into whatever hotel room with the keycard Molly gave me. Molly, she'd leave my bag there for me, right?"

"Yes," I say. "I did. Every night."

"That bag, it was never mine. It was Mr. Rodney's. His drugs were inside. Cocaine. And some other things too. He used to bring more drugs later in the night when no one else was around. And then he'd leave. All night, he made me work—sometimes alone, sometimes with Mr. Rodney's men—and we'd prepare the cocaine for sale. I didn't know nothing about these things before, I swear. But I learned. I had to learn. Fast."

"When you say he made you, what do you mean exactly?" Charlotte asks.

Juan Manuel wrings his hands as he speaks. "I told Mr. Rodney, 'I won't do this. I can't. I'd rather be deported than do this. This is wrong.' But things got worse when I said that. He said he'd kill me. I said, 'I don't care. Kill me. This is no life.'" Juan Manuel pauses, looks down at his lap, then continues. "But in the end, Mr. Rodney found a way to make me do his bad business."

Juan Manuel's face tightens. I notice the dark rings around his eyes and the redness in them. We look the same, he and I—all of our sorrows on full display.

"What did Rodney do then?" Charlotte asks.

"He said if I don't keep quiet and do his dirty work, he would kill my family back home. You don't understand. He has bad friends. He knew my address in Mazatlán. He's a bad man. Sometimes, when I was working late, I got so tired I'd fall asleep in my chair. I'd wake up, forget where I was. Mr. Rodney's men, they would hit me, throw water at me to keep me awake. Sometimes they burned me with cigars to punish me." He holds out his arm.

"Molly," Juan Manuel says. "I made up lies about the dishwasher burning me; I'm sorry. It's not the truth." His voice catches and he dissolves into tears. "It's wrong," he says. "I know a grown man should not cry like a baby," he says. He looks up at me. "Molly, when you came in the hotel room that day and saw me with Rodney and his men, I tried to tell you to run away, to go tell someone. I didn't want them to get you like they got me. But they did. They found a way to get you too."

Mr. Preston is shaking his head as Juan Manuel continues to sob. My own tears begin to fall.

Suddenly, I feel very tired, more tired than I've ever felt in my life. All I want is to get up from the sofa, pad down the hallway to my bedroom, wrap myself up in Gran's lone-star quilt, and fall asleep forever. I think back to Gran in her last days. Is this what she felt near the end, drained of the will to carry on?

"Looks like we found our rat," Mr. Preston says.

"Where there's one, there are more," Charlotte adds. She turns to Juan Manuel. "Was Rodney working for Mr. Black? Did you ever hear or see anything—anything at all—that might suggest Mr. Black was actually behind this drug operation?"

Juan Manuel wipes the tears from his face. "Mr. Rodney never said much about Mr. Black, but sometimes he took calls. He thinks I'm so stupid that I don't understand English. But I heard everything. Mr. Rodney would sometimes come into the room late at night with lots and lots of money. He'd set up meetings to give money to Mr. Black. Like more money than I ever seen in my life. Like this." He makes a gesture with his hands.

"Stacks of bills," Charlotte said.

"Yes. New. Fresh."

"There were bundles like that in Mr. Black's safe the day I found him dead," I say. "Perfect, clean stacks."

Juan Manuel continues. "Once, Rodney was really upset because there wasn't much money coming in that night. He went to meet Mr. Black and when he came back, he had a scar just like mine. But not on his arms. On his chest. That's how I knew I wasn't the only one getting punished."

The pieces come together. I remember the V of Rodney's crisp, white shirt and the strange round blemish marring his perfectly smooth chest.

"I've seen that scar," I say.

"There's another thing," Juan Manuel says. "Mr. Rodney never talked to me directly about Mr. Black. But I know he knows the wife. The new wife. Mrs. Giselle."

"That's not possible," I say. "Rodney assured me he barely ever spoke to her." But even as I say it, I realize I'm a fool.

"How do you know Rodney knows Giselle?" Charlotte asks.

Juan Manuel takes out his phone from his pocket and flicks through some photos until he finds the one he's looking for. "Because I caught him," he says. "How do you say in English *en flagrante delito* . . ."

"In flagrante?" Mr. Preston offers.

"Like this," he says, and turns his phone around to show us a picture.

It's Rodney and Giselle. They are kissing so passionately in a shadowy hallway of the hotel that they most certainly would not have noticed Juan Manuel taking the picture. My heart feels sore and heavy as I stare at the photo, registering the details—her hair swept across his shoulder, his hand on the small of her arched back. I fear my heart may stop altogether.

"Wow," says Charlotte. "Can you send that to me?"

"Yes," Juan Manuel says. They exchange numbers and he texts the photo to her. It takes only a few seconds for the vile proof to replicate on her phone.

Charlotte stands and paces the living room. "It's becoming more and more clear that Giselle and Rodney had multiple reasons to want Mr. Black dead. But the only way we can prove Molly is innocent is by finding irrefutable proof that one or both of them killed Mr. Black."

"It wasn't Giselle," I say. "She didn't do it."

Many skeptical eyes turn my way.

"Oh, Molly. How do you know that?" Charlotte asks.

"I do. I just do."

Charlotte and Mr. Preston exchange that look again, the look of doubt.

Mr. Preston rises to his feet. "I have an idea," he announces.

"Uh-oh," Charlotte replies.

"Just hear me out," he says. "It's not going to be easy, and we'll have to work as a team. . . ."

"That's a given," says Charlotte.

"I like this team idea," says Juan Manuel. "It's not right, the way they treat us."

"We'll have to be conniving," says Mr. Preston. "We'll have to make a plan that's ironclad."

"A plan," Charlotte says.

"Yes," Mr. Preston answers. "A plan. To outsmart the fox."

Chapter 20

It took well over an hour to hash out the details. During that time, I said, "No" and "I can't" so repeatedly that I sounded, as Gran used to say, like the Little Engine That Couldn't.

"Yes, you can," Mr. Preston told me over and over. "Would Columbo give up?"

"You've got this, Miss Molly," Juan Manuel chimed in.

"If I didn't think you could do this, I wouldn't be suggesting it," Charlotte reasoned.

We practiced and practiced. We ran through scenarios and I perfected my answers to all the questions they could come up with. We acted out the possible things that could go wrong. I had to get past the feeling of dissimulating, of not presenting my true thoughts, but Juan Manuel said something that eased my mind: "Sometimes, you must do one thing bad to do another thing good." He's right in so many ways, and I know so from experience.

We rehearsed with Juan Manuel playing opposite me, then with Mr. Preston playing opposite me. I had to forget they were my kind friends. I had to think of them as very bad eggs when in fact they are nothing of the sort. We hashed through details, noted key lines, and came up with contingency plans to deal with any eventuality.

And now we're finished. Charlotte, Mr. Preston, and Juan Manuel are all smiling and sitting taller in their chairs as they stare at me. I can't quite be sure, but I think I understand what I see in their faces—pride. They believe I can do this. If Gran were here, she'd say, *See, Molly? You can do it if you put your mind to it.*

I'm feeling better after so much practice, calmer about the entire plan. I must say, I do feel a little like Columbo, with a team of crack investigators around me. Together, we've devised a trap that will hopefully result in Rodney being caught in flagrante again—but this time, in a different way entirely.

The first step begins immediately, with me texting him. We've strategized exactly what I'll write. "I'm too nervous," I say, once I type the message into my phone. "Can someone check it before I press Send?"

Juan Manuel, Mr. Preston, and Charlotte gather round me on the sofa, reading over my shoulder.

"It sounds good," Juan Manuel says. "The way you speak, it's so nice all the time. More people should talk like you, Molly."

He smiles and I feel a tingle of warmth. "Thank you. That's very kind."

"I'd add the word 'urgently' to your text," Mr. Preston suggests.

"Yes, that's good," says Charlotte. "Urgently."

I adjust the message: *Rodney, we must meet: urgently. Mr. Black was MURDERED. I made revelations to the police of which you should be aware. I'm sincerely sorry!*

"Okay?" I ask, looking for approval from all of them.

"Do it, Molly. Press Send," Charlotte says.

I squeeze my eyes shut and press the button. I can hear the *swoosh* of the message leaving my device.

When I open my eyes a few seconds later, three circles appear in a new text box below my sent message.

"Well, well, well," says Mr. Preston. "Looks like our cretin is in a real hurry to respond."

My phone trills as Rodney's message appears: *Molly, WTF? Meet me in twenty minutes at the OG.*

"OG?" Mr. Preston asks. "What's that?"

"Original gangster?" Juan Manuel replies.

"What's that supposed to mean?" Charlotte asks.

Then it comes to me in a flash, and I figure it out. "The Olive Garden," I say. "That's where I'm to meet him. Shall I answer?"

"Tell him you'll be there soon," Charlotte says.

I try to type a response, but my hands are shaking too much.

"Do you want me to do it?" Charlotte asks.

"Yes, please," I say.

I hand her the phone and we all watch over her shoulder as she types: *K. CU in 20 min.*

She's about to press Send when Juan Manuel stops her. "That doesn't sound like Molly at all. She'd never write that."

"Really?" Charlotte says. "What's wrong with it?"

"You have to make it more pretty," Juan Manuel offers. "Use respectful language. Maybe use the word 'delightful.' Molly uses this word a lot: *deelightful.* So nice."

Charlotte erases what she wrote and tries again: *This plan sounds delightful, even if the circumstances bringing us together are not. See you soon.*

"Yes," I say. "That's what I'd say. That's very good."

"That's my Miss Molly," Juan Manuel adds.

Swoosh. Charlotte sends the message and then hands me my phone.

"Molly," says Mr. Preston, putting a reassuring hand on my shoulder. "Are you ready? You know what to say to him, what to do?"

Three concerned faces await my response.

"I'm ready," I reply.

"You can do this, Molly," Charlotte says.

"We have faith in you," Mr. Preston adds.

Juan Manuel gives me a thumbs-up.

They have all put their faith in me. They believe in me. The only one who isn't sure is me.

You can do it if you put your mind to it.

I take a deep breath, put my phone in my pocket, and walk out the front door.

CHAPTER 21

I'm at the Olive Garden eighteen minutes later, which is two minutes sooner than my ETA, mostly because I'm so nervous that I speed-walked the entire way. I'm sitting at our booth under the glow of the pendant light, only this time, it doesn't feel like our booth at all. It will never be our booth ever again.

Rodney hasn't arrived yet. As I wait, horrific visions loop in my mind—Mr. Black, his skin ashen and drawn, the photo of Rodney and Giselle, two slippery serpents entwined, Gran's last few minutes of life. I don't know why these things replay in my mind, but it's doing nothing to quell my extreme jitters. How I'm going to get through this, I do not know. How will I act normally when the tension is already jangling the core of my being?

When I next look up, there he is, rushing into the restaurant, searching for me. His hair is tousled, the top two buttons of his shirt are open, revealing his exasperatingly smooth chest. I imagine taking the fork from my place setting and stabbing him with it, right there, where the V of his shirt frames his naked skin. But then I see his scar, and my dark desire evaporates.

"Molly," he says as he slides into the booth across from me, "I made an excuse to take off from work for a bit, but I don't have much time. Let's make this quick, okay? Tell me everything."

A waitress comes to our table. "Welcome to the Olive Garden. Can I get you started with some free salad and bread?"

"We're here for a quick drink," Rodney replies. "A beer for me."

I put a finger in the air. "Actually, salad and bread would be lovely. And I'll also take an appetizer plate and a large pepperoni pizza, please. Oh, and some water? Very, very cold. With ice." No Chardonnay for me today—I must remain clearheaded. Also, this is not a celebration, not in any way. "Thank you," I say to the waitress.

Rodney runs his fingers through his hair and sighs.

"Thank you for coming," I say once the waitress is gone. "It means the world to me that you're always there when I need you. Such a reliable friend you are." My face feels stiff and forced as I say this, but Rodney doesn't seem to notice.

"I'm here for you, Molly. Just tell me what happened, okay?"

"Well," I say as I conceal my shaking hands under the table, "after the detective took me to the station, she told me Mr. Black did not die naturally. She said he was asphyxiated."

I wait for this to sink in.

"Whoa," Rodney says. "And you're the obvious suspect."

"In fact, I'm not. They're looking for someone else." These are the exact words Charlotte instructed me to say.

I watch him carefully. His Adam's apple bobs up and down. The waitress returns with bread, salad, and our drinks. I take a long sip of cold water and revel in Rodney's growing discomfort. I do not touch the food at all. I'm far too nervous. Plus, it's for later.

"Detective Stark said the persons of interest were most likely motivated by Mr. Black's will. She thinks they maybe even discussed his will with him before they killed him. Poor Giselle. Do you know that Mr. Black didn't leave her a thing? Not a single thing, the poor, poor woman."

"What? The detective told you that? But that can't be. I know for a fact it can't be."

"Do you? I thought you weren't well acquainted with Giselle," I say.

"I'm not," he says. He appears to be sweating though it's not unduly warm in here. "But I know people who know her well. Anyhow, this isn't what they told me. So it's . . . well, it's a bit of a surprise." He takes a gulp of beer and puts his elbows on the table.

"Rude," I say.

"What?"

"Your elbows on the table. This is a restaurant. That is a dinner table. Proper etiquette requires you to keep your elbows off it."

He shakes his head but takes his offensive appendages off the table. Victory.

"Salad? Bread?" I offer.

"No," he replies. "Let's just get to the point. Didn't Mr. Black leave Giselle the villa in the Caymans? Did the detective mention that?"

"Hmm," I say. I pick up my napkin and grip it under the table between my perspiring hands. "I don't recall anything about a villa. I think the detective said almost everything goes to the first Mrs. Black and the children." Another tidbit doled out as planned.

"You're telling me the police volunteered all of this information to you for no good reason?"

"What? Of course not," I say. "Who would tell me anything? I'm just the maid. Detective Stark left me in a room by myself, and you know how it is. People forget I'm there. Or perhaps they think I'm too daft to understand? I overheard all of this at the station."

"And weren't the detectives concerned about the gun in your vacuum? I mean, I'm assuming that's why they nabbed you, right?"

"Yes," I say. "It seems Cheryl found the gun and alerted them. Interesting that she knew where to look. For someone so lazy, it's hard to imagine her searching a dusty vacuum bag."

Rodney's face changes. "You're not suggesting I told her, are you? Molly, you know I would never—"

"I'd never suggest that about you, Rodney. You're blameless. An innocent," I say. "Much like me."

He nods. "Good. I'm glad there's no misunderstanding here." He shakes his head the way a wet dog would when it comes out of the water. "So what did you tell the police when they asked about the gun?"

"I simply explained whose gun it was, and where I found it," I reply. "That raised two eyebrows. Meaning I believe Detective Stark was surprised."

"So you narced on Giselle, your *friend*?" he asks. His elbows make an aggravating reappearance on the table.

"I would never betray a true friend," I say. "But there's something dreadful I have to tell you. It's why I called you here." Here it comes, the moment I've prepared for.

"What is it already?" he asks, barely able to keep the rage out of his voice.

"Oh, Rodney. You know how nervous I get in social situations, and I must say that being interrogated by detectives caused me much consternation, as I have very little experience in such matters. Perhaps you're more accustomed to such ordeals?"

"Molly, get to the point."

"Right," I say, wringing my napkin in my hands. "Once the issue of Giselle's gun was out of the bag—I suppose that's both literal and figurative in this case—the detective said they would sweep the former Black suite yet again." I bring my napkin to my eyes as I try to gauge his response to this.

"Go on," he says.

"I said, 'Oh, you can't do that! Juan Manuel is staying in that suite.' And the detective asked, 'Who's Juan Manuel?' And so I told them. Oh, Rodney, I probably shouldn't have. I told them how Juan Manuel is your friend and how you've been helping him because he has no work permit and—"

"You mentioned me to the detective?"

"Yes," I say. "And I told them about the overnight bags and the cleaning up after Juan Manuel and your friends, and how good and kind you've all been—"

"They're his friends, not mine."

"Well, whoever they are, they sure do drag a lot of mess into rooms.

But don't worry, I made sure to let the detective know what a good man you are, even if your friends are a little . . . dusty."

He takes his head in his hands. "Oh, Molly. What have you done?"

"I told the truth," I say. "But I realize I have caused a bit of an issue for Juan Manuel. What if he's still in the Black suite when they check it again? I'd hate for him to get in any kind of trouble. You'd hate that, too, wouldn't you, Rodney?"

He nods vigorously. "I would. Yeah. I mean, we've got to make sure he's not in there when they check. And we've got to clean that room out, fast, before the police arrive. You know, so there are no traces of Juan Manuel."

"Of course," I say. "My thoughts exactly." I smile at Rodney, but inside I'm pouring a full kettle of boiling water onto his dirty, lying face.

"So you'll do it?" he asks.

"Do what?" I reply.

"Sneak in and clean the suite. Now. Before the cops get there. You're the only one besides Chernobyl and Snow who has access. If Mr. Snow catches Juan Manuel there—or worse, if the police do—he'll be deported."

"But I'm not supposed to be going to work today. Mr. Snow says I'm 'a person of interest' to the police, so—"

"Please, Molly! This is important." He reaches out and grabs my hand. I want to wrench mine away, but I know I must not move.

We have faith in you.

I hear it in my head, but it's not Gran's voice this time. It's Mr. Preston's. Then Charlotte's. Then Juan Manuel's.

I keep my hand steady under his, my gaze neutral. "You know," I say, "I'm not allowed to enter the hotel, but that doesn't mean *you* can't enter. What if I quickly sneak into the hotel, grab the right room key, and give it to you? You can then use my trolley and clean up the room yourself! Wouldn't that be something—you cleaning up your own mess?— I mean, Juan Manuel's mess."

His eyes are darting all over the place. The sheen on his forehead is condensing into droplets.

After a few moments, he says, "Okay. All right. You get me the suite key, I clean the room."

"The suite key *tout suite*," I say, but he fails to register my cleverness.

The waitress arrives at our table with the pepperoni pizza and the appetizer plate.

"Would you mind boxing that up, please?" I ask.

"Sure," she says. "Was there something wrong with the bread and salad? You didn't even touch them."

"Oh no," I say. "It's all delightful. It's just that we're in a bit of a rush."

"Of course," she says. "I'll box everything." She gestures to a colleague, and the two of them take care of the food.

"He'll have the bill, please," I say, pointing to Rodney.

His mouth drops open, but he doesn't say anything, not so much as a word.

Our waitress retrieves the bill from her apron and hands it to him. He pulls out a crisp, fresh $100 bill from his wallet, passes it to her, and says, "Keep the change." He stands abruptly. "I better run, Molly. I should get back to the hotel and do this right away."

"Of course," I say. "I'll take all this food home. Then I'll text you as soon as I make it to the hotel. Oh, and Rodney?"

"What?" he asks.

"It really is a shame that you don't like jigsaw puzzles."

"Why?"

"Because," I say, "I don't think you quite know the pleasure one feels when suddenly, all the pieces come together."

He looks at me, his lip curled. It's so clear, the meaning of the look. I'm an idiot. A fool. And I'm too daft to even know it.

That's the expression that's smeared all over his vulgar, lying face.

CHAPTER 22

I walk quickly all the way home, takeout bags in tow. I'm eager to report back to Mr. Preston, Charlotte, and especially Juan Manuel.

Once I'm in my building, I climb the stairs two by two. I'm rounding the corner to my hallway when I see Mr. Rosso's door open a sliver. He peeks out, spots me, then slinks back inside, closing the door behind him.

I put down the takeout bags to turn the key in my lock, then I walk through the entrance. "I'm home!" I announce.

Mr. Preston springs to his feet. "Oh, dear girl, you're back. Thank goodness."

Charlotte and Juan Manuel are seated in the living room. They, too, jump to their feet the moment they see me.

"How did it go?" Charlotte asks.

Before I can answer Charlotte's question, Juan Manuel is beside me. He's grabbed the takeout bags and is now getting out the polishing cloth from the closet. The moment I remove my shoes, he takes them, cleans the bottoms, and puts them away.

"You don't have to do that," I say.

"It's okay. Do you need anything? Are you okay?" he asks.

"I'm fine," I reply. "I brought takeout. I hope everyone likes the Olive Garden."

"Like it? I love it," Juan Manuel replies. He picks up the bags and whisks them away to the kitchen.

"You better tell us how it went," Charlotte says. "Dad and Juan Manuel have been a nervous wreck since you stepped out that door."

"Everything went according to plan," I say. "Rodney's heading back to the hotel now. He's none the wiser that I'm the one who's been arrested, and he believes the police are coming back to search the suite. I told him I'd be there shortly to get him the suite key." I can't help but smile as I say this, because I've accomplished something I wasn't sure that I could.

"Perfect. Well done," Charlotte replies.

"I knew you could do it!" Juan Manuel calls out from the kitchen.

"Dad," Charlotte says, "your shift starts at six o'clock, right? Are you sure you can get your hands on the key to the Black suite?"

"I have a few tricks up my sleeve," he replies.

"They better be foolproof ones, Dad, because the last thing we need right now is you in trouble too."

"Don't you worry. It's all going to go tickety-boo. Trust your ol' pa."

Juan Manuel emerges from the kitchen carrying Gran's tea tray filled with appetizers and pizza from the Olive Garden.

"I was supposed to be back at work a while ago," he says. "They keep calling me." He sets the tray on the coffee table and sits down.

Charlotte shuffles her chair closer to him. "It's up to you, Juan Manuel, but I'm concerned that if you go back to work today—in fact, if you go to that hotel ever again—Rodney will find a way to use you as he always does, and then you're going to be the one caught in a trap, not him."

Juan Manuel looks down at his feet. "Yes, I know," he says. "I'll call the kitchen back and tell them I'm sick and can't finish my shift."

"Good," Charlotte says.

"I'll figure the rest out later," Juan Manuel adds.

"The rest?" Mr. Preston asks.

"Where to sleep tonight," he says. "First, we must concentrate on catching the fox." He nods and smiles, but it's not the real kind of smile, not the kind that reaches his eyes.

Charlotte looks at Mr. Preston.

"Oh Juan Manuel," Mr. Preston says. "We weren't thinking. If you don't go back to the hotel, that means you have nowhere to sleep tonight."

"This is my problem, not yours," he says without looking up. "Don't worry."

It occurs to me that there's an obvious solution, but it's one that's also a little bit awkward for me. I've never had a guest stay overnight before, but I do think that in this particular instance Gran would urge me to do the right thing. "You can stay here, for tonight," I say. "There's plenty of space. You can have my room and I'll stay in Gran's room. It will give you some time to consider alternative arrangements."

He's looking at me like he doesn't believe what I'm saying. "Really? Are you serious? You'd let me stay here?"

"Isn't that what friends are for? To help each other out of binds?"

He's shaking his head slowly back and forth. "I can't believe you'd do this for me after everything that's happened. Thank you. And don't worry—I'm very quiet. I'm like a good oven—self-cleaning."

Mr. Preston chuckles and grabs a small plate from the tea tray, filling it with bruschetta, pizza, and fried mozzarella.

I follow his lead and prepare first a small plate for Juan Manuel, then one for myself.

"Courtesy of Rodney," I say. "He owes us both much more."

"He does," Juan Manuel says.

Charlotte gets up and grabs the remote control on the television, turns it to the twenty-four-hour local news channel.

I'm just about to take my first bite of fried mozzarella when what I hear stops me mid-bite.

"... and police will be holding a special press conference in one hour to release important updates on the search for real-estate magnate Charles Black's killer. We don't know for sure, but we expect to hear details on the charges and very possibly the identity of the accused, as well as ..."

I feel all eyes on me. All of my confidence ebbs away in just a few seconds. "What now?" I ask.

Charlotte sighs. "I was worried about this. The police are eager to reassure the public and take credit for catching the killer."

"This is not good," Juan Manuel adds as he puts his plate down on the table.

"What if they say my name? What if Rodney finds out before he even gets to the hotel?"

"It's five o'clock now. We've still got an hour," Mr. Preston says.

"That's right," Charlotte says. "Let's not panic. I say we stick to the plan. But we don't have a lot of time."

The newscaster is reviewing the details of the death and the findings of the autopsy—death by asphyxiation. We all watch in silence. ". . . and inside sources say that Mr. Black's wife, socialite Giselle Black, may *not* be the accused and that she remains a guest at the hotel. But we'll know more for sure in an hour when—"

Charlotte turns the TV off. "Let's hope Rodney doesn't see this and disappear. And that Giselle doesn't check out anytime soon," she says.

"She won't," I say. "She has nowhere else to go."

Mr. Preston puts down his plate and gets to his feet. "Looks like I'm heading to work early today," he says. "Molly, are you ready? You understand the next steps?"

I can't seem to form words. I feel the world tilt a little, but I know I must forge onward. "I'm ready," I say.

"Charlotte, when you receive the text from me, you'll contact Detective Stark?"

"Yes, Dad. I'm actually going to wait right outside the station."

"Juan Manuel, will you act as mission control from here? We'll call you when we need your help."

"Yes, of course," he says. "You call, I'm on it. I won't rest until we catch him."

There is nothing else for me to say or do. I've lost my appetite, so I put down my plate.

The deep-fried mozzarella sticks will have to wait.

CHAPTER 23

Mr. Preston insists we take a cab over to the hotel to save time. We've now pulled over just around the corner so the taxi can drop me off. I'm embarrassed when he pays, but I've really no choice but to accept his generosity.

"Molly, are you sure you're okay to walk from here? You know the plan?"

"Yes, Mr. Preston. I'm fine. I'm ready." I'm saying the words with the hope that the feelings will follow, but the truth is that I'm trembling and the world around me is spinning too fast.

I'm about to step out of the taxi when Mr. Preston puts a hand on my arm. "Molly, your gran would be proud of you."

The mention of her makes my emotions bubble up, but I will them back down. "Thank you, Mr. Preston," I manage before slipping out the door.

I watch as Mr. Preston drives away without me.

I walk the last block on my own and wait for ten minutes hidden in an alleyway across from the hotel. It's eerily beautiful in the late afternoon. The golden light strikes the brass and glass of the entranceway, bathing it in a mysterious glow. The Chens are on their way to an early dinner. He's wearing a pinstripe suit and she's all in black, except for a bright-pink corsage pinned to her bodice. A young family jumps out of a taxi after a long day of sightseeing, the parents lethargic and slow. Their two children dash up the scarlet steps, holding up souvenirs for the valets to see. It's always like this at dusk—as if the day is throwing the last of its energy up the steps while the hotel itself patiently waits for the calm of night to come.

The podium is the only spot that's forlorn and empty. Mr. Preston has not yet arrived. No doubt he's still downstairs, donning his great coat and hat and signing in early for his shift.

Time is going by unbearably slowly. Nervous tension makes my entire body tremble. I don't know if I can do this. I'm unsuited to this level of performance. The only thing that gives me strength is the fact that Mr. Preston, Charlotte, and Juan Manuel are in on it.

When you believe in yourself, nothing can stop you.

I'm trying my best, Gran. I am.

It's time.

I remain where I am, tucked in the alleyway, hiding in the shadows of the coffee shop, up against the wall. At long last he appears, Mr. Preston, smartly uniformed. He walks calmly through the revolving doors and stands at his podium on the hotel landing. He pulls out his phone and sends a text, then tucks it back into his pocket. I lean against the wall even though I know it's dirty. If all goes well, there will be time for washing later. If it doesn't go well, I'll never be clean again.

A couple more minutes go by. Just when I'm starting to fully panic, I spot him down the street—Rodney, walking quickly toward the hotel. I'll admit that my feelings upon seeing him are mixed. On the one hand, his appearance means things are going according to plan; on the other, the very sight of his lying, cheating face fills me with murderous rage.

He runs up the front steps and stops at the podium. He talks to Mr. Preston. The conversation lasts no more than a minute. Then Rodney heads into the hotel.

Mr. Preston pulls out his phone and dials. I practically jump out of my skin when my pocket starts to vibrate.

I grab my phone. "Hello?" I whisper. "Yes, I saw it all. What did he want?"

"He heard about the press conference," Mr. Preston explains. "He was asking if I knew who was arrested."

"What did you tell him?" I ask.

"That I saw Giselle talking with the police. And that she looked upset."

"Oh dear. That wasn't part of the plan," I say.

"I had to think fast on my big ol' feet. You'll do the same if you have to. You can do this. I know it."

I take a deep breath. "Anything else?"

"The news conference begins in under forty minutes. We have to be fast. It's time. Text him now. Proceed as planned."

"Roger, Mr. Preston. Over and out."

I end the call and watch Mr. Preston slip his phone away.

I open a text to Rodney:

Help. I'm at the front door of the hotel and they won't let me in! If I can't get that keycard for you, whatever will we do?

Rodney's response is immediate: BRT DGA

What? What on earth is that supposed to mean? I haven't the faintest clue. Think, Molly, think.

You're never alone as long as you have a friend.

The answer is literally right at my fingertips. I find Juan Manuel in my contacts and dial his number. He picks up before the end of the first ring.

"Molly? What's happening? Is everything okay?"

"Yes, everything's fine. The plan is in progress. But . . . Juan Manuel, I'm in a bit of pickle and I need hasty assistance." I read Rodney's text to him.

"You think *I* know what that means?" he asks. "I feel like I'm on that TV show where you call a friend and they give you the answer and you win big money. But Molly, you called the wrong friend!" He pauses. "Wait. Hold on." I hear some rustling on the end of the line.

"Okay, Molly? Are you still there?"

"Yes."

"I checked Google. Rodney means Be Right There. Don't Go Anywhere. Okay? Does that make sense?"

It does. It absolutely does. I'm back on track. "Juan Manuel, I could..."

I could kiss him. That's what I want to say—that I'm so grateful I could kiss him. But it's such a bold and ridiculous thought, so unlike me, that it catches in my throat and doesn't make it out.

"Thank you," I say instead.

"Go get the fox, Molly," he replies. "I will BRT when you get back home."

I know he's not here with me, but it feels like he is. It's like he's holding my hand through the line.

"Yes. Thank you, Juan Manuel."

I hang up and tuck my phone away.

It's time.

I take a deep breath, then walk out of the shadows onto the sidewalk.

Always look both ways. . . .

I cross the street, trying to do so normally, without rushing, reminding myself to act as though it's just another ordinary day. I steady myself at the landing, holding tightly to the brass rail. Then I put one foot in front of the other, and I climb the plush red stairs.

Mr. Preston sees me. He picks up the hotel phone on his podium and makes a call. I can hear him sounding perfectly believable when he says, "Yes. Urgently. She's here at the front door and she won't leave."

As planned, Mr. Preston is wearing white gloves, not part of his regular uniform. He usually wears these only on special occasions, but they'll come in handy today.

"Molly," he says loudly and brusquely. "What are you doing here? You can't be at the hotel today. I'm going to have to ask you to leave." He looks around to make sure people are watching. Several guests are streaming in and out of the hotel. A couple of valets on the sidewalk stop what they're doing and watch as well. It's as though I'm an engaging spectator sport.

Though it feels so strange to do so, it's time to play my part, to draw even more attention my way. "I have every right to be here," I call out in a confident, booming voice. "I'm an esteemed employee of this hotel, and—"

I stop short when Mr. Snow emerges from the revolving doors.

Mr. Preston swiftly moves toward him. "I'll get Security," he tells Mr. Snow, then heads through the revolving doors.

Mr. Snow rushes over to me. "Molly," he says. "I'm sorry to inform you that you are no longer employed at the Regency Grand Hotel. You must leave the grounds immediately."

The words are a shock to me, and I must say I feel utterly bereft when I hear them. Still, I breathe deeply and stick to my performance, delivering my next lines even louder than my previous ones. "But I'm a model employee! You can't just fire me without cause!"

"As you well know, there *is* cause, Molly," Mr. Snow says. "We need you off these steps. Now."

"This is inconceivable," I say. "I won't leave."

Mr. Snow straightens his glasses. "You're disturbing the guests," he hisses.

I look around and see that more guests have gathered. It seems the valets have tipped off Reception. Several employees from the concierge desk are standing by them, whispering to one another. They're all looking my way.

For the next few minutes, I keep Mr. Snow engaged on the stairs, demanding explanations, begging him to reconsider, talking at length about the added value of my devotion to hygiene and the high level of quality I bring to the hotel with each guest room that I clean. I channel Gran, how she used to be in the morning, how she would chirp and chirp and chirp without so much as a pause for breath. The whole time, I'm aware that we have only a few minutes left before the whole plan falls apart. I'm also aware that I'm not in uniform, which adds to my distress and general discomfort. *Come back, Mr. Preston. Quickly!* I think to myself.

At long last, he walks briskly through the revolving doors and stands beside Mr. Snow.

"I can't find Security, sir," he announces.

"I can't get her to leave," Mr. Snow replies.

"Let me handle this," Mr. Preston says. Mr. Snow nods and steps aside. "Molly, a word . . ."

Mr. Preston gently pulls me aside, out of earshot. We both turn our backs to the curious crowd.

"Did it work?" I whisper.

"It did. I found Cheryl."

"And then what?" I ask.

"I got what I wanted."

"How?" I ask.

"I told her I knew she was stealing tips from other maids. She got so flustered she didn't even notice me pocketing her master keycard from her trolley. Not so much as a fingerprint left behind either," he adds, wiggling his white-gloved fingers. "Here," he says, holding out one hand. "Shake."

I take the cue and shake. When I do, I feel the master keycard transfer seamlessly into my palm.

"You take good care, Molly," he says in a voice loud enough for the entire neighborhood to hear. "You run home now. You have no place being here today." He nods to Mr. Snow and Mr. Snow nods back.

Of course, Mr. Preston knows as well as I do that I cannot leave. Not yet. I'm about to start a whole new monologue about worker bees when at long last Rodney emerges through the revolving doors and bounds down the steps toward me.

"I don't understand any of this!" I shout. "I'm a good maid! Rodney, you're just the person I wanted to see. Can you believe this?"

Mr. Snow approaches. "Rodney," he says, "we're trying to explain to Miss Molly that she is no longer welcome in this hotel. But we're having a hard time delivering the message."

"I understand," Rodney says. "Let me talk to her."

I'm pulled away again. Once we're out of earshot, Rodney says, "Molly, don't worry. I'll talk to Snow later and find out what's up with your job. Okay? Probably just a misunderstanding. Did you get the key? To the Black suite? There's no time to lose."

"You're right, there isn't," I say. "Here's the key." I discreetly pass him the card.

"Thanks, Molly. You're the best. Hey, I heard the police announced a news conference that's just about to happen. Do you know what that's all about?"

"I'm afraid not," I say.

I watch him carefully, hoping this answer appeases. "Right. Okay. I'd better get this done before Owl Eyes lets the cops in."

"Yes. As quickly as you can. Good luck."

He turns and starts up the stairs. "Oh, Rodney," I say. He turns back, looks down at me. "It really is remarkable the lengths to which you'll go for a friend."

"You don't know the half of it," he says. "There's nothing I wouldn't do."

Before I can say anything else, he's at the top of the stairs. "Don't worry," he tells Mr. Snow. "She's leaving." He says it just like that, as though I wasn't even there.

After that, I hurry down the scarlet steps, turning back only once to see Rodney rushing through the revolving doors and Mr. Preston behind him, one hand out, the other guiding Mr. Snow into the hotel.

I check my phone: 5:45.

It's time.

—

Chapter 24

I'm sitting at the coffee shop directly across from the hotel. I'm right by the window, so I have a perfect view of the entrance to the Regency Grand. The light is fading. Sharp shadows fall upon the entrance, turning the scarlet staircase a different shade, closer to the color of dried blood. It won't be too long before the wrought iron gaslights will flicker on and their flames will glow richly as dusk gives way to dark.

I have a metal teapot in front of me, the kind that dribbles and never pours cleanly, and a thick mug. I prefer Gran's porcelain to this, but beggars can't be choosers. I also splurged on a freshly baked raisin-bran muffin, which I've divided into four pieces, but I'm too nervous to eat it right now.

A few minutes ago, Mr. Preston emerged from the revolving doors and resumed his position at the doorman's podium. He made a call. It was very quick, very quick indeed. I can see him look up and across the street at this very window. He probably can't see me in the fading light, but he knows I'm here. And I know he's there. Which is a comfort.

My phone buzzes. It's a text from Charlotte. A thumbs-up emoji, which we agreed beforehand would be our sign for "Everything is going according to plan."

Another text arrives from her: *Wait where you are.*

I send her a thumbs-up emoji back even though I am not feeling thumbs-up at all. I am decidedly thumbs-down and won't feel thumbs-up until I see some movement on those steps, until I see signs—any signs beyond an emoji—that the plan is actually working. And so far, nothing.

It's 5:59 P.M.

It's time.

I wrap my anxious hands around my mug, even though it's tepid now and not much comfort. I have a good view of the TV screen to the right of my table. There's no sound, but it's tuned as it always is to the twenty-four-hour news channel. A young police officer I recognize as Detective Stark's colleague is about to speak at the press conference. He's reading from the papers in front of him. The captions are scrolling:

. . . that an arrest has been made in connection to what police have now confirmed is the murder of Mr. Charles Black, on Monday at the Regency Grand Hotel. Photographed here is the accused, Molly Gray, hotel room maid at the Regency Grand. She is under arrest for first-degree murder, possession of a firearm, and drug charges.

I take a sip of tea and nearly choke when I see my face appear on the screen. It's a photograph that was taken when I was hired, for my HR file. I didn't smile for the picture, but at least I look professional. I'm wearing my uniform. It's clean, freshly pressed. The captions continue to scroll:

. . . currently out on bail. Anyone requiring further information is invited to . . .

I tune out then because I hear cars coming to a screeching halt. Across the street, right in front of the hotel, are four dark cruisers. Several armed officers jump out of the vehicles and run up the stairs. I watch as Mr. Preston ushers them in. The whole event lasts only a few seconds. Mr. Preston emerges again from the revolving doors, followed by Mr. Snow. They exchange a few words and then turn to the various guests on the landing, no doubt reassuring them that everything is fine when everything is most definitely not fine. I feel completely helpless as I watch from afar. There's nothing to do except wait and hope. And make a call. One important call.

It's time.

This is the only part of the plan that I have kept to myself all this time. I never shared it with anyone—not with Mr. Preston or Charlotte or even Juan Manuel. There are still some things that only I know, things only I can understand because I've lived them. I know what it's like to be alone, to be so alone that you make the wrong choices, that out of desperation you trust the wrong people.

I open my contacts on my phone. I call Giselle.

It rings once, twice, three times, and just when I think that she won't answer . . .

"Hello?"

"Good evening, Giselle. It's Molly, Molly the maid. Your friend."

"Oh my God, Molly. I've been waiting for you to call. I haven't seen you at the hotel. I've missed you. Is everything all right?"

I don't have time for niceties, and I do believe this is one of the few situations in life when skipping the rules of etiquette is entirely appropriate. "You lied to me," I say. "Rodney's your boyfriend. Your secret boyfriend. You never told me that."

There's a pause on the other end of the line.

"Oh, Molly," she says after a time, "I'm so sorry." I can hear it in her voice, that little catch that tells me she is near tears.

"I thought we were friends."

"We *are* friends," she replies.

I feel the sting of this like a barb.

"Molly, I'm lost. I'm . . . I'm so lost," she says. She's crying openly now, her voice meek and scared.

"You made me move your gun," I say.

"I know. I shouldn't have gotten you involved in my mess. I was scared, scared the police would find it and then everything would point to me. And I figured they'd never suspect you."

"The police found your gun in my vacuum. Everything's pointing to me now, Giselle. I've been arrested on many charges. It was publicly announced a few minutes ago."

"Oh God. This can't be happening," she says.

"It is happening. To me. And I did not kill Mr. Black."

"I know that," she says. "But I didn't either, Molly. I swear."

"I know," I say. "Did you realize that Rodney would frame me?"

"Molly, I swear I didn't. And the stuff Rodney made you do, cleaning rooms after his shipments? I only found that out on Monday morning. Before that, I had no idea. That black eye he has? That's because I hit him when he told me. We had a big fight about it. I told him it wasn't right, that you were an innocent, good person, and that he couldn't just use people like that. I flung my purse at him, Molly. I was so mad. The chain whopped him right in the eye."

That was one mystery solved, but only one. "Did you know that Rodney and Mr. Black were partners in illicit activity?" I ask. "Did you know that they were running an illegal operation through the hotel?"

I hear her shift and shuffle on the end of the line. "Yes," she says. "I've known for a while. That's why we spent so much time in this fucking hotel. But the part about you? About Rodney involving you in his dirty work? I didn't know that until this week. If I'd known earlier, I swear, I would have put a stop to it. And I'm telling you, I had nothing to do with Charles's murder. Rodney and I joked about it, sure, how we would fix our lives and finally be able to be together openly, just by offing his boss and my husband with the same bullet. We even planned running away together, far away."

It clicks then. The flight itinerary, two one-way tickets. "To the Caymans," I say.

"Yes, to the Caymans. That's why I asked Charles to put that property in my name. I was going to leave him and run away, file for divorce from afar. Rodney and I were going to start a new life, a better life. Just the two of us. But I never actually thought . . . I didn't know Rodney could actually be capable of . . ."

She trails off. "Have you ever felt betrayed, Giselle?" I ask. "Have you ever put a great deal of faith in someone who then let you down?"

"You know I have. You know it all too well," she says.

"Mr. Black, he let you down."

"He did," she says. "But he's not the only one. Rodney too. It seems I'm an expert at trusting assholes."

"It may be something else we have in common," I say.

"Yeah," says Giselle. "But I'm not like them, Molly. Charles and Rodney, I'm not like them at all."

"Aren't you?" I ask. "My gran used to say, *If you want to know where someone's going, don't watch their mouths, watch their feet.* I never understood that until now. She also said, *The proof is in the pudding.*"

"The proof's in the . . . what?"

"It means I won't trust your words anymore. I won't."

"Molly, I made a mistake is all. I made a stupid fucking mistake in asking you to go back into that suite and do my dirty work for me. Please. I won't let you go down for this. They can't get away with it."

Her voice is raw and real, but can I trust what I hear?

"Giselle, you're at the hotel now? You're in your room?"

"Yeah. A princess locked in the tower. Molly, you have to let me help you. I'm going to speak out, okay? I'll tell the police it was my gun and I told you to get it. I'll even tell them that Rodney and Charles were running a cartel. I'm going to get you cleared, I promise. Molly, you're the only true friend I've ever had."

I feel the rush of tears break over the banks of my eyes. I hope it's true, I really do. I hope she's a good egg caught in a rotten basket. It's time to put her to the test.

"Giselle, you need to listen to me. You need to listen very, very carefully, okay?"

"Okay," she says, through sniffles.

"Can you get to the Cayman Islands?"

"Yeah. I have open tickets. I can go anytime."

"Do you still have your passport?"

"Yes."

"Do *not* contact Rodney. Do you understand?"

"But shouldn't I let him know that—"

"He doesn't care a jot about you, Giselle. Can't you see that? He'll take you down, too, at the first chance. You're just another pawn in his game."

I hear her struggle to draw in breath. "Oh, Molly, I wish I were more like you. I'm not. I'm not at all. You're strong. You're honest. You're good. I don't know if I can do it. I don't know if I can be alone."

"You've always been alone, Giselle. Poor company is worse than none."

"Let me guess. Your gran told you that?"

"She did," I say. "And she's right."

"How could I have ever fallen for a man so . . ."

"Vile?" I offer.

"Yes," she says. "So vile."

"Vile and evil are composed of the same letters. One begets the other."

"Rodney and Charles," she says.

"Vile and evil," I reply. "Giselle, we don't have much time. I need you to do as I say. And it has to be fast."

"Okay," she says. "Whatever you ask, Molly."

"I want you to pack your basic necessities into a single bag. I want you to carry your passport and whatever money you have right next to your heart. And I want you to run. Not out the front doors of the hotel, but out the back ones. Right now. Do you hear me?"

"But what about you? I can't just let you—"

"If you are a friend, you will do this for me. I'm not alone anymore. I have real friends, true ones. I'm going to be fine. I'm asking you to do as I say. Go now, Giselle. Run."

She keeps talking, but I don't listen because I've said everything I need to say. I know it's rude, and if this weren't an extraordinary situation, I certainly wouldn't behave in this curt and clipped manner. I hang up on her without another word.

When I look up from my phone, there's a coffee-shop employee standing by my table. She's shifting awkwardly from one foot to the other. I recognize this behavior. It's what I do when I'm waiting for my turn to speak.

"Was that you?" she asks. She points to the TV screen.

How am I supposed to answer?

Honesty is the best policy.

"That was me. Yes."

There's a pause as she takes this in.

"Oh, I should add that I didn't do it. Murder Mr. Black, I mean. I'm not a killer. You have nothing at all to worry about." I take a sip from my mug.

The coffee-shop employee stiffens and sidles away from my table. She turns her back on me only once she's safely behind the counter. I watch as she rushes to the kitchen, where she is no doubt talking to her supervisor, who will soon come out and look at me with wide eyes. I will recognize the expression instantly. I will know that it means fear because I'm getting better at this—understanding the subtle cues, the body language that expresses emotional states.

The more you live, the more you learn.

That same supervisor will look me up and down and verify that it's me, the one on the news. She will call the police. The police will say something to calm her down, tell her not to worry or that the news conference had the details wrong.

All will be well. In the end.

I take a deep breath. I enjoy another calming sip of tea. I wait and I watch the hotel entrance.

And then: there it is at last—what I've been waiting for. . . .

The police emerge through the revolving doors with a man in front of them—Rodney, his white shirtsleeves rolled up, making it easy to see his lovely forearms in handcuffs. Trailing behind him is Detective Stark. She's carrying a navy-blue duffel bag that I recognize immediately. The zipper is half-open. Even from here, I can tell it's not filled with a dishwasher's clothes and personal effects but with bags containing white powder.

I pick up one neat quarter of my raisin-bran muffin. How lovely. It's fresh. Isn't it interesting that this shop bakes goods in the late afternoon? You wouldn't think many people would choose muffins in the afternoon, but there you have it. Perhaps there are others out there in the world just like me.

People are a mystery that can never be solved.

It's true, Gran. Very true indeed.

The muffin is delightful. It melts in my mouth. It feels good to eat. It's something so human, so satisfying. It's something we all have to do to live, something every person on Earth has in common. I eat, therefore I am.

Rodney's head is pushed down into the backseat of one of the police cruisers. Several of the officers who ran into the hotel a few minutes ago are standing guard at the bottom stair. Nervous hotel guests huddle on the landing, seeking comfort and reassurance from their doorman.

Detective Stark climbs the stairs, says something to Mr. Preston. I see them both look my way. There's no way they can see me, not with the late-afternoon light hitting the shop window.

Detective Stark nods my way, almost imperceptibly, but still, it's a nod. It's meant for me. I'm certain of it. What I'm not certain of is what it means, this small gesture from afar. I've definitely had my fair share of trouble interpreting Detective Stark, so all guesses are just that—suppositions, not certainties.

I have never been one for gambling, mostly because money has been so hard for me to earn and so easy to lose. But were I to place a bet, I'd say that Detective Stark's nod carried a specific meaning. And what it meant was: *I was wrong.*

CHAPTER 25

I walk at a leisurely pace back to my apartment. It's funny how when you're feeling the impact of stress, it's hard to appreciate the small, inspiring things around you—the birds chirping their last lullabies before puffing up for a night's sleep, the cotton-candy sky as the sun sets, the fact that you're on your way home and unlike every other day for the last several months, when you open your front door, there will be a friend there waiting for you. It may be the first time since Gran's death that I feel such a sense of hope.

Everything will be okay in the end. If it's not okay, it's not the end.

My building is up ahead. I quicken my pace. I know Juan Manuel will be desperate for news, real news, not just a thumbs-up emoji.

I glide through the front doors and take the steps to my floor two by two. I turn down my hallway, take out my key and enter.

"I'm home!" I call out.

Juan Manuel rushes my way and is standing much closer than a trolley-length away from me, not that his proximity bothers me. I've never had an issue with people being near me. My issue has always been the opposite—that people keep their distance.

"*Híjole,* you're home," he says, his hands together. He opens the closet, grabs the shoe cloth, and waits as I take off my shoes.

"Did it work?" he asks. "Did they catch the fox?"

"Yes," I say. "I saw it with my own eyes. They caught Rodney."

"Oh, thank you, thank you. You must tell me everything. You're okay? Tell me—you're okay?"

"Juan Manuel, I'm fine. I'm very well indeed."

"Good," he says, exhaling. "Very good." He grabs my shoes and rubs at the soles as if a genie were going to materialize from them. His aggressive polishing mercifully concludes and he puts my shoes and the cloth away in the closet. Then he hugs me. I'm so surprised by this sudden display of affection that my arms flail out and I forget that the correct thing to do is to hug back. Just when I realize this, he lets go.

"What was that for?" I ask.

"For getting home safe," he says. "Come. To the kitchen. I prepared a small dinner for us. I tried to have hope, Molly, but I was worried. I thought maybe the police would come and take me away or maybe you would never come back. I had bad, bad thoughts about if they . . ." He trails off.

"If they what?" I ask.

"Rodney and his men," he says. "If they . . . hurt you the way they hurt me."

I feel the room tilt thirty degrees at the very thought, but I breathe deeply to settle myself.

"Come," Juan Manuel says.

I follow him to the kitchen, where he's laid out a spread. It's the leftovers from the Olive Garden, put together beautifully on plates for each of us. He's even lain Gran's black-and-white-checkered tablecloth for additional Italian ambience. The effect is charming. Our tiny kitchen nook is transformed into a scene on a tourist postcard. It feels as though I'm in a dream, and it takes me a moment to recover my voice.

"This looks so lovely, Juan Manuel," I manage to say. "Do you know that for the first time in a long time, I think I can eat a full meal?"

"We eat, and you tell me everything," he says.

We sit down together, but no sooner than he's seated does he spring to his feet once more. "Oh, I forgot," he says.

He hurries to the living room and returns with one of Gran's candlesticks and a matchbox. "Can we light this?" he asks. "I know it's special, but today is special, too, no? Today, they catch the right man?"

"Yes, they drove him away in a police car," I say. "And I hope this means good things for both of us." Even as the words leave my lips, doubt creeps in. One thing is to have hope; another thing is to trust that all will end the way it should—for Juan Manuel, and for me.

He places the candle between us. Just as we're about to pick up our forks, my phone rings in my pocket and I practically jump out of my chair. It's Charlotte. Thank goodness.

"Charlotte?" I say. "This is Molly. Molly Gray."

"Yes," she answers. "I know. Are you okay?"

"Yes," I say. "I'm quite well. Thank you for asking. I'm here at home with Juan Manuel and we are about to take a Tour of Italy."

"I'm sorry?"

"It's not important. Can you tell me how things went inside the hotel? I saw it happen, from the coffee shop, but did the plan work? Did they catch Rodney in flagrante?"

"Things went very well, Molly. Listen, I can't talk much now. I'm at the police station. Detective Stark wants me in her office. You and Juan Manuel stay right there, okay? Dad and I will be your way as soon as we can. This will probably take a couple of hours. And I think you'll be very pleased with the results."

"Okay, yes. Thank you, Charlotte," I say. "Give my regards to Detective Stark."

"You want me to . . . are you sure?"

"There's no reason to be impolite."

"Okay, Molly. I'll say hello from you."

"Please tell her I can read nods."

"You can what?"

"Just say that, please, exactly that. And thank you."

"Okay," Charlotte says. Then she ends the call. I put my phone away.

"I'm terribly sorry for the interruption. I'll have you know that it's not my usual practice to take calls during dinner. I don't intend to make a habit of it."

"Molly, you worry too much about 'this is right' and 'this is not right.' I just want to know what Charlotte said."

"They caught him in the act. Rodney."

"*En flagrante delito?*"

"In flagrante, yes."

A smile spreads across Juan Manuel's face and into his dark-brown eyes. Gran once told me that a real smile happens in the eyes, something I never really understood until right now.

"Molly, I never had a chance before to speak with just you, to say sorry. I never wanted you to be involved in any of this."

I have picked up my fork, but I immediately put it down.

"Juan Manuel," I say, "you tried to keep me out of this. You even tried to warn me."

"Maybe I should have tried harder. Maybe I should have told the police everything. The problem is I don't trust the police. When they look at people like me, sometimes all they see is bad. And not all police are good, Molly. How can you tell who is who? I worried if I talked about the drugs and the hotel, maybe things would get even worse—for me and for you."

"Yes," I say. "I understand. I've had my own troubles telling who is who."

"And Rodney and Mr. Black," he continues. "I no longer cared if they killed me. But my mother? My family? I was so scared they'd hurt them. And I was scared they'd hurt you too. I thought, if I just take the pain, if I stay quiet, maybe no one else gets hurt."

His wrists are on the table, not his elbows. I'm struggling to focus on his face because all I can see are the scars on his forearms, some healed over and one or two still raw.

I point to Juan Manuel's arms. "Was it him?" I ask. "Did Rodney do that to you?"

"Not Rodney," he says. "His friends. The big ones. But Rodney gave the orders. Mr. Black burns Rodney, so Rodney burns me. This is what I get for complaining, for saying I don't want to do Rodney's dirty work. And for having a family I love when he doesn't have one."

"It's so wrong, what they did to you."

"Yes," he says. "It is. And what they did to you."

"Your arms. They look sore," I say.

"They were. But today, they're okay. Today, I feel a little bit better. I don't even know what will happen to me, but I still feel good because Rodney is caught. And we have a candle to light. And so there's hope." He takes a match out of the matchbox and lights the candle. Then he says, "We shouldn't let the food get cold. Let's eat."

We pick up our forks, and we enjoy the meal. I have ample time, not only to chew the correct number of times but also to savor each and every bite. Between bites, I recount every detail of the afternoon—how I sat at the coffee shop, how I waited and worried, how I saw myself on TV, how the cars screeched to a halt, how it felt to see Rodney's head being unceremoniously pushed into the backseat of a cruiser. When I tell him about the woman at the coffee shop recognizing me from the news, he starts to laugh out loud. For a moment, I'm frozen. I can't tell if he's laughing at me or with me.

"What's so funny?" I ask.

"She thought you were a murderer! In her shop. Drinking tea and eating a cake!"

"It wasn't a cake," I say. "It was a muffin, a raisin-bran muffin."

He laughs even harder at that, and I don't know why, but what becomes clear is that he's laughing with me. Suddenly, I find myself laughing, too, laughing at a raisin-bran muffin without even knowing why.

After dinner, Juan Manuel starts clearing the dishes.

"No," I say. "You were very kind to serve dinner. I'll clean up."

"Not fair," he replies. "You think you're the only one who likes to clean? Why do you take away my joy?"

He smiles again in that way of his, and he grabs Gran's apron from behind the kitchen door. It's blue-and-pink paisley with flowers, but he doesn't seem to care. He loops it over his head and hums to himself as he ties the string. I haven't seen that apron on anyone in so long; even Gran herself was too ill to use it in her final months. And to see it become three-dimensional, to see a body give it shape again . . . I don't know why, but it makes me look away.

I turn to the table and gather the remaining dishes as Juan Manuel prepares the sink with soapy water.

Together, we make quick progress on the mess, and in just a few minutes, the entire kitchen is perfectly gleaming.

"See?" he says. "I've worked in kitchens all my life—big ones, small ones, family ones—and at the end of the day to see a clean counter makes the heart jump with joy."

"Jump *for* joy?" I say.

"Ah yes. Jump for joy."

I look at him in the glow of Gran's candle, and it's as if I've never really looked properly. I've seen this man every day at work for months on end, and now, suddenly, he is more handsome than I've ever noticed before.

"Do you ever feel invisible?" I ask. "At work, I mean. Do you ever feel like people don't see you?"

He's taking off Gran's apron, replacing it on the hook by the door.

"Yes, of course," he says. "I'm used to this feeling. I know what it's like to be completely invisible, to feel alone in a strange world. To be afraid for the future."

"It must have been terrible for you," I say. "To be forced to help Rodney even though you knew it was a bad thing to do."

"Sometimes, you must do one thing bad to do another thing good. It's not always so clear, so black and white like everyone thinks. Especially when you don't have choices."

Yes. He's absolutely right.

"Tell me something, Juan Manuel," I say. "Do you like puzzles? Jigsaw puzzles?"

"Do I like them? I *love* them."

Just then, there's a knock at the door. I feel my stomach sink and find my legs are glued to the floor.

"Molly, can we open? . . . Molly?"

"Yes, of course," I say.

I force my legs to move. We both reach the door. I unlock and open it.

Charlotte and Mr. Preston are standing there, and behind them, Detective Stark.

My knees weaken and I brace myself against the doorframe.

"It's okay, Molly," Mr. Preston says. "It's okay."

"The detective is here with good news," Charlotte adds.

I hear the words, but I'm unable to move. Juan Manuel is at my side, keeping me upright. I hear a door open down the hall and the next thing I see is Mr. Rosso standing behind Detective Stark. It's like a party at my front door.

"I knew it!" he yells. "I knew you were no good, Molly Gray. I saw you on the news! I want you out of this building, you hear me? Officer, get her out of here!"

I can feel the rush of shame burning into my cheeks, robbing me of my voice.

Detective Stark turns to Mr. Rosso. "Actually, sir. That news report was misinformed. There'll be a correction issued in about an hour. Molly is entirely innocent of any wrongdoing. In fact, she's tried to help with this case, and that wasn't understood at first. That's why I'm here."

"Sir," Charlotte says to Mr. Rosso, "as I'm sure you're aware, you can't simply evict tenants with no cause. Has Ms. Gray paid the rent?"

"Late, but yes, she paid," he replies.

"Ms. Gray is a model tenant who does not deserve your harassment," Charlotte says. "Also, Detective Stark," she says, "did you notice any elevator in this—"

"I'm sorry, I must go," Mr. Rosso says, and begins to rush away.

"Goodbye!" Charlotte calls after him.

The hall is quiet. We're all standing at my door. All eyes are on me. I don't know what to do.

Mr. Preston clears his throat. "Molly, would you be so kind as to invite us in?"

My legs rouse themselves from their torpor. As I regain my strength, Juan Manuel's grip releases.

"My apologies," I say. "I'm not accustomed to receiving so many guests. But it's not unwelcome company. Do come in."

Juan Manuel stands like a sentinel to the side of the door, greeting each guest and asking them to take off their shoes, which he wipes down with shaky hands and neatly places in the front closet.

All of my guests walk into the sitting room and stand awkwardly. What are they waiting for?

"Please," I say. "Have a seat."

Mr. Preston goes to the kitchen and comes back with two chairs, which he places across from the sofa.

"Would anyone like tea?" I ask.

"I'd murder for a cuppa," Mr. Preston says.

"Dad!"

"Poor choice of words. Apologies."

"That's quite all right, Mr. Preston," I say. I turn to Detective Stark. "We all make mistakes from time to time, don't we, Detective?"

Detective Stark appears very interested in her own stockinged feet. It must be unusual for her, to take off her boots on a work call, to have her tender tootsies so exposed.

"So," I say. "What about that tea?"

"I will make it," Juan Manuel replies. His eyes flit to the detective and then he makes a hasty retreat into the kitchen.

Mr. Preston offers Detective Stark a seat, and she obliges. Charlotte sits in her usual chair. I take my place on the sofa, with Mr. Preston beside me in the spot where Gran always sat, before.

"As you can imagine," I say, "I'm most curious to know what has transpired in the last few hours. I would most expressly appreciate knowing if I remain accused of murder."

I hear a spoon clatter against the tiled floor in the kitchen.

"Sorry!" Juan Manuel calls out.

"All charges against you are dropped," Detective Stark says.

"All of them," Charlotte repeats. "The detective wanted you to come to the station so she could tell you in person, but I insisted she face you here instead."

"Thank you," I say to Charlotte.

She leans forward in her chair, looking right into my eyes. "You're innocent, Molly. You understand? They know that now."

I hear the words. They register in my head, but I don't quite believe them. Words without action can be deceiving.

Mr. Preston gives my knee a little pat. "There, there. All's well that ends well." It's exactly what Gran would have said, were she still alive.

"Molly," Detective Stark says, "I'm here because we're going to need your help. We received a call from Mr. Snow this afternoon urging us to come to the hotel immediately. He was tipping us off to new developments."

Juan Manuel emerges from the kitchen, his face pale and drawn. He's carrying Gran's tea tray, which he sets on the table. He backs away then, several trolley-lengths from the detective.

Detective Stark doesn't notice. She eyes the tray and chooses Gran's cup, which bothers me no end, but never mind.

"Juan Manuel," I say as I stand up. "Please take my seat." I wish I had another chair to offer him, but alas, I do not.

"No, no," he says. "Please, you sit, Molly. I stand."

"Good idea," Detective Stark says. "Less chance of her fainting again." I sit back down.

The detective adds some sugar to her tea, stirs, then continues. "When we entered the former Black suite today, the bartender of the Social Bar & Grill, Rodney Stiles, and two of his associates, were inside."

"Two imposing gentlemen with an interesting array of facial tattoos?" I ask.

"Yes, you know them?"

"I thought they were guests of the hotel," I say. "I was told they were Juan Manuel's friends." As soon as I say it, I regret it.

It's as though Mr. Preston can read my mind, for he immediately says, "Don't worry, Molly. The detective knows all about Rodney and the blackmailing against Juan Manuel. And the . . . violent acts against him too."

Juan Manuel is standing motionless just outside of the kitchen. I know what this feels like—to be discussed as if you're not even there.

"Molly, can you tell the detective why you cleaned rooms for Rodney whenever he asked? Just tell the detective the truth," Charlotte says.

I look to Juan Manuel. I won't say another word without his consent. "It's okay," he says. "You can tell them."

I then proceed to explain everything, how Rodney lied, that he told me Juan Manuel was his friend and that he was homeless, how he had me clean rooms without me realizing what it was I was wiping away, how he deceived me—and how he used Juan Manuel.

"I didn't know what was actually going on in those rooms every night. I didn't realize Juan Manuel was being violently assaulted. I thought I was helping a friend."

"Why did you believe him, though?" Detective Stark asks. "Why did you believe Rodney when it was pretty obvious that drugs were involved?"

"What's obvious for you, Detective, isn't always obvious for everyone else. As my gran used to say, 'We're all the same in different ways.' The truth is, I trusted Rodney. I trusted a bad egg."

Juan Manuel remains statue-still outside of the kitchen.

"Rodney used me and Juan Manuel to make himself invisible," I say. "I see that now."

"You're right," Detective Stark replies. "We've caught him, though. We found large quantities of benzodiazepine and cocaine in that suite. It was literally right in his hands."

I think of Giselle's "benz friends" in an unmarked bottle, most likely supplied by Rodney.

"We've charged him with several drug-related offenses, possession of an illegal firearm, and threatening an officer."

"Threatening an officer?" I say.

"He pulled a handgun when the door of the suite opened. Same make and model as the one we found in your vacuum, Molly."

It's hard to imagine—Rodney in his white shirt with the sleeves rolled, pulling a gun rather than a pint of beer at the bar.

It's Juan Manuel who notices what I do not. All eyes turn to him as he speaks. "You mentioned many charges. But you never mentioned murder."

Detective Stark nods. "We have also charged Rodney with the first-degree murder of Mr. Black. But to be perfectly honest, we're going to need your help to make that charge stick. There are still a few things we can't figure out."

"Such as?" Charlotte prompts.

"When we first went into the Black suite the day you found him dead, Molly, there were no traces of Rodney's fingerprints anywhere in that whole suite. In fact, there were hardly any prints anywhere. And traces of your cleaning solution were found on Mr. Black's neck."

"Because I checked his pulse. Because—"

"Yes. We know, Molly. We know you didn't kill him."

It occurs to me then. "It's my fault."

Everyone looks my way.

"What could you possibly mean by that?" Mr. Preston asks.

"The fact that you couldn't find Rodney's prints anywhere. When I clean a room, I leave it in a state of perfection. If Rodney ever entered that room and left prints behind, I would have wiped them away without even knowing it. I'm a good maid. Maybe too good."

"You may be right," Detective Stark says. She smiles then, but not a full smile, not the kind that reaches the eyes. "We're wondering if you know anything about Giselle Black's whereabouts. After we arrested Rodney, we rushed to her hotel room, but she was already gone. Seems she saw us ambush the hotel and took off in a real hurry. She left a note on Regency Grand stationery."

"What did it say?" I ask.

"It said, 'Ask Molly the Maid. She'll tell you. I didn't do it. Rodney and Charles = BFFs.'"

"BFFs?" I say.

"Best friends forever," Charlotte offers. "She's saying Rodney and Charles were accomplices."

"Yes," says Juan Manuel. "They were accomplices." All eyes turn his way. He continues to speak. "Rodney and Mr. Black talked a lot on the phone. Sometimes, they argued. About money. About shipments and territories and deals. Nobody thinks I hear anything, but I do."

The detective turns her chair to face Juan Manuel. "We'd be very interested in taking your witness statement," she says.

A look of alarm crosses Juan Manuel's face.

"They're not going to charge you," Charlotte says. "Or deport you. They know you're a victim of crime. And they need your help to try the perpetrator."

"That's right," the detective says. "We understand that you were threatened and coerced to cooperate with Rodney, that you suffered ... physical assault. And we know you had a work permit that ran out."

"It didn't just 'run out,'" Juan Manuel says. "It ran into Rodney."

Detective Stark cocks her head to one side. "What's that supposed to mean?"

Juan Manuel explains how Rodney put him in touch with an immigration lawyer, only to have his money disappear and his papers never materialize.

"This 'lawyer.' You have his name?"

Juan Manuel nods.

The detective shakes her head. "Looks like we have another case to pursue."

Charlotte jumps in. "Juan Manuel, if you support us as a key witness in the case against Rodney, maybe we can also catch this so-called lawyer. Catch him before he does this to more people."

"No one else should go through this," Juan Manuel says.

"That's right. And Juan Manuel," Charlotte says. "My partner García handles immigration law in our firm. If you want, I can introduce you to him, see if he can get your work permit reinstated."

"I would like to talk to him, yes," Juan Manuel says. "I have many concerns—Mr. Snow, for one thing. He knows what I did. He knows I stayed quiet when I should have talked. He will fire me for sure."

"He won't," Mr. Preston says. "He needs you now more than ever."

"We all do," Detective Stark adds. "We need you to corroborate that Rodney and Mr. Black were running a cartel through the hotel, that they were using and abusing you. With your help, we might also be able to figure out what pushed Rodney to commit murder. He maintains he's innocent on that charge. Admits to the drug charges, but not to murder. Not yet."

Juan Manuel is quiet for a moment. Then he says, "I will help you if I can."

"Thank you," Detective Stark says. "And Molly, is there anything else you can tell us about Giselle? Do you have any idea where she could be?"

"She'll appear, when she's ready," I say.

"Let's hope," Detective Stark says.

I imagine Giselle on a faraway white-sand beach, clicking through news feeds on her phone and learning of Rodney's arrest. She'll find out that I'm no longer a suspect. What will she do then? Will she reach out to the police? Or will she put it all behind her? Will she grift her way into another rich man's wallet or will she actually grow and change?

I have never been a very good judge of character. I see the truth too late. It's like Juan Manuel said: sometimes, you have to do one thing bad to do another thing good. Perhaps this time, Giselle will do one thing good. Or perhaps not.

"What happens now?" I ask. "For Juan Manuel? For me?"

"Well," Detective Stark says. "You're free. All charges are dropped."

"But am I still fired?" I ask. The very thought of it makes me feel like I'm falling off a cliff to my doom.

"No, Molly," Mr. Preston says. "You won't lose your job. In fact, Mr. Snow will talk to you and to Juan Manuel about that himself."

"Really?" I say. "He won't fire either of us?"

"He said you're both model workers and that you exemplify what it means to be Regency Grand employees," Mr. Preston says.

"But what about the trial?" I ask.

"That won't be for a long while," Charlotte replies. "We'll prepare for it, and that will take many months. But hopefully, by working with Detective Stark and her team, we'll be able to put Rodney behind bars for a long time."

"That seems appropriate," I say. "He's a liar, an abuser, and a cheat."

"He's also a murderer," Mr. Preston adds.

I say nothing.

"Detective," Charlotte says, "I'm sensing my client is tired. It's been quite a day for her, given that this morning she was wrongly accused of murder and now she's having tea in her living room with her accuser. Was there anything else you wanted to say to her?"

Detective Stark clears her throat. "Just that I, uh, regret that you were . . . detained."

"That's very kind of you, Detective," I say. "I hope you've learned an important lesson."

The detective shifts in her chair as if she's seated on a sharp pin. "I'm sorry?" she says.

"Perhaps you jumped to some conclusions about me. You expected certain reactions that you consider normal, and when you didn't see those reactions, you assumed I was guilty. You made an A-S-S out of U and Me."

"That's one way to put it," she says.

"My gran always said that to live is to learn. Maybe next time you'll avoid assumptions."

"We're all the same in different ways," Juan Manuel adds.

"Huh," she says. "I suppose."

With that she stands, thanks us for our time, puts on her boots, and leaves.

Once the door clicks shut behind her, I slide the rusty dead bolt across it and breathe a huge sigh of relief.

I turn around and instead of emptiness, in my living room I see the faces of my three friends. They are all smiling, the kind of smiles that reach their eyes. For the first time in my life, I think I understand what a true friend is. It isn't just someone who likes you; it's someone willing to take action on your behalf.

"Well?" Mr. Preston says. "That detective just ate so much humble pie I think she might explode. How does it feel, Molly?"

I'm relieved beyond measure, but there's more to it than that. "I . . . I'm not quite certain what I did to deserve this," I say.

"You didn't deserve any of it," Charlotte says. "You're innocent."

"I don't mean the crimes. I mean the kindness the three of you have shown me, for no good reason."

"There's always a reason for kindness," Juan Manuel says.

"You're right," Mr. Preston says. "And you know who used to say that to me all the time?"

"No," I say.

"Your good ol' gran."

"She never did tell me how you two knew each other," I say.

"No, I expect she didn't," he replies. He takes a deep breath. "We were engaged, once upon a time."

"You were *what*?" Charlotte says.

"That's right, I had a life before you, my dear, a life you know very little about."

"I can't believe this," Charlotte says. "I'm learning this only now?"

"So what happened?" Juan Manuel asks. He settles himself into the detective's empty chair.

"Your grandmother, Flora, she was a wonderful lady, Molly. She was kind and sensitive. She was so different from other girls her age, and I was completely besotted. I proposed to her when we were both sixteen, and she said yes. But her parents wouldn't allow it. They were well-to-do, you know. She was miles above my station, yet she never acted that way."

I'm surprised by what I'm hearing, utterly shocked. But perhaps I should have known that Gran had her secrets. We all do, all of us.

"Oh, how your gran loved you, Molly," Mr. Preston says. "More than you'll ever know."

"And you kept in touch with her over the years?" I ask.

"Yes. She was friendly with my wife, Mary. And from time to time, when Flora was in trouble, she'd call me. But the real trouble happened early."

"What do you mean?" I ask.

"Did it ever occur to you that you had a grandfather?"

"Yes," I say. "Gran called him a 'fly-by-night too.'"

"Did she?" he says. "He was many things, but never that. He'd never have flown away if he'd had a choice. He was forced. Anyhow, he was known to me. A friend, you could say. And you know how things happen when love is fresh and the blush is still on the rose." Mr. Preston pauses to clear his throat. "As it turns out, Flora was with child. And when she could hide it no longer and her parents found out, that's when they really turned their backs on her, for good. Poor girl. She wasn't yet seventeen. She was just a child secretly running away with a child of her own. That's why she became a domestic."

It's hard to imagine, Gran on her own like that, losing everything, everyone. I feel a heaviness on my shoulders, a sadness that I can't quite name.

"She was bright, your gran. Could have won scholarships to any school," Mr. Preston says. "But in those days, as an unwed woman with child, say goodbye to education."

"Now, wait just a second, Dad," Charlotte says. "Something doesn't make sense. Who was this friend of yours? And where is he now?"

"The last I heard, he has a family of his own that he loves very much. But he's never forgotten Flora. Never."

Charlotte's head cocks to the side. She eyes her father in a funny way that I don't quite understand. "Dad?" she says. "Is there anything else you want to tell me?"

"My dear girl," he says. "I think I've said quite enough already."

"Did you know my mother too?" I ask him.

"Yes. Now, she was a true fly-by-night, I'm afraid. Your gran had me try to talk some sense into her when she shacked up with the wrong fellow. I went to see her, tried to pry her from the flophouse she was living in, but she wouldn't listen. Your poor gran, the pain of that . . . of losing a child the way she did . . ." Mr. Preston's eyes fill with tears. Charlotte grabs his hand.

"Your gran was so good, that she was," Mr. Preston says. "When my Mary was struggling near the end, your gran came to her rescue."

"What do you mean?" I ask.

"Mary was in extreme pain and so was I. I sat by her bedside holding her hand, saying, 'Please don't go. Not yet.' Flora watched it all, then drew me aside. She said, 'Don't you see? She won't leave you until you tell her it's time.'"

That's exactly what Gran would have said. I hear her words echo in my head. "Then what happened?" I ask.

"I told Mary I loved her and I did as Flora said. That's all my wife needed to rest in peace."

Mr. Preston can't hold back his sobs any longer.

"You did the right thing, Dad," Charlotte says. "Mom was suffering."

"I always wanted to repay your gran, for showing me the way."

"You have repaid her, Mr. Preston," I say. "You've come to my aid, and Gran would be grateful."

"Oh no, that's not me," Mr. Preston says. "That's Charlotte."

"No, Dad. You insisted on this. You convinced me we had to help this young maid you worked with. I think I'm starting to see why it was so important to you."

"A friend in need is a friend indeed," I say. "Gran thanks you. All of you. If she were here, she'd say it herself."

With that, Mr. Preston stands, as does Charlotte. "Well, let's not get too soggy then," he says as he wipes his cheeks. "We best be going."

"It's been a long day," Charlotte adds. "Juan Manuel, we brought your real overnight bag from your locker at the hotel. It's by the front closet."

"Thank you," he says.

It strikes me suddenly, an urgent feeling. I don't want them to leave. What if they walk out of my life and never come back? It's not the first time that has happened. The thought puts me instantly on edge.

"Will I be seeing you again?" I ask. I can't keep the anxiety out of my voice.

Mr. Preston chuckles. "Whether you like it or not, Molly."

"You'll be seeing us plenty," Charlotte replies. "We have a case to pre-pare."

"And besides the case, you're stuck with us, Molly. You know, I'm old, and I'm a widower who's become a bit set in my ways. It may seem odd, but this has been good for me. All of this. All of you. It feels like . . ."

"Family?" Juan Manuel suggests.

"Yes," Mr. Preston says. "That's exactly what it feels like."

"You know," Juan Manuel says, "in my family, the rule is that on Sun-days, we all have dinner together. That's the thing I miss the most from back home."

"That's easily remedied," I say. "Charlotte, Mr. Preston, would you be so kind as to join us for dinner this Sunday?"

"I'll cook!" Juan Manuel says. "You've probably never had real Mexi-can food, the kind my mother makes. I'll make the Tour of Mexico. Oh, you'll love it."

Mr. Preston looks to Charlotte. She nods.

"We'll bring dessert," Mr. Preston says.

"And a bottle of champagne to celebrate," Charlotte adds.

At the doorway, I stand and wait as Charlotte and Mr. Preston put on their shoes. I'm not sure of the proper etiquette for saying goodbye to two people who have just saved you from life in prison.

"Well, what are you waiting for?" Mr. Preston says. "Give your ol' friend a hug."

I do as I'm told and am surprised by the sensation—I feel like Goldi-locks hugging Papa Bear.

I hug Charlotte as well, and it's pleasant but entirely different, like caressing the wing of a butterfly.

They leave arm in arm, and I close the door behind them. Juan Man-uel stands in the entryway, shifting from foot to foot.

"Are you sure, Molly, that you're okay with me staying here tonight?"

"Yes," I say. "Just for tonight." The words that follow cascade out of my mouth. "You'll take my room, and I'll take Gran's room. I'll change the sheets right now. I always bleach and iron my sheets and keep two pairs at the ready, and you can rest assured that the bathroom is sanitary and disinfected on a regular basis. And if you do require any extra amenities, such as a toothbrush or soap, I'm most certain that I—"

"Molly, it's good. I'm fine. It's okay."

My verbal rush comes to a halt. "I'm not terribly good at this. I know how to treat guests at the hotel, but not in my own home."

"You don't have to treat me in any special way. I'll just try to be clean and quiet, and to help out where I can. You like breakfast?"

"Yes, I like breakfast."

"Good," he says. "Me too."

I try to change the sheets in my room by myself, but Juan Manuel will have none of it. We peel back Gran's lone-star quilt and remove the sheets, replacing them with fresh ones. We do it together as he tells me stories of his three-year-old nephew back home, Teodoro, who always jumped on the bed when he was trying to make it. When he tells his stories, they come to life in my mind. I can see that little boy jumping and playing. It's like he's right there with us.

When we are done, Juan Manuel goes quiet. "Okay. I'll get ready for bed now, Molly."

"Do you need anything else? Perhaps a cup of Ovaltine, or some toiletries for the bath?"

"No. Thank you."

"Very well," I say as I leave the room. "Good night."

"Good night, Miss Molly," he replies, and then quietly closes my bedroom door.

I pad down the hallway to the washroom. I change into my pajamas. I brush my teeth slowly. I sing "Happy Birthday" three times to make sure that I've brushed every last molar properly.

I wash my face, use the toilet, scrub my hands. I take the Windex from under the sink and do a quick polish of the mirror. There I am, shining back at myself, spotless. Clean.

There's no point dallying any longer.

It's time.

I walk down the hallway and stand in front of Gran's door. I remember the last time I closed this door, after the coroner and his aides wheeled out Gran's body, after I cleaned the room from top to bottom, after I washed her sheets and remade the bed, after I fluffed her pillows and dusted every last one of her trinkets, after I took her house sweater off the hook behind the door, the last remaining stitch of her clothing I had not washed and held it to my face to breathe in the vestiges of her before putting even that into the hamper. The sharp click of this door closing was as final as death itself.

I reach out and put my hand on the doorknob. I turn it. I open it. The room is exactly as I left it. Gran's Royal Doulton figurines dance statically in petticoats on her bureau. The ruffles on her baby-blue bed skirts remain pristine. Her pillows are plump and wrinkle-free.

"Oh Gran," I say. I feel it, a tidal wave of grief, a wave so strong that it carries me to her bed. I lie down on it, feeling suddenly like I'm on a life raft lost at sea. I hug one of her pillows, put it to my face, but I've washed it too well. There's no scent of her left. She is gone.

On the last day of her life, I sat with her. She was lying where I am now. I'd carried the chair by the front door—the one with her serenity pillow on it—and set it up beside her. A week earlier, I'd moved the television, setting it up on her chest of drawers so she could watch nature shows and National Geographic while I was at work. I didn't want to leave her alone, not even for a few hours. I knew she was in great pain, though she took great pains to deny it.

"Dear girl, they need you at work. You're an important part of the hive. I'm fine here. I've got my tea, and my pills. And my *Columbo*."

As the days passed, her color changed. She stopped humming songs to herself. Even in the morning, she was quieter, each thought belabored, each trip to the bathroom an epic journey.

I tried desperately to make her see reason. "Gran, we need to call an ambulance. We need to get you to a hospital."

She'd shake her head slowly, her gray, feathery tufts trembling on the pillow. "No need. I am content. I have my pills for the pain. I'm where I want to be. Home, sweet home."

"But maybe they can do something. Maybe the doctors can—"

"Shhhh," she said whenever I refused to listen. "We made a promise, you and I. And what did we agree about promises?"

"Promises are meant to be kept."

"Yes," she said. "That's my girl."

On the last day, her pain was worse than ever. I tried yet again to convince her to go to the hospital, to no avail.

"*Columbo* is coming on," she said.

I turned on the television, and we watched the episode, or rather I watched and she closed her eyes, her hands gripping the bedsheets.

"I'm listening," she said, her voice a mere whisper. "Be my eyes. Tell me what I need to see."

I watched the screen and narrated the action. Columbo was interviewing a trophy wife who didn't seem terribly distraught to learn that her millionaire husband was probably not the main suspect in a murder case. I described the restaurant they were in, the green tablecloth, the way her head moved, the way she fidgeted at the table. I told Gran when I knew Columbo was onto her, that look that showed he knew the truth before anyone else.

"Yes," she said. "Very good. You're learning expressions."

Halfway through the episode, Gran became agitated. The pain was so bad that she was wincing and tears were running down her face.

"Gran? How can I help? What can I do?"

I could hear her labored breath. There was a catch to each intake, like water gurgling in a drain.

"Molly," she said. "It's time."

Columbo continued his investigations in the background. He was onto the wife. The pieces were coming together. I turned the volume down.

"No, Gran. No, I can't."

"Yes," she said. "You promised."

I protested. I tried to reason. I begged her to please, please, please let me call the hospital.

She waited for my storm to pass. And when it did, she said it again.

"Make me a cup of tea. It's time."

I was so grateful to have instruction that I leaped to my feet. I rushed to the kitchen and had her tea ready, in her favorite cup—the one with the pretty cottage scene—in record time.

I took it back to her and set it on the bedside table. I put a pillow underneath her so she was more upright, but no matter how gently I touched her, she moaned pitifully, like an animal in a trap.

"My pills," she said. "Whatever's left of them."

"It won't work, Gran," I said. "There aren't enough. Next week we'll have more." I begged her yet again. I pleaded.

"Promises . . ."

She no longer had enough breath to complete the phrase.

In the end, I relented. I opened the bottle and put it on the edge of her saucer. I brought the teacup to her hands.

"Put them in," she said.

"Gran—"

"Please."

I emptied the rest of the painkillers into her tea—four pills, that's all. Not enough. It would be five days before we could fill another prescription, five days of agony.

I looked at Gran through my tears. She blinked and looked at the spoon on the saucer.

I took it and stirred and stirred, until a minute later she blinked again. I stopped stirring.

With great effort, she leaned forward, enough that I could put the cup to her gray lips. Even as I fed her the liquid, I begged. "Don't drink. Don't . . ."

But she did. She drank the whole thing.

"Delightful," she whispered when she was done. Then she eased herself back on her pillows. She put her hands to her chest. Her lips moved. She was speaking. I had to come right up to her lips to hear.

"I love you, my dear girl," she said. "You know what to do."

"Gran," I said. "I can't!"

But I could see it. I could see her body stiffen, the pain seizing her once more. Her breathing became even more shallow and the rattle was louder, like a drum.

We'd discussed it. I'd promised. She was always so rational, so logical, and I could not deny her this last wish. I knew it was what she wanted. She did not deserve to suffer.

God grant me the serenity to accept the things I cannot change, the courage to change the things I can, and the wisdom to know the difference.

I took her serenity pillow from behind me on the chair. I put the pillow over Gran's face and held it there.

I couldn't look at the pillow. I concentrated instead on her hands, a worker's hands, a maid's hands, hands so much like mine—clean, nails trimmed short, callused knuckles, the skin thin and papery, the blue rivers beneath them receding, their flow ebbing. Once, they extended out, her fingers grasping, reaching, but it was too late. We'd decided. Before they could reach anything, they relaxed. They let go.

It didn't take long. When all was silent, I moved the pillow away. I hugged it to my chest with all my strength.

There she was, my gran. She looked for all the world as though she was fast asleep, her eyes closed, her mouth slightly open, her face serene. At rest.

Now, as I lie awake in her bed over nine months later, with Juan Manuel just down the hall, I think of everything that has come to pass, of these past few days that have turned my life upside down.

"Gran, I miss you so much. And I can't believe I'll never see you again."

Count your blessings.

"Yes, Gran, I will," I said out loud. "It's so much better than counting sheep."

FRIDAY

I wake to the familiar sounds and smells of breakfast being made—the coffee brewing, the shuffling of slippers in the kitchen. Even the sound of humming.

But it's not Gran.

And I'm not in my own bed. I'm in hers.

It all comes back to me.

Rise and shine, dear girl. It's a new day.

I shift out of bed, slip my feet into slippers, and put Gran's housecoat on over my pajamas. I tiptoe to the bathroom to freshen up and then walk to the kitchen.

There he is, Juan Manuel. He has showered—his hair is still wet. He's humming his little tune, clattering dishes and scrambling eggs on the stovetop.

"Good morning!" he says, looking up from the pan. "I hope you don't mind. I ran to the store and came back very quiet. You didn't have eggs. And this bread?" He points to the crumpets on the counter. "For me it is strange. I don't know how to cook it. Too many holes."

"They are crumpets," I say. "And they're delicious. You toast them, then add butter and marmalade."

I grab the bag and pop two into the toaster.

"I hope you don't mind that I make breakfast."

"Not at all," I say. "It's very kind of you."

"I bought some coffee. I like coffee in the morning. With milk. And eggs. And tortilla, but today, I try something new—I try your holey crumb-pets."

Together, we bustle around the kitchen getting breakfast ready. It's incredibly strange, to move around the kitchen like this with someone who isn't Gran, but we're done in a flash. We sit and I prepare our crumpets with butter and marmalade.

"Do you mind? I washed my hands."

"If there's anyone I know who is clean, it's you," Juan Manuel says.

I smile at the compliment. "Thank you very much."

The eggs are unusually delicious. He's prepared them with some kind of sauce that has a bit of spice. It's tangy and delightful. It goes remarkably well with the marmalade and crumpets. I'm able to savor every bite in silence because he is chattering on and on, like a morning sparrow. He's holding his fork as he speaks, and I can't help but marvel at how he keeps his elbows politely off the table.

"I FaceTimed with my family this morning. They don't know about all the other stuff, and I won't tell them. But they do know I stayed here last night with a friend. I showed them your room, your kitchen, your living room. Your photo." He takes a sip of coffee. "I hope you don't mind."

I can't answer because my mouth is full, and it's rude to speak with your mouth full. But I don't mind. I don't mind at all.

"Oh, my cousin, Fernando? His daughter is turning fifteen next month. I can't even believe it! In my country, when a girl turns fifteen, there's a big family party, and we hire mariachis, and we make a big meal, and we dance all night. My mom, she had a cold, but now she's all better. This Sunday, they'll take a family picture at dinner and they'll send it to us. You'll see everyone. And my nephew, Teodoro. He went to the farm and rode a donkey. Now all he does is pretend to be a donkey. So funny. . . . Oh, I miss them so much."

I swallow the last of my crumpet and wash it down with some coffee.

"It must be so difficult," I say. "Seeing them only through FaceTime."

"They're far away," he replies. "But they're also still here."

I think of his father and of Gran. "Yes," I say. "You are right."

Before we can talk more, my cell phone rings. I've left it in the living room.

"Excuse me," I say. "I don't normally take calls during meals, but—"

"I know, I know," he replies.

I walk to the sitting room and grab my phone.

"Hello?" I say. "This is Molly. How may I be of assistance?"

"Molly, it's Mr. Snow."

"Yes, hello."

"How are you?" he asks.

"I am well. Thank you for asking. And you?"

"It's been a trying time. And I owe you an apology. The police led me to believe things about you that were simply not true. I should have known better, Molly. Our rooms could use your care, and I'm hoping you'll be coming back to work in the near future."

I'm pleased to hear this, extremely pleased. "I'm afraid I can't make it to work just this minute. I'm right in the middle of breakfast."

"Oh no. I didn't expect you to come in immediately. I meant, when you're ready. You take all the time you need, of course."

"How's tomorrow?" I ask.

I can hear Mr. Snow breathe a sigh of relief. "That would be most excellent, Molly. Cheryl has unfortunately declared herself unwell, and the other maids are doing double duty. They miss you terribly and they're worried about you. They'll be so glad to hear you're coming back."

"Please send them my regards," I say.

Something is niggling at me, and I decide to voice it. "Mr. Snow," I say. "It was brought to my attention that some of my coworkers find me to be . . . odd. I believe one term used was 'weirdo.' I'm wondering if you might provide me with your opinion on this matter."

Mr. Snow is quiet for moment. Then he says, "My opinion is that some of your colleagues ought to grow up. We are running a hotel, not a preschool. My opinion is that you're one of a kind in all the right ways. And you're the best maid the Regency Grand has ever known."

I feel pride lift me. I may very well have grown a couple of inches as a result of his words.

"Mr. Snow?" I say.

"Yes, Molly."

"What about Juan Manuel?"

"I'll be calling him as well to make sure he knows he has a job here as long as he wants one. Apparently, his work permit situation is resolvable. None of what happened was his fault."

"I know that," I say. "He's right here. Would you like to speak with him?"

"He's . . . what? Oh. Yes, that would be fine."

I walk to the kitchen and pass Juan Manuel my phone.

"Hello?" he says. "Yes, yes . . . I'm so sorry, Mr. Snow, I . . . no, I . . ."

At first, Juan Manuel can barely get a word in edgewise. "Yes, sir. . . . I know, sir. You didn't know. But thank you for saying that. . . ."

As the conversation continues, it turns back to work. "Of course, sir. I will be talking to a lawyer today. . . . I appreciate that. And I'm very happy to have my job."

There's a bit more back and forth between them. Then, at last, Juan Manuel says, "I'll be back at work as soon as I can. Goodbye, Mr. Snow."

Juan Manuel hangs up and places my phone on the table.

"I can't believe it. I still have my job."

"Me too," I say. I feel a warmth spread through me, a *je ne sais quoi* verve I haven't felt in some time.

He claps his hands together. "So," he says. "It looks like two people in this kitchen have the day off. I wonder what they will do. . . ."

"Tell me something, Juan Manuel," I say. "Do you by any chance like ice cream?"

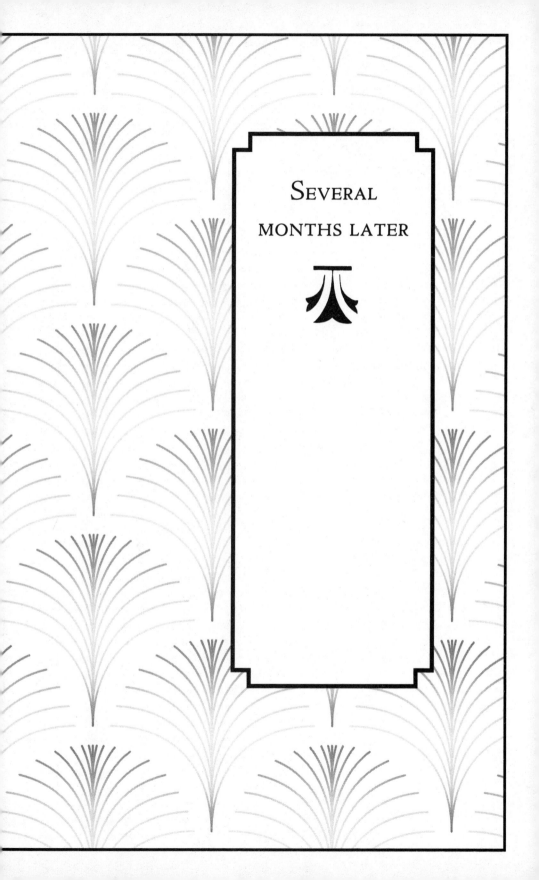

SEVERAL
MONTHS LATER

CHAPTER 27

Today is a beautiful day for so many reasons. Just last night when I went to bed and began to count my blessings, there were so many that I made it over a hundred in no time. I must have fallen asleep eventually, but I could have kept counting the whole night through and never run out.

And today, there are even more good things, too many to count.

The sun is shining. It's warm outside, with no clouds in the sky. I have just arrived at the Regency Grand, and I'm bounding up the scarlet steps toward Mr. Preston, who has just relieved some incoming guests of their luggage.

"Molly!" he says, his whole face a smile. "It's nice to see you at work instead of across a crowded courtroom."

"Isn't it a beautiful day, Mr. Preston?"

"That it is," he replies. "We're at work, and Rodney is behind bars. All's right with the world."

I wonder if there will ever come a day when hearing Rodney's name won't produce an acidic churn in my stomach and a tightening in my jaw.

"Where's Juan Manuel?" Mr. Preston asks.

"He'll be along shortly. His shift starts in an hour."

"Are we still on for Sunday? I'm looking forward to his enchiladas. You know, I'm not the most adventurous when it comes to food, and with my wife long gone, I don't get up to much in the kitchen. But that man of yours, he's opened my palate. Maybe a little too much," he says, chuckling and patting his belly.

"He'll be very pleased to hear it, Mr. Preston. And yes, we'll see you and Charlotte on Sunday at the usual time. I best be going. Much to do today! There's a wedding and a conference. Mr. Snow says all rooms have been booked for a solid week. Say hello to Charlotte."

"I will, dear girl. Take care."

Mr. Preston turns to help some guests. I push through the revolving doors and take in the lobby. It's as grand as the first day I laid eyes on it—the austere marble staircase, the golden serpent railings, the plush emerald love seats, the buzz and hum of guests and valets and porters bustling to and fro. I breathe deeply, then head toward the basement. But just as I'm about to take the stairs down, I notice the neat penguins behind the reception desk. They've stopped working. They're all looking my way. Several are whispering to one another in a way I don't care for, not in the least.

Mr. Snow emerges from a door behind Reception. He sees me.

"Molly!" he says. He comes rushing over. "You were brilliant. Absolutely brilliant."

I'm having trouble focusing on his words. I'm watching the penguins, trying to understand why they're so fixated on me this time.

"I merely told my truth," I tell Mr. Snow.

"Yes, but it's your truth, your testimony that clinched it. You were so calm and steady on the stand. And you do have a gift for words, you know, and for remembering details. The judge saw that and knew you were a reliable witness."

"Why are they staring?" I ask.

"I'm sorry?" Mr. Snow says. He follows my eyes to the reception desk. "Oh, I see," he says. "If I had to guess, I'd say they're in awe. I'd say the look they're giving you is respect."

Respect. I'm so unaccustomed to being the object of such an expression that I can't even recognize it.

"Thank you, Mr. Snow," I say. "I best be going. I have many rooms that must be returned to a state of perfection, and as you know, rooms don't clean themselves."

"They most certainly do not. Good day, Molly."

I head downstairs to the housekeeping quarters. It's stuffy and close as usual, but I've never minded it, not in the least. I'm standing in front of my locker, where my uniform, freshly dry cleaned and crisply pressed, hangs in gossamer-thin plastic wrap. My uniform is yet another blessing. It is a thing of great beauty.

I take it into a change room and put it on. Then I return to my locker and open it. Detective Stark returned Giselle's timer to me long ago, and I keep it on the top shelf to remind me. Of her. Of us. Of our strange friendship that was and wasn't.

It's time.

I have a new bit of accoutrement that I also keep in my locker, an addition to my uniform. It's an oblong gilt pin that I wear just above my heart. It reads MOLLY GRAY, HEAD MAID.

In a bold and unexpected move, Mr. Snow promoted me about a month ago. Far be it from me to tell tales, but it would seem that Cheryl's work ethic was not meeting Mr. Snow's high professional standards, for she was stripped of her supervisory role and it was bestowed unto me.

I have since instantiated some new best practices to improve the overall functioning and morale in the hive. First, before every shift, I see to it that each maid's trolley is fully and properly supplied. I love this part of my job—arranging the soaps and tiny shampoos in their trays, replenishing the polishing cloths and detergents, stacking the fresh, white towels in perfect piles. On special days—such as Mother's Day—I leave little gifts for the maids in their trolleys, such as a box of chocolates with a little tag: *From Molly the Maid. Know this: your work is sweet.*

Another new best practice is how we begin a shift. All of us maids gather with our trolleys and agree to a fair and equitable room distribution, both in terms of the quantity of rooms each and the potential to earn tips. I have made it abundantly clear to Cheryl that she is not to "preview" rooms assigned to other maids and that if she so much as takes a dime off another maid's pillow, I will eject her unceremoniously from the hive and run her over with her own trolley.

We have a new maid on our team. His name is Ricky, and he is Sunshine's son. Cheryl was quick to point out that he has a lisp and wears eyeliner, two facts which, to be perfectly honest, are so irrelevant that I failed to notice either over the entire course of his month-long training. What I did notice, however, is what a quick study he is, how he delights in making a bed with no creases, how he polishes glass to a high shine, and how he greets guests with the manners of a fine courtier. He is, as managers say, a keeper.

I received a raise when I was promoted, and between that and the fact that I'm now sharing the cost of rent, I've been able to start my very own Fabergé. It's not much yet, just a few hundred dollars, but I have a plan. I'll keep growing the egg until I have enough to enroll once more in the hotel management and hospitality program at the nearby college. With Mr. Snow's permission, I will work around my class schedule, and in a year or two, I will graduate, magna cum laude, and return to full-time work at the Regency Grand with even better skills and a more complete knowledge of hotel management.

Perhaps the biggest change in my life is that it's now official: I have a beau. I'm told it's in vogue to refer to him as my partner, and I'm trying to get used to that term, though every time I say it I think of partner in crime, which in some ways we were, though I didn't know it at the time.

When Juan Manuel eventually received a work permit and returned to the kitchen, Mr. Snow offered him his own room in the hotel for as long as he needed to get back on his feet. But on evenings and weekends, when we weren't working, Juan Manuel and I spent a lot of time together. It took some time for me to fully trust that he really is what he appears to be—which is a good egg. And I believe it took him some time, too, to trust that so am I.

I've learned to judge friends through their actions, and Juan Manuel's actions speak volumes. There are the big things, like standing up for me in court and saying that I didn't know a thing about the illegal activities going on at the hotel. But there are also the small actions, like the brown paper bag lunches he prepares for me, which I pick up from the kitchen at precisely noon each workday. Inside the bag is a delightful sandwich and a sweet treat that he knows I will like—shortbread biscuits, a chocolate, and from time to time, a raisin-bran muffin.

There are still days when I feel very sad about Gran, and when I text Juan Manuel to say I'm blue, he responds immediately—*BRT! DGA!* He'll bring a jigsaw puzzle that we'll tackle together, or he'll help me with my daily cleaning chore. If there's anything that raises the spirits more than a good tidy, it's a good tidy with company. And for my part, when I know Juan Manuel is blue and misses his family, I refrain from offering tissues. I offer hugs and kisses instead.

Two months ago, I asked Juan Manuel if he wanted to move out of the hotel and in with me. "For cost-saving purposes," I clarified. "Among others."

"I'll only agree if I'm allowed to do *all* the dishes."

Reluctantly, I agreed.

We've been living quite happily together ever since—splitting the rent, making meals together, calling his family together, shopping together, going to the Olive Garden together . . . and more. Juan Manuel shares my love of the Tour of Italy platter. We often play a game where we have to choose just one part of the Tour of Italy to eat if we one day become stranded on a desert island.

"You can choose only one—the chicken parmigiana, the lasagna, or the fettucine Alfredo."

"No, I can't choose. It's impossible, Molly."

"But you must. You have to choose."

"I can't choose. I'd rather die."

"I'd rather you stay alive and well, thank you very much!"

The last time we played this game, we were at the Olive Garden. He leaned forward and kissed me across the table, right under the pendant light, all without ever putting his elbows on the table, because that's just the kind of man he is.

Tonight, we will go out, just the two of us, to the Olive Garden. After all, we have reason to celebrate. Yesterday was a big day for both of us. We each took the stand in the trial against Rodney. Charlotte spent weeks preparing us for cross-examination, for every difficult question the defense could throw at us. In the end, Juan Manuel took the stand before I did and told the court his very sad and terrible truth. He told them how his papers were taken from him, how Rodney threatened his life and those of his family members, how he was forced to work for Rodney, and how he was burned repeatedly. In the end, it wasn't Juan Manuel who was attacked on the stand. It was me.

Do you truly expect this court to believe you didn't know anything when you were literally wiping cocaine off tables every morning?

Is it accurate to say that you were Mr. Black's accomplice?

Is Giselle your friend? Is that why you're protecting her?

I wanted to tell them that Giselle doesn't need my protection, not anymore, not since her abuser, Mr. Black, is dead. But I learned from Charlotte that in court, when a question assumes, you don't have to answer it. And since I didn't want to make an A-S-S out of myself, I allowed Charlotte to object. And I said nothing.

Detective Stark tried many times to get Giselle to appear in court, but to no avail. Once, she managed to get her on the phone. She located Giselle at a hotel in Saint-Tropez. Detective Stark begged her to come back to the country and take the stand. She asked who the charges were against, and when she learned they were against Rodney, not me, she said, "Hell no. I'm not going back."

"Did she say why?" I asked.

"She said she's wasted enough of her life on guilty men. She said that everything's different for her now, that she's free for the first time ever.

She said that unless I can track her down and serve her a subpoena, she'll come back when hell freezes over. She also said I'm the detective, not her, that it's my job to put the villain behind bars."

That sounded like Giselle. I could almost hear her saying it.

In the end, I took the stand with only Juan Manuel to corroborate my side of the story.

Apparently, I did well. Apparently, I had a calm demeanor on the stand and the judge took notice. Charlotte says that most witnesses feel attacked up there, and they either lash out or break down.

I'm used to name-calling and insinuations about my character. I'm used to verbal jousts and jabs. They're fired my way every day, often without me even being aware of them. I'm used to my words being my only defense.

For the most part, being on the stand was not difficult. All I had to do was listen to the questions and respond with the truth, my truth.

The hardest part was when Charlotte asked me to walk the court through my memory of the day I found Mr. Black dead in his bed. I told them about Mr. Black almost bowling me over outside the suite. I told them how I entered later that day and Giselle was gone, how I turned the corner to the bedroom and saw Mr. Black lying there. I told them every detail I could remember—the drinks on the sitting-room table, the open safe, the spilled bottle of pills, Mr. Black's shoes akimbo on the floor, three pillows on the bed, not four.

"Three pillows," Charlotte said. "How many are usually on a bed at the Regency Grand?"

"Four is our house standard. Two firm, two soft. And I can assure you, I always kept four clean pillows on that bed. I'm a very detail-oriented person."

A muffled eruption of laughter traveled through the courtroom, laughter at my expense. The judge called for order, and Charlotte asked me to continue.

"Tell the court, Molly. Did you see anyone in the suite or in the hallways, anyone who might have had the missing pillow?"

Here came the tricky part, the part I'd never discussed with anyone, not even Charlotte. But I'd prepared myself for this moment. I'd practiced night after night, in between counting blessings and sheep.

I steadied my gaze and my voice. I concentrated my mind on the pleasant sound of my own blood. I could hear it in my ears, the rushing flow, in and out, rolling waves on a faraway beach. *What's right is right. What's done is done.*

"I wasn't alone. In the room," I said. "I thought I was at first, but I wasn't."

Charlotte swiveled on her heel and turned my way.

"Molly?" she said. "What are you talking about?"

I swallowed, then spoke. "After I called down to Reception for help the first time, I put the receiver down. Then I turned toward the bedroom door. And that's when I saw it."

"Molly, I want you to think very carefully before you speak," Charlotte calmly advised, though her eyes were wide with alarm. "I'm going to ask you a question, and you're to tell the absolute truth. What did you see?" Her head tilted to one side as if nothing made sense.

"There was a mirror on the far wall in front of me."

I paused and waited for Charlotte to catch up. It didn't take her long.

"A mirror," she said. "And what was reflected in it?"

"First, myself, my terrified face staring back at me. Then behind me, to my left, in the shadowy corner by Giselle's armoire was . . . a person."

My eyes locked with Charlotte's. It was as though her mind were an intricate machine, reading me, deliberating on how to proceed.

"And . . . was this person holding anything?" she asked.

"A pillow."

Murmurs traveled through the crowded courtroom. The judge called for order.

"Molly, is the person you saw standing in that dark corner present in this courtroom today?"

"I'm afraid I would not be comfortable saying," I said.

"Because you don't know?"

"Because at that precise moment, when I turned from the mirror to get a direct look at the figure in the dark corner, I fainted. And when I woke up, the person wasn't there anymore."

Charlotte nodded slowly. She took her time. "Of course," she said. "You have a history of fainting spells, don't you, Molly? Detective Stark testified that you fainted once at your front door upon arrest and once at the station, is that correct?"

"Yes. I faint when under extreme duress. And I most certainly was under extreme duress upon wrongful arrest. I was also under extreme duress when I looked into that mirror and realized I wasn't alone in that hotel room."

Charlotte began to pace in front of the stand. She stopped directly in front of me. "What happened when you came to?" she asked.

"When I regained consciousness, I called Reception for the second time. But there was no one in the room at that point. Just me. Well, me and the corpse of Mr. Black," I said.

"Is it possible, Molly—I'm not saying it *was*—but is it possible that the person in that dark corner was Rodney Stiles?"

Rodney's lawyer jumped to his feet. "Objection. Leading the witness," he said.

"Sustained," the judge replied. "Counsel, do you wish to rephrase your question?"

Charlotte paused for a moment, though I doubt it was because she was thinking. I took that time to study Rodney. His lawyer was leaning forward, whispering something in his ear. I wondered what I was being called this time, not that it mattered. Rodney was wearing what appeared to be a very expensive suit. I used to think he was so handsome, but as I looked at him in that moment, I couldn't imagine what I'd ever seen in him.

After a long interval, Charlotte finally said, "No further questions, Your Honor." She turned to me. "Thank you, Molly," she said.

For a moment I thought it was over, but then I remembered we were only halfway through. Rodney's lawyer sauntered toward me, stopping right in front of me and staring me down. It did little to unnerve me. I'm used to such looks. The world had prepared me well.

I can't recall every word that was said, but I do remember treading the same old ground, telling the same story the same way every time I was asked. I didn't trip up even once because it's easy to tell the truth when you know what it is and what it isn't, and when you've drawn your own line in the sand. There was just one moment during cross-examination when Rodney's lawyer drilled into me with particular vigor.

"Molly, there's something I still don't understand about your story. You were brought to the police station several times. You were given ample opportunity to tell Detective Stark about the figure in the corner of the hotel suite that day. Doing so might have even exonerated you. And yet, time after time, you never mentioned seeing someone in that room. You never said a word about that. And if your lawyer's behavior means anything, it sure seems like she didn't know until today either. Now, why is that, Molly? Is that because no one was actually there? Is it because you're protecting someone else, or is it because when you looked in that mirror, all you saw was your own guilty face reflected back at you?"

"Objection. Badgering. Of the very worst kind," Charlotte said.

"Sustained, minus the last bit," said the judge.

The whispers fluttered through the courtroom.

"I'll rephrase my question," Rodney's lawyer said. "Did you *lie* to Detective Stark when you first told her about what you saw in that hotel room?"

"I did not lie," I say. "On the contrary. You've all read the transcripts. Perhaps you've even watched the video of my testimony on the very first day I was interrogated at that filthy police station. One of the first things I said to Detective Stark, in no uncertain terms, was that when I announced my arrival in the suite, I thought someone was there with me. I asked her specifically to write that detail down."

"But the detective obviously assumed you meant Mr. Black."

"And that's why assumptions are dangerous," I said.

"Ah," he replied as he paced back and forth in front of the stand. "So you omitted the whole truth. You refused to clarify. That, too, is a lie, Molly." He eyed the judge, who tilted her chin down ever so slightly. I thought that maybe Charlotte would intervene, but she didn't. She was still and quiet at her bench.

"And can you please enlighten us, Molly, as to why you failed—countless times—to clarify to investigators your claim that 'someone else was in the room' and that this person was holding a pillow?"

"Because I was . . ."

"Was what, Molly? You strike me as someone rarely at a loss for words, so have out with it. This is your chance."

"I wasn't one hundred percent sure what it was I'd seen. I've learned to doubt myself and my perceptions of the world around me. I do realize I'm different, you know, different from most. What I perceive isn't what you perceive. Plus, people don't always listen to me. I'm often afraid I won't be believed, that my thoughts will be discounted. I'm just a maid, a nobody. And what I saw in that moment, it felt like a dream, but I know now that it was real. Someone with a deep motive killed Mr. Black. And that wasn't me," I said. I looked at Rodney then, and he looked at me. There was a look on his face that was entirely new. It was as though, for the very first time, he was seeing me for who I really am.

The courtroom erupted and the judge called for order once more. I was asked several other questions, which I answered, clearly and politely. But I knew nothing else I said would matter. I knew this because I could see Charlotte on the bench. And she was smiling, a smile that was new for me, one that I would add to the catalog in my mind, filed under A for "awe." I'd surprised her, shocked her completely, but I had not made a total mess of things. Everything was going our way. That's what her smile said.

And she was right. Things did go our way.

As I think back on it now, on everything that happened in that courtroom yesterday, I can't help but smile myself.

I snap out of my recollections when I see Sunitha and Sunshine heading toward me. They've just arrived for the start of our shift.

They're perfectly dressed in their uniforms, their hair neatly pinned back. They stand in front of me silently, which is quite usual for Sunitha and most unusual for Sunshine.

"Good morning, ladies," I say. "I hope you're looking forward to another day of returning rooms to a state of perfection."

They still say nothing. Finally, Sunshine speaks. "Just go on. Tell her!"

Sunitha takes a step forward. "I wanted to say: you caught the snake. The grass is clean now, thank you."

I don't exactly know what she's trying to say, but I can tell she's paying me a compliment.

"We all want a clean hotel, do we not?"

"Oh yes," she says. "Clean means green!"

This pleases me immensely because she's quoting something I said in a recent maid training session. *If we work to make things clean, we'll make a lot of green.* By green, I meant money—tips, bills. I thought that was quite clever, and I'm pleased she remembered.

"Big tips today and big tips in the future!" she says.

"Which is good for us all," I say. "Shall we?"

And without further delay, we get behind our trolleys and push onward.

But just as we make it to the elevators, my phone buzzes in my pocket.

The elevator doors open. "You two go ahead. I'll take the next one up," I say.

Off they go together, which gives me a moment to check my phone. It's probably Juan Manuel. He often sends text messages throughout the day, little things to make me smile—a picture of us eating ice cream at the park, or an update about his family back home.

But it's not Juan Manuel. It's an email from my bank. Instantly, I feel my stomach sink. I can't bear the thought of bad financial news. I open it and read the message:

SANDY CAYMAN has sent you $10,000 (U.S.) and the money has been automatically deposited into your account.

And under "Special message," three words: Debt of Gratitude.

At first, I think it must be a mistake. But then it dawns on me. Sandy Cayman. Sandy beaches. The Cayman Islands.

Giselle.

Giselle sent me a gift. And that's where she is—on her favorite island in the villa that she wanted so badly, a villa she asked Mr. Black to put in her name hours before his death. Mr. Black relented. He gave in. That was revealed in court by Rodney's defense team. When he left the suite on the last day of his life, after throwing his wedding ring at Giselle, he had a change of heart. He grabbed the deed for the villa in the Caymans out of the safe. I happened to see it in his breast pocket when he nearly bowled me over in the hallway. Despite the argument with Giselle, he went directly to his lawyers and had them put the villa in Giselle's name. That was the last bit of business he conducted before returning to the hotel. It explained a lot. . . .

I imagined Giselle on a lounge chair in the sun, finally getting what she always wanted, just not the way she expected. Somehow, she had money now, too, even if it wasn't Mr. Black's—money to make amends.

She'd sent me a gift. An enormous, Fabergé-enhancing gift.

A gift I wouldn't know how to give back even if I wanted to.

A gift that I intended to put to very good use.

—

Epilogue

G ran always said that the truth is subjective, which is something I failed to comprehend until my own life experience proved her wisdom. Now I understand. My truth is not the same as yours because we don't experience life in the same way.

We are all the same in different ways.

This more flexible notion of truth is something I can live with—more than that, it's something that gives me great comfort these days.

I am learning to be less literal, less absolute about most things. The world is a better place seen through a prism of colors rather than merely in black and white. In this new world, there is room for versions and variations, for shades of gray.

The version of the truth I told on the stand on my day in court is exactly that—a version of my experiences and memories on the day that I found Mr. Black dead in his bed. My truth highlights and prioritizes my lens on the world; it focuses on what I see best and obscures what I fail to understand—or what I choose not to examine too closely.

Justice is like truth—it, too, is subjective. So many of those who deserve to be punished never receive their just deserts, and in the meantime, good people, decent people, are charged with the wrong crimes. It's a flawed system—justice—a dirty, messy, imperfect system. But if the good people accept personal responsibility for exacting justice, would we not have a better chance of cleaning the entire world, of holding the liars, the cheaters, the users, and the abusers to account?

I do not share my views on this subject widely. Who would care? After all, I'm just a maid.

On my day in court, I told those gathered about the day I found Mr. Black dead in his bed. I told it how I saw it, how I lived it, only I cut the story short. Yes, I did check Mr. Black's neck for a pulse only to find none. I did call down to Reception asking for help. I did turn to the bedroom door and catch a glimpse of myself in the mirror. Only then did I realize I was not alone in the room. There was in fact a figure standing in the corner. A dark shadow fell across the person's face, but I could see their hands clearly, and a pillow, clutched close to their heart. This figure reminded me so much of myself, and of Gran. It was as if I was seeing myself reflected twice in the mirror. That's when I fainted.

The story continues after that. Much like an episode of *Columbo*: there's always something more that wasn't seen before.

It wasn't a man, the figure in the corner.

When I awoke, I found myself on the floor beside the bed. Someone was fanning my face with hotel stationery. After a few deep breaths, my vision sharpened. It was a woman. She was middle-aged, with salt-and-pepper hair held back by the sunglasses propped on her head. Her hair was cut neatly into a bob, styled straight, much like my own. She was wearing a loose-fitting white blouse and dark pants. She was crouched over me, a worried look on her face. I didn't recognize her face, not at first.

"Are you all right?" she asked as she stopped her fanning.

My first instinct was to reach for the phone again.

"Please," she said. "You don't need to do that."

I brought myself to a seated position, pushing my back against the bedside table. She took two steps backward, giving me space, but she kept her eyes on me.

"I'm terribly sorry," I said. "I didn't realize there was another guest in the room. But I must—"

"You must nothing. Please. Hear me out before you touch the phone."

She did not sound angry or even tense. She was merely offering a suggestion.

I did as I was told.

"Would you like a glass of water?" she asked. "And maybe something sweet?"

I wasn't ready to stand. I didn't trust my legs. "Yes," I said. "That would be most kind."

She nodded once and left the room. I could hear her rummaging around in the sitting room. Then I heard the rush of water from the bathroom tap.

A moment later, she was back in the bedroom, crouching in front of me. She passed me a glass of water, which I took in my shaky hands and drank greedily.

"Here," she said once I'd finished, "I found this in your cleaning cart."

It was a chocolate, for turn-down services. Strictly speaking, it was not mine to eat, but this was an extraordinary circumstance and she'd already opened the wrapper.

"You'll feel better," she said.

She passed me the square of chocolate, put it right into the palm of my hand.

"Thank you," I replied. I placed the whole square on my tongue. It dissolved instantly, the sugar working its magic.

She waited a moment, then asked, "Can I help you?" She reached out her hand.

I put my unsteady hand in hers and with her assistance, I was soon standing beside her. The room came into sharper focus. The ground was solid beneath my feet.

We stood there beside the bed, looking at each other for a moment, neither of us daring to look away.

"We don't have much time," she said. "Do you know who I am?"

I studied her more closely. She looked vaguely familiar, but she also looked like every other middle-aged female guest who frequented the hotel.

"My apologies, I'm afraid . . ."

And that's when it hit me. From the newspapers. From our one brief encounter in the elevator. It was Mrs. Black. Not the second Mrs. Black, Giselle, but the first Mrs. Black, the original wife.

"Ah," she said as she neatly tucked the chocolate wrapper into her pants pocket. "Recognition dawns."

"Mrs. Black, I'm terribly sorry to intrude, but I do believe that your former husband . . . I believe Mr. Black is dead."

She nodded slowly. "My ex-husband was a cheater and a thief and an abuser and a criminal."

I started to put it together then, only then. "Mrs. Black," I asked. "Did you . . . did you kill Mr. Black?"

"I suppose that depends on your point of view," she said. "I believe he killed himself, slowly, over time, that he became infected by his own greed, that he robbed his children and me of a normal life, that he modeled corruption and evil in just about every way a man can. My two sons are his clones, and they're now drug-addled slobs who flit from party to party, spending their father's money. And my daughter, Victoria, all she wants is to clean up the family business, to run it with some decency, but her own father wants to disown her. He wouldn't have stopped until Victoria and I were both destitute. And he did this even though she's a forty-nine-percent shareholder. Well, she *was* a forty-nine-percent shareholder. She'll be more than that now. . . ."

She looked at Mr. Black, dead on the bed, then back at me.

"I came only to talk to him, to ask him to give Victoria a chance. But when he let me in, he was drunk, popping pills, slurring his words, muttering about Giselle being a gold-digging bitch, just like me, how we're both good-for-nothing bimbo wives, the two biggest mistakes of his life. He was obnoxious and a bully. In other words, he was his usual self."

She paused.

"He grabbed me by the wrists. I'll have bruises."

"Just like Giselle," I said.

"Yes. Just like the new and improved Mrs. Black. I tried to warn her. Giselle. But she didn't listen. Too young to know any better."

"He beats her too," I said.

"Not anymore," she replied. "He would have done worse to me, but he started to heave and pant. He let go of my wrists. Then he stumbled to the bed, kicked off his shoes and lay down, just like that."

Her eyes darted to the pillow on the floor, then away. "Tell me," she said. "Do you ever feel like the world is backward? Like the villains prosper and the good suffer?"

It was as though she were reading my deepest thoughts. My mind flitted through a short list of those who had taken from me unjustly and had caused me to suffer—Cheryl, Wilbur . . . and a man I'd never met, my own father.

"Yes," I said. "I feel that way all the time."

"Me too," she replied. "In my experience, there are times when a good person must do something that's not quite right, but it's still the right thing to do."

Yes, she was right.

"What if it were different this time?" she asked. "What if we took matters into our own hands and balanced the scales? What if you didn't see me? What if I just walked out of the hotel and never looked back?"

"You'd be recognized, would you not?"

"If people actually read the newspapers delivered to their doors, but I doubt they do. I'm largely invisible. Just another gray-haired, middle-aged woman in loose-fitting clothes and sunglasses walking out the back door of the Regency Grand. Just another nobody."

Invisible in plain sight, just like me.

"What did you touch?" I asked her.

"Excuse me?"

"When you entered the suite, what did you touch?"

"Oh . . . I touched the doorknob and probably the door itself. I think I laid a hand on the bureau by the door. I didn't sit down. I couldn't. He was chasing me around the room, yelling and spitting in my face. He grabbed my wrists, so I don't think I ever actually touched him. I took that pillow off the bed and . . . That's it, I believe."

We were both silent for a moment, staring at the pillow on the floor. I thought again of Gran. I didn't understand her back then, not entirely, but during that moment with Mrs. Black, I suddenly saw it clearly— how mercy takes unexpected forms.

I looked up at her, this virtual stranger who was so much like me.

"They're not coming," she said. "Whoever you called earlier."

"No, they won't. They don't listen well. Not to me. I'll have to call again."

"Now?"

"No, not yet."

I didn't know what else to say. My feet turned to stone as they do when I'm nervous. "You best be going," I eventually said. "Please don't let me delay you." I offered a slight curtsy.

"And what will you do? When I'm gone?"

"I'll do what I always do. I'll clean everything up. I'll take away my water glass. I'll wipe down the front doorknob and the bureau. I'll polish the faucet in the bathroom. I'll put that pillow on the floor in my laundry hamper. It will be cleaned in the basement and returned to another room in a state of perfection. No one will ever know it was here."

"Just like me?"

"Yes," I said. "And after I've returned those few areas of the suite to a state of perfection, I'll call Reception again and reiterate my urgent request for help."

"You never saw me," she said.

"And you never saw me," I replied.

She left then. She simply walked out of the bedroom and out the front door of the suite. I didn't move until I heard the front door click behind her.

That was the last time I saw Mrs. Black, the first Mrs. Black. Or didn't see her. So much depends on your point of view.

Once she was gone, I cleaned things up as I said I would. I put the pillow she left behind into the laundry hamper in my trolley. I called down to Reception, for the second time, once I fully regained conscious-ness, just like I said in court. And at long last, a few minutes later, help arrived.

I sleep well at night now, perhaps better than I ever have before be-cause I lie beside Juan Manuel, my dearest friend in all the world. He's a heavy sleeper, just like Gran was—he falls asleep before his head hits the pillow. We sleep together under Gran's lone-star quilt because some things are better kept the same, whereas other things are better when they change a little. On the walls around us I've taken down Gran's landscape paintings, replacing them with framed photos of Juan Manuel and me.

I listen to his breathing, like rolling waves—in, out, in. And I count my blessings. There are so many of them it's daunting. I know my con-science is clean because I make it through fewer and fewer blessings each night before I fall into pleasant dreams. I wake up refreshed and joyful, ready to seize the day.

If all of this has taught me anything, it is this: there's a power in me I never knew was there. I always knew there was power in my hands—to clean, to wipe away dirt, to scour and disinfect, to set things right. But now I know there's power elsewhere—in my mind. And in my heart too.

Gran was correct after all. About all of it. About everything.

The longer you live, the more you learn.

People are a mystery that can never be solved.

Life has a way of sorting itself out.

Everything will be okay in the end. If it's not okay, it's not the end.